Time Will Tell

Sandy Loyd

Published by Sandy Loyd

Cover design by Kelli Ann Morgan at Inspire Creative Services
Edited by Pam Berehulke at Bulletproof Editing
ISBN: 978-0-9891995-3-7

 This book is a work of fiction. The characters, events, and places portrayed in this book are products of the author's imagination and are either fictitious or are used fictitiously. Any similarity to real persons, living or dead, is purely coincidental and not intended by the author.

For more information on the author and her works, please see www.SandyLoyd.com

This book is also available in print from some online retailers.

DEDICATION

As always, I dedicate this book to my husband. He's the one I want to go through time with.

Also, this book is dedicated to friendship. I'm thankful for those new friends I've met since I've begun my writing journey. I'm more thankful for those lasting friendships that span decades. You know who you are. I love you all.

Amazon Links to Other books by Sandy Loyd

Contemporary Romances

The California Series

Winter Interlude – Book One – http://amzn.to/VsPzQ3
Promises, Promises – Book Two – http://amzn.to/X6901Q
James – Book Three – http://amzn.to/SuwaTR

Second Chances Series

Tropical Spice – Book One – http://amzn.to/Vz0QCZ

Christmas Short Stories

A Christmas Miracle – http://amzn.to/15WK1Ub

Contemporary/Time Travel/Historical

Timeless Series

Time Will Tell – Book One - http://amzn.to/10zmPM0
Games – Book Two - http://amzn.to/13fG635
Temptation – Book Three – http://amzn.to/14tBpq7

Romantic Suspense

D.C. Bad Boys Series

The Sin Factor – Book One – http://amzn.to/SJvBlx

Running Series

Running Out of Fear – http://amzn.to/VsSoAA

Deadly Series

Deadly Misconceptions – http://amzn.to/WgdSEF

A Matter Of Trust – http://amzn.to/XWJsZ1

Chapter 1

“““Libby—Libby? Are you listening to me?”

Libby Edwards shook off her daydreams and looked at her fiancé. “What did you say?”

“Come on, Libby. Stay focused.” He frowned. “You’re miles away. I might as well not even be in the car.”

She sighed. “I’m sorry. I guess I’m just tired from helping Mrs. Meyers move into a retirement home today. I wasn’t expecting to go out tonight.”

“You’re on your feet all the time at work. You should relax and not help neighbors on your day off.”

“The poor woman has no one else.” His comment confused her, considering his main reason for practicing medicine—to *help* people—was what she loved most about Dave.

“Well, you can relax now.” He patted her thigh. “An evening at the opera should do the trick.”

Libby offered a slight smile, wishing she didn’t hate opera. “You’re so sweet.” Where was the *Enterprise* when she needed it most? Oh, how she’d loved to have Scotty beam her up so she wouldn’t have to endure another night of Dave’s surprises. Last week, it was a new wave art show that she had no interest in. Why couldn’t he be content to just watch a ball game on TV on Sunday night? Once she started analyzing the reasons, she couldn’t stop, which lead to more analyzing, ending at her relationship with Dave. In the last month, he’d started on this kick to do more with his friends. “Which isn’t working,” she said, thinking out loud.

“What’s not working?” He glanced at her, those soulful brown eyes narrowing.

“I don’t know.” She shrugged. “I feel as if your friends don’t like me. That I’m not good enough.” Or maybe she lacked something. The niggling feeling kept returning. The more she was with his group of friends, the more she wondered if she'd ever feel comfortable around them. She'd always led a simple life, and the hoity-toity stuff they were into didn't interest her.

"You just need to be a little friendlier."

"Maybe." She moved to look out the window without seeing the streets of Louisville whiz by. She could do somersaults in an attempt to please them and they would still ignore her.

"You worry too much." Dave shook his head, dismissing her concern. "You have nothing to fear. You're about to become a doctor's wife. You'll do fine."

His smug tone drew her gaze and Libby could only stare at him, dumbfounded. Did he really believe that marriage to him would make up for their differences? Did Dave find her lacking, like the wives of his friends obviously did? Those women treated her as if she had a contagious disease. With only three months to go before their wedding, was being a doctor's wife what she really wanted? She'd never really thought about it before, but now doubts assailed her. The knot, already in the pit of her stomach, tightened.

The car stopped. A valet opened Libby's door, saving her from further commentary. She climbed out of the expensive BMW and waited briefly as Dave ran around to her side to escort her into the Kentucky Center for the Arts.

"Maybe if you didn't hang around with Bev so much, you'd fit in better with my friends and their wives." A disapproving look passed over his face as he reached the top step. "She's too wild—not the kind of influence you should be subjecting yourself to."

"I don't understand why you don't like her." Sure, Bev moved to a different beat. After all, she was one of those Trekkies who wouldn't miss a Star Trek convention, but so what? Libby loved her, despite their differences. "You've never given her a chance," she defended. Unfortunately, her best friend didn't like Dave either. The two repelled each other worse than Cutters did a mosquito and Libby felt stuck in the middle, always playing referee.

"I merely wish you wouldn't spend so much time with her." Dave took her hand and placed it in his bent elbow after entering the double glass doors.

"You know, I don't tell you who your friends should be." Libby just couldn't seem to make him understand. An important part of Libby's life, their friendship went all the way back to her teens, to just after her mom's fatal car accident. Bev Jorgensen was like a sister. Her only family besides her dad, and Libby couldn't imagine a life without her.

"That's because my friends are respectable. Don't look like Kewpie dolls," Dave said as if he were espousing some momentous secret to life and happiness. "Nor do they have tattoos or weird body piercings. I can assure you, they're all upstanding pillars of the community."

Please, Scotty, beam me up! Where was that damn ship when she needed it most?

"Take John Miller and Terrance Young. They both have beautiful wives with thriving careers. You should try harder to make friends with them. Bev's a little crass. I can't believe you let her get away with calling me Dr. Bull."

"Yeah, yeah! I know. They're doctors' wives who walk on water." She didn't add that, lately, there were times—like right now—when she wholeheartedly agreed with Bev's nickname. Dr. David R. Phillips could definitely be full of it, especially when it came to his friends. "It's hard to hang with those two when I feel uncomfortable around them."

"You need to relax and just be yourself. They'll come to like you. Give it time."

Libby stiffened. "I have given it time." She exhaled a long sigh and pasted a smile on her face, wishing he'd take her feelings on the subject a little more seriously.

He didn't answer as they found their seats.

When the curtain finally closed after a long, drawn-out show, Libby heaved a sigh of relief. She rubbed her temples in an effort to ease her splitting headache. All she wanted to do was go home, take some aspirin, and climb into bed. Instead, once they hit the lobby, Dave spotted Dr. Terrance Young and his wife, along with the other couple.

Libby groaned when he caught her hand and headed straight for them. "Terry…John…wait up."

"Why, Libby." Candace Young's nod indicated her mother's brooch. "Is that a bee?"

"Yes." Libby fingered it and smiled. "I cherish this pin." She felt closer to her mom when she wore it.

"How nice." Her tone said otherwise. "And it matches that lovely dress." She glanced at Victoria Miller and smirked. "I thought it the perfect color for your complexion the last time you wore it."

Libby looked down at her favorite gown—one that even on sale and with her discount cost a week's salary. So what if she'd worn it more than once? Was that a crime? Her gaze moved higher. Her smile deepened as she eyed the two women she secretly thought of as the Stepford wives. Victoria and Candace appeared much as they always did. Too perfect. Too polished. And definitely too phony to wear something twice, even if they liked it.

Dave cleared his throat. "It's a beautiful pin and I love that dress."

She glanced at him. A hint of pink flooded his face. Oh my God! He's trying to smooth over my gaffe, she realized. Does he see me as gauche and unsophisticated? Her smile died as more concerns about her not ever fitting in with his friends or his lifestyle came to mind. She was a simple person at heart. Until recently, she'd thought that was something they shared. But lately?

"We were just heading to McVey's," Terry said about a trendy bar up the street, interrupting the uncomfortable silence. "Would you like to join us?"

"Sounds great," Dave said too quickly, paying no attention to her surprised look. With his hand on the small of her back, he fell into step with the others.

Libby followed, even adding a comment now and then that everyone but Dave totally ignored.

The entire time she walked, Bev's concern about Libby changing to fit into the mold of what Dave needed as a partner filled her thoughts. It seemed Libby Edwards was disappearing right in front of her eyes.

Maybe that's how it was for Victoria and Candace, before they became Stepford wives.

At the bar she nursed a drink, mulling over her predicament. She didn't like Dave's friends any more than they liked her.

The drive back to her apartment was quick. He parked and then looked at her, seeming only now to notice her silence. "You're awfully quiet. Is something wrong?"

"I had a busy day and I'm beat. I wish you would've asked me if I wanted to go to that bar before you accepted their invitation."

"Why? We agreed that we need to socialize more. You'll never get them to accept you unless you show an interest and do things with them."

No. She hadn't agreed. She just hadn't disagreed.

Dave waved her reservations away as if his explanation solved the problem. "Listen, I don't have to be at the hospital until ten in the morning. Why don't I spend the night? There are some things I'd like to discuss."

Libby's hands fisted to the point of pain when her nails dug into her palms. If only she were a more superficial person, they'd like her. Flexing her fingers, Libby sighed and swallowed her aggravation. Still, she had no intention of listening to a lecture about how to win over women like Victoria and Candace.

"Can we do it another time? I'm tired and have a headache. Plus, I have an early morning meeting at the store." She closed her eyes and tried to soften her refusal with a smile. "If you'd given me your schedule, I wouldn't have planned the meeting." Actually, Libby planned to go in to work early so she could take a long break to have breakfast with Bev. Yet, if she relayed that information, he'd spend another hour trying to convince her to cancel.

Dave shrugged and ushered her out of the car. At her door, he kissed her good night—a quick peck on the lips—and soon drove away, blissfully unaware of how much Libby's misgivings bothered her.

At that moment, all her fears about the future and what it would really be like being married to him flooded her thoughts. Did she really want to turn into a Stepford wife?

Her shoulders slumped and she blinked back tears. Dave loved her and she loved him, but obviously love wasn't enough.

ଓଃ

"Here you are, ma'am," Libby said to an unhappy customer who refused to be placated. This was the third time she'd assembled a boxed lamp. If this one had some imagined flaw, she'd just have to lose the sale because there were no more in stock.

"That's it," a voice said from behind her. "I want that lamp."

"This one is mine." The old biddy clutched the rod so close to her chest the lampshade almost fell off. "Ms. Edwards brought it from the stock room specifically for me." She then took her charge card out of her purse and waved it, indicating the others off to the side. "But there are three more to choose from."

Taking the card, Libby nodded to Bev and gave a quick wink that her customer couldn't see. "I'll be right with you as soon as I finish with this lady."

Bev winked back. "No problem." She placed one of the discarded lamps next to the register. "I like this one, but I also want to look around."

Libby rang up the sale and watched the demanding customer leave in a self-righteous haze of happiness. "Probably to bug another manager," she said under her breath as Mrs. Thompson didn't like having mere salespeople wait on her. An image of Victoria and Candace in twenty years appeared in her mind's eye. Would they become self-absorbed older women? Would she, if she married Dave? As she rushed over to Bev and gave her a hug, the thought added to all her other misgivings. "Thanks for rescuing me. How'd you know she'd buy it if you wanted it?"

"Classic human behavior of a selfish person. Think of a three-year-old who may not want a toy, but doesn't want anyone else to have it either."

"I wish I could ignore people like her." Dealing with the Mrs. Thompsons of the world always put her in a funk. They seemed to come out in droves during a sale. She sighed, glancing around at a room full of lamps feeling even more down. "My group sales manager is always on me to make my displays look fresh. How in the heck am I supposed to make lamps look fresh? Put bows on them?"

"I have a solution." Bev laughed and her oversized earrings

bounced as her head bobbed slightly. "A job opportunity. Out at the farm." Bev was a horse handler at Twin Oaks Farm, a place that was near and dear to Libby's heart and where the two originally met. "A couple of hands just quit on Doug."

She'd worked with Bev on the farm as a teen, until her sophomore year of college when her dad told her she needed to concentrate on her future. Trouble was, after almost four years, she hadn't found anything she'd loved as much, especially her current stint at Dillard's. "Do you think he'd be interested in hiring me?"

She couldn't care less about being on the fast track for a buyer, as her manager kept reminding her at every opportunity, a promotion all the manager trainees drooled over. Every trainee but her.

"Hell, yes, he'd be interested." Bev's excited voice drew her focus. "He hated losing you to begin with. Besides, he really needs the help with the season starting back up. At least go and talk to him, then you can decide."

A thrill tingled up her spine. "OK. I'll do it. I get off early today since I came in early." She hadn't felt such a sense of fun in a long time, just another warning flag to add to her list of concerns.

"Awesome! I'll set it up. You won't be sorry."

She left Bev full of resolve. In fact, while taking the escalator to the third floor, she decided it was time to do something just because it made *her* happy. Not Dave or her dad. Instead of going back to her department, she veered toward her manager's office and asked for a personal half day. After that, she called Bev to set up an earlier appointment.

Libby spun out of Dillard's parking lot, feeling like she'd been let out of prison. That alone made her realize it was time to make some changes in her life, and quitting Dillard's would be the first one.

At her apartment, she quickly donned jeans and riding boots, grabbed her vest, then hurried back to her car and soon was heading east on US 60. Excitement welled up inside her, building to near-bursting proportions. She'd finally chosen a path and it felt like the best decision she'd ever made. Kismet; meant to be. She mentally kicked herself for not acting sooner. If only she could fast-forward the next few weeks, her life would be perfect.

Well, almost perfect. Thoughts of Dave sprang forth. She doubted he'd like her decision, but she didn't want to worry about his disapproval. Not now.

She tapped the brake pedal, slowing, and turned onto the shaded gravel road leading to Twin Oaks Farm. As she drove, her gaze wandered. Various shades of green emerged everywhere. The main stables and outbuildings eventually came into view. Beyond them, open meadows and Kentucky bluegrass spread out as far as Libby could see. Overhead, giant oak trees that, even without leaves, formed a canopy across the road, hiding the sunlight behind dark branches that stretched toward the heavens.

When she spotted a group of horses in the distance, running together in the same direction, she pulled over to the side of the road. While watching the herd run with wild abandon, contentment warmed her. Despite civilization looming only eight miles away, Libby imagined herself slipping back in time.

This place was special and made her feel comfortable. She remembered her first trip to the farm like it was yesterday instead of nine years ago. She'd never forget why she came. To heal. Twin Oaks and the horses had helped her deal with the overwhelming grief of losing her mom.

I made the right decision to return, she mused happily. I belong here.

Smiling, she looked at the clock on her dashboard. "Shoot. Better get a move on. Don't want to be late for my interview."

She put the car in gear and, after a quick glance to check the side mirror, a couple of giant oaks grabbed her notice. The two stood side by side, about fifteen feet away from the road. They towered over the other trees lining the drive, appearing out of place. Not only that, she caught whispering in her thoughts. Like they were mentally calling to her.

Yeah, right! Giant oaks didn't call to people in their minds. She laughed, hit the gas pedal, and peeled out. Boy, she'd escaped from the crazies at Dillard's just in time.

Around the bend, her best friend rushed to unlatch the gate. When the car came to a stop, Bev ran over and opened Libby's door.

"I'm so excited you made it."

"Me too! I can't believe I'm actually here." The "William Tell Overture" sounded from her pocket. Libby pulled out her cell phone and glanced at the caller ID. "It's Dave."

Bev shrugged. "Just text him and tell him you can't talk right now and you'll call him back later."

"Good idea." When the message light blinked, she typed a quick message and after sending it, turned the phone off. The thought about feeling as if she couldn't share her excitement with him didn't ease her anxiety any. She could already hear his words about irresponsibility and immaturity, not to mention what he'd say when he learned she'd be working with Bev. Candace and Victoria would certainly mock her choice. But none of that mattered. She'd made up her mind. Retail and messing with displays day after day, fresh or otherwise, just weren't her thing. Horses were.

"So, where'd Dr. Bull take you last night? You never said this morning."

She sighed. "I wish you wouldn't call him that."

"If the name didn't fit, I wouldn't use it."

"Can't you try to get along," she asked, tired of playing referee. "And be nice to him?"

"I have tried." Bev's chin lifted. "He treats me like I'm a pariah because I don't fit his mold of what he thinks is respectable."

Wasn't that the truth? Still, if Bev didn't respond to his little barbs so negatively, it would help. "Then be the bigger person and be nice for my sake."

"OK. I promise I'll try harder." Bev hesitated a beat, then her eyebrows rose. "So, where'd you guys go last night?"

"The opera." Libby exhaled slowly, blowing on her bangs. "I'm sure he thinks I'm uncultured."

"Be still my heart." Bev placed her hand over her chest, patting, and rolled her eyes. "How'd you get roped into doing something so *fun*?"

"I don't know." She shrugged. "It just sort of happened. You know, another surprise."

"It seems a lot of things are just sort of happening." Bev

clucked and shook her spiky red head. Her overlarge dangling earrings followed the movement, dancing back and forth. "But hey, you're the one who's going to spend the rest of your life with him. Not me."

Another truth Libby didn't want to reflect upon as Dave's comment about Kewpie dolls entered her thoughts. She smiled, thinking it an apt description. Her friend did tend to use makeup, clothing, and jewelry to attract attention, even when working with her precious horses.

A loud neigh rent the air. A hoof impatiently pawed the ground and the horse blew a huge breath out of her nostrils. "Is that Black Mystic?" Libby nodded at the mare Bev had been working with when she drove up.

"Yes. And as you can see, she hates to be ignored." Bev reached for Libby's arm and tugged. "Come on and get reacquainted."

"I'd love to." Libby climbed out of the car and turned a full circle, taking everything in.

Another snort erupted. Black Mystic pranced, clearly growing more impatient by the second.

"Cool your jets, Mystic. We're coming." Bev latched on to Libby's hand, pulling her behind. The mare's head rose and her ears twitched. Nostrils flaring, the mare nudged Bev when she got close enough to grab her halter. "She's my favorite, and she abuses the knowledge." She rubbed soothingly over her long face. "Behave, you beast. Black Mystic, this is Libby. You remember her? She remembers you."

"It's nice to see you again." Stifling pure joy, Libby stroked the animal, letting her gaze wander farther.

"Sam's added more horses and enlarged the bunkhouse to accommodate another fifteen kids."

She nodded. Twin Oaks Farm was an unusual one in these parts. A camp for kids. A place where children came to heal. Whether from a serious illness such as cancer or from traumatic problems like Libby's, Sam's horses helped them.

A few grazed in the adjacent pasture.

Most of the thoroughbreds on the farm were castoffs taken in or bought after being on the racing circuit. Some were injured early on, ending their racing careers before they had a chance to become breeding champions. Others were too old to race and not good enough to breed, meaning they hadn't won many races in their careers.

Libby grinned. "I'm glad they can bring a little pleasure to kids who need them." All were dead broke and gentle, needing their own place to heal as they aged. "They're proud animals and deserve to be useful."

"I agree."

"It feels right!" Familiar smells and sounds assaulted Libby's senses. She spent long seconds enjoying the sensation of returning home after a long journey.

"Doug's right over there, talking with Sam." Bev indicated the house with a nod. "Good luck. Not that you need it. I'll be here when you're done."

Libby's gaze followed Bev's as two men stepped farther onto the porch. She recognized Doug, the farm's manager, a balding, tall, lean man in his early to mid-forties, deep in conversation with the owner, Sam Thorpe.

Libby approached the house.

Doug Williams glanced up. "Can we finish this later?" He turned to Sam and nodded in her direction. "There's the new handler I'm interviewing. But unless she's changed significantly since she was last here, I think it's only a formality. You remember her?"

Sam looked over and a smile lit his face. No one could miss his shock of snowy white hair. That and the deep crinkles around his warm blue eyes gave his age of sixty-nine years away. "Is that Libby Edwards?" When Doug nodded, Sam added, his voice full of amazement, "She's all grown up. How many years has it been?"

"At least four."

Libby started up the stairs, meeting Sam halfway.

"Well, well, well. It's about time you came back."

"Hi, Mr. Thorpe." Libby's smile was as wide as his when they shook hands. "It's good to be here." She turned to the younger man, still grinning. "Mr. Williams, I'm ready for my interview."

"What's this Mr. Williams stuff? You can call me Doug. If you don't, I'll feel old."

"OK, Doug. I'm here to work. How about a job?" Libby replied, laughing.

Doug glanced at Sam with eyebrows cocked. "Can we finish going over the schedule later?"

"Fine." Sam grunted. "No big hurry since we have a few days before the season begins." He gave Libby a brief nod. "The first session starts next weekend and then we're up and running until the end of October." He turned toward the front door.

Doug's eyes sparkled. "Well, little lady, I bet you haven't lost your touch with the horses."

"I hope not, but it's been awhile."

"Ha! It's like riding a bicycle. Once you get comfortable, it'll be like you never left. I feel blessed that you're interested. Of course the pay's not the main attraction, but I think you'll love the benefits. Heck, you can even live out here. In order to attract better trainers, we've added a few cabins with all of the amenities—bed, bath, and kitchen. Would you like a tour?"

Libby nodded. "I'd love one."

While they walked, memories flooded Libby's thoughts. Besides the two weeks as a camper at age fourteen, she'd spent too many summers after that as a counselor. When she left, at the start of her sophomore year of college, she never thought to return because her father had been dead set against it. Even now, his main argument replayed in her mind. She'd never done anything else, so how could she know what she wanted. Libby had no answer at the time and quitting had been the hardest thing she'd ever done. Six jobs later, she could finally answer the question more definitively.

Libby hurried to keep up with Doug, at the same time noting her surroundings more closely. At first glance it appeared as if nothing much had changed, but now, the new additions stood out.

"Twin Oaks Farm has been in Sam's family for over a hundred years," he said. "His great-great-grandfather started it with two horses back in the 1870s."

Libby knew all this, but never tired of hearing it. They entered the main stable. Her gaze went directly to the third stall on the right. And there stood Thorpe's Pride.

At their intrusion, the mare's head shot up and her nostrils flared.

"I wonder if she remembers you." Doug strode toward her stall.

The exquisite animal immediately nuzzled her hand when she stepped close enough to hold it out. "Hey there, Pride. It's good to see you again." She caressed her nose and rubbed a hand along her sleek neck. "You're such a beauty."

"She is that. And big too. Sixteen hands." He nodded, absently stroking the horse. "Still, she can be stubborn at times."

Libby leaned in close and whispered, "Are you giving these nice people a hard time, Pride?"

Doug laughed. "Sam usually does most of her handling because when she does get a burr up her butt, she's a handful. If it were up to me, I'd get rid of her. I think she knows it, too."

"Oh, Pride. I can't believe you've become such a naughty girl." Libby turned back to Doug. "I'm sure I can still handle her." She'd never had trouble in the past, though, a twinge of guilt tugged on her heartstrings for never visiting the horse in all this time. The two shared something special. Libby had been present at her birth; even helped train her. Yet, as much as she missed Pride, returning would have been too painful.

"If anyone can handle her, that'd be you. She's always had a soft spot for you." Doug continued rubbing her neck. "She's just finicky. She's definitely happy to see you. It'll be nice to have help. Hell, we both know Sam will never part with her. He loves her. Besides, Pride has also become quite the mare for breeding and too valuable. Never hurts to be a direct descendant of Aristide, the first Derby winner back in 1875." Doug stopped talking, then looked over at Libby and blushed. "Sorry, I forgot you already know all that. Don't know why I'm rattling on. Habit, I guess."

Libby smiled. "That's OK, I don't mind."

"Well, good, because I'm likely to repeat a lot of information. Anyway, back to Pride. Sam doesn't race her. He quit all that back when he started the camp, but her foals add to the farm's income. Sam runs her daily, which gives her a chance to show us she knows what she was bred for." He let go of the horse and faced her. "Well? Have I convinced you yet?"

She indicated Pride with her nod. "Brought out the big guns, huh? You didn't need her. I was ready to sign on the minute I drove up the gravel road."

"Great. There's more to see. Then I'll need to get to work." He turned to leave. "When can you start?"

"Not for two weeks." Libby stroked Pride one more time and whispered good-bye before catching up with Doug. "I still have to give a notice. I can be here after work and on my days off, if that's OK?"

"I'll take any time I can get. Just let me know your schedule and I'll work around it." They walked through the stable with him pointing things out as he went. "The last ten are pregnant mares we saved a couple of months ago from a farm in Montana—that's all we could take. We'll sell the foals to help with finances. They're outside right now. Since they're used to harsher climates, we're able to let them graze more in the open. It helps with the workload and overhead. I only bring them in when the temperature gets too cold at night."

"They must have been the horses running free that I saw on my way in."

"Yeah, the left pasture. Close to the road." The two departed the main stable and headed toward a two-story building. Doug continued talking. "The good thing about having more horses is that after they foal and the foals are weaned and sold, we'll be able to help more kids. We've renovated the bunkhouse. Added a few more rooms."

He stopped and looked around. His chest puffed up with pride. "We can accommodate up to fifty-five kids at a time. Of course it doesn't always work out that we're full, given that some kids stay only a week and some stay the full month. It's best if each child cares for the same horse for his or her entire stay. That always creates a few scheduling dilemmas."

She smiled. "I take it Thorpe's Pride isn't one the kids practice on?"

"Hardly." Doug grunted. "Thorpe's Pride, Black Mystic, and

Mary's Choice are the only three mares we breed. They're descendants from the farm's original two horses and each has a special place in Sam's heart. We geld the stallions. They're easier for the kids to handle. Sam takes care of Thorpe's Pride and Bev takes care of the other two. She works with our vet the rest of the time."

They toured the bunkhouse. On the way out, Doug glanced at Libby. "Does it bring back memories?"

Boy did it ever! Images of the kids and the camp rushed into her head. This place was as unique as the kids who came through it, sometimes providing solace to a dying child, and at other times the means to aid in confidence-building or nurturing the healing process. Nodding, she said, "Yes. I've always loved it here."

"Are you interested in seeing the cabins?"

She nodded. "I'm thinking of moving here full time."

"They're not too far." He headed down the same path they'd come. Within minutes, ten small cabins came into view through the trees. "Sam wanted these built away from the house for privacy. He hates people living right on top of him. That's why he's out here. Come on, I'll show you a vacant one and you can decide if you like it."

At the third cabin, he took out a ring of keys, unlocked and then opened the door, and stepped aside. "It's not the Ritz, but the cabins are insulated, and all have adequate furnishings."

Libby strolled through the modest unit. Cheery and comfortable came to mind. The bath and kitchen were adequate and held possibilities. "This is nicer than my apartment." She offered a slight smile. Dave wasn't going to like it. For that matter, neither would her dad. Thinking of the two men, Libby wondered how she was going to tell either. "Sold."

"Now that we have that solved, let's go find Sam. Once you've talked to him, we can go over the schedule and I can put you to work. That is, if you're willing?"

"Of course I'm willing." She increased her gait to catch up with him.

When they neared the house, Doug slowed. "I'll be in the rear stable. One of the Montana mares is due to foal any time now. Sam should be in his office. Go on up, I'll see you later." He turned in the direction of the stables.

Libby ran up the porch stairs and into the house. She'd been here before, so she knew where his office was located. Sam glanced up from his desk as she approached. He stood and smiled expectantly. "So, what'd you think of all the changes?"

"You've added a lot since I was last here. The cabins are really nice."

"Have a seat." He sat back down and motioned toward a chair across from the desk. "It helps with the bottom line. They're very basic; believe it or not they were fairly inexpensive to build."

"I'm impressed." Sam had told Libby long ago that Twin Oaks was his and Mrs. Thorpe's dream of leaving something for future generations to appreciate. This part of Kentucky had always been horse country, yet more and more farms were selling out to big developers, who in turn were chopping up the land and creating urban sprawl. The way Sam saw it, stud farms like the one that had been his family's livelihood for generations were all too quickly disappearing.

"It's part of my long-term plans. Since none of my kids want the hassle of running it, I've begun the task of putting the farm in a trust."

Libby nodded. "So is Mrs. Thorpe around? I'd like to say hello." She wondered why she hadn't seen her during the tour.

"No." Sorrow crept over Sam's face. He shook his head, sighing sadly. "She died last year, so it's just me and Doug now."

"I didn't know," Libby said softly, wishing she could disappear. "I'm so sorry."

"Don't be." His wistful smile replaced sadness. "She's no longer suffering and we had thirty-nine wonderful years. Now I just need to make sure this place lives on after I'm gone, mainly for Mary. It was her idea to turn the farm into the camp once we retired. Her death taught me things happen quickly. One minute she was healthy and then three months later I'm mourning her passing." His smile turned warmer. "I can't believe it's been eleven years since we helped our first camper."

Sam stood, came around the desk, and leaned against it. "Do

you have any questions? I know Doug's pretty thorough. In case he missed something, feel free to ask."

"Well, I do have one question. Is it OK if I ride Thorpe's Pride?"

The edges of his eyes crinkled into deep lines when his grin widened. "Most people would want to know about the pay or if there is medical coverage."

"I guess I should ask those questions, too."

"You're not going to get rich working here. Most of our hands love what they do and they love the kids, so turnover isn't too much of a problem. We do offer a basic health policy, but we only kick in fifty percent," he explained briefly. Then he chuckled. "To answer your question—you can ride Pride whenever you feel up to the challenge. Maybe I should go with you for your first time. She can be stubborn when the mood strikes."

Libby's grin stretched. "How about now?"

"I can use a break." Sam straightened and motioned toward the door. "Let's go."

After saddling Thorpe's Pride and Mary's Choice, both riders spent time warming the horses up. Having worked the highjinks out of the mares, they headed out at a slow trot, which built until both mounts were given full freedom to run.

Libby's laughter caught on the wind. She leaned in, urging Thorpe's Pride faster as the mare's swift gait ate up the ground. Libby had forgotten how energized she'd always felt riding this magnificent animal—the air rushing past her face and the countryside speeding past in a blur of green—her idea of heaven.

When they neared a stream, Libby pulled back on the reins and slowed, allowing Pride to catch her breath. Sam followed. They ambled. All the while she scanned the spectacular scenery.

"I'd forgotten how beautiful it is." It was still too early for the deciduous trees to leaf. But the hearty wild flowers bloomed in the meadows, adding purple and yellow to the rain-soaked bluegrass, laid out along the rolling hills like a carpet for miles. "Makes me feel alive, like I belong here," she added fervently.

Since no job in the past four years had made her feel this way, Libby realized her sentiments spoke volumes.

Sam nodded but didn't speak.

The two rode in companionable silence for more than a mile, still on Thorpe land. On the return trip, they traveled along the same gravel road Libby had driven in on, paralleling the same white fence that seemed to go on into infinity. While passing the trees that had caught her attention earlier, trees she'd seen a million times, Libby once again felt their pull. Strange thoughts of having been here in another era flitted through her mind, which was totally crazy.

She pointed to the oaks. "I've never noticed before, but those trees look so out of place out there."

Sam's gaze followed her hand. His features lit with amusement. "Those two trees are special."

Libby squinted. "Oh?"

"Yep. The kids started calling them wishing trees a few years back."

"Wishing trees?"

"Yeah, you know like a well? Only with trees." He winked and added in a conspiratorial whisper, "According to family legend, all sorts of things have happened under them over the years."

"I believe it." Libby nodded. "Don't laugh, but when I passed by here earlier, they seemed to call to me. Like right now. I have this funny feeling that I'm here for a reason."

"Trees or no trees, that's not so hard to figure out. You belong at Twin Oaks." The crinkles surrounding Sam's eyes deepened as his grin widened. "I know how you are around horses. It's a rare gift few people possess."

Libby glanced at the oaks again and shrugged. "They look old."

Nodding, Sam looked in the same direction. "They are. Maybe even centuries. For over a hundred years, the number one rule in the Thorpe family has been to leave them alone. That's what my daddy told me, and his daddy told him, all the way back to my great-grandfather."

"And no one's cut them down? How amazing that something lasts so long." That right there made them special.

"About sixty years ago, my daddy planted the other trees away from those two and made the road where it is, but he left those two intact. I only know that I can't touch them and my kids have been given the same instructions. Of course, our rule has only added to their mystique."

Libby shot Sam a questioning glance. "Do they work?"

"Who knows? I wished for a long and happy life with Mary when we got engaged under them and my wish came true." He chuckled. "I would've liked more time, but sometimes we have to be happy with what life or the trees give us." Sam sighed. "One thing's for sure. No one in the near future will cut them down. They're timeless. Add continuity and peace to the surroundings."

"You're right," Libby agreed. "I do feel at peace here. Time seems to stand still." Then she laughed and rolled her eyes. "Don't mind me. I've been having strange thoughts all afternoon."

"The trees have a way of making people feel that way. It's not new. I've heard it before and I'll probably hear it again."

They approached the paddocks surrounding the stables.

"Thanks for the company." Sam dismounted and opened the gate. "I'm glad you're back, because I meant what I said. You belong here."

Libby nodded and guided Pride through the gate before dismounting. Sam led his horse inside before closing the gate behind him.

In the stable at one of the crossties, Libby relieved Thorpe's Pride of her bridle and saddle. She began grooming the mare as Sam groomed Mary's Choice in a similar area several stalls away.

First, she grabbed a hoof pick to check each hoof for caked dirt and small pebbles, then working her way up the leg, she inspected for strains. Finally, Libby took a dandy brush and started to brush the dust, mud, and other debris off the legs in short, quick strokes, using another brush to rub down her back. Done and with everything put away, she guided the mare to her stall. Before leaving, she stroked Pride's neck and whispered how happy she was to be back.

Libby met Sam on his way out of Choice's stall.

"It's a lot of work." He stretched. "I'm just happy it keeps me in such good shape."

Libby smiled. Her arms ached from the exertion. "I forgot

how hard it is."

"You'll be up to it in no time. You're young. I have to work on my scheduling, so I'll see you later."

"OK. Thanks for the company. I enjoyed the ride." She turned to look for Doug as Sam started off in the opposite direction.

"I ride every day," he said over his shoulder. "Let me know when you can be here and I'll ride with you if I can."

"Thanks, Mr. Thorpe. I will."

"Oh, and Libby?"

He stopped his retreat as she halted in midstride and glanced back at him with eyebrows raised. "Yes, Mr. Thorpe?"

"Unlike Doug, I know I'm old. But I still don't cotton to all that formality around here. I like things friendly and informal—so call me Sam, OK?"

Grinning wide, Libby nodded. "OK, Sam it is." She left him to find Doug and quickly immersed herself in her new duties with the horses.

By quitting time she could barely move, even noted how much effort it took to turn the wheel of her car as she sped out to the main road on the way home. Libby couldn't remember a time in the last three years when she'd worked so hard.

Inside her apartment, she turned on her cell and noticed someone had left a message. There were four. All from Dave. She connected to voice mail. The device came alive with his voice. The first two were friendly, but the last two indicated definite displeasure with her absence.

Libby sighed, then checked her text messages. Dave had sent three in all. Her shoulders slumped. She'd have to call him back, but first she needed a hot shower.

Chapter 2

The doorbell rang, interrupting Libby's peaceful breakfast. She took a deep breath and gathered the morning paper into a pile, stalling as the impatient pealing continued.

He's your fiancé, not an executioner. The thought didn't ease her trepidation, nor did she hasten her pace in answering his urgent summons. She wiped her hands on her slacks, took another deep breath, and braced herself as she swung open the door.

Dave pushed past her into the room, annoyance stamped over his expression.

At least I've had a good night's sleep so I can deal with him, she thought. Libby kept quiet as he moved through her apartment, edgily pacing back and forth, reminding her of a caged tiger.

He stopped and glared at her. "Don't you answer your phone anymore?" His tone was sharp. "Or return your messages?"

Libby decided to ignore his testy disposition. "Sorry. I got wrapped up in something and forgot I'd turned off my cell." She offered a contrite shrug. "And when I got your messages, I'd planned to call you back after a quick shower, but I fell asleep. So let's start over, OK? Good morning! Would you like some coffee?"

"I'm not in the mood for games. Where were you yesterday afternoon and last night? I was worried about you."

She sighed. "Sit down, Dave. We need to talk."

"I don't want to sit down. You've been acting weird lately and I want to know why."

"Sit!" Libby demanded. "And I'll tell you. My shift at the store starts at nine, so I don't have a lot of time. You can either listen to what I have to say, or you can leave."

Dave pulled out a chair and sat, then impatiently drummed his fingers on the table.

Libby poured a cup of coffee and placed it in front of him.

"I'm quitting my job today. I've found another one."

He practically shot out of the chair. "You what?" Total shock replaced annoyance in his expression. "You've only been a manager with Dillard's for ten months. I thought we went over this."

Libby held on to her rising temper, but the effort cost her. "No. You told me your opinion and I listened. Now I'm doing what I feel is right for me."

"You can't keep quitting, Libby. Five jobs in four years doesn't look good on a résumé. It's immature and irresponsible."

Though the real number was six, she remained silent, eyeing the handsome man spouting off his explanation as if he were talking to a child. She couldn't help but smile. He sounded so much like her father. Dave Phillips was really a wonderful guy—the perfect height for her at five feet ten inches with wavy dark brown hair and soulful brown eyes—when he wasn't telling her how to behave. In a sudden rush of insight, their relationship became clearer.

Libby already had a father, which was why she needed to take a stand now. Holding on to her determination, she asked, "Do you like your job?

Dave's brow furrowed and the bluster went out of his expression. "Why?"

Libby eyed him thoughtfully. "Just answer my question. Do you?"

His yes came out in a long sigh and he nodded.

"Did you always want to become a doctor?"

He rubbed the back of his neck. "For the most part, yes." Whether out of frustration or agitation, Libby wasn't quite sure as he added, "I knew it was something I wanted fairly early on." He aimed a narrow-eyed gaze at her. "How does my wanting to be a doctor have any bearing on what we're discussing?"

"I'm done doing what everyone else wants me to do. I'm going to do what I love." She took a deep breath, reaching for the courage to venture forth. "I've taken a job at the horse farm where I used to work in my teens."

Deafening silence followed and Dave only stared at her like

she'd grown horns.

Libby had to force herself to breathe…to relax. She couldn't stop now. She took one more deep breath and kept going, ignoring the censure in his expression. "I see this news comes as a shock. I don't know why. And I don't know why I didn't do it three years ago, since it's why I've had so many jobs. I never should've quit. Working with kids and horses is what I wanted to do—what I love. I'm also moving out to the farm for the time being."

"Libby, you're much too bright to be mucking out stalls, filling hay bins, and playing camp counselor," he finally said after a prolonged moment. "What about us? We're going to be married the last week in June. That's only three months away."

Might as well go for broke! Still, Libby couldn't meet his eyes. "I want to postpone the wedding."

"What?" Dave shouted, coming out of his chair. "Where's all of this coming from? Bev! That's where. This is her idea, isn't it?" He raked a hand through his hair and began pacing. The caged tiger was back.

"This isn't about Bev."

"The woman is bad news," he stated in a clipped tone. "You should stay away from her."

"Who are you? The friend police?" She clenched her fist.

He didn't seem to notice, just kept talking along with his pacing. "Changing our date will be expensive, so that's not the most viable option. Why don't you work at your farm and even live there, but I'm sure once we're man and wife, you'll be too busy to work as a common laborer. Maybe you can buy a horse and stable it somewhere. That way we're both happy."

"You can't be serious?" She gaped at him when he nodded. What was wrong with working with horses? He spoke as if his opinion was the only valid one, which did nothing to ease her worst fears. Did he really know her? Why had she never noticed before that he seemed to be molding her into someone he wanted her to be, rather than who she was?

Libby had no one to blame but herself for his attitude, having let him get away with telling her what to do for too long in their year-long relationship. It hit her just then what she wanted—a partner who accepted her and loved her—faults and all—so this was worth the fight.

"How's this for serious? Either we postpone the wedding or it's off." Libby stormed toward her front door. "I need to leave for work. You can show yourself out." If she stayed, she'd end up saying something to make things worse.

"You can't leave now." His stunned tone stopped her cold.

She looked back and caught Dave staring at the empty space she once occupied, confusion clouding his eyes. She gave a mental snort and continued walking. Well, what did he think? That she'd just roll over and become someone else?

"Libby…wait!" He followed her, pleading while she grabbed her things, but she was past the point of waiting. She'd waited too long as it was to say something.

"Let's not be rash. This is our future we're talking about."

"No, Dave. You're talking about your future—not ours." Her words, once out, were liberating, like a cinched belt being loosened so she could take a deep breath again. She'd finally verbalized her feelings after months of holding them in and she wasn't about to back down now. "Your future involves only what you want. If I'm to be part of it, you need to include my wants and my needs in there. So far, all I see are yours. That's just not good enough." She yanked her coat off the hanger and headed to the door. "I have to go. Call me when you want to talk about us, OK?"

She stalked to her car with Dave on her heels. "Libby, you can't drop a bombshell like that and leave. Damn it all. We need to sit down and discuss this rationally."

"Fine. But I'm not changing my mind now that I've made my decision."

"I'll pick you up for dinner tonight."

"No. I can't. I'm going out to the farm after work."

"Come on, Libby," Dave pleaded. "Why are you doing this?"

Libby continued walking and said over her shoulder, "I'm not doing anything but following my heart and being who I am. If you honestly loved me, you'd want me to be happy. Somehow, I'm starting to doubt that you really know me at all."

"That's not true. I love you just the way you are."

The fervency in his voice tugged on Libby's emotional cord, causing her to stop and turn. She looked him directly in the eye and said in a tormented whisper, "Then why do I feel you're trying to change me? Why am I not good enough the way I am?"

He halted and stared, his eyes big as quarters, seeming surprised by her questions.

Observing him, Libby sighed as sadness filled her soul. She just didn't think she could ever be what he seemed to need. She wasn't a college graduate nor was she any great beauty. She'd never have a high-powered job, or look like she stepped out of a magazine, the way Candace and Victoria did. Her face was nondescript, with eyes that all but disappeared without makeup because her blonde eyelashes were the same shade as her hair. With a lean, five-foot-three-inch frame, she appeared almost juvenile, much younger than her twenty-three years.

Slowly, he shook his head, his gaze pleading. "Please, Libby, don't do this."

Tears sprang to her eyes. Yet she couldn't back down now or let that mournful brown gaze affect her. She opened her car door and slid into the driver's seat. "I've got to be at work in ten minutes. Think about what I said, Dave. Tomorrow's my day off and I'm moving into one of the cabins at the farm. It'd be nice to have your help."

"I can't. I've got a horrendous day tomorrow."

"I see." She hesitated. "I was hoping to show you around a bit after I moved in so you could meet everyone. I thought maybe then you'd understand why this job is so important to me." She swallowed the lump in her throat and pulled the door shut. She gunned the engine, backed up, put the car in drive, and sped out of the parking lot, leaving Dave staring dumbfounded.

Libby shed tears all the way to work. Damn it all. Why should she have to choose between her horses or Dave? Did having Dave mean becoming a Stepford wife? Definitely not her idea of wedded bliss.

I want it all, she thought angrily. I want someone who loves me for me and I want to do what I love. Is that so much to ask?

Her chest felt tight as she drove. The only thing that kept her going was the pleasure she'd derived from working at the farm the day before. Libby parked, then pushed all of the problems out of her mind and headed into Dillard's. She intended to give notice right away, which meant only ten work days left before she could pursue her dream full time.

Thankfully, the day passed quickly. Libby drove to her apartment and changed into loose-fitting jeans, leather riding boots, and a tailored oxford shirt. She glanced in the mirror and noticed her fair complexion lacked color. She shrugged. Didn't matter what she looked like. No one but the horses would see her.

She ran a brush through short blonde hair, not bothering to redo her scant makeup, then grabbed a vest and rushed out the door. Her new job waited.

Like the previous day, when she neared the two trees, Libby felt their pull. This time, curiosity conflicted with common sense and won. She stopped the car and climbed out. After walking over to the trees and peering up at the monstrous branches, she remained rooted for countless moments, trying to understand why they seemed so important. Maybe they really were wishing trees and her problems with Dave could be solved as easily as wishing.

As silly as it seemed, she decided what the heck. She closed her eyes. "I want it all. I want him to love me for me, to work at what I love, and to fit into his world."

Suddenly, she felt a jolt.

The earth shook. Panic engulfed her when everything seemed to break apart and she felt herself falling. Her mind went blank as the world around her flew by in a hazy blur.

Time seemed to stand still as the scene came back into focus. Eventually, her equilibrium returned and she could think again. Libby pivoted. Oh my God, her mind screamed at the two big oaks standing before her, only much smaller than just seconds ago.

What had just happened?

The other majestic trees lining the drive were gone, so were the accompanying white fences and outbuildings. The scene looked bare, yet recognizable. Libby tried to make sense of it. There was something familiar about the experience, yet at the same time totally different. Was this a dream just like the last episode had been? Or was this some kind of answer to her wish?

She pinched herself. Other than hurting a bit, it did nothing to wake her up or change the scenery as she took another look around. The only thing that made sense was that she'd gone back in time somehow.

No.

She had to be dreaming. How did going back in time grant her wish? Maybe the last two days had been a dream and she'd wake up still employed at Dillard's. She halted, stood completely still, and closed her eyes.

"Wake up," she said none too softly, pinching herself again, only harder. When she opened her eyes, the two smaller trees were still visible. This definitely wasn't a dream. A bit of fear mixed with complete wonderment filled her. Had she actually been transported back in time? She could barely believe it possible, but she was here, wasn't she?

But how? And why? Maybe that other time hadn't been a dream either. Maybe she really had gone back in time to see her mother. She vaguely remembered wishing to see her mom back then, but wishing seemed to be the only similarity. She darned sure had no wish to be in the past.

Giggling interrupted Libby's thoughts.

Chapter 3

Libby heard the laughter again. That's when she noticed the heat—not terribly hot—but warmer than minutes earlier. She looked up into the green tree, now fully leafed. Through a narrowed gaze, she spotted a boy about ten years old, dressed in what looked to be homespun clothes. He
hung on to a tree limb while standing on the branch below.

"Hello." Her voice held none of the apprehension coursing through her. She forced herself to remain calm.

"How'd you do that?"

"Do what?"

"Appear from nothing. Are you magic?"

"No. I'm Libby. What's your name?" she replied, hoping to distract him from asking more about her appearing from nothing, because she had no ready answer. She glanced around, still trying to figure it all out.

"Nathan."

"Nathan? That's a nice name." Libby placed a hand over her eyes to shade them. "Hey, Nathan? What's the date?"

"Are you daft?" Everything about his look said he thought so. "How come you don't know?"

She laughed and shrugged. "I must be daft because I don't know. It's also why I'm asking."

He contemplated her reply before nodding. "It's June nineteenth."

"And," she prompted.

"Huh?"

"What year?"

He stared at her as if she were a Rubik's cube. Finally he smiled. "Eighteen seventy-four."

Libby blinked. "Eighteen seventy-four? Are you sure?"

When he nodded, his look now indicating he thought she'd lost more than just her marbles, she fought to keep the panic out of her voice. "Where do you live, Nathan?"

He pointed toward the main house. Without the treelined drive, the roof was barely visible from where Libby stood. "We live in the caretaker's house. Behind the big house. My ma is Mr. Thorpe's housekeeper and my pa runs his stables."

"Stables?" Libby looked to where the boy pointed.

Nathan nodded. "Mr. Thorpe breeds horses."

With her eyes on the landscape, reality hit her. Thorpe? The same name of the man who owned this land in her own time—Sam Thorpe. Of course. That made sense, but what in the world should she do now? Libby kept her shaded eyes on Nathan as her mind churned.

The trees. It had to be the trees, especially since she'd made a wish under them. Only, being in 1874 wasn't exactly the answer she'd expected.

Thoughts of Dave, Bev, and her dad, along with Sam, Doug, and her new job went through her mind, as did the memory of riding Thorpe's Pride the day before. As much as the idea of seeing the past intrigued her, she had no desire to be here. Apparently her wish had something to do with it, and she just had to figure out what. If the oaks truly had some kind of power to make wishes come true, then they had to be her ticket home. Or maybe all she had to do was wish herself home. She closed her eyes and wished. "Please take me home!" Libby chanted the words over and over.

"Whatcha doin'?"

Nathan's voice slipped into her thoughts and was a clear indication that wishing wasn't working.

"I'm thinking out loud." Maybe she needed to do something while she was here. Or learn something. Yeah, that seemed like a decent explanation. Maybe discovering something in the past would help her deal with Dave so that her wish could come true. Or maybe she was just plumb crazy. Either way, it didn't matter.

Blend in and stay by these trees. That's what she needed to do.

Libby looked down at her clothing and an indelicate snort

popped out. Yeah, right. I'll blend in. The same way pepper blends with salt. She was pretty sure women didn't run around in the late nineteenth century in jeans and short hair.

She sighed. Considering her gender and the time period, one where men ruled, blending in might be a bit of a problem.

So, what could she do? Pretend to be a boy?

"That's it," she said out loud, laughing because it made perfect sense. With her size, everyone would think she was a young male teenager. It shouldn't be too hard to pull off. Without makeup, Libby knew she was pretty plain. "Not real original, but so what?" It always worked in all those novels she'd read.

"What'd you say?"

"Nothing." Libby craned her neck and grinned at the boy now situated on the branch with his legs swinging freely. "Nathan, do you think your dad—er, pa—could use some help with the horses?" She needed this kid. He was her lifeline to survival. "I'm looking for work and I'm a pretty good handler." She slipped off her engagement ring and stuck it in her pocket. Boys didn't wear diamond rings in 1874.

"I dunno." Nathan shrugged. "I wanna help him, but he ain't got time." Then his voice became suspicious and his eyes narrowed. "Hey, where'd you come from? How come you just appeared outta nowhere?"

Libby smiled. Smart little guy. Hopefully he'd be an ally. Taking a chance, she confessed. "I came from the future. See these trees?" He nodded, his expression solemn. "Well, I think they brought me here. Only I don't know why. I'm hoping you'll help me."

"Sure." Nathan's legs started swinging faster. "I'll help ya if'n you'll be my frien'. I ain't got any since Tobby left to work on the docks in Lou'ville. I get to see him when we go to town. But that ain't very often. 'Course, he was older'n me. But we're still friends. Now all I have to play with're prissy girls." He hesitated a heartbeat. "So how 'bout it? You wanna be my frien'?"

"I'd love to be your friend, but you'll have to keep my secret. You can't say anything to anyone about me appearing out of nowhere, especially adults. They'll think we're crazy. OK?"

"Sure." Nathan beamed and scooted over on the branch. "Wanna join me?"

"OK." Libby lifted herself up into the tree and climbed. In moments, she sat with her legs swinging back and forth, imitating Nathan.

"Great." The boy grabbed a branch to pull himself up and stood. "I'm glad you're not some prissy girl."

She stilled the impulse to smile. "I take it you don't like prissy girls?"

He shook his head.

"How come?" Libby would have to make sure he didn't discover her true gender.

"They're bossy an' think they know everythin'. Take Clara May Johnson." Nathan rolled his eyes. "She's as prissy as they come. Always bossin' me aroun', tellin' me what to do. She thinks she's so smart. She's my sister's best friend." He stopped to take a deep breath. "My sister Sarah's not so bad—only when she's aroun' Clara May. An' I have a new baby brother. He's only two though. It'll be awhile before he can climb trees like us." His words died and he remained quiet for a drawn-out moment, eyeing her thoughtfully. "So where in th' future are ya from?"

"Same place, only a hundred and thirty-eight years from now," Libby answered honestly, propping her chin on her hand and looking out over the landscape. From her position she could see for miles and the view didn't look much different than it did in the future, except for the missing buildings. Twin Oaks, the horse farm in her time, had more stables along with another bunkhouse. Also missing were the cabins. "I'm pretty sure the trees brought me through time."

"Really?"

She nodded.

Nathan's eyes grew rounder. "They're magical, just like you. I can tell."

Libby offered a conspiratorial wink. "Remember, no one can know." Hopefully, returning home would be as simple as wishing herself there. It had to work. Of course, it might take some time to figure out the correlation between her being here and her wish. In the meantime, it would be fun to have a look around and experience life in the past. At least for a day or so.

"It'll be our secret." She made the motion of locking her mouth with a pretend key. "Most adults don't believe in magic."

"Yeah, I know. I'll keep yer secret. I like havin' you for a frien'."

"I like having you for one, too."

"Hey, do you like to fish? My pa can't take me fishin' on account he has to work. The mares're foaling."

"As a matter of fact, I love to fish," she lied, crossing her fingers. He didn't have to know she hated the slimy things. Hopefully he wouldn't want to catch frogs too, which might be more than she, a true prissy girl, could handle. "That's too bad about your pa having to work, though. Maybe he could use my help," she asked, broaching the subject of work again. "I need to stay near these oaks to get home, so I need a job. What do you think?"

"Mr. Thorpe's always lookin' for hands, 'cuz my pa's says good hands tend to drift, whatever that means." He pointed toward the stables, visible from their high perch. "There's Pa now. He's with Mr. Thorpe."

Libby's gaze followed his finger. A group of men were leaving the main stable. Two, who were complete opposites in coloring but physically very similar, stood out among them. They split from the others and stopped to talk. Both were tall and broad-shouldered, sporting the lean, muscular build of active males, one blond and one with jet-black hair. She couldn't see their faces and figured they'd both be good-looking, but it was the darker-haired man who caught her attention. Something about his presence held her gaze. She spent a long moment staring, sensing a strong connection and trying to understand why.

"Does Mr. Thorpe have black hair?" Since the blond boy was paler than her, with startling blue eyes, it seemed a good guess.

Nathan nodded.

Her gaze returned to the two men, and Libby watched them disappear into the main house. Would they believe she was a boy and let her work until she figured things out? Or would they tell her to get lost?

"What's Mr. Thorpe like?" Maybe Nathan could enlighten her more about the owner, which might help her secure a job working with his horses until she found her way home.

"I dunno. Nice, I s'pose. My pa's helping him build a thoroughbred stud farm."

Libby looked around the land. Was this the beginnings of the original farm?

Just then she saw a man riding a horse off in the distance. The animal had rivulets of sweat running down his sides and looked to be struggling. When the horse flat-out stopped, the man began whipping the beast.

Incensed, Libby pointed. "Look at that! Do all of Mr. Thorpe's men ride their horses to death?"

Nathan squinted. His gaze followed her finger. He shook his head. "He must be new. If Pa saw anyone riding a horse too hard or beating 'im, he'd take the whip away and start using it on the fellow doin' the whippin'. I seen him do it."

Her anger mounting, Libby clenched her fists as the rider bullied the horse into obeying him. As they rode out of sight, she tamped down the frustration of feeling helpless. Even if it were possible to catch up with him, she was powerless to act. This was another era, one where men who treated animals cruelly usually got away with it. Those same men probably got away with abusing women and children too.

"Don't worry, Libby," Nathan said, patting her hand. "I'll tell Pa. He'll send him packing. You just wait and see if he don't."

Libby nodded and offered a slight smile. Then remembering her plight, she asked, "Do you think now might be a good time to see about that job?"

"Sure." He climbed down with a minimum of movements and waited for her at the tree's base. When she had both feet planted firmly on the ground, he grabbed her hand, pulling her along. "Hell an' tarnation, let's go before they leave the stables."

"Hell and tarnation?" Libby eyed him with raised eyebrows, grinning.

"Yeah. Heard my pa say it once." Nathan shrugged. "Sounds

important. I like saying important stuff." As they walked toward the main house, he pointed to the left. "The fishin' hole's that way. Maybe we can fish after you get your job."

"I don't see why not." Two pressing questions consumed Libby as she kept up with the boy. What was so important to bring her all this way, and would she be able to wish herself back home once she learned it?

Along their short trek, the two came up with a believable story. Libby heard about the Thorpe farm through word of mouth. She, or he in this case, had come on foot from Louisville after arriving on a steamboat from Cincinnati looking for fame and fortune, like so many others who preceded her.

They neared the main stable. Libby looked around in awe. Though the structure stood in the same spot as the one in the twenty-first century, the other buildings were missing. Everything looked timeless. Even the Thorpe house appeared much the same as the house she was very familiar with. The differences were so minor. The trees were smaller and the main landscaping had changed.

A loud whinny cut into the air, the piercing sound of distress belying the peaceful setting. Libby ran the few feet to the stable door and shoved it open. Nathan followed.

"Stop that," Libby shouted as the man she'd seen from atop her perch struck the overridden, sweating horse.

Enraged, she rushed over to him and yanked the whip out of his hand. Unable to control her temper at seeing such a beautiful animal being abused, not just once, but twice, she drew the whip back and hit him with it as hard as she could.

"Why, you little bastard." Anger flared in his eyes. "I'll teach you to mind your betters." He backhanded her, sending her flat on her back.

For a moment Libby could only see stars. Never in her life had anyone struck her. Shaking her head to clear it, she spied Nathan grab on to the monster's arm to keep him from laying into her. The boy, half her size, clearly waged a losing battle. The monster broke free and she closed her eyes, bracing for the next blow. In those few seconds, her life flashed inside her brain, a quick video telling her she was too young to die.

"What the hell is going on?" said a booming voice. Libby opened her eyes just as the whip her attacker was about to wield on her was torn from his grasp. Her focus trailed down her savior's arm to a broad chest, then moved higher to take in a handsome face, reddened in anger.

"He was whipping the horse," Nathan said, wiping his tears and sniffling. "When my frien' Libby stopped him, he hit him. He knocked me down and was meanin' to whip my frien'."

The black-haired man, obviously Mr. Thorpe, considering the boy had pointed him out earlier, turned his focus to her attacker. While he dealt with him, Libby jumped up, more concerned with calming the heavily panting horse. "That's OK, big guy," she crooned, grabbing his bridle and staying out of kicking range. "That bad man won't hurt you anymore. I'll make sure of it." She stroked his sweaty neck, digging her fingers in to soothe him.

"You were warned, Smithers. I want you off my land." As her attacker walked to the animal Libby was trying to calm, Thorpe shook his head. "Without the horse."

"I ain't going nowhere without my mount."

Ignoring the two men, Libby continued her deep strokes, talking to the stallion in a soft tone the entire time. Eventually, the horse's nervous panting became even breathing and he quieted, even nudging Libby for more when she dropped her hand. She laughed. "You like that, do you?"

By this point, several men had gathered to form a half circle around them.

"Pay the man for his mount." Thorpe turned to the tall blond man in the center, the same one Nathan had identified as his dad. "And have someone escort him to the edge of my property."

"I won't forget this." Smithers looked over at Libby and she swore hatred shone in those beady eyes. "You should learn to mind yer own business, boy," he said, sneering. "You'll be sorry you ever messed with Clyde Smithers." He picked his hat off the ground and dusted it off. "You'll all be sorry." He shoved the hat on his head, took the offered money, and stormed out, shrugging off the hands belonging to the two men heeding their boss's order.

"I'll take care of the stallion, son," Nathan's dad said. Libby handed him the reins. As he led the horse away, she glanced up and got her first good look at Colin Thorpe. In an attempt to ascertain what he was like, she stared at him for a minute, startled at how attractive he was. He wore dark, formfitting pants that tapered to fit inside worn riding boots and a white muslin shirt with the sleeves rolled up, showing off well-defined forearms. He could easily grace the cover of one of her romance novels.

He noticed her attention and their gazes met.

For several moments, steady oceanic eyes held hers. Time seemed to stand still. A deer in headlights came to mind when she couldn't look away. His eyes conveyed a warm intelligence, but they were curious at the same time. Finally, Libby cast her gaze down at her feet. Heat crept up her face and she knew it was probably beet red, a by-product of being blonde and female. Don't let him realize I'm a girl, she prayed, busying herself with brushing off her jeans. That would bring up questions she did not want to even begin to attempt to answer.

"Are you OK, young man?" He touched her shoulder and his fingers slid higher to take her chin. He studied her face, concern etched into his expression. "Doesn't look too bad."

He smiled, and it was all she could do to continue breathing. That devastating smile, along with that intense gaze, did strange things to her insides.

"I'm Colin Thorpe."

Unable to speak, she just nodded and took his offered hand. She cleared her throat, trying to ignore the warmth of his fingers, also trying to figure out why he affected her so.

"This is my frien' Libby," Nathan chimed in, coming to her rescue. "He's lookin' for work."

"Is he now?" Colin dropped her hand and turned to the blond man striding up behind him. "What do you think, Gus?"

"*Ja*." Gus nodded. "We could always use a hand like you." Even though his gaze wasn't as troubling, the fact that she was lying about her gender added to the warmth in her cheeks. "You've a way with horses, boy."

"Yes," she croaked out. "I love horses. I've worked around

them most of my life." Libby took a deep breath and added, sounding more convincing, "Some even say I'm gifted."

"I say hire the boy." Gus turned to Colin.

Colin nodded. "Hell, it's the least we can do to thank him for risking his neck to save that fine animal from more abuse." He clapped her on the back and offered another smile—one so irresistible, Libby had to look away. "In fact, we could use your help right now, since I had to fire Smithers."

"Can I help too," Nathan asked.

Colin shrugged. "I don't see why not. You can help your friend there." He glanced at Gus for confirmation. "If that's OK with your pa."

"*Ja*, you two can muck out the dirty stalls. Just try to stay out of everyone's way, son."

As they strode away, Libby exhaled a sigh of relief.

A beaming Nathan grabbed her hand. "Did you hear that? He's letting me help you." He started walking in the same direction the two had taken. "Pa likes you. An' I think Mr. Thorpe does too." Libby had no choice but to follow. This was turning into an interesting adventure, she decided, even as her main question about being here still loomed.

She and Nathan cleaned out the first of several stalls. Both picked up horse manure with pitchforks and tossed it into a wheelbarrow before adding fresh straw and moving to the next stall. While silently working, she thought back to her wish and what it meant to no avail.

When the wheelbarrow was full, Libby hefted up the handles and unsteadily pushed it toward the rear of the stable door. Her arms ached from exertion and it was hard to keep her forward momentum. The wheel hit a small hole in the dirt floor and her load almost tipped over.

"Here, let me help you with that, young fellow," said a booming voice that had become all too familiar during the last few hours.

Libby looked up and sure enough, Colin Thorpe stood right behind her.

He relieved her of the bulky burden and their fingers touched.

It hadn't helped that too many times he'd caught her staring at him when he'd pass by. He must really think she was daft.

Her face warmed and Libby cleared her throat, stilling the urge to run. She doubted the trees sent her here to find another man attractive, but she wouldn't be female and not be affected by him when he appeared so handsome, like some rugged horseman modeling men's cologne.

She got a whiff of her own perfume, *eau de* horse, looked down, and groaned. Her blouse and jeans were covered in sweat and grime and her once clean boots had clumps of manure around the soles. There was no avoiding it with this many horses. Here she was, staring into the eyes of one of the most striking males on the planet, and she just happened to look worse than usual. Of course, none of that should matter because he assumed she was a boy. Not to mention Libby was an engaged woman.

It would certainly be nice if the trees helped her figure out what to do about Dave. Yet, having bigger issues to deal with at the moment than the purpose of her time travel, she followed Colin out the door.

He easily emptied the barrow and offered it back to her. Unfortunately, he also offered that thousand-watt smile that kept doing funny things to her insides whenever she saw it.

Averting her gaze, Libby tried hard not to gush as he walked away. The man would definitely be a heartthrob in her day. Too bad he's here in the past, she thought, veering the now easier conveyance back to the stall where Nathan waited. But then it really didn't matter. She wasn't the type to draw the attention of men like that. Not that she even wanted to.

She hadn't dated much in high school, too busy spending time with her horses. In college, she had little interest in dating and had never had a serious relationship until Dave. Her thoughts flew back to when they'd first met and a smile broke free. He'd been so romantic. The memory of their courtship resurfaced and she remembered why she fell in love with him. A rush of homesickness pulsed through her and a thought struck. Maybe this trip into the past was meant to make her aware of what was important in relationships. Dave had some wonderful qualities and she really did love him. Maybe her answer lay in communicating her feelings better.

Libby grabbed the pitchfork, barely able to lift it, and prayed for it to be so. Then wishing would take her home.

☙

As Libby guided the bulky wheelbarrow back inside, Colin wondered about those few instances earlier in the day when he would walk past the boy, offering a quick glance, only to catch him staring. Each time their gazes had locked, he'd felt a tug—a connection. Even more peculiar, there was something about the lad that brought out his protective instinct. The same instinct he felt for each of his three children, who were all under the age of five.

Colin shrugged the thoughts off when out of the corner of his eye he saw Gus leading Zeus and turned in his manager's direction.

The stallion's ears perked up and his head bobbed as he drew near. "How'd he do today?"

Gus grinned, halting the horse. "Two seconds faster than yesterday, so I'd say he's coming along nicely."

"I wish Abby was here to see him run," Colin said, rubbing his long nose. His wife had died in childbirth nine months earlier. That sad burden only added to his guilt of bringing Abigail to Kentucky, far away from her beloved Virginia. As a result, her last years had been miserable. "Maybe then she'd finally understand why this land is so important."

"She missed her home, Colin. Some people just aren't of a mind to leave those they love."

He eyed Gus. "You and Berta did." As immigrants, they'd traveled much farther, all the way from Norway. At least Abby had been able to visit her family now and again. Unlike Gus and Berta. Besides, it wasn't as if she hadn't known about his plans to leave Virginia before they married.

His friend nodded. "*Ja*, but my wife wanted the opportunity America offered as much as I did."

And Berta loves you, he thought wistfully. His and Abby's hadn't been a love match, but they'd been good friends in the beginning of their marriage, which is how he liked to remember her. That's the woman he grieved for. He loved his new home. His thoroughbreds thrived here, and so did his children. Abby was the only one who hadn't.

When the horse neighed, Colin realized he'd stopped stroking his neck. Nuzzling closer, he whispered, "You're a champion, aren't you?" He was breeding faster and stronger animals. Zeus was just the beginning.

"*Ja*," Gus said, turning to lead the stallion back inside. "It'll only be a matter of time before this brute makes you famous. He's one of the best runners I've ever seen."

Following, Colin grinned. "Which will be soon, I hope." His entire future was riding on all the horses in this barn, but this one was special.

"He's definitely gaining more speed day by day. But the mare he sired might just give him some competition."

"Good. He'll have plenty of incentive to run faster." Thinking of all he'd achieved in ten years, Colin's grin spread. His dream was coming to fruition. It really was too damned bad that Abby couldn't be here to experience his small gains.

At this point, they neared the stall Libby and Nathan were cleaning. Colin ignored the same sense of protectiveness that crept over him every time he came close. A few feet away, he stopped to observe the lad.

Gus looked at him with questioning eyes.

His nod indicated Libby. "He looks so young." And scrawny, he thought. A stiff wind could easily blow him over. "But he seems to be pulling his weight."

Gus grunted an assent. "Actually he's pulling a hell of a lot more than his weight and shows promise. He's worked wonders with Nathan. I only hope he's as good with horses as he claims. It sure would be nice to have a decent hand who understands equines."

Colin sighed. "His small size will be an asset for training, but I'm just not sure how effective he'll be if one of the stallions acts up."

"Don't count the lad out yet," Gus said. "You saw how quickly he eased Smithers's overridden horse. He's got a gentle touch. We both know it's not the size. It's the heart and spirit of the man that horses respond to."

Wiping the sweat off his brow, Colin couldn't argue that point. "Damn, it's a hot one today," he said, changing the subject. "What do you say to a quick dip in the spring to cool off?" Most of his men utilized the spring during the summer months.

"You don't have to ask me twice. Definitely makes working in this heat more bearable." Gus started toward the stallion's stall. "I just have to finish with Zeus."

"I'll help." Colin used his thumb to point to the stall behind him. "Those boys have been working like fiends. They could probably use a swim too, don't you think?"

"*Ja.* They definitely deserve a break." Gus kept walking. "I'll tell them on the way out."

☙

"We're going swimming at the spring." Gus came up behind Libby and his voice startled her. "You boys can take a break and join us."

She turned and stared at him as if he'd grown an extra head. "We're, um, we're…almost done." She glanced down so as not to reveal her rising panic. Libby still wore her vest to aid in her deception, but it was like having a forest fire on her back. Her breasts pretty much disappeared behind it, but the second she took it off, her ruse would be up. There was no possible way she could go swimming. "We'll finish here and meet you there."

Gus nodded and then met up with Colin, who waited a few feet away.

The minute the two were out of earshot, Libby turned to Nathan. "What happens if we don't go swimming at the spring?"

"I dunno." The boy shrugged. "I ain't never been before. But it sounds like fun."

"We can't go."

Nathan scrunched up his nose. "Why not?"

"'Cuz we were supposed to go fishing, remember?"

Nathan nodded. "Oh, yeah." A sly grin made an appearance.

Libby returned his smile. "And while we're fishing, we can take our own swim." She'd just keep her clothes on. Nathan would understand. Then at least she could rinse off the stench of the day in order to feel normal again.

As soon as they completed raking the straw, Nathan grabbed her hand. "C'mon. We gotta tell Pa we're going fishing. I hope he won't mind."

As they neared the spring, it was all Libby could do to hold herself back from jumping into the inviting pool of water. The desire to cool off and to rid herself of grime and the scent of *eau de* horses was too overwhelming to ignore. Except, that would just raise questions, which would lead to other questions.

Colin stepped onto the bank in all his glory. Water sluiced off his shoulders. Droplets ran down the length of a well-built chest, going lower all the way to… Libby's breath hitched in her throat and she forced her focus higher. She knew she was practically gawking, but he had a gorgeous body. His muscles bunched as he wiped drips off his face and hair, holding her rapt attention.

"Come join us," Colin called. Her gaze slid to his eyes and Libby couldn't look away from that same heart-stopping stare. "The water's great."

She was tempted to do exactly as he requested. Thankfully her senses returned just in the nick of time. Good grief! Heat engulfed her face. *Remember, Libby, you're an engaged woman who has no business drooling over some Adonis-like model who lives in the past. Don't look at him.* She cast her focus at her feet and cleared her throat, struggling for an intelligent reply.

"We're goin' fishin' instead," Nathan piped up, saving her from making more of an idiot of herself. "Is that OK, Pa?" He turned to look at Gus. "We'll cool off at the fishin' hole."

"*Ja.*" Gus emerged from the water, drawing Libby's focus. And even though he was just as well built as Colin, seeing his blue-eyed gaze or watching water sluice off his back did nothing to make her heartbeat falter. "Fishing sounds like a good way to spend the rest of a lazy afternoon."

Libby glanced from him to Colin.

Colin's grin widened. "If we didn't have so much work, we might be inclined to join you."

"C'mon, Libby." Nathan reached for her hand and tugged.

Still red-faced and unable to articulate a decent farewell, Libby offered a quick smile and waved. The entire time they walked away, she felt the heat of the two men's gazes on her back. But only one gaze concerned her.

Maybe sticking around a day or so wasn't such a good idea. Unfortunately, the thought of making it home right now was just as unsettling.

Chapter 4

"The fishin' hole is this way." Nathan ran ahead. By now the two were out of earshot from Colin and Gus.

Libby shrugged. "Sure." Heaven help her. What she had gotten herself into? She shuddered over the idea of actually touching live bait or slimy fish.

"Great."

Libby only laughed, praying for the fortitude to last a day or two. She wasn't sure she was up to it, especially considering what she'd just witnessed.

Hopefully she could figure out why she was here and make the trip home sooner rather than later. Colin Thorpe was just too tempting to be around for long without somehow giving herself away.

They walked about a mile to a small lake with trees clustered around the perimeter, creating an idyllic scene. The clear, calm water mirrored the surrounding countryside in a vivid display. Every now and then a fish would jump and produce a ripple, distorting the image for a few seconds. She grasped that she was seeing a view of the past that no longer existed. She would have remembered something this breathtaking in her own time.

Nathan walked over to a bush and moved a rock, yielding two hidden poles. "Since Pa's swimmin', he won't mind if you use his."

Looking at the odd-looking poles and then at Nathan, Libby felt stuck. Just the thought of wiggling worms sent chills down her spine. *Don't think about it. Just do it, like the ad says.*

This boy was her lifeline and she needed his cooperation. "OK." She took the pole, acting as if she did this kind of thing all the time, but when the hook pricked her finger, she dropped it on the ground.

Nathan squinted against the sun in his eyes. "You ain't never fished before, huh?"

Libby lifted her shoulders and slowly shook her head. "What can I say? I lied."

"Well, I guess I can teach you." He smiled. "First, we need worms. So, c'mon—let's go get 'em." He ran to a spot ten feet away and started digging in the damp dirt. She followed him and copied his movements. After digging for mere minutes, they each had worms in a pile of moist dirt, except Nathan had twice as many.

He's such a boy.

He picked up the moist dirt, worms and all, and started toward the lake. Libby scooped her pile into both hands, held it away from her, and fell in step behind him. She tried not to think about carrying worms. Where was the *Enterprise* when she needed it most?

At the water's edge, she dropped the pile and waded into the inviting pool, more to cool off at this point, having become accustomed to the scent of *eau de* horses.

"You're not taking your boots off?"

"Nah." Keeping them on while in the water would get rid of the horse manure. "I'm not taking my clothes off either. It'll be cooler to fish in wet clothes."

In seconds, he joined her fully clothed.

The two swam for a few refreshing minutes, after which she followed Nathan out of the water. Her wet shirt and jeans felt good against the warm breeze. Both would probably dry in no time.

Libby eyed him, still grinning. "OK, now what?"

"Now we move over there because we scared all the fish away." At the spot he'd indicated, both plopped down. When Libby removed her boots and laid them on a flat rock in the sun, so did Nathan.

He put a worm on the hook for her and showed her how to toss the line out. He spent a moment explaining how to hook a fish if she caught one, which wasn't her goal, but he didn't need to know that.

"So, tell me about the future," Nathan said after a few minutes of comfortable silence. "What's it like?"

"Not much different than here. I have a best friend. We're

sworn confidants, just like us." A vague memory of praying to see her mom again before going to sleep entered her consciousness just then. It happened on that first night she'd returned home after spending two therapeutic weeks at Twin Oaks. "Actually, I think I may have traveled through time before." The memory sharpened. Could it have been real? Looking around, Libby wondered. Bev had believed it hadn't been a dream. Plus, she had wished to see her mother again at least a hundred times in those two weeks. Maybe the trees had made it possible back then, too.

"So you are magical!" Nathan's eyes grew as big as saucers.

"I guess I am." She was here, wasn't she?

"Yer so lucky. I wish I could do that."

"I think I went back in the past after being on this very farm in the future." Her being here now brought the memory to the forefront of her mind. "Want to hear about it?" Maybe talking would help her figure things out.

When he nodded, she smiled distractedly and began to tell him what happened all those years ago.

ଔ

Learning to feed, groom, and ride the horses had eased Libby's heartache. Still, guilt tormented her, and her most fervent wish had been to see Liz Edwards one more time to undo her last ugly words. Libby had fought with her mom, and her only memory of the night before the accident was of her yelling, "I hate you and I wish I'd never been born." Libby's biggest regret was never getting a chance to apologize. She felt responsible. That because of those horrible words, Liz Edwards had died.

The night Libby returned home from her two weeks at Twin Oaks, she dreamed of her mom. She woke up feeling weird in a bigger bed. Her pink room had changed to blue, and the curtains on the window were not Libby's curtains.

She heard voices. Seconds later she was at the door to listen and recognized her parents' voices. They talked about having children. Stunned, Libby cautiously stepped into the hall, tiptoed to the top of the stairs, and looked down.

Her mom and dad appeared much younger. It was too much to take in!

Tom and Liz Edwards obviously loved each other by the way they interacted. Libby couldn't look away when her father kissed the top of her mother's head and said, "I didn't realize how important this was to you. We can start our family whenever you want." Then he chuckled. "In fact, we can get started tonight."

Liz practically purred. "Oh, Tom, I love you." They kissed, something Libby had observed many times before, but this scene filled Libby with love and hope. She'd never seen her parents so in love and so happy.

"Why don't you go up?" He patted Liz's butt after releasing her. "I need to do a few things before coming to bed." He turned to go into the other room, but not before adding, "And Lizzie, I like that flimsy thing you wore last week. Wear it again, OK?"

Liz gave a throaty laugh. "Anything for my Tommy."

Libby darted back into the bedroom and waited until her mother walked past. After listening for several minutes and not hearing anything, she headed for her parents' bedroom.

"Go away—I'm not ready yet." Her mom reached up to take off an earring, obviously mistaking Libby for her husband. Liz glanced over her shoulder and jumped slightly when she caught Libby watching her.

She sensed her mother shouldn't see her and didn't even know if Liz could hear her. Yet, unwilling to waste this chance to apologize, she took a deep breath and blurted out, "I know this seems odd. But I've come to tell you I love you. I'm sorry I hurt you and I just wanted you to know."

"Who are you?" Fear and confusion clouded Liz's eyes. She blinked. "How did you get in here?"

"Don't be frightened. I'm your child. From the future." Libby moved over to her mother and wrapped her arms around the shocked woman's waist. "Somehow I've been able to travel back here. I don't know how, but I've been granted this opportunity, and I have to use it. Mom, please remember, whenever we fight after I'm born, know that I will always love you."

☙

Libby stopped talking and glanced at a wide-eyed Nathan. "Then I found myself back in my own bed, in my own bedroom." Despite never being able to explain Liz's earring nestled in the palm of her hand that morning, she'd always believed the whole incident had been a dream.

"I don't like fighting with my ma either." No one could miss the gravity in Nathan's voice as he added, "But I'll try not to from now on. I don't want her to die."

"Most moms don't die like mine did." She patted his hand reassuringly. "I apparently got the chance to say I was sorry." Libby smiled. "Of course, I told my best friend all about it. And Bev, being Bev, decided that I'd zapped back in time." Just like Scotty used to beam Captain Kirk and Mr. Spock off the *Enterprise.* "Exactly like I came to be here." As implausible as that seemed. Dream or not, the fact that she'd had a friend to discuss such a weird experience with was the biggest reason she'd never give up their friendship.

"Bev?" Nathan glanced at her with a speculative gleam in his eye. "That sounds like a girl's name. Is she a girl?"

Her grin expanded. "Yeah, but not a prissy one, so you'd like her."

"Does she travel through time, like you?"

"No."

"Wow." His total belief reminded her so much of Bev. "I'd love to be able to travel through time just by wishing."

If only it could be so easy. Libby sighed. Another sudden wave of homesickness assailed her senses. She decided to be more proactive about trying to make it home and visit the trees every night until she made it home. Hopefully, she'd be a quick study and figure it out sooner rather than later. "Remember, Nathan. You need to keep my secret."

"I will, 'cuz yer my frien' and yer magical."

The two fished for a while. Finally, Nathan stood. "I need to get home. Sun's getting low and we can't dawdle."

"Dawdle?" Libby stifled a laugh and put on her boots. Thankfully, everything had dried.

"Sure, ya know—my ma says I dawdle when I'm late. I think

that means I should get home fast. I'm not sure, but it sounds important so I like the word. C'mon. Don't dawdle." His mischievous expression charmed Libby all over again.

He strung up his fish and handed them to her. She gave him her pole and he carefully put both away behind the bushes.

Then he skipped back to her. "Here, I can carry those."

Libby didn't have to be asked twice to get rid of the smelly things. She watched him run ahead. He seemed so grown-up for such a little guy.

They quickly retraced their steps. At the oak trees, she looked around. Dusk was setting in. She had nowhere to go, which brought to mind her predicament. She closed her eyes and fervently wished herself home. When that didn't work, she glanced at Nathan. "Do you think I can stay with you?"

"I'm sure Pa will say yes, 'cuz he likes you." He grabbed her hand and started for the caretaker's house behind the big house.

The two walked into the kitchen, and Libby noticed at once how warm and inviting the room appeared.

"There you are, Nathan. 'Bout time you made your way home," said a large-boned woman with Nordic good looks—blonde hair, blue eyes, and fair complexion. She saw Libby and her eyebrows shot up. "Who's that with you?"

Nathan smiled and said in a grown-up voice, "This here's my frien' Libby. I helped him work fer Pa today, then we went fishin'. He has nowhere to go, so I invited him to stay with us."

"Set another place then." Berta Gunderson nodded toward the cabinets. "Dinner's almost ready." Her curious attention returned to Libby. "So you work with horses?"

"Yes." Libby angled her chin higher and prayed Nathan's mom wouldn't send her packing. "I've trained thoroughbreds most of my life. I heard about this place in Louisville."

Berta clucked. "You don't look big enough to do such strenuous work."

"I'm plenty big and I am a really good handler."

"I hope so." She sighed, seeming unconvinced. "Gus and Mr. Thorpe could use a good hand." Then her eyes narrowed and she studied Libby's face for a few minutes before nodding at Nathan.

"We'll eat in a few minutes. Why don't you go wash up? There's a bowl with warm water and soap on the counter over there."

By the time she'd washed, the others had joined in at the table.

Nathan introduced her to his sister, Sarah, and baby brother, Christophe. Gus didn't offer much more than a grunt when Nathan explained that he'd brought Libby home with him.

Libby sat.

Gus handed her a bowl of sweet potatoes. "So, where'd you say you were from?" He had features similar to Berta's, but was slightly darker in coloring and towered over his wife by six inches.

"Cincinnati." Libby placed a couple of wedges on her plate and passed on the bowl. "I came by riverboat."

"You traveled from Cincinnati all by yourself," Berta asked.

"Yes." Libby nodded and began to eat, trying to act like a boy.

Berta took a drumstick off the platter. "Where are your parents?"

"Dead and gone." It wasn't a lie. Her mom was dead and her dad was gone from this time. She then offered the rendition she and Nathan had created earlier.

Skepticism shone in Gus's eyes and she prayed it was due to her story, not the fact that she was female rather than male. His wife's warm gaze held a more understanding glint.

They discussed more of her past and Gus told a little of his.

He and Berta were immigrants who'd come from Norway as newlyweds eleven years earlier with dreams of prosperity. Gus originally worked with Colin Thorpe's father soon after arriving in the US. "In the postwar years of the late 1860s and early 1870s, opportunity abounds for anyone willing to work hard enough to take advantage of it," he said, ending his autobiographical spiel.

"You showed some real gumption today." Gus grunted and took another bite. He chewed thoughtfully, then swallowed. "Even still, you don't look old enough to be on your own, boy."

Libby's chin lifted. "I'm old enough."

He eyed her a long minute before nodding. "Maybe tomorrow I'll try you out in other areas. I sure could use a hand who understands horses." Gus shook his head. "Thoroughbreds are a touchy bunch—spirited and high-strung."

"A fact I'm well aware of after spending plenty of time working with them," Libby countered. "I've trained thoroughbreds for years." Her voice held conviction. "I'm willing to work hard and earn my keep." She couldn't leave just yet, so why not try to get a closer look at Colin's prized horseflesh, as she was dying to do?

"I don't know." Gus let out an audible sigh. "This is foaling and breeding season and the work is brutal."

"Gus, why not give him a chance," Berta chimed in. "You're working yourself to death, toiling seven days a week. At least try him out for a time."

His gaze trailed to his wife's before wandering to Libby's, where it stayed. He appeared deep in thought. "You're right." He refocused on Berta. "Everyone needs a chance to prove himself now and again. That's what this great country is all about, taking and giving chances. Besides, the boy proved his mettle earlier." He broke off. His focus returned to Libby again and he silently observed her for another moment. Finally he nodded, saying gruffly, "We start early around here. Right now we're working every day, even tomorrow, Sunday. Be in the stables at sunup and I'll give you more than a try. It's backbreaking work, and as you've already experienced firsthand, I don't mollycoddle my workers. You continue to pull your weight, boy, and you'll have a job for as long as you want."

Libby exhaled the breath she'd been holding. "Thank you, sir. You won't be sorry."

"I hope not." Gus stabbed at a wedge of sweet potato and resumed eating. He took a few more bites, then glanced at her. "Libby's a strange name. Don't think I've ever heard of anyone called Libby before."

"It's a nickname." Libby shrugged. "Short for Liberty. What can I say? My mom was patriotic."

This answer seemed to appease him and he went back to his meal.

But Berta didn't appear to be fooled. She just shook her head and clucked.

When the dinner was over, Libby leaped from her chair,

intending to do her part to help clean up. While carrying dishes to the sink, she felt a hand on her arm. Libby looked over her shoulder to see Berta shaking her head.

"You best be getting ready for bed. This here's woman's work. You can bunk with Nathan tonight."

"I can take him to the bunkhouse," Gus said. "He'll be fine there."

"No." A look of horror crossed Berta's face. "He can bunk with Nathan. I wouldn't let this child stay with those animals in the bunkhouse."

"Now, Berta, if he's going to be working here, he needs to be with the rest of the hands. They're not animals. Just young bucks with wild oats to sow."

"*Ja*—you say that, but I'll not have this child corrupted by those young bucks. Keep them away from him. He's too young to be around such hooligans."

Gus heaved a resigned sigh. "OK, but bear in mind, this boy isn't our responsibility. He needs to earn his keep or he'll be gone."

Libby watched the entire exchange with interest, only too happy not to have to sleep in the bunkhouse with the other hands. They *were* a hardened bunch. Besides, she liked this family. She felt comfortable here. The Gundersons were good people. Maybe they were the reason she'd been sent here. To see how a loving family interacted with each other, and to discover what was important in a marriage, so she could apply it to her own life.

Berta grabbed her hand. "Come with me. I'll show you where you'll be. The house has three bedrooms on the second floor. The outhouse is right outside. We don't have an inside bathing room like the big house does, but we have a tub with a pump that drains out."

They climbed the staircase and were soon heading toward a bedroom, well out of range of her husband's hearing, when Berta harrumphed.

"Men! They can't see what's right in front of their noses." She aimed her stare at Libby. "You, child, are no boy. But I will keep your secret. Whatever your reasons, it's your business, *ja*? I'll help you all I can. I only hope you're as good with horses as you say you are."

Berta stopped, opened a cupboard, sorted through it, and took out several items. Then she continued speaking while tearing up an old sheet. "You can wear these old clothes. Here's an old hat that can help with your ruse, *ja*? Wrap yourself with the strips—they will hide your budding."

Stunned, Libby grabbed the clothes, along with a hat that had seen better days and asked softly, "You're not mad?"

"No, I'm worried." Berta offered an apprehensive smile. "What's a child like you doing out here on your own?"

Relieved, Libby bestowed her own smile and brushed aside the notion of her just starting to develop. Her buds were fully bloomed. Berta had obviously mistaken her age, assuming she was much younger than her twenty-three years. "It's a long story."

She should probably be incensed over the insult. Geez. Even in the past, women had to have a rack to be considered fully grown. "If I told you, you'd have a hard time believing it. I'll do my best to help your husband with his work. I am good with horses."

Berta shrugged. "*Ja*, well, time will tell. I'm a pretty good judge of character. Just don't make me regret helping you." Her voice held warning and Libby realized she never wanted to tangle with the woman. "Here's Nathan's room. There's an extra bed since Christophe, his younger brother, is still in with us. Sarah, my oldest, has her own room down the hall."

"Thanks so much." Libby hesitated a moment, then stepped up and hugged Berta. "I don't know how I can repay you."

The older woman cleared her throat and patted her back, offering a flustered, "*Ja*, just work hard and help my husband. That will be thanks enough for me. He works too much. Let's take it one day at a time, shall we?" Berta then turned and left her alone.

Libby quickly discarded her jeans and blouse, and wrapped the strips around her breasts, thankful not to have to rely on the hot vest any longer. She pulled the muslin shirt over her head. Amazingly, her shape disappeared. The old garments resulted in her looking more the part. She'd take her own clothes to the tree and hide them in order to keep them handy for when she tried to wish herself back to her own time. She'd already given it one attempt earlier and decided to try again tomorrow. If this was like her last experience, she would probably be zapped right back to within minutes from when she'd left. Or at least, she hoped so.

Nathan came in and climbed into his bed, while she slid into the bed next to him.

"I'm glad you came to visit us, Libby." His sleepy voice drifted to her ears. "G'night."

Libby smiled in the dark. "Good night, Nathan. Sweet dreams."

Though her muscles ached from exertion, too many questions kept her awake.

Her conversation with Nathan while fishing entered her thoughts as Bev and her dream came to mind. Suddenly a wave of homesickness washed over her. Hopefully, she would figure out what she needed to learn so she could return to her own time.

Libby closed her eyes and prayed for the means to get back home. She missed her friend. Sighing, she hit the pillow. She missed Dave. Heck, she even missed Dr. Bull.

Chapter 5

Libby sprang out of bed eager for a chance to try out the trees. She followed Nathan down the stairs, rounded the corner, and was met with a scene straight out of *Little House on the Prairie*. In daylight everything appeared rustic. The countertops might fit in her century, considering they were honed hardwood that was all the rage, but the room lacked other contemporary amenities. Like a dishwasher, a microwave, or a refrigerator with French doors. A potbellied stove took the place of a cook top with oven.

Even Berta fit the part of the mom, who stood at the stove, hair tied back with a kerchief and wearing an apron over a faded calico print dress. "Privy's out back." Berta pointed to the door with the long fork she'd been using to turn the bacon.

Libby sniffed the mouthwatering scent. Her stomach gurgled as she headed outside.

She had no trouble finding the BB, or bathroom in a box as she'd dubbed it. Libby made her way back to the house with a newfound appreciation for modern times. The toilet paper looked nothing like paper and there was no running water. She vowed never to take a flushing toilet for granted ever again.

"The washbasin's on the counter," Berta said. "Just fill it with fresh water." The elder woman nodded at the sink and hand pump, which was better than having to get water from the nearby creek.

Libby noticed the bowl. Next to it was a cloth and small towel, along with what looked like a bar of soap. She moved to the sink, picked up the bowl, and started pumping. It was hard work pulling and pushing the handle up and down to get a decent flow. Even worse, it was ice cold. What Libby wouldn't give for warm tap water.

"There's a ladle to make it bearable," Berta said as if reading her mind. Her nod indicated a bucket atop the potbellied stove.

"You don't need much. That bucket stays there during the day." One by one, Berta added cooked strips of bacon onto a platter, then poured what looked to be scrambled eggs into the hot grease. "All I ask is that you fill it up when the water gets low. Make sure you use a hot pad, though. Otherwise you'll burn yourself. Also, I put out an extra toothbrush." She grabbed a wooden spoon and stirred the contents in the cast iron pan. "I cleaned it with lye soap, so it should do for now. The tooth powder's in the tin right there."

Libby nodded and murmured her thanks. The toothbrush in question looked worn. Was she supposed to use that? Apparently so.

After washing, she did feel more human. Even the worn toothbrush and salty-tasting powder weren't too bad, especially since they did help to take away morning breath.

She emptied the basin of dirty water in the big sink, then took in more of her surroundings. Despite the fact that there were few comforts from her century, the scene was cozy. The fireplace across from the stove wasn't lit this morning, but in her mind's eye, she saw how warm the room would be once winter set in.

Now done with the eggs, Berta added them to the bacon, set the fork down, and wiped her hands on her apron. With hot pad in hand, she bent to take biscuits out of the oven before placing them in a napkin-lined basket.

"All ready." Berta smiled and picked up the huge platter containing bacon, ham, sausage, and eggs that still sizzled and smelled heavenly.

Libby's stomach growled again. "Do you need any help?"

"No, child, I've been doing this a long time. You'll be working hard enough in no time." Berta's smile softened. "You just sit there and enjoy a hearty breakfast."

Libby pulled out her chair as the rest of the family filed in. Berta set the food on the table and joined them.

After a quick blessing, Libby ate with zest, preparing for the strenuous work ahead. She wasn't willing to take any chances on not meeting Gus's expectations.

When Gus finished his meal, he shoved away from the table. "Time's a-wasting. You best hurry, Libby. We have a full day ahead." He proceeded to lean down and kiss Berta's forehead. "We usually don't work on the Lord's day, but too many mares are in foal." He grabbed his hat and strode toward the door.

Libby took one last drink of milk and jumped up. "Thanks, Berta. Wish me luck."

Berta shook her head. "Child, you'll need more than luck. Now, go on with you."

Nathan stood too. "Can I help you, Libby?"

"Nathan—" Berta frowned. "You leave him alone. He has enough to do without worrying about keeping you out of trouble. You and your sister have your own chores. You'd do well to get busy with those. After that we'll be going to church."

"I know, but I was thinking 'bout later once my chores're done an' after church. How 'bout it, Libby?"

Libby shrugged. "Sure. If it's OK with your mom."

Nathan offered a lopsided grin. "Okey-dokey."

"Okey-dokey, friend." She returned his grin and then hurried out the door to catch up with Gus.

At the stables, she and Gus did the usual mundane tasks for the first couple of hours. There were at least six men she recognized from the day before, and a dozen she didn't, all ranging in age from early to late twenties. As Berta had said, they were a tough-looking bunch, appearing weathered and hard. They all looked mean enough to fit in with any gang in any bad neighborhood. All that was missing were the tattoos and the baggy pants.

One burly guy stopped to relieve himself barely a few feet from where Libby stood with Gus, who'd been giving her a more complete tour of the stables.

The guy then laughed and spit out a wad of chewing tobacco before buttoning his jeans. Watching him walk off, Libby sent up another prayer of thanks that she didn't have to bunk with guys like him. Hopefully, no one would pay her any mind if she used the outhouse. Heck, hopefully, she would not have to stay here that long. Using an outhouse was the pits. Twice she'd used it that morning, walking past the trees and wishing her heart out. Both times nothing happened.

"Our goal is to produce the best thoroughbreds around, but we mainly breed workhorses right now." Drawn out of her thoughts, Libby refocused on what Gus was saying. "The farm's income depends on the sturdier animal. The need for racehorses dried up because of the war. Colin's convinced the demand for Kentucky's racehorses will pick up eventually. And when it does, we'll be ready."

It dawned on her that Gus was talking about the War between the States. If nothing else, Libby decided to enjoy the physical history lesson as he added, "Let's go check on the mares in foal. That way I can see how you handle yourself around fidgety females."

Thankfully, Colin Thorpe hadn't made an appearance yet this morning. If Libby were lucky, he would not come by at all.

Gus stopped at a stall door and opened it. "We need to examine the horse to see if her bag has dropped and filled."

Having done this type of work before, Libby nodded and proceeded to the first mare, then checked her teats. This was more Bev's expertise and Libby tried to remember what to look for. She turned back to Gus with the question in her eyes.

"As a mare gets closer to her time, wax forms on their ends," he said, pointing to one teat. "This mare isn't ready yet." He offered a slight smile.

They moved on.

The horse in the next stall was definitely closer to dropping her foal. "We'll check her in a couple of hours. Now, let's see how well you handle yourself in the saddle." He entered another stall. Libby halted at the gate and watched as he harnessed a fine-looking gelding. He led the animal toward her and pointed to another stall with tack hanging on the post. "Go ahead and ready him up."

Horses saddled, she and Gus led them toward the entrance just as Colin Thorpe walked through the stable door.

Libby tried not to stare, but there was something about him that grabbed her attention. She was again struck by how attractive he was. He wore similar clothes as the previous day—dark, formfitting pants that tapered down to fit inside worn riding boots, and a white muslin shirt with the sleeves rolled up, showing off well-defined forearms. Colin Thorpe looked every bit of what she imagined a Regency-era hero would look like.

He would have to pick that precise moment to glance at her.

Heat flooded Libby's cheeks as their gazes locked. For too long, blue eyes held hers. That déjà-vu feeling washed over her as the strength to look away evaporated on the spot. Time seemed to stand still. Finally, Libby forced herself to avert her gaze. She resisted the urge to cover her flaming face. Damn! How on earth was she going to keep up her ruse when he flustered her every time she saw him?

Gus handed her the reins to his horse. "Why don't you take them out to the pastures and turn them out. I'll be with you shortly." He indicated the horse Libby had saddled. "If you want to keep busy, you can start exercising that one."

Eager to make a quick escape, she turned to leave. Hopefully, she'd find her way home soon. It was bad enough to have to be subjected to men peeing, passing gas, and making lewd comments all day long, but what worried her more were the thoughts bouncing around inside her own mind whenever she caught sight of Colin Thorpe. They definitely weren't those of someone in a committed relationship.

☙

Colin walked up to Gus and nodded at Libby's departing back. "How's the new lad doing today?"

"He's coming along nicely. We can definitely use him with the mares."

"Have you learned any more about him? Like where he came from?"

"*Ja.* Libby, short for Liberty, Edwards hails from Cincinnati. I'd think he'd rather be called Lib, but Libby suits him well enough. He wasn't boasting when he said he knows horses." Gus wiped the sweat off his brow with his shirtsleeve. "I've never seen anyone with such a calming touch. He seemed to understand the mares he checked out this morning. They quickly bonded with him."

Colin nodded. Earlier, when he entered the stable and met the boy's stare, he felt a tug. A connection. Just like the day before. It was most peculiar…like the lad needed him. He turned to the stable entrance and stared at the spot the boy had just vacated. "Think we can use him for training the thoroughbreds?" They were short-handed as it was and time was of the essence if they were to be ready by spring. Experienced and effective handlers were hard to find, and those who were small enough to jockey even harder, not to mention expensive.

"Don't know. But I plan to find out. The lad's exercising Wild Black."

Colin grunted. The aptly-named cantankerous beast was used for breeding until he got too hard to handle and had to be gelded. Wild Black had the potential to make a decent workhorse, but he needed more training before being sold. "My money's on the boy. We can definitely use someone as talented as he appears to be. Keep an eye on him, OK?"

Gus smiled. "I'd already planned to spend more time with him today to see what else he's made of." He chuckled. "But you needn't worry about him. Berta's already taken him under her wing. Says he's too young to be in the bunkhouse, so he's staying in Nathan's room."

"Really?" Colin raised his eyebrows. Maybe Berta felt the same protective instinct he did toward the lad.

Nodding, Gus said, "Says our hands would corrupt a saint."

Colin laughed. "She's right about that." He glanced back at the stable door for several more minutes, wondering about the child.

Shaking his thoughts, he remembered why he'd searched Gus out to begin with. "I'm taking the train to Louisville in the morning."

"You were just there."

"Yes, but another meeting about the racetrack has come up. The committee hopes to make their recommendation on whether to invest or not."

"You don't think it's a good investment?" Gus glanced at Colin with a concerned expression.

Scuttlebutt in the river city concerning the proposed racetrack had spread. An idea was about to become a part of history. Whether good or bad, Colin was still undecided. "I'm still not convinced the public will support another track."

Promoters were selling shares for a new jockey club at a hundred dollars each in order to build a racetrack for Louisville.

"It's a perfect spot and I believe the time is right."

Only three miles from the city limits, the flat sand and clay land packed and drained well. Unfortunately, that same parcel, used for horse racing years ago, now sat empty because of economic decline. In the past twenty years, two others had gone bust. "It's only been a couple of years since Woodlawn was sold off and divided for homesteads. What's to stop this one from going belly-up too?" He rubbed his neck and sighed. "Before I invest, I plan to check out a few more details."

"*Ja*, information is good. It would be nice to have a track closer to home. Lexington's twice the distance."

As Colin grunted an assent, they moved out of the way of several handlers leading horses through the stable.

"The war changed people," he mused. "Life's tougher. Racing has fallen behind basics, like survival. Supposedly, this track is different. You know, similar to successful ventures, like the Metairie Club in New Orleans or the Jockey Club in New York." He met Gus's gaze. "Clark's pushing for creating an event race that will bring in the masses," he said, referring to M. Lewis Clark Jr., the main promoter. "Much like the Epsom Derby in England. Tomorrow's meeting should finalize his idea. A committee is working on the articles of incorporation."

"I'd best get outside with Libby." Gus turned to leave. "I hope you find good news. I'll take care of things here."

"Thanks, Gus. I know the farm's in good hands with you. And the young'uns will be OK with Minnie and Maizie. I shouldn't be gone too long."

He followed Gus out the stable door, but couldn't keep his eyes from wandering to where Libby worked. With much interest, he watched the boy ride Wild Black, effortlessly putting him through his paces in the pasture. The lad definitely had a knack with horses. He'd never seen the gelding so completely willing to cooperate. Maybe Libby Edwards was the answer to his prayers.

Money was tight and hiring a decent jockey and a trainer other than Gus wasn't in his budget. His stud farm had to survive first and foremost.

☙

The moment Colin Thorpe stepped out of the stable, Libby sensed his attention. While controlling the gelding, she fought to ignore his presence, but little good that did when the man fascinated her. Even more unsettling, she found it next to impossible to keep that fascination from showing in her eyes every time his gaze would lock on to hers. Which seemed way too often for Libby's peace of mind. If she continued in the same vein, Colin would eventually figure out her true gender.

Libby shuddered to think what would happen then. Besides, she was an engaged woman. As such, she darned well should not be having fantasies about one sexy horse breeder who lived over a hundred thirty years in her past.

The horse beneath her legs grew restless as Colin headed in the other direction. Libby breathed a little easier and centered her full concentration on dealing with the unruly gelding.

Gus eventually joined her and together they worked with the two horses until a clanging sounded.

"That's Cookie's signal." Gus dismounted. The stables emptied of humans as twenty or so men rushed toward the noise. "Time for lunch. But first we need to take care of these boys."

He helped Libby down and together they led the horses back to the stable. They worked quickly and were soon heading toward the bunkhouse mess.

Now sitting among the others, whose table manners left a lot to be desired, Libby could not remember a time when basic food tasted so good.

She had just finished eating when Gus entered her line of vision. "C'mon. Time's a-wasting. We need to check on the mares." She jumped up. He was almost to the door when she finally caught up with him.

For the rest of the afternoon, Libby labored alongside Gus. Not much had changed in over a hundred years. Whether the nineteenth or the twenty-first century, the basics of taking care of horses, even pregnant ones, were the same. They needed to be groomed, fed, and exercised, and their stalls needed to be cleaned out.

Gus mentioned earlier that he didn't let just anyone around his mares, which made her feel special. Yet, after working nonstop since lunch, every muscle in her body ached. What Libby wouldn't give for a nice hot bath. She would never take water and electricity for granted again. She squirmed in an effort to loosen the constricting bindings that were rubbing her skin raw. She didn't dare go without them.

The men around her could walk off the set of a Western, and none of them would wear a white hat. They made Dave seem like a choirboy. Maybe that was why she'd come all this way. To appreciate what she had, rather than what she didn't have.

She poured a bucket of water into the trough and sluiced some liquid over her face and neck, reveling in the cool feel of it. Heck, when she made it back to her own time, she would never take anything for granted again.

"Day's pretty much over." Gus relieved her of the empty bucket and set it aside. "You've earned yourself a spot. Berta will be having dinner soon."

"Thank God." Libby stretched. Wiping the remaining droplets off her face, she nodded at the pile of hay that still needed spreading. "I'm almost finished."

"Here, I'll help." He grabbed a nearby pitchfork and started to spread the hay. "It's been a long time since I've seen someone with a soothing touch like yours with the horses."

"They've always responded to me." Libby shrugged, trying to maintain her dignity when she felt like a glow stick. She doubted Colin's manager gave such praise to every worker. From what she'd seen, he was a fair boss, but he was one who expected as much as he gave.

He grunted approvingly. "Looks like I'm getting a better deal with you than I thought. Can you ride?"

When Libby nodded, Gus said, "Maybe tomorrow I'll let you help me train the thoroughbreds."

"Really?" She stopped in the middle of pulling the fork back and looked at him. "I'd love that. They're beautiful animals."

It didn't take much longer before all the hay was spread. Gus set his pitchfork aside, then grabbed hers out of her hand and stuck it with the other. "Let me introduce you to a couple."

He then motioned for her to follow him.

Curiosity set in as she walked beside him. "Tell me about this farm. You seem to know a lot about horses, too."

"*Ja*, I share in Colin's dream of building one of the finest stud farms in the country. That's what brought us to Kentucky." Gus halted in front of a stall. "This here's Zeus." The horse's nostrils flared and he slowly walked toward the gate. "Colin does the breeding and I train and manage the place. Originally, I worked with Colin's father. Managed his stables in Virginia. That's where Colin and his wife were from."

"Colin's married?" The thought saddened her, and it should not have.

"He's a widower."

"I'm sorry to hear that." She sounded more contrite than she felt, which bothered her even more.

"It was awhile ago." Gus sighed and continued speaking as Libby leaned against the stall post.

"Colin heard about the bluegrass and bear grass, touted as being the best natural food source for thoroughbreds in the US, while in England. That's where he met Richard Ten Broeck, another breeder, whose horses are considered some of the best in the world. American thoroughbreds are bred from the top English thoroughbreds and other hardier American breeds." Gus stroked Zeus's long face and rubbed behind his ears. The stallion whinnied and pawed the ground. "This brute is one of our finest achievements." He smiled and gave Zeus one last pat before turning to go.

Libby hurried to keep up with him. "Wow, what a story."

"We made our first trip here together and both of us fell in love with this area."

Nodding, she understood completely because she also loved Kentucky.

"*Ja*, I have the best of both worlds. I'd love to have my own farm, but raising and racing thoroughbreds are expensive and risky endeavors. My expertise is the stable, while Colin has the eye for good horseflesh."

"I don't think I've seen such gorgeous animals." Other than at Churchill Downs during racing season, Libby amended silently. Every stall they passed held a horse that would be worth millions in her day.

"Wait till tomorrow and you can see for yourself what they'll do. Colin can trace his original pair's bloodlines back to English thoroughbreds." Gus practically beamed with obvious pride. "In the last five years this farm has made a modest name, and despite the fact that demand for Kentucky racehorses died with the war, Colin's studs are kept busy and his mares are producing champions." They reached the entrance. "We're done for the day. Let's go see what Berta has for dinner."

Libby needed no further prodding. Her stomach was already growling from hunger.

He held the door open and she slipped past him. "I admire your skill, Libby," he said, breaking the comfortable silence that sprang up between them as they walked. "You definitely have a gift. I'm glad you found Twin Oaks."

Looking around, Libby sighed contentedly. If only Dave could see her gift as something worthwhile, she would be the happiest person on earth. A thought struck. Maybe that was her lesson—to realize the value of what she loved to do. If she believed it, then it might be easier to make Dave understand. Libby spotted the twin oaks and smiled. A couple of days in the past should do much to give her all the confidence she needed. Then she would wish herself home. Hopefully, it would work. She sure as heck didn't want to get stuck here.

With her plan set firmly in place, she followed Gus into his kitchen and was surrounded with the aroma of baked bread and roasting meat.

"Do you need any help?" Libby offered a smile, wanting to be helpful. "I can set the table."

"No, you relax." Berta wiped her hands on her apron. "I'm sure your day was hard and long. In fact, dinner won't be for about an hour. Would you like to take a bath?"

Gus scoffed. "Berta, let the lad be. He doesn't want a bath. And if he did, he can just use the creek like the other hands."

As much as she was dying to take a bath, Libby shook her head and smiled at Berta, whose gaze held sympathy. "Maybe later I'll try the creek."

After a wonderful meal that was very much like the night before, Libby excused herself. "I think I'll go and wash up a bit before turning in."

Nathan stayed right behind her until Berta called to him. "Nathan, you still have chores to do before bed. Best get to them. No need to bother poor Libby. He may want to be by himself a spell."

"Ah, Ma. Do I haf to?" the little boy said in a resigned voice.

"*Ja*, and it's have to, not haf to. You need to practice. People will think less of you if you can't speak properly. Now get to your chores."

"Yes, Ma."

Libby hurried to the creek and let out a sigh of relief that no one was around. She undid the restrictive bindings and took a deep breath. Crouching, she swished the strips in the cold water, raised them over her head, and squeezed. Her body jerked as the freezing drops rolled off her neck and back. This sucks, she thought as a cool breeze sent goose bumps over her arms and shoulders. Her hands quickly grew numb after doing it several times. Shivering, she then used the strips to wash off the stench of the day. She gave them one final rinse and squeeze and began wrapping them back into place. On the third wrap she quit, unable to go any farther. The icy cloth chilled her to the bone.

The entire walk back up the hill, Libby thought about home and Dave and why she was sent here. Uncomfortable memories of the day spent working in the past bombarded her. Finding a secluded spot to relieve herself topped the list of bad experiences. The thought of continuing held little appeal. She looked around at the beauty but only saw inconvenience and savagery. Even the lure of riding thoroughbreds wasn't enough to stop the yearning to go home.

She changed directions and headed for the bushes to quickly change into her own clothes hidden there. It felt good to be out of the ill-fitting trousers and scratchy homespun shirt. After undoing the icy strips around her breasts, she took a deep breath before slipping into her own shirt and vest, and quickly hid the old clothes in the same spot.

Now at the base of one of the oaks, she stared up at the massive branches. Her most fervent wish was to go home. Please, please take me home, she prayed. Libby closed her eyes and continued wishing.

☙

Unbeknownst to Libby, she had an unwitting observer.

Colin Thorpe walked out of the house to check on the horses, a task he'd decided on since Smithers's hasty departure. A rustling noise near the path to the creek drew his attention. He stopped to listen and quickly stepped into the shadows to wait when it was obvious someone was heading his way. Seconds later, Libby, the new stable hand, walked by, not even a foot away from his hiding spot.

Intrigued, Colin followed, keeping a safe distance to remain hidden from the boy's notice.

When Libby moved behind the bushes and came out wearing different clothes, Colin's curiosity rose higher. He was just about to step out of his hiding spot for a confrontation, only she disappeared before he'd taken one step.

"What in the hell?" Stunned, Colin gaped at the empty spot that Libby had just occupied.

Chapter 6

Libby stirred, glanced around, and smiled. Her plan had worked. She actually landed back in her own time. The trees had somehow brought her home. She wanted to kiss them. Instead, she hopped up, ran over to her car, and climbed inside. Libby turned the key in the ignition. As the car idled, she picked up her cell phone and glanced at it. According to the date and time, only ten minutes had elapsed since the trees had called to her, even after spending almost two days in the past.

She threw one last look at the two oaks, put the car in gear, and peeled out onto the road, leaving a dusty trail behind her.

Around the bend, Bev was walking toward the Twin Oaks stable. She quickly parked and hurried in her direction. "Bev, wait up."

At Choice's stall, Bev halted and spun around. A smile lit her face. "Hey, Libby. What's up?"

"I need to talk to you." Libby didn't bother to keep the excitement out of her voice.

"What happened?" Bev's gaze narrowed. "Did you have your talk with Dr. Bull?"

"No. I mean yes, I had my talk with him, but that isn't why I'm here. I went back today. After making a wish."

Bev was in the process of opening the gate to Choice's stall. With her hand on the latch, she glanced back, her brow furrowing in question. "What are you talking about? What happened?"

"I went back in time. Here on the farm. Not in my sleep like the last time, remember?" She nodded and Libby added, "Bev, it was the weirdest thing. I can't explain it. The trees called to me. I know it sounds crazy. I'm having a hard time believing it myself, except look at this." She pulled the old hat Berta had given her out from under her vest. The hat Libby found on the ground next to her after waking up was proof enough, at least for her, that her ordeal hadn't been a dream.

Bev took the hat and examined it. "Looks old." She remained silent for a few seconds. "It *is* just like before, but different. You know. Than when you went back to see your mom. What do you think it means? Why would you go back here?"

Libby shrugged. "I don't know. But to be honest, I loved seeing the farm in its beginning stages."

Bev sighed and a wistful yearning entered her expression. "Think of all that history."

She followed Bev into the stall, wanting to hug her friend for believing in the impossible.

Brush in hand, Bev ran it over the mare's back. "So, what's it like? Back then? I gotta tell you, Libby, I wish it had been me."

"Geez, Bev, I don't know what I'd do if I couldn't talk to you about something so outlandish." Merely thinking about Dave's reaction had her mentally groaning. She rolled her eyes, then smiled. "Just the fact that I can sit here and discuss this experience with you calms me. I feel better already."

"You didn't answer my question." Bev's gaze sparkled with curiosity. "What's it like?"

"Different, yet in some weird way it's the same. There's so much to tell you and no time since I have to meet Doug in the other stable. How about getting together after work for a beer?"

Her grin spread. "I'm always game for a beer. I'll meet you in the parking lot at nine."

Upon entering the other stable, Libby spotted Doug in a stall housing one of the Montana mares.

He looked up when she approached. "Good to see you. Can you start grooming the bay mare in stall five? I'll be there when I'm done here."

"Hey, beauty," Libby said to the mare as she entered the stall and reached for a brush. She spent a few minutes brushing before Doug joined her.

They worked side by side for a few moments before he said, "These mares haven't been named yet. Thought the kids coming through in the first session could give us their ideas and we can draw the names out of a hat. What do you think?"

Libby smiled, remembering coming up with a few quirky names as a teen. "I think it's a great idea, as long as you don't mind what the kids might dream up."

"I'm not particular and I'm pretty sure the horse won't know the difference as long as she is loved and taken care of." Doug nodded to the mare. "Help me check her foal's position."

Libby heaved a contented sigh, positive that quitting her job at the store to return to the farm had been the right thing to do. Still, as she let tasks she loved absorb her attention, her time travel adventure stayed in the forefront of her thoughts, as did her resolve to somehow make Dave understand her dream.

Finally, she looked at her watch. Eight fifty-five. Time to meet Bev to talk things out.

Despite Libby's long day in the past and an additional three hours doing much the same thing in the present, renewed energy coursed through her system.

Her step was light as she headed in the direction of her car. She turned and caught sight of Bev, who waved and called, "Let's go to Giorgio's."

Libby nodded, an abrupt movement that mirrored her excitement.

"Libby! Bev!" The shout resonated across the room the moment they walked into the noisy bar and grill. "Long time no see. Where have you two been hiding? We've missed you." Giorgio, the owner and bartender, waved.

"I saved those just for you." Giorgio nodded to the only two empty spots at the huge mahogany bar and proceeded to pour them each a beer from the tap, their usual.

Smiling, Libby grabbed a stool and sat. "Hey, Giorgio, how's business?"

"Never better, my lovely, never better." He bestowed a grin showing straight white teeth made brighter with his dark, suntanned complexion. He set their drinks down in front of them. "Especially now that you're here."

Bev tossed out a throaty laugh. "I thought you were after me, not my best friend."

Giorgio chuckled. "There's room in my heart for both of you." He bowed. "Now, if you two beauties will excuse me, I have work to do. But I'll be back," he added in his best Arnold Schwarzenegger impression, waggling his eyebrows up and down. He left to attend to the several customers who held up empty glasses at the other end of the packed bar.

Libby nursed her beer and let her mind wander as her gaze swept the crowded room.

Bev set down her glass and crossed her arms, giving her a penetrating look. "OK, tell me what happened. Start from the beginning and let's see if we can figure this out."

Libby reached over and squeezed Bev's wrist. "I knew I could count on you." For the next thirty minutes she recounted her adventure as Bev listened intently.

"Wow, what a fantastic story," she said once Libby finished. "Hot damn! Maybe I should try wishing under these trees. It sounds like fun. Just thinking about living in 1874 makes the hair on the back of my neck stand up. It really is magical—you know, the fairies at work." She winked.

Smiling, Libby took a drink. Leave it to her friend to veer off the main topic of conversation and allude to her precious fairies and their magic. Bev even had a fairy tattoo. In fact, she had two tattoos, both hidden from the casual eye and both commemorated her beliefs. One, a small unicorn, was just below her right hip bone. The other, on her left buttock, was a fairy with wings and Bev's personal tribute to their friendship. Bev never doubted Libby's time travel dream and always said how could she believe in one and not the other?

"Well? What do you make of it?" Libby prodded when she hadn't said anything else. "I can't think of any reason I would go back to that particular time in history after making my wish."

Bev took a swig of beer. She put the glass on the bar and wiped her mouth with a paper napkin. "I'm still reeling over the fact that you went back in time. I need to think about it for a minute." She put her chin on her hand, her elbow supported with her opposite hand. After a minute, she shook her head. "I'm coming up empty."

"I have a theory." Libby shrugged. "I was meant to see the farm in the beginning. My theory falls apart because there's enough known about the original place that I already had a good idea of what it must have been like. Of course, nothing is as good as reality. I mean, being there sure beats reading about it in some book." Just remembering it all sent chills up and down her spine. "The rolling hills, different landscape with a timeless feel, clean air that makes it seem as if a gray lens was peeled away from everything in sight, and the silence of no traffic, it was all so unbelievable." She left out all the negatives. "I only wish I knew why the trees took me back to that specific time and why the farm?"

Bev's sigh came out in one long exhale. "Maybe it was some quirk of nature and we'll never know."

"Maybe. I still feel there's a reason. It's hard to explain. Like I needed to be there to realize why I exist."

"That makes sense. Do the trees still call to you?"

"I'm not sure." Libby offered a wan smile. Bev had a way of simplifying things. "I didn't feel it when I woke up. I'm kind of afraid to go near them. What if they take me to the past again?" She frowned at the thought.

"You worry too much." Bev waved away her concerns. "You came back once. So you'd do it again, if you had to."

"Yeah, you're right. I did come back."

Bev set her elbows on the bar and directed her focus on Libby. "You said you talked to Dr. Bull." Her eyebrows lifted and the gleam in her eyes said she wasn't about to let it drop. "What'd you say to him? I'm dying to know."

Libby sighed. Talking about Dave sounded depressing. Then again, maybe it would be good to hash out that conversation. "I told him I quit and that I was working at the stables. He wasn't too happy. No surprise there. To be honest, he was such a jerk that I also asked him to postpone the wedding."

"Oh my gosh!" Bev's jaw dropped, her mouth forming the perfect *O*. "You postponed the wedding? What was his response?"

"I stunned him. You know, by speaking my mind. I can't believe I kept quiet all those times he pushed me to do things I really didn't want to do."

"Well, it's about time you let him know what you think." Bev's harrumph sounded more like a snort. "Libby, if you're planning on spending the rest of your life with him, he's got to know what you're really like."

"I honest to God am coming to believe he thinks of me as some kid without any sense." Libby picked up her beer and stared into the glass as if the amber liquid held the answers to her problems. "That I'll meekly accept anything he says as gospel," she added a second later. She took a long draft and shook her head. "He won't be making that mistake again."

"Good for you." Bev clapped her hands and practically jumped up and down.

"I'm not even sure I want to get married. I thought Dave was the one when I said yes, but too much has happened since then to change my mind." With all these doubts, canceling seemed the best thing to do, but then her trip to the past came to mind and she looked at it from a different angle. Bev was right. Dave had no clue as to what she was really like because Libby had never stood up and let him see the real person. That thought only depressed her more.

"I'm sure he didn't like that. Dave's never struck me as the kind of guy who lets a little thing like his bride's reluctance get in his way," Bev warned.

"He will if I dig in my heels and say no. I'm part of the couple, I just realized. If he wants to talk about our future, not just his, I'm willing to listen." Libby crossed her arms, unwilling to yield on this stipulation. "I was pretty clear about not accepting that my wants and needs are taking a back seat to his. There are two of us."

"My sentiments exactly." Bev slammed down her empty beer mug. "I hope you stick to your guns."

"When I think of it all I get so mad at myself. I can't believe I was so naive as to change who I am to please him." The idea set off a nerve and anger filled her all over again. No wonder he made all the decisions.

"Don't be too hard on yourself. He's your first love, so you have no one to compare him to. Now that you have a firmer grasp on you, he'll come around. That is, if you want him to."

Libby blew at her bangs and nodded. "Yeah, you're absolutely right." She set her empty glass next to Bev's, wondering how her life got so mixed up in just a few short days.

Giorgio set a separate check in front of each of them. "Don't stay away so long next time."

Libby smiled and thanked him, paying no attention to her friend's usual bantering.

Bev's lips curled into a pout. "Giorgio, if you keep making goo-goo eyes at my friend, I'm going to think you don't love me anymore."

Giorgio laughed in obvious enjoyment. "I told you, sweetcakes, I have a big heart. You name the time and place and I'm yours." He then reached across the bar to take Bev's face in his hands and gave her a big, noisy kiss before striding away like a peacock.

Hiding her smile, Libby turned to leave. Bev was usually immune to guys and their come-ons, but her blush spoke volumes as she followed Libby out of the crowded bar.

Thinking about her friend's reaction was a heck of a lot better than thinking about her own mess. Libby headed to her car having come to one big conclusion. She had a lot to think about.

Chapter 7

Eager to move into her cabin on Twin Oaks, Libby woke early the next morning. She stretched the kinks out of her muscles. Without the bindings and able to breathe easier, she jumped out of bed and took an extra-long, hot shower. It felt wonderful, she thought, drying off. With the light on, she added mentally, flipping the switch after brushing her teeth. She glanced at the toilet and moved to flush it one more time, just because she could.

In the kitchen, she lovingly touched the coffeepot before filling it with water. Inhaling the aroma of freshly ground Italian roast, she smiled. The smile stayed glued to her face as she watched the strong liquid brew. Once done, she poured a quick cup and sat at the table to read the newspaper.

Her cell phone rang. Dave's picture flashed on her caller ID. Unease gripped her. She had no idea how to react.

Libby pushed the ON button, deciding to go for normal. "Hey, Dave. What's up?"

"Hi, Libby. Have you got a minute? I wanted to catch you before you left and was worried you wouldn't keep your cell on."

"Yeah, I have a few minutes to spare." She cleared her throat and studied her fingernail. Was that a speck of mud from her worm hunt? Shivering at the thought, she dropped her hand and focused on Dave. "Have you thought about what I said?"

"How could I think about anything else, considering the bombshell you dropped on me yesterday. I do want us to work. I want to see your side of things, but I still can't help thinking you're making a mistake."

"I know," she said on another sigh. "You've been quite clear. But it's my life and my mistakes to make. To be honest, that's only part of it. Did you think about the rest?"

"Yes. We need to talk. I rescheduled my appointments this afternoon. If you still need help moving, I'm offering my services."

Libby sat silent for a minute, too astonished to speak. Dave had *never* rearranged his schedule for her before. She smiled, suddenly feeling lighthearted and wishing she'd made a stand earlier. "I'd love the help."

"I can be at your apartment around two. Is that too late?"

"No, I'll make sure I'm here."

"Great. I'll see you then. 'Bye."

Libby disconnected and eyed the phone, not sure if things were changing or if he was manipulating her as he'd done in the past. "Time will tell," she murmured, remembering Berta's comment, which in turn made her think of the Gundersons.

A smile broke free. From her perspective, Berta and Gus had a strong marriage. Libby had noted the love and commitment between the two. Each had a definite role and both were happy fulfilling those roles. *I mean to have that type of relationship with Dave.* Or she wanted nothing at all. She understood that now.

The trees had granted her wish by sending her back to witness something that had been lacking in her life since her mom's death. The more she thought about it, the more convinced she became while hurrying to finish her coffee. Minutes later, she grabbed her jacket and was soon out the door.

Her first item on the list was a trip to her apartment complex's rental office to give her thirty days' notice. With the task out of the way and a promise to get her deposit back if she left the apartment clean, she packed, but only loaded a few boxes into her car. She would utilize Dave's help later in the day with the majority and to clean the place.

Two hours later, she sped up along the treelined drive as she neared the trees. Silly or not, she hadn't realized how much the two large oaks bothered her until she passed them and nothing happened. She half expected them to hurl her back in time again.

Libby unpacked and organized her belongings. A satisfied grin took hold as she noted her progress. She quickly locked up with just enough time to meet Dave, who emerged from his car when she pulled into the space next to him. Libby quickly climbed out and gave him a welcoming hug. "You don't know how much your help means to me."

"Yeah, well you got through to me," Dave answered after giving her a quick peck on the cheek. "Maybe I have been a little self-absorbed."

"Just a little?" Libby teased.

"No gloating allowed. Let's get busy. We have a lot to talk about."

"Sorry. I couldn't help it. I really do appreciate your being here. I'm all packed." She tried not to think about how her life fit into a few boxes. Dave had a huge house in one of the nicest subdivisions in the area. Libby had been ambivalent about moving there after their wedding. Now she realized why. It wasn't hers and she'd always felt intimidated when spending time there. That would have to change. "After loading the rest of the stuff, we need to clean."

Dave raised his eyebrows. She laughed and socked his shoulder playfully, loving the reappearance of the man she fell in love with present in his grin. "It shouldn't take too long. I'm not a slob and there's not much to do. I need to make sure it looks good to get my deposit back. If you start on the boxes, I'll start cleaning."

"Lead the way." Dave followed her up the walkway. "I'm your most humble servant."

Libby unlocked the door and they went inside. She had stacked all the boxes to the side of her living room.

Nodding, Dave took note of them. "This shouldn't take more than an hour. That'll give us more time to talk. I realize I've made a mess of things."

He made quick work of the boxes. "So, what do you want me to do now," he asked, coming into the kitchen.

She directed him to the bathroom and handed him a bucket of supplies. "When you're done in there and I'm done in the kitchen, we'll be ready to go."

Earlier she'd set the self-cleaning oven. Her only task left was wiping out the ashes at the bottom of the oven, which didn't take long. She rinsed off her hands and went in to fetch Dave.

Soon Libby was driving out to the farm with Dave following, because he'd never been there before. When Libby zipped past the two trees and nothing happened, she heaved a sigh of relief and wove her way around to the cabin. Dave unloaded the boxes and Libby unpacked them.

"Whew! That didn't take as much time as I thought." Libby put her mom's picture on the end table and wiped the dust off her jeans. She turned to Dave, who had his attention on the scene outside her window. "Thanks to you." She grazed her bottom lip between her teeth, then pushed a strand of hair behind her ear, and hesitated. "You wanted to talk?"

"Yes." He turned away from the window, ran a hand through his hair, and rested it on the back of his neck. "I've thought about everything you said. I want to understand you. I had no idea you felt this way." He caught Libby's gaze. "What's going on?"

Libby shrugged. "I've changed jobs and I need your support in my decisions."

Dave released her gaze and shook his head, rubbing his neck. "What about us?"

She threw up her hands in exasperation. "This has nothing to do with us. It's about me."

"Did you take our upcoming wedding or my feelings into account when you considered your change?"

Libby noted a hint of hurt in his voice. "I shouldn't have to for something that's this important to me." Damn it all. She shouldn't have to defend herself either.

"Don't I count? My career? My needs?" Dave's earnest gaze sought hers again. "Being a doctor is very demanding. I need someone I can count on to be there for me. I thought you were the one."

"How does my working here at the farm for forty hours a week instead of a department store change all that?" She began to pace the perimeter of the small room, feeling hemmed in.

"Is this really what you want to do?" He sat on the edge of her sofa, his expression incredulous.

She stopped, then knelt beside him. "Yes! Haven't you been listening? This is what I love."

"It doesn't make sense to me." His eyes clouded in confusion. "You're much too bright to be settling for working as a common laborer."

"A common laborer?" Libby tossed out a half laugh. "That sounds so stuffy. It's honest work and something to be proud of." She stood up straight, frustrated that he could be so obtuse. Rather than say something that would make things worse, she decided to think about how best to continue. "Can I make you a cup of coffee?"

"I'd like that." He offered a self-deprecating smile that only added to her frustration.

Dave definitely had a few hang-ups, but he was a good guy. He also deserved an explanation, especially since part of their problem stemmed from her refusing to take a stand earlier.

He followed her into the kitchen.

She got everything together and poured the water in the pot. As the coffeemaker churned, she leaned against the counter. "I'm a counselor and a horse handler. I'm damned good at both. Like you, I'm helping people heal—in my case, it's the kids at to the camp who need someone like me." She looked him in the eye, holding on to her solemn expression. "More importantly, I'd hoped you'd be happy I've found something that I love. It's part of who I am and I can't…no, I won't change just to be someone else." She hesitated and added, "Even if it means calling off the wedding."

"You honestly mean you'd call off the wedding?" When she nodded, he remained silent. Finally he said, "I'm sorry. I didn't realize how much this meant to you." He sighed and swiped a hand through his hair. "I guess the next step is to postpone the wedding." After another long exhale, he said, "For how long?"

"I don't know. I need time to figure this out." The coffee was finally ready. Thankful for a diversion, Libby grabbed two mugs and poured. She then handed him one of the mugs and met his gaze. "I don't want to make a mistake."

"Libby, we're not a mistake." Dave's voice was as earnest as Libby's had been pleading. "How can you say that? I love you." He set his coffee down and gripped her arms. "I want to spend the rest of my life with you. I thought you felt the same way." His soulful brown eyes added to the intensity of his expression. "Am I wrong?"

Libby sighed. She had to make him understand how she felt. "I need a partner who sees me as an equal, regardless of what I do. Someone I can trust."

"You don't trust me?"

Peering into his shocked face, she wondered what he'd do if she let him in on her secret. *Actually, that didn't seem like such a bad idea.* Yet, knowing him, he'd have a coronary and think she'd lost her marbles. The more she thought about it, the more convinced she became that she needed to say something. Besides, Bev was right. If they were going to spend the rest of their life together, he would need to understand that aspect of her personality. The knowledge would either make or break them as a couple.

"Sit down. I have something I want you to know."

Dave retrieved his coffee, followed her to the table.

Libby pulled out the chair next to him. "What would you say if I told you I've been back in time?"

"You're joking, right?" He snorted and rolled his eyes. "We're getting off the subject."

Libby closed her eyes, seeking patience. She opened them and offered a sad smile. "No, Dave. I'm not trying to veer off the subject. I'm trying to be honest here. I've gone back in time. Not once, but twice."

"Quit messing around. You have to know how ludicrous that sounds."

"It's true. How can I convince you?"

"That's not possible."

She didn't know how to make him believe her. She remembered the old hat and jumped up to find it. "Here, look at this." She held it out. "I brought this back from my last trip."

"Yeah, sure, and I've been to the moon," Dave said in a derisive voice, ignoring the hat. He sighed and shook his head. "I don't know what's gotten into you lately."

"I'm trying to confide in you. Please, look at the hat. You can see how old it is. Doesn't that prove anything?" She shoved the hat into his hands.

"OK, so you have an old hat. You can find them in any Goodwill store. How does that prove you went back in time?"

"It's true." She knew he would have a hard time believing her, but she never felt he would totally dismiss her claim or ridicule her. Bev accepted it and believed her wholeheartedly. She thought he'd at least open his mind to the possibility. "What do I have to say to get you to believe me?"

"I'm a scientist, for crying out loud. I know about these things. What you're suggesting is physically impossible." His eyes narrowed in confusion. "Why are you so insistent about this? I know I've been a jerk, but I can make it up to you. I promise."

"I want you to listen to me. Please!"

"I can't, Libby. You're asking the impossible."

"All I wanted was a little understanding." Libby choked back tears. His reaction hurt. More than she thought possible. "I wanted you to know more about me so you could understand me. Now I'm beginning to think that will never happen." Without his cooperation, they had nothing.

Dave gripped her shoulders and waited until she met his gaze. "I want to understand you. Honest I do, but what you're trying to convince me of is absurd."

A tear broke free. Libby wiped it off and looked away, shaking her head. In admitting to the trip, she'd finally faced that fact.

He reached over and took her chin between his forefinger and thumb, forcing her to look at him. "It's just not feasible. There has to be some reasonable explanation."

"Why is it so hard to believe?" Tears began streaming down her face. Libby didn't bother wiping them away. "Do you think I'd make this up?"

"No. I'm sure you think it's true, judging by your reaction."

Libby stared through a watery gaze, too stunned to say more, her heart tearing in two as his pleading gaze begged her to back down. She couldn't.

Finally she found her voice. "I think it's time you left." She pointed to the door. "This isn't getting us anywhere. What's more, I think we should call off the wedding."

"You're overreacting." Frustration was evident in every one of Dave's syllables.

With a sad smile, Libby shook her head. "No, Dave, I've finally come to my senses. Please leave. I'll take care of canceling the plans for the wedding."

"Libby, don't do this. It's crazy. Please give it some time. We'll work it out."

More tears broke free. She didn't know what upset her more—his attempt to placate her or his refusal to acknowledge what she had to say. It all hurt so much. Still, she shouldn't have been surprised, knowing him as she did. Dave Phillips was too stuffy to believe in magic. How could she have thought that he'd ever be able to understand or accept her?

"Please go," she said on a resigned sigh. "I can't discuss this any more right now."

"OK. I'll leave." Dave's pleading eyes said it all. He was clearly at a loss as to what to do next. "I know you're upset and this conversation is leading nowhere. But this isn't over. Please don't throw us away. I'll give you a little time before you cancel our plans."

Her shoulders slumped. Too exhausted to argue further, she didn't add that she just didn't see how marriage between them would ever work.

Dave moved toward the door. With his hand on the doorknob, he looked back at her with a worried expression. "Will you be OK?"

She nodded.

"Please, Libby. Give this a few days, OK?"

"Sure," she said with a wobbly attempt at a smile. "But I don't think a few days will matter when it's obvious I can't be the type of wife you need."

"Don't say that! You are exactly what I need. I'll call you in a few days." And then he was gone.

Libby stared at the empty spot that Dave had just vacated for the longest time, feeling emotionally drained, but at the same time feeling relieved. It seemed as if a big weight had been taken off her shoulders. She had expressed her feelings to Dave and had told him what was in her heart. That in itself was cathartic—gave her a sense of liberation. Maybe things would work out.

☙

Libby began avoiding the oak trees. After her argument with Dave, she'd felt their pull too many times while passing by them. That alone was scary enough and kept her wondering. It was as if she hadn't learned her lesson or completed her wish, which made some kind of weird sense, considering she and Dave were still at odds. Still, she had no intention of going anywhere but her own century. How women stood the constraints back then, she had no idea.

Thankfully, her final days at the store had flown by in a blur, and in that time she hadn't seen or talked to Dave. Instead, she texted him and poured all of her energies into the farm, as the camping sessions were in full swing. Working with the horses and the children acted as a balm. When immersed in her duties, nothing else mattered. Unfortunately, Dave and her postponed wedding still lurked in the back of her mind, which is why Libby agreed to have dinner with him later that evening. She did love him and wanted to fit into his world. He deserved a second chance to fit into hers.

Then, there was her dad. Tom Edwards was furious to learn of the postponement. Libby lacked the nerve to tell him she was reconsidering it altogether when he'd practically had a stroke after hearing her news about quitting Dillard's to go back to Twin Oaks.

The only person who made the whole mess endurable was Bev, Libby's rock. Their conversations always steered away from her love life, and the two mostly rehashed Libby's time travel and the reasons for it. Today, Bev wanted to meet for lunch under the trees. She wouldn't say why, only that it was important.

Determined to ignore any and all mental calls, Libby grabbed the picnic basket she'd filled earlier and headed out.

Bev was already sitting on a blanket when Libby plopped down next to her. "What's up?"

"Did anything out of the ordinary happen when you went back in time?"

The concern in Bev's tone drew her gaze. Her brow furrowed. "I don't follow."

Sighing, Bev leaned against one of the giant oaks. "Sam's having trouble forming his trust. Someone contested the property's ownership. He has to appear in court with proper documentation in order for the title to clear."

"What does that have to do with me going back in time?" she said, reaching for the basket.

"Sam's deed isn't just missing, it's as if it never existed. I believe someone messed with the county's records between the time you went back and now."

Sandwiches in hand, Libby froze. "That's impossible."

Bev's eyebrows shot up. "Is it?"

A sense of dread nestled in her stomach. She handed Bev a sandwich. "What's this someone's name?"

"T. P. Smithers."

"Smithers?" Libby's heart skipped a beat. "Oh my God. That's the name of the guy who rode that horse into the ground. You know—the jerk Colin got rid of. He said he'd get even."

"I googled him." Bev's earrings danced as she nodded excitedly. "He's a slick lawyer out of Louisville with a shady background. Not much nicer than your guy, which means they're probably related. I always wondered how guys like him pass the bar."

"Did my going back in time change history?" Libby sat back on her heels, not wanting to believe it. She glanced up at the trees and heard their call—one much stronger than before. Was that why she'd started feeling their pull again? The thought had merit and was worth considering, especially if her actions caused trouble for Sam and his plans.

As realization filtered into her expression, she glanced at Bev, who gave her a "what else could it be?" look.

"You have to go back to undo it." Bev's expression hardened. "We can't let Mary's dream die. It will kill Sam to see this land subdivided and sold off."

That would kill Libby too. "How do I undo it?"

"By getting the original deed."

The dread thickened, weighing her down. "There has to be another way!" She had no idea of how to do what Bev was asking, nor did she want to. Her gaze flew to the trees again. Their cry grew louder, almost a wail, as thoughts of what awaited her if she heeded their call overwhelmed her. "I can't do it," she whispered, shaking her head. "I'm too scared." Of what, she wasn't sure. She just had this ominous gut feeling that her life would never be the same if she did what Bev was asking.

"You have to."

"How," she asked, even though she knew the answer.

"Simple. Just wish yourself back there. Otherwise the farm could be sold at auction."

"What if it doesn't work?" Libby took one more look at the trees, and stupid as it sounded, they seemed to mock her.

"Then we'll figure out something else, but you have to at least try."

"Let me think about it."

"Don't think too long. Sam only has ten days before the hearing."

The two ate in silence. Finally, Libby sighed. "If I do decide to try, let's make a plan, in case something happens and I can't get home."

Bev sat up straighter. "Why would you think you can't get home again? You returned twice before, didn't you?"

"Yeah. It's a feeling. I can't get rid of it, so I'm going with it. If for some reason I can't come home, I'll bury information right here."

Fear crept into Bev's eyes. "You're scaring me. You make it sound ominous. That if you do go, you're not coming back."

Smiling, Libby shook her head. "I'm merely taking precautions." Her mother's death taught her that events she had no control over happened, no matter what. Her smile stretched and she patted Bev's shoulder. "Your friendship and loyalty mean the world to me. You're the best friend anyone could ask for. I love you. I'm sure we'll be sitting under these trees for the next fifty years."

Clutching her arm, Bev blinked back tears. "Oh, Libby. I feel the same way. You accept me for who I am. You've always looked beneath the surface and seen the real me." She wiped the moisture at her eyes. "Your belief in me is what made it so easy to believe in you. Here, let's make a toast. To friendship! May it last through time!"

Humbled, Libby held up her cola. "I can drink to that."

They clinked soft drink cans together and laughed.

Libby took a sip, wishing all things in her life could be as easy as her friendship with Bev. She looked up at the trees, still feeling their pull, before glancing at Bev. "So, promise me if something happens, you'll check the trees? OK?"

Nodding, Bev agreed. "I promise."

Satisfied, Libby placed her arm beneath her head, lay back on the blanket and closed her eyes.

Bev's voice interrupted the quiet. "So, are you still avoiding Dave?"

Shrugging, Libby said, "We're having dinner tonight."

"Are you still having second thoughts about the wedding?"

Libby opened her eyes and sighed. "I'm confused more than anything right now. Dave is trying. It's funny. It took me threatening to back out of the wedding for him to take my concerns seriously. Why did it have to come to that? Why does it take so much effort for us to be together?" She stopped talking and scanned the horizon, then frowned. "I only wish he believed me about my time travel."

Bev snorted outright. "Libby, give the guy a break. It's going to take more than blind faith for someone like Dave to believe you can go back in time."

"You believed me."

"Yes, but I've always believed in the unbelievable. That's one of my many faults. Don't worry. Things will work out the way they're supposed to." She tossed the empty baggie that held her sandwich in the basket and brushed a few crumbs off her lap. "Let's talk about something more pleasant than being stuck in time or Dr. Bull." She glanced at Libby. "Answer me this, will you? Are we going to Thunder Over Louisville this year?"

"I don't know. I'll probably be working during the air show. And the traffic's always such a pain after the fireworks. Why?"

Bev grinned. "You need a diversion to forget all of your problems."

"I'll think about it."

"While you're thinking, add this to your thoughts. You can stay with me and we can walk, so we can avoid the traffic. We should go and have fun, even hit Giorgio's on the way back. Make it a night. Come on. It'll be fun."

Leave it to Bev to make big plans on a big day. Thunder Over Louisville, one of the largest air shows and fireworks displays in the country, marked the start of Louisville's Kentucky Derby Festival. The two-week celebration ended with the Kentucky Derby thoroughbred horse race on the first Saturday in May. "I'm not up for crowds."

"Oh, come on, Libby. You sound like my mother. The crowds are what make it fun."

"Maybe," she said, standing and helping Bev pack everything away.

Both needed to get back to work.

Later that afternoon, Libby rode out alone on Thorpe's Pride before working with a group of kids going out for their first ride. After a good run, the mare was always more docile and willing to go at the slower pace the kids needed.

Giving Pride full rein, Libby loved the feeling of becoming one with the horse. The wind whipped her hair. Greens and browns whizzed by as they galloped through the Kentucky countryside. Libby eventually slowed the mare, having traveled a good distance.

Horse and rider eased to a stop at the top of a rise, a spot where she could see rolling hills for miles. The timeless scenery tugged at Libby. This part of Kentucky hadn't changed in over a hundred years. The continuity of the land was a constant. People came and went, they were born, gave birth, and died, and still the land remained.

A sense of peace engulfed Libby, leaving nothing of the fear or uncertainty she'd experienced on and off for the past two weeks. Suddenly it dawned on her that this land was somehow her destiny. That thought brought a broad smile to her face.

Yes! This land held the key to what was ahead for her. Sam couldn't lose it. Not to something that happened because of her. She no longer felt reticent about what would happen. Whatever was in store for her, she would meet it head on. Libby turned the mare toward the stables and started back.

Nearing the pastures, she slowed Pride to a walk. She still had plenty of time to meet the kids. As she rode by the two oaks, she glanced their way and quickly wished she hadn't because their call was more urgent. So much so, that this time she couldn't ignore it.

She stopped the horse, dismounted, and led her over to the trees, where she tied Pride to a low branch. Libby then walked around the trees, looking up with full understanding of why they were calling. She needed to return and undo her mistake. The thought no longer frightened her. Instead she stood there, looking up into the new green leaves that were just making an appearance, and accepted the trees' call, at the same time wishing to be taken back to the moment she left the past.

In seconds the world turned upside down and she felt herself floating through time again.

Chapter 8

Blinking several times, Colin worked to clear his vision, positive his eyes deceived him. The boy was there one minute and then gone. Less than thirty seconds passed before he was back, but only in a different position. Even stranger—he was no longer wearing his sleeveless jacket. Plus his shirt was a different color. Colin narrowed his gaze and watched in stunned silence as the boy went over to the bushes and emerged a little later in the garb he'd worn earlier in the day. He then strolled past him not more than a few feet from his hiding spot.

Fascinated, Colin stared after him. A dozen questions swirled inside his brain, his most pressing running along the lines of what the hell had just transpired. There was more to Liberty Edwards than met the eye. Since Nathan had befriended him, he decided to talk to Berta about his new stable hand. Berta knew everything going on in her household. What she didn't know, she would easily glean, once her curiosity was spiked.

Colin remained in his hiding spot until the boy was out of sight before finally heading back to the stable. Just as he pushed through the main door, a noise at the rear of the building drew his attention. The earlier scene he'd witnessed faded somewhat as he hurried to check on his favorite stallion.

Zeus greeted him with a loud neigh and one hoof pawing the ground. The horse's ears perked up and he bobbed his head as Colin held out the carrot he'd taken out of his pocket and said in a soothing tone, "Hey, big fellow. Was that you making that racket?" The stallion nudged his hand and captured the bribe. Colin grinned. Must have been, he decided, since all was quiet. Zeus probably sensed his presence and didn't want to go unnoticed.

As Colin shrugged aside his concern, the memory of the boy disappearing and reappearing entered his thoughts again. While the horse chewed on his carrot, Colin grabbed a brush and began stroking and talking about what he'd seen out by the twin oaks.

"So, what do you think, Zeus," he asked after ending his spiel. "Am I crazy?" Colin smiled when Zeus eyed him thoughtfully. Then the horse shook his head and neighed, as if to say no, like the horse understood the question. Suddenly, the thought of seeing an apparition wasn't as disturbing as it had been a few minutes earlier. "You're good for the soul, Zeus. I'm going to be gone for a few days. I'll miss you." Colin put away the brush. "There are several new mares needing your attention, my good fellow. You'll be busy enough—too busy to miss me."

His entire future was riding on all the horses in this barn, but this one was special. So was Asapurna, the mare two stalls down. Both horses were the basis of his prized stable.

He stroked Zeus's sleek neck, thinking it an appropriate name. In fact, all of his horses were named after mythological gods or goddesses, which seemed fitting considering their ancestors. Mythology and the legends of ancient people had always fascinated Colin.

With Lexington as Zeus's sire, the stallion was a god among horses and one of the best runners he'd ever seen. Four years earlier, when Colin had first purchased the pair from Woodburn Farm, Lexington's owner, his deal had included breeding Asapurna with Lexington. The result was a little filly he named Fortuna—the goddess of chance.

Lexington had been a descendant of Diomed, a champion thoroughbred and the winner of England's first Epsom Derby in 1780; a race that Colin knew was still run today. Diomed's blood ran through some of the finest American thoroughbreds of the nineteenth century. Having never seen a better champion, Colin saw a sure thing in Lexington. Bred with the right mares, the stallion's offspring would produce legendary horses. Zeus was one of those offspring. Fortuna was another.

"Well, good buddy, I need to get going." He gave Zeus a final pat, then walked the distance to Asapurna's stall. When he leaned against the gate, it unlatched and opened. He froze as an eerie sensation settled on the back of his neck. Colin spun around and listened as his searching gaze swept the stable. Everything appeared normal and only the sound of chirping insects or croaking tree frogs filled the air.

Still not satisfied that all was right, considering the earlier noise, he did a quick inspection of the stables. Near the door he spotted a dirty bandana on the ground and bent to pick it up. He studied the red cloth and remembered that Smithers had worn a bandana exactly like this.

The thought of canceling his trip flitted past his mind, but that meant missing the meeting at the Galt House in Louisville with the instigators of the new racetrack. Colin started back to the house with the intention of finding Gus and warning him to keep a sharper eye out while he was gone.

As Colin neared the caretaker's house, light from a gas lantern illuminated Berta and Gus on their porch swing. The couple was obviously taking advantage of the cooler evening air.

Gus stood. "Something wrong?"

Taking the steps two at a time, Colin held out the bandana. "Found this a few feet from the stable door. Earlier I thought I heard something and then found Asapurna's stall gate unlatched.

Eyeing the red cloth, Gus scratched his head. "What do you make of it," he asked as Berta came up behind him.

"Do you know who it belongs to," she asked in a worried tone.

"Smithers wore a red bandana," Colin said. "If it's his, the man has to be up to no good, sneaking his way into the stable." He exhaled heavily and let his gaze roam over the countryside before settling it on Gus once more. "I've decided to take the train from Shelbyville to Louisville in the morning. That way I can get back a little sooner in case there's trouble."

Then remembering the Edwards boy and what he saw, he turned to Berta. "I wanted to ask you about our new stable hand."

"You mean the boy, Libby," she asked, clearing her throat.

"Yes," he said, nodding. "The boy." Unable to think of a delicate way of putting it, he blurted out, "Does he seem a mite strange to you?"

"Strange?" Her eyes narrowed as she studied his face. "What do you mean by strange?"

Colin shrugged, feeling rather silly for even bringing it up, but he couldn't dismiss what he'd seen. "I mean, is there anything peculiar about the boy that makes you think he's not what he seems?"

Shaking her head, Berta looked away and brushed at her calico skirt. "I'll keep my eye on him, just to be sure. You can depend on that."

"So will I, Colin," Gus chimed in. "We'll take care of things while you're gone. I'll put a couple more hands in the stable at night, just in case Smithers is up to anything."

Thankful to have that out of the way, he smiled. "Good. This mating season is too important to the farm's survival. I don't want anything to go wrong."

They said their good-nights, and Colin retraced his steps to his big house. First, he checked on his children. All three were tucked in their bed. He stared for long moments, just enjoying their innocent, angelic faces softened in sleep.

Sam, his oldest at five, had Colin's coloring and temperament as did three-year-old Melanie. Rebecca, his baby, was a miniature of Abby. Sometimes when looking at her his guilt would get the better of him, and he'd want to hug her to him, as if doing so would assuage the emotion.

He left them sleeping and walked toward his bedroom with the realization that Abigail hadn't entered his thoughts until that moment, since before spying his young handler out by the trees, a novelty since her death. He was tired of feeling guilty and being reminded of how much his wife had hated being here. He often wondered why she'd married him when he'd made it abundantly clear during their short courtship that he wasn't content to stay in Virginia. He'd always planned to find a place where he could start his own farm without the interference of his domineering father.

Colin had specific ideas of what he wanted for his farm that were more forward thinking, not at all like his father's tried and true ways of generations. These ideas always created tension between the two men. Colin was more apt to experiment with his breeding and bring in new blood to his American thoroughbreds. He had a good eye for horseflesh. If he saw certain traits in a mare he liked, he had no qualms of putting her in with one of his stallions to see what she produced.

In the four years he'd been in business, his methods were generating incredible horses. Most of these he sold off, providing a good income. His dream of owning one of the best horse farms in the country was beginning to take shape. If Abigail had embraced his dream, he would have been the happiest man in the world. Unfortunately, his dream had played too big a part in her unhappiness, which kept him awake far into the night, staring at the dark ceiling and wishing it hadn't been so.

☙

Thankfully, when Libby made it back to the small house, no one but Nathan paid her any attention. At first she was nervous. After all, she'd been gone in the future for several weeks, but it was obvious no more than an hour had passed here.

Nathan ran up to her and grabbed her hand. "Libby, I've finished my chores. Do you want to play checkers before bed?"

Smiling at his eagerness, Libby let him lead her to the table. "I guess I could play one game."

"Great. What color do you want to be?"

"Hmmm." She stroked her chin, appearing deep in thought. "Black. I need to warn you, I'm pretty good at this."

Nathan giggled. "So am I."

Once Libby sat, he went over to a cabinet and retrieved a checkerboard and a cup that held carved round wood pieces painted either red or black. As Nathan laid the board on the table and proceeded to place the pieces on the checkerboard in the appropriate spaces, Libby wondered how to go about getting her hands on Colin's deed. It wasn't as if she was experienced in this type of thing.

"Since yer my frien', you can go first," he said, looking up at her.

His smile was so engaging that Libby was drawn out of her thoughts. Tomorrow was soon enough to figure out how to be a thief. "OK. Prepare to be beaten." She moved her piece one space and the game began.

"King me," he said, jumping two of her pieces and landing at the end square.

Libby grunted and did as he asked. The little guy played a lot of checkers. She'd always thought it was a simple game requiring a basic skill, but Nathan seemed to have a strategy. Within the next five minutes, he soundly beat her. She stared at the board in awe, unable to believe a ten-year-old boy had trounced her so quickly.

"Best two out of three," she said, while setting up the board again for another round. "And this time, I'm putting on my boxing gloves. No more Mr. Nice Guy. You are clearly a worthy opponent."

Nathan laughed, clearly pleased by her praise of his abilities. The second game took fifteen minutes longer, but the outcome was no different than the first game. Nathan emerged the winner. When that happened, Libby eyed him speculatively. "I think I've been hustled."

Chuckling, Gus came into the room and walked toward the gas wall sconce as Berta followed, only to disappear into the kitchen. "Nathan's been playing checkers since he was in nappies," he said, turning out the flame. "He loves the game and he hates to lose." He moved to the other one across the room. "It's a good thing you lost. Otherwise, he'd never let you walk away from the table until he won. Come on, it's time for bed. We all have a long day tomorrow. You can try for a win tomorrow night, Libby."

"I guess I am pretty tired." She got up from the table. Near Nathan's chair, she placed her hand on his shoulder and squeezed. "Come on, friend. I'll have to work on my strategy."

By the time she and Nathan were nestled in their beds, a little over an hour had passed since Libby was transported back in time. She wasn't tired at all. Then she remembered it was afternoon when she had left the future. She mused that she was probably suffering from a time zone change of sorts.

Lying there, she could only marvel at how similar this experience was to the last time she was here.

This entire process no longer frightened her. Now it seemed like an adventure or quest she had to conquer before she could go home for good. Until then, she planned to enjoy her visit here in the past. After all, everything about this farm was worth the trip—the people, the horses, and the land. Sighing, Libby brought her arm around and put it under her head. Everything would work out in the end. Somehow she just had to believe that it would.

The next morning's rituals were no different than those other mornings she'd previously spent in 1874. Berta was in the kitchen when Libby returned from the privy. The toothbrush, bowl, cloth, and soap were on the counter. She promptly pumped water into the bowl, added a bit of hot water, and washed. After brushing her teeth with the weird-tasting powder and emptying the basin and rinsing it out, she turned to go to the table.

Breakfast was also much the same affair as always, but this time Libby had come to accept the camaraderie of the family and joined in. When she'd lived with her father before she went to college, nothing had ever been this easy. Libby couldn't remember what it had been like when her mom was alive, having very little memory of everyday happenings. Mostly the big events were what stayed in her mind. She wasn't sure if her mother's death changed things.

Soon Gus pushed away from the table and gave his wife a peck on the cheek. "We have a full day ahead. Come on, Libby," he said, glancing at her. "We'd best get started."

After waving at Berta and pretending to hit Nathan's shoulder, Libby followed.

The June morning was crisp and cool, with very little humidity in the air as she fell into step next to Gus.

"Colin is leaving this morning, so we'll need to take over his duties," he said on the way. "That shouldn't be a problem, since you're so good with horses. I'm thinking you ride as well as you work with them?"

Libby shrugged, holding in her excitement. "Yeah," she said as nonchalantly as she could. "I can ride. I was hoping you'd let me."

Gus only grunted. "I'm working on training two of the mares for racing. You can take over for me. That way I can then work with the stallions. Our track's out by the north pasture. Early morning is the best time to give them a couple of runs. We usually work two at a time—they run faster when they have a little competition."

Libby cleared her throat. "I've never raced on a track before. I'm used to riding thoroughbreds and giving them a good run," she said, swallowing her disappointment. "I'm not sure I'm ready to race on a track."

"Ha!" Gus clapped her on the back. "If you can race through the countryside, you can race on a course. The horse may be a bit faster, but the even ground more than makes up for the extra speed." He practically cackled in glee. "You're in for a treat. Nothing compares to running these beauties around the track, encouraging them to reach their peak speeds."

Open-jawed, Libby could only stare at him. Oh my God. She was going to race a horse. That alone was worth the inconvenience of having to return to 1874. Her grin widened. Every bit of the excitement running through her system came out in her voice as she said, "OK, I'm game."

They entered the stables amid shouts and activity. Libby had to step back to avoid running into two men leading horses in their direction.

"Come on over here and meet the four we'll be working with this morning," Gus said, walking up to the beauty she'd seen him with on her earlier visit. "This is Zeus and here we have Asapurna, Fortuna, and Hercules," Gus said as he took her to each horse, introducing her one by one.

Libby rubbed Asapurna's neck and the mare nuzzled her in greeting. Up close she was gorgeous. All of them absolutely stole her breath with their magnificence. The thought of riding any one of them overwhelmed her. It was like she'd gone to sleep and a dream she hadn't ever known she had was turning into reality.

"Once we exercise them, we'll set them out to graze," he said, handing Asapurna's reins to one of the handlers.

"Do you put them to pasture because it's summer," she asked, wanting to know all there was to know about how horses were trained in the past.

"*Ja*. We also do it in the winter as much as we can. The grasses here in Kentucky are better than any grain we can buy." He stopped for a minute to grab some tack off the wall. Then he began to help ready the four horses for their workouts. "The only problem is we have to monitor how long they are out eating. Otherwise the horses have a tendency to get fat."

"So the grasses really make better horses?" Like everyone else in her century, Libby had come to take for granted what was right in her backyard. The grasses became a background, hardly noticeable because they were forever present.

Gus nodded. "Our soil's rich in nutrients. Some believe the limestone in the natural terrain leaches out into the grass, which in turn, is eaten by the horses and helps build a strong skeleton on the young foals."

"All that from grass," she asked distractedly, brushing Asapurna. A native of Kentucky, she never thought about something as simple as grass being so important.

"*Ja*, bluegrass and bear grass are considered indigenous to this part of the country, but we don't know if it was always here or if other settlers brought it," Gus said, warming to his subject. "Many farms harvest the seed to sell in other parts of the US. Doesn't matter to Colin or me. We only care that these native grasses help make the thoroughbred stronger and better. Before the war, most races were endurance races of at least four miles and for sure the horses were fast. Now races are shorter distances, usually about a mile or so, but the horses run much faster. Of course the horses from our stables do both—run faster and last longer. They have the endurance to last four miles or longer and are some of the fastest horses alive." Pride rang out loud and clear in Gus's voice.

"Well, these horses are definitely superior," Libby said, putting the brush down and following him through the stable.

Until that moment, Libby never understood how important the landscape was to the health and well-being of the horses. The terrain seemed forever green—whether rolling hills or neighborhood yards—always the lushest in the late springtime and early summer after the spring rains. No wonder the best thoroughbreds in the country were raised within a fifty-mile radius of this land.

When everything was ready, they headed in the direction of the course. Along the way, Libby could only stare. The scene could be part of a Monet painting. The various greens of the grass and the lush deciduous trees, with their assorted shades of brown trunks that dotted the landscape, contrasted sharply with a sand-colored stone wall that circled the pasture. The focal point of the entire scene was the reddish-brown sand and clay track, surrounded by a white fence and centered in all of the hues of greens and browns. Libby sighed. This truly was an adventure. There was nowhere else she'd rather be at that moment in time than here, preparing to race thoroughbreds.

"I thought you'd be halfway to Louisville," Gus said, drawing her attention to a man she hadn't noticed—Colin Thorpe. He was dressed more formally, wearing a jacket and necktie, than when Libby last saw him.

Pretending her heart wasn't beating wildly, she followed Gus and Colin over to the head trainer she'd met earlier. Jake took the reins to all four horses they'd been leading.

"I had a little time to kill before my train departs." Without looking at Libby, Colin nodded in her direction. "What's the lad doing here?" he said in an accusing voice that made her back straighten with determination to convince him that she belonged here, even if she didn't.

"He's proven his mettle," Gus said, taking the sting away from Colin's comment. "He says he's ridden before, so I'm trying him out with the mares."

"Really?" He then gave her a cursory glance and grunted. "He must've impressed you if you're letting him ride one of the thoroughbreds. You're usually very protective of them."

"I still am. Just watch. See if I'm not right," was all Gus said before nodding to Libby for her to follow him.

"I'll watch, all right. I'm very interested in what the lad does after last night," Colin said, then turned and walked toward Jake.

Libby tried not to let the comment bother her, but something about his tone of voice struck a nerve. She risked a glance back at Colin and watched as he and Jake exchanged a few words. Unfortunately, he chose that moment to look up and catch her staring. Averting her gaze, she inhaled deeply, praying her face wasn't as red as it felt. She did not want to find that blue gaze so compelling, especially when he already seemed suspicious of her. "Remember, Libby, you're here for a purpose, so don't get sidetracked," she said under her breath. She needed to make a good showing during the race to ensure her job here. Going home without a copy of the deed wasn't an option.

The men scrambled about setting up for the race. Mounting Asapurna, Libby allowed the excitement of the moment to help her shove Colin and his compelling gaze out of her mind. Gus rode Zeus. A handler, keeping a grip on both reins, walked with them to the starting point.

Jake held a stopwatch in one hand and gun in the other. He looked to Gus to give him the signal before firing.

At the sharp report, Asapurna leaped onto the course and took off with surprising speed. Libby quickly caught her balance and leaned forward, moving in sync and watching the scenery whiz by. Spurring the mare on, she'd never felt more liberated or happier. "Come on, girl," she whispered, laughing at the rush she felt, knowing they were ahead. Riding this mount, with the wind blowing through her hair as the mare's gait ate up ground, was indescribable.

She saw Gus on Zeus out of her peripheral vision, riding at warp speed, catching up fast. As the other horse and rider slowly took the lead, she leaned in and urged, "Come on, you're too good to let him win." Libby whooped and hollered as Asapurna did her damnedest to regain the lead, staying less than a length behind the stallion until the end.

When the race was over, both riders allowed their mounts to slow to a steady walk, then guided them back to where the group had gathered.

Gus dismounted and handed his reins to one of the other handlers. "Cool them off. They both gave a good showing." Then he looked to Jake. "What'd he do? It has to be good."

"It was." Jake grinned. "Knocked two seconds off his best time. The mare set a record too."

"I thought so." Laughing, he walked over to Libby, who still sat atop of Asapurna. "I've never seen anything like it. Asapurna's never run that fast. I had to push Zeus to keep his lead."

Pure delight welled up in Libby. With her gaze on the ground, she dismounted with Gus's help, just as Colin walked up.

"Where did you learn to ride like that?"

She looked up and noted those startling eyes again, only this time rather than being filled with suspicion, they held approval. As Colin continued holding her focus, her mind went blank. Not the best time to be tongue-tied. Geez, why did this guy affect her like this?

Finally, she was able to clear her throat and managed to croak out, "I don't know. I've always liked horses and they like me. I've been told I have a way with them."

And even more disconcerting? During their brief stare-off, she sensed a connection. He seemed as bothered by it as she was, considering afterward he quickly looked away, appearing embarrassed.

"Whoever told you that spoke the truth," he said, recovering almost immediately. The warmth in his voice wrapped around her being like a blanket, casting off the rest of his earlier coolness.

"Our job just got easier," he said, looking at Gus, practically beaming, which added another ten degrees to the heat spreading throughout her system. "Are you going to work the other two now? I can't wait to see what they can do."

"*Ja*," Gus said. "This should be good."

Libby kept quiet as they all headed to the starting point where Fortuna and Hercules stood waiting patiently for their turn. Never in her life had she felt such a pull as when Colin held out his joined hands to give her a lift up. The instant attraction filling her senses unsettled her. For God's sake, even though she and Dave still hadn't worked things out, she wasn't free to go daydreaming about horse breeders who lived in the wrong century.

When the gun went off, Libby had no more time to contemplate her love life. She had her hands full with Fortuna. The mare was that much faster than Asapurna and every rider's dream. Libby was bound and determined to make a good showing.

"Come on, girl, show me what you've got," she said, leaning into the mare, feeling the rush as the wind hit her face and the landscape flew by in a whirl of greens, browns, and grays. Instantly, it was as if she and the horse became one with a common goal. Fortuna, responding to her slightest touch and voice commands, stayed with the other horse, trying with all her might to take the lead. Hercules crossed the finish line first, but if the race had been longer, Fortuna might have won.

Libby eventually slowed to a walk to cool down the mare, honored to be sitting atop this special thoroughbred bearing the heart and the soul of a champion. The experience of riding this horse would stay with her for a lifetime.

Gus, having already dismounted, strode toward her with a big grin on his face. "Fortuna has never run that well against Hercules. What did you do to get her to run like that?" He grabbed the reins to steady the mare. "You, my boy, have a magical touch."

Libby's smile matched his. "It's easy when you have such a good partner." She then bent from the waist to nuzzle the horse and whispered, "Next time, we'll beat that ol' Hercules." Fortuna bobbed her head several times, pulling out of Gus's grasp. Her strut became more pronounced and Libby laughed in pure enjoyment.

Colin hurried up to them, his gaze trained on Jake. "Was that a record for Fortuna?"

Jake nodded. "By eight seconds and Hercules cut three seconds off his best time, Mr. Thorpe."

"You were right, as usual." Colin clapped Gus on the back, practically gloating. "I'm as impressed as you are." Then he turned to Libby and said, "Can you ride like that all the time?"

Shrugging, Libby struggled to act nonchalant as warmth spread up her neck. Thankfully, he refocused on Gus, too busy talking to pay her reaction any mind. "This boy certainly has a knack for getting the best out of our mares. I've never seen anything like it. Next race, you let him ride Hercules against Zeus and see what happens. Then I want you to let him ride Fortuna against Asapurna. Do the same tomorrow. Mix it up a bit while I'm gone." His disquieting gaze settled on her once more. "When I get back, I want to work with you. You have the makings of a good jockey." He shook his head. "By God, I've never seen anything like that performance."

Having never had such praise before, Libby didn't know how to respond other than, "It's not hard when you have such a good mount."

"All the mounts in our stables are good—better than good." Colin grunted. "No, you can't dismiss your talent. You, my boy, take your mounts to the next level." He took his watch out of his pocket and flipped the gold timepiece open. "Damn, it's almost eight o'clock. I have to leave." With resignation, he turned to Gus. "I'd love to stay and help, but I have to go or I'll miss my train."

"Don't worry. You'll be back before you know it. The boy'll be here when you do. He and I will start working together, then you can take over."

Not if I complete my mission first, Libby thought, watching Colin head back the way he'd come. She needed to find the deed, and soon, so she could go home. His trip away gave her the perfect opportunity for snooping. Her time in 1874 was only temporary—the people only a means to an end. Becoming attached wasn't an option when she had a life to return to.

Thoughts of returning home brought on a sudden twinge of sadness. This whole adventure was taking on a new dimension and made her wish for the best of both worlds. Ignoring the thrill of excitement humming through her body, she decided to stick to the basics. Work on getting the deed, then making it back to her own time without getting any more involved here in 1874 than she already was.

Without the distraction of one sexy stud farmer, Libby was able to focus more on racing.

The sun rose higher, along with the temperature.

Finally, Gus called it a day and said, "We need to check out the pregnant mares. I'm worried about two that are soon to foal." He continued talking, telling her they were separated from the other horses and stabled when it was close to their due date. The farm had fifteen mares expecting and several were due any day. That by itself was an adventure. Gus showed her how to check out the mare, making sure the placement of the foal in the mare's belly would present no problems for delivery. Even though she'd done this sort of thing in her own time, Libby was fascinated that other than not having the use of fancy X-ray machines, not much had changed in regard to the birthing of horses in over a hundred years.

"It's important that the feet and head come out first, otherwise complications set in. It's usually not a problem. But if it is, we can turn the foal if we catch it in time," Gus said, walking into one of the pregnant mare's stalls. Watching the nervous mare calm when Libby started stroking her, he grunted. "I think I'll have you with me all the time on my daily checks." Libby's face lit in pleasure as he added, "We have a couple of foals already out in the pasture. They're up in a matter of minutes and soon running all over the place." After they finished with the last pregnant mare, he said, closing the stall door, "Come on, I'll show you how we work on the young foals until they're weaned to get them used to being handled."

Libby followed him outside to one of the pastures.

As they neared the gate, he started speaking again. "When they're old enough, the training becomes a little more intense. June is a busy time here on the farm. We have foals being born, foals being conceived, and yearlings being sold. The whole process can take two or three years and is ongoing. During it all, we're always on the lookout for specific traits. Colin usually spots them. He has a good eye and knows what he wants. When we see certain traits in a foal or yearling, we pull 'em and then we work with that horse separately. If a colt or filly shows promise, he or she may join our small stable of thoroughbreds. So far we've averaged about one a year."

Gus spent a couple of hours showing Libby what he did with the foals. He told her that when they finished here, they'd be working with the yearlings. Libby followed his actions. It wasn't long before the foals were nuzzling her and following her around if she didn't get too far away from their dam. Their playful, curious antics charmed her.

After they left the foals, they went to the house and ate lunch. It was well past one in the afternoon and Libby was starving.

When lunch was over they headed for another pasture. All of the land they'd hit during the course of the workday amazed Libby. Colin's property went on forever and most of it was being used for one purpose or another.

Gus stopped at the gated fence, circling a vast area where the young horses grazed. "The yearlings stay out here most of the time." He re-latched the gate once they were inside. "Most of these will be sold soon. As soon as they carry a saddle and can follow a lead, they're ready to be sold. But rest assured, the minute they are gone, there are new yearlings to take their place."

It didn't take Libby long to get the knack of working with these wonderful, quick animals. With every new chore and every new horse, she began to fall a little more in love with the place. She loved all aspects of working on this farm. The work was hard and there was so much to learn, but she'd never had so much fun.

Gus came up to her just after she'd finally gotten a yearling named Jessie to take the bit into her mouth. "Time to quit."

Surprised it was so late, she glanced up.

"You've earned your pay for today. Come on, Berta'll have dinner ready soon."

Libby stretched. Her muscles told her she'd put in a good day. Smiling, she asked, "What time is it?"

Gus chuckled. "A little past six. We've been at it almost twelve hours. A normal day for me. The other hands don't work as long. Things will slow down eventually. Then I won't be too busy to take Nathan fishing."

Thinking of the boy, Libby remembered her promise. "You know, Gus, Nathan asked me if he could help with the horses. Have you ever thought of training him?"

"*Ja.* He would love it and probably be good at it. But he's still too young. I don't have the time to deal with his childishness."

"What if I work with him a couple of hours every day? I'll start with something simple—like working with the foals or yearlings. Surely he can do that?" Frisky for sure, but much easier than dealing with high-strung adult horses.

Gus thought about her offer for a long moment before nodding. "*Ja*, Nathan is eager to learn. Maybe it would work. But I have to warn you, he can be a handful."

What an understatement, Libby thought, laughing inwardly. "He can teach me to play checkers and I'll teach him to work with yearlings."

Grinning, Gus grunted. "It seems you know him well. He's a natural with horses. I just haven't found the time to spend with him." He remained quiet for several more minutes. "You're a godsend. You've been here for less than a week and already you're making an impact."

Libby thought about his comment, wondering if she could actually make a difference while on her quest. The idea provided a heady feeling for someone whose father and fiancé considered her an immature screw-up unable to hold a job. Since she had a few days before Colin would return, there was no reason not to spend some of that time with Nathan, passing on her skills.

As the two walked back to the caretaker's house nestled behind the big house, she decided on a bigger issue that weighed heavily on her mind. Tonight would be a perfect time to snoop for Colin's deed.

Chapter 9

When the westbound train pulled into the Shelbyville station, Colin boarded, having spent most of the hour-long horseback ride reflecting on his mares' performances. After finding a seat, he stared out the window as his mind drifted once again to his new stable hand.

Unanswered questions about what he'd seen the night before still concerned him. He honest to God didn't know what to believe. Yet because he needed someone with the boy's gift, he was tempted to overlook the anomaly. After witnessing Libby shave seconds off his mares' best times, he couldn't dismiss what that meant. Weight was more important than they'd figured. The boy looked to be about a hundred pounds, maybe one hundred and ten, at least eighty pounds lighter than Gus and sixty lighter than himself.

It was difficult to gauge a real race, since most of the jockeys racing weighed less than a hundred and thirty pounds. So far he and Gus were able to train their horses on their own. Their heavier weight actually gave them a slight advantage. Up to a point. Early on, they'd decided to forgo the expense of employing a jockey on the farm until the need became more urgent.

As luck would have it, they no longer had the problem of finding a competent one. In fact, they were ahead of the game.

Colin had never seen a jockey just hop on and encourage that type of speed without working with either horse for days. Apparition or not, he would be a fool to expose the lad without knowing more. He had no doubts that when he returned, his stallions' times will have improved under the boy's touch. He was that good.

His thoughts then turned to his meeting later that day at the Galt House, where he'd booked a room. Besides the meeting, Colin had pressing business with his solicitor, and he'd planned on taking the time to scout out the site of the new track. He also wanted to talk to several businessmen to gain more information.

He was anxious to have the issue resolved one way or the other. After thinking about it, he realized why he was antsy. He was in a hurry to get back to his farm. Funny, he was in no hurry yesterday. But after seeing Libby on his mares, he couldn't contain his budding excitement at the thought of working with him.

The fierce shrill of a train whistle interrupted his thoughts. Looking out the window, he was shocked to see the Louisville sign. Totally absorbed in his thoughts, he'd completely missed the other stops along the way.

The train lurched to a stop and he quickly disembarked. Avoiding horse-drawn wagons and pedestrians alike, he hurried up Main Street toward the livery stable to rent a horse for later that afternoon. The sun's rays beat on his shoulders. Near midday, the temperature was climbing.

His mission accomplished, he started for Mr. Malcolm Webster's office on Fourth and Main. His appointment wasn't until the next morning, but if Malcolm could see him now, Colin would be able to tie up his business concerns and return to Shelbyville on the morning train.

Inside Malcolm's office, he nodded to the clerk who sat at a desk near the door.

The young man immediately stood up. "Good morning, Mr. Thorpe," he said in an anxious voice, wringing his hands. "How may I help you?"

Colin smiled to put him at ease. "Good morning, Mr. Pettibone. Is Mr. Webster in? I realize my appointment isn't until tomorrow. I had some free time now and thought I could get my business out of the way."

"I'm not sure," he answered awkwardly, glancing a little nervously at his employer's closed door. "Mr. Webster's been in there for quite a while with his earlier appointment. He should be finished any time." He took a deep breath as if trying to relax before saying, "Why don't you have a seat and when he's free, I'll let him know you are here."

"Thank you." He started to sit then stood back up. "On second thought, if he comes out, let him know I'd like to change my appointment if I can. In the meantime, I'll go check in at the hotel. That way I can drop my satchels off."

"Very well, sir. I'll tell him." The clerk smiled in a more confident manner.

"I shouldn't be too long." Colin walked out of the office, impatient to conclude his business. Normally he relished a trip to bustling Louisville with all of the amenities—restaurants and shops were plentiful But today, he simply wanted to get going.

He swiftly walked the short distance to Second Street and the hotel's entrance. After checking in and putting his bags in his room, he promptly made his way back to Webster's office.

Mr. Pettibone stood at his approach. "Mr. Webster is free now." He went to the closed door, knocked, then opened the door and stuck his head inside.

Malcolm, a stocky man a few inches shorter than Colin with reddish-brown hair and a ready smile, hurried out of the room and over to him. "Colin. Come on in." He offered his hand. "It's good to see you."

"Thanks for rearranging your schedule."

He waved his thanks away. "You know I always have time for you. In fact, why don't I take you to lunch?"

Colin shook his hand. Having used his services since moving into the area, the two had become friends. "Hello, Malcolm. Thanks for rearranging things. I would love lunch, but only if you let me buy."

"I'd be honored." Malcolm laughed. "Where would you like to go?"

"You know the restaurants better than I do."

"There's a new one I've been meaning to try up the street. Let's go there, shall we?" He grabbed his jacket and led Colin out the door.

When seated, the two proceeded to order.

After being served, Malcolm started talking. "The news isn't what we'd hoped. My audit's confirmed that while your breeding farm is exceeding your expectations, your expenses are much higher than anticipated." He handed him a file, going over the numbers in detail. "You're still not making a profit."

Colin closed the file and frowned. "I knew we had a few setbacks, but I wasn't expecting it to be quite this bad." Forcing himself to relax, he took a deep breath, thankful to have the boy, Libby, already working for him. This way he could circumvent the added expense of an experienced jockey. Money wasn't an issue; Colin had been a wealthy man before he started his farm. It was a matter of personal pride. If his farm was profitable, then he could meet his father one-on-one—as an equal. If the farm didn't pan out, his father would never know it. But Colin would know. His farm's success was more than his livelihood. More than a dream. His measurement of being a man was gauged by that success.

Once business was out of the way, their conversation led to more personal interests.

Watching the waiter leave after serving them, Colin asked, "You're going to the meeting later, aren't you?"

"Wouldn't miss it. The prospect of having another track in Louisville is all anyone's talking about." Malcolm sighed. "I only hope this one lasts."

Colin nodded. Those backing the proposed racetrack felt the time was ripe to build, that it was exactly what the city needed. "Personally, I'm unsure of demand. Businesses are still having trouble bouncing back from the Panic of '73." The economy was sluggish, even if picking up in Louisville. Economic troubles could easily hamper their vision. In Colin's opinion, the city's enthusiasm for such a venue was crucial to success. "Clark's presenting ideas to overcome the negatives at this meeting, so I'm remaining optimistic."

As he picked up a fork to begin eating, he remembered that Malcolm had handled several of the sales when the old track went bankrupt and was sold off in lots. Though he'd made a lot of money on the sales, Malcolm had believed the social cost of losing the track seemed too high a price to pay for monetary gain. Colin felt the same way. Horse racing had been a way of life in Louisville from its early history. It was a damned shame the city had no track on which to enjoy the sport today.

"Our city needs this track," Malcolm said. "Too much has happened in the past thirteen years to change our way of life."

"The war all but destroyed horse racing in the South," Colin said, thinking of all the ramifications of the War between the States. The South's breeding centers had been raided during the war, and the taxes assessed after its end had crippled landowners who had anything left. The end of slavery also affected the economy in the Southern states. Colin's family hadn't owned slaves—they didn't believe in owning another individual. With a solid industrial basis before 1861, Louisville had only a minimal dependence on slaves compared to the rest of the state, but horse racing still died out in the city. Saratoga, in New York, became the new mecca of the sport and American thoroughbred racing shifted north after the war.

"The business community from here to Lexington is interested," Malcolm said, warming to his subject. "Breeders, shopkeepers, landowners, and the railroad owners are curious about the new proposed track. Be prepared for a packed meeting."

By the time the check came, they'd discussed the topic thoroughly.

Colin paid and both men rose from the table. Once outside, they started back the way they'd come.

At Malcolm's two-story office building, Malcolm turned to Colin and shook his hand. "Save a spot for me at the meeting." He turned to go into his office, but stopped and said over his shoulder. "Oh, by the by, I'm to tell you that if I saw you that Caroline Hillier wants me to convey her best wishes. She's back in town. You remember her? Seems her husband died recently and she's now a widow. Better watch it, old boy. She's heard about Abby's death and I think she's on the prowl. You were always in her sights."

Unimpressed, Colin rolled his eyes. Caroline was a fast piece who caused more than a minor annoyance during the few parties and activities he and Abby had attended right after they'd first moved into the area. Colin had had little interest in such activities. But Abigail had enjoyed them. It seemed a small price to pay to give her that little bit of happiness. Yet Caroline's outrageous flirting dimmed some of that enjoyment. "Give her my best, will you?" he said without conviction. Caroline Hillier was the least of his problems.

"I think you'll have the opportunity to tell her yourself, if she gets wind you're in town," Malcolm said, smiling. "I've got to tell you, my friend, I don't envy you. She's a tough one to ignore."

"Thanks for the warning. Just be glad you've got Susan to keep her from digging her claws into you."

"Like that ever stopped the woman," Malcolm sneered. "I'll see you in a bit."

Colin nodded. "Until later, then." As he walked back to the hotel, Colin truly hoped he wouldn't see her. Caroline always made him feel like he was a fox on the run. His thoughts turned to Emily Jones, a widow he'd struck up a friendship with several months earlier. She was the complete opposite of Caroline. Emily's husband died three years ago, leaving her a wealthy woman. The widow laughed at anyone's attempts to marry her off. This made her the perfect partner for him because he had no intention of marrying again either, seeing no need. He had his children, and his farm was his life. After Abby's death, he vowed never to marry again. In his opinion, there wasn't a woman out there who could be happy sharing his dream with him.

Emily's shared disdain of marriage made her the perfect woman for him to escort to dinner without feeling pressured. The relationship worked for both of them. She most likely expected to see him tonight, but after talking to Malcolm, he had no desire to socialize.

Shrugging off the thought, he walked into his hotel and up to his room. Once inside, he took out his pocket watch. Having an hour to kill, he decided to finish reading a book detailing the latest ideas in animal husbandry. He read anything he could get his hands on concerning breeding. In his mind, knowledge was power. That, coupled with experience, was the road to success.

Colin read until it was time to go downstairs. Outside the room where the meeting was to be held, he spied M. Lewis Clark, Jr., or Lutie, as his friends called him.

Clark was in the middle of speaking. When Colin walked up, he stopped and smiled warmly. They shook hands. "I was explaining that the property I have in mind belongs to my uncles."

"Yes, but it's so far out. Why not the Falls City grounds? It's much closer," said one man in the small group.

"Vision!" Clark answered. "My vision includes a grandstand for two hundred people and stables for four hundred horses built on sixty-five acres of prime land once used as a track that sits unused and can be leased for a reasonable price. The soil is superb. Springy sand mixed with clay and drains well. It's a mile-long oval. Eighty feet wide on the homestretch—sixty feet on the backstretch. The turns are a quarter of a mile each, which means it'll be one of the safest racetracks in the country."

More men had filed into the packed room that was soon standing room only. Clark cleared his throat. "I'll start the meeting now. If you still have concerns afterward, let me know. Hopefully I can allay your fears."

Colin sat next to Malcolm, who'd saved him a seat.

Clark's speech was persuasive. He'd obviously investigated this thoroughly, traveling through England and France extensively. For almost a century, people came from all over England to witness the Epsom Derby, an annual event. Louisville needed something similar to draw in the masses—Louisville's own derby. His proposal involved creating the Louisville Jockey Club and Driving Park Association, along with the new racetrack. Both would sponsor the event and hold it in the middle of the spring meet. The railroad could lay track to the park, which would provide transportation for the masses.

The next part of Clark's plans included using the Paris Mutuel machine, invented by a Frenchman, which calculated the bets. The total amount bet on any one race would be divided between all of the winners of that race, minus the five percent the house would take for their services, ensuring profitability. The machines were currently being used in France, and had been for a couple of years. The process worked. Clark was very excited when he ended his speech with, "My friends, this is our opportunity to bring Kentucky back into horse racing."

There was silence in the room before the questions started flying and were promptly answered. By the time the meeting was over, the men had come to an agreement. The Articles of Incorporation were adopted for the new Louisville Jockey Club and Driving Park Association. Three hundred and twenty men pledged one hundred dollars each for work to begin on the new grandstand and stables to be finished by May, in time for the 1875 spring meet.

Though still a gamble, Colin pledged his and Gus's money before walking the few blocks to retrieve his horse. He rode down Third Street toward the outskirts of town, intending to check out the track. Weaving in and out of passersby, horse-drawn wagons, and men on horseback, Colin was surprised to find the road so crowded well after six o'clock on this Monday evening. The sun was no longer high, but dusk wouldn't come for a couple of hours.

Near the edge of town, walkers and riders still filled the promenade, but as he continued riding, the crowds started thinning. By the time he reached his destination, three miles south of the city limits, Colin was totally alone. The only sound, other than his horse's hooves hitting the dirt, was that of bees buzzing or birds chirping. It was peaceful and quiet.

Colin dismounted and walked around, noticing at once what his friend had seen—a perfect spot for Louisville's premier racetrack. Though a ways from town, Colin could see this area surrounded by houses and activity in no time. Louisville had been slowly stretching its boundaries since its beginnings in the late 1700s.

Having achieved his goal, Colin quickly mounted his horse and headed back the way he'd come. By the time he reached Main Street, the city's gaslights were being lit.

He dropped his horse off at the livery and settled his account. While walking back to the hotel, he ran into several friends. One in particular, Ian Stevens, invited him to dinner at the hotel. An hour later he finished eating and departed the restaurant. Energy still consumed him. Colin wasn't ready to turn in yet. When he pushed the heavy door to go out, he almost ran into Emily Jones.

A smile lit Emily's face as recognition set in. "Why, I thought you might be in town tonight." Then the smile slowly faded. "I'm surprised you didn't call."

Colin caught the hurt look in her eyes before she quickly lowered her gaze.

Damn, this was getting complicated. "Emily, I'm sorry," he said, feeling torn. "I did mean to call, but my business ran later than I expected. Time got ahead of me. I was just out for a bit of air—a night stroll." He offered a bent elbow. "Would you care to join me?"

Emily nodded. "A stroll sounds lovely." She placed her hand on his arm.

Together, they walked out into the street. Despite the fact that the time was nearing ten o'clock, there were many out and about, also enjoying the pleasant evening.

They'd gone half a block when Emily said, "How was your meeting?"

"It went well." Colin smiled. "We actually set the gears in motion."

"People are talking about nothing else. There is so much speculation."

Colin chuckled. "I don't have a crystal ball, but I'm optimistic. Time will tell."

Small talk went back and forth for a few minutes, eventually lapsing into silence.

Colin wondered how he could gracefully decline the invitation he knew she would be issuing for a late dinner as she sometimes did. He had too many pressing issues on his mind to deal with hurting her feelings. It seemed callous and cruel, but it was how he felt. He knew his not calling on her had also hurt her feelings, because he could still see sadness in her eyes when he happened to gaze into them.

After being so careful, he couldn't believe he'd done what he'd sworn never to do. Hurt her. He didn't want to hurt anyone, especially someone he cared about. He cared about Emily, but he didn't love her. Suddenly, he felt in the exact position he'd been in when he was married. No matter what he did, his actions hurt his wife. Now the past was repeating itself.

Looking at Emily now, her gaze shielded by the corner of her hat, he sighed.

"You seem distracted," she said in a quiet voice. "I hope you're not merely being polite." She paused, momentarily watching him. Then her invitation came tumbling out quickly. "Would you like to have a late dinner? I'd love the company."

The hope in her voice tugged at Colin, tearing his insides. It seemed he could hurt her a little now by being honest. Or be dishonest and carry on the lie, which would probably hurt her more later on. Thinking about it for a moment, he finally opted for honesty, mainly because he wasn't in the mood to placate a woman who shouldn't need to be placated.

"I'd love nothing more, but I have a lot on my mind. I don't think

I'd be good company," he said in a gentle voice. "That's the main reason I didn't call. I know you were expecting it, and I am sorry."

"I don't believe you wouldn't be good company," Emily countered hopefully. "You always are, no matter what. Besides, maybe I can help."

He shook his head. "Not tonight." He stopped and looked down at her. When she raised her head so that he could hold her gaze, he smiled wanly. "Were you at the Galt House for a reason? Are you going back? If so, I'll escort you there."

She blinked back tears and shook her head. Her voice was just above a whisper when she spoke. "No, I only went there to see if I might bump into you. I guess I am the one who should be sorry."

Noticing the tears, Colin felt as low as the dirt under his feet. Still, he'd wanted no entanglements and he couldn't relent. That would be too cruel in the end. "There's no need for you to apologize. Come, I'll escort you home."

They started in the direction of her house. When they reached her porch, Colin stopped. He turned to her and said in a solemn voice filled with sadness, "I believe you are starting to want something I can't give."

"That's not true, Colin."

He winced at the desperation in her voice. He was silent for several minutes. Finally, he met her gaze so she could see the truth in his eyes. "We've always dealt with each other honestly. And you know where I stand. Where I've always stood on marriage. I'm not going to change my mind. I don't want another wife, especially one from the city who's afraid of horses. My God. I could never make that mistake again. Think about it. You're a city girl. You've lived in the city your entire life. My farm is my first love and I have three children to think of, leaving me time for little else. After this racetrack settles, I'll have even less time."

"But Colin, I love you. I would love being with you anywhere."

"That's not good enough," he said in a resigned voice, shaking his head. "That may work for a little while, but what about after that? I can't handle being the cause of another woman's unhappiness. You are too much like my wife. I see too many similarities."

"Then let's continue as before," she said a little too quickly. "I'll ask nothing of you."

"No, it will never be as before and you know it." His tone gentled. "You need to find someone to share your life with. I know you say you don't want it, but your actions prove otherwise. I care about you, Emily, but not enough to marry you. I'm sorry. I think it's best if we didn't see each other anymore. In time, you'll see I was right." With those words he turned to go.

Colin's walk back to the hotel took only a matter of minutes. The entire time his thoughts had been on Emily and the relief he felt in speaking his mind. During their last few times together, he sensed she was beginning to see much more in him than he did in her. As he pushed his way through the entrance to his hotel, one truth hit him between the eyes. He doubted he'd ever find a suitable mate, so he should just quit trying.

Chapter 10

Libby hurried along the trail to the big house, having found Berta's suggestion of a bath in the creek a perfect opportunity to snoop for the deed to Colin's land. Gus was still at the stables, staying later to work out a guard detail. Nathan was busy with chores.

According to Berta, two older nannies, Minnie and Maizie, were prone to eat in their room and turn in early when Colin wasn't in residence. Approaching the house, Libby spent a moment looking around, praying the two women weren't in the parlor.

Everything appeared quiet. Even the insects hadn't begun to chirp yet. With fingers crossed that the coast would stay clear, she sneaked up the porch steps. She eased the door open and listened. Her heart pounded so loud, she was sure the noise would alert either one of the nannies or another servant. She inhaled deeply, using the technique to calm her nerves. When nothing happened for the longest time, she slipped inside. Afraid to move too quickly, she edged her way along the wall, listening for any noise other than her rapid heartbeat that still hadn't slowed to normal.

A door opening sounded above and Libby stopped short, her heart in her throat. The pounding inside her chest grew louder as someone on the second floor walked in her direction. Another door opened and total silence followed. Libby stood watching the staircase for the longest time, then quickly ventured toward the study door and slipped inside.

Taking several deep breaths to still her rapid heartbeat, she shook her hands and rolled her shoulders. Being a thief required the kind of gall Libby didn't think she had. But now that she was here, she had no time to waste questioning her sanity and moved quietly across the room. The large dark wood desk suited a man like Colin, she thought, sitting in his oversized chair and methodically opening the side drawers one by one. It didn't take much searching to spot a locked strongbox. Figuring the deed was probably inside, Libby continued looking for a key.

At the sound of a thump, she froze with her hand on the locked box on top of the desk. Her gaze flew to the door. When all was silent for an extended moment, she let out the breath she'd been holding and picked up a letter opener to jimmy the lock.

The lock clicked open. Her glee-filled grin broke free, and she couldn't contain the triumphant excitement running through her. Nestled inside with other documents, Libby found the deed, which she quickly grabbed and stuck inside her shirt. She jiggled the makeshift key to relock the box, put everything back the way she'd found it, and hurried out of the house the way she'd come. Staying near the bushes, she made her way toward the twin oak trees to wish herself home. Hopefully, she'd be able to make notarized copies and then return to replace the deed before anyone knew it was missing. Only then would her task be complete. The thought of being nestled in her own bed in her own century tonight had her rushing.

At the base of one of the trees, she stood and glanced up into its monstrous fully-leaved branches. Closing her eyes, she wished to go home.

Nothing happened. Looking at the trees, she tamped down the rising trepidation and said more forcefully than was necessary, "Come on. You're supposed to be wishing trees and I'm wishing to go home." Maybe she wasn't wishing hard enough. Giving it another try, she closed her eyes and wished with all her might. When that didn't work she did it again. Several times.

What was wrong? Why wasn't she going home? The thought of being stuck here sent another streak of fear down her spine. Yet, no matter how much she wished, it did no good. She definitely wasn't going anywhere tonight. Finally, her shoulders rounded in defeat and she slowly headed back to the smaller house, beyond the big one. There had to be a reason she couldn't go home. Nothing would let her believe she was stuck in the wrong century. She'd try again later. In the meantime she'd keep the deed hidden and pray no one would realize it was missing.

As usual, the scents coming from the kitchen were strong enough to make Libby's mouth water. Only tonight, eating was the last thing on her mind.

Gus joined them a minute later and bowed his head to say grace.

Dinner was another boisterous affair that Libby usually enjoyed when the Gundersons shared the events of their day. She tried to stay focused on the conversation rather than on her failure at the trees.

"Minnie and Maizie certainly have their hands full with those poor angels," Berta said, warming to one of her favorite topics, Colin's three motherless children. "Yesterday Sam had turned the parlor into a stable and had Melanie acting like a horse he was training. Where that child gets his imagination, Lord only knows. Soon, he had both women playing in the game."

Libby did the math in her head. The boy Berta mentioned must be the future Sam's grandfather. She wondered what he looked like.

"Sam's interest in horses is inherited." Gus reached for the platter going around the table. He probably had his father's and grandson's blue eyes, Libby thought as he added, "Colin will train him properly."

Berta clucked. "He's only five, much too young to lose his mother."

In Libby's book, fourteen was too young too. "That's sad," she said, feeling a strange sort of kinship with kids she'd never met.

"Now, Berta, you know Minnie and Maizie love those kids—more than their own mother ever did, if you ask me."

Libby would have liked to learn more about Colin's children and was disappointed when the conversation turned to other topics. Since it didn't seem fitting for a boy to be too interested, she let her mind drift back to her time travel problem as Gus shared his day with Berta, even encouraging Nathan and his sister, Sarah, to share their experiences.

"Libby can certainly ride. Zeus and Fortuna beat their records today," Gus said, pulling her interest back to the conversation. "Colin and I have found our jockey."

Humbled at the genuine praise in his voice, Libby prayed her warm face wasn't beet red. Having spent so much of her life vying for her father's approval, she couldn't stop the smile forming. Gus's expression said it all. So did Berta's. More happiness welled up inside her. They appreciated her skills. She ignored the slight twinge of discomfort resting on her conscience over the thought of never seeing them again once she finished her mission. Would they miss her?

As Nathan talked about finding tadpoles, Libby wished for a family like this one. Being an only child, she'd never enjoyed dinners like this with her father. When the two of them had dinner together the conversation was usually stilted, because Libby felt as if she'd somehow disappointed her father.

That led to other conflicting thoughts, like those of Dave. She hadn't thought of him in a while. Could they have something similar ten years down the road? Somehow it didn't seem possible. Dave never relaxed enough to enjoy simple things like discussing the day's events. Her fiancé didn't usually talk openly about anything. Maybe she could draw him out and get him to open up to her—to show his inner self, as Gus was doing to Berta? The idea intrigued her. Maybe that was the reason she hadn't been able to go home yet. She needed to learn something here in the past in order to have her wish answered in the future.

That seemed reasonable. What could it hurt to spend more time here in the past to figure it all out? Besides, she'd be training thoroughbreds and also be able to work with Nathan.

"What do you think about letting Nathan help with the yearlings?" she said, leveling her gaze on Gus. "I'll take responsibility for him." She'd use the lessons to let the boy in on the fact that their time together was limited. It was the least she could do before visiting the trees tomorrow night.

The thought of leaving shouldn't disturb her, but it did.

The next morning, Gus pushed away from the table and stood. He bent to kiss Berta, then glanced at Libby. "Best get a move on. We have much to do today."

Libby waved good-bye to Berta and Nathan and followed Gus out the door.

They trained at the track until the heat of midday started to affect the horses. From there they moved to the stables.

"What do you think?" Gus looked askance at her after stopping at a stall holding a pregnant mare.

Clearing her throat, she realized he wanted her opinion on the mare's condition. Sure, she'd been around pregnant horses before and even helped when Pride was born, but her experiences were limited. Bev had been the expert in dealing with foaling mares.

Besides, Gus had known her for less than a week. As Colin had said, he was overly protective of these thoroughbreds, as well he should be. The farm's future rode on the foals these mares produced. His faith in her added to the sense of belonging she'd felt last night.

A similar sense of sadness tugged on her heartstrings as she eased closer and rubbed the mare's neck in an attempt to introduce herself. This would be the last morning to be around these beautiful animals.

The horse nickered and took a few steps back. "Easy, Electra." Using the name Gus had provided, Libby kept her tone soothing and continued stroking. "I just need to check you out. It will only take a minute and you won't even feel it." Her examination was quick. "She's ready to foal." The udders were enlarged and a waxy substance appeared on the edge of her teats.

Approval evident in both his eyes and his smile, Gus nodded. "We'll keep a closer eye on her today." While he continued watching Libby's progress, she examined the others. None were as far along as Electra.

Gus led her out of the stable and up to the paddock gate. Inside the fence, three yearlings grazed. "I need to check on the stallions." He took off his hat and wiped at his brow with his shirt sleeve. "With so many mares in heat, I can't ignore them any longer."

"What do you do? Just put them together and let the process begin," Libby asked, interested in the differences in mating throughout the centuries.

"*Ja*, basically. Thorpe's farm uses a process called teasing, which is safer for the two animals involved, but it takes longer and is more work. We put the animals in a separate, specially built corral that keeps the animals from getting hurt," he replied. "A stallion can be overly aggressive and unmanageable when picking up the scent of a mare in estrus." Gus stuck his hat back on his head and grunted. "Sometimes it's downright violent, especially if a mare isn't ready." He spent a little time telling her about the process. The mare and stallion would be separated in a corral with a divided partition. If the mare exhibited signs—adopting the position and moving her tail to the side—she was ready, which made his job easier. If she bared her teeth or tried to kick and bite the stallion through the fence, she still had a day or so to go, which could be dangerous.

Libby knew all about how dangerous the situation could be. In her own time, most farms used artificial insemination to avoid injuring either horse.

"I love it when it's over, because that is where it all begins," Gus said, grinning. "The prospect of a new colt or filly next year makes all the work worthwhile." He broke off for a moment, then nodded at the yearlings. "Now might be a good time to work with Nathan." When her gaze turned questioning, Gus shook his head. "It's not that I don't trust you. I don't trust the stallions. Maybe next year, when you've grown a bit." He started for the gate. "Nathan's just finishing his chores and should be here shortly."

Eventually Nathan joined her. While showing him how to clip the horse's hair to create a bridle path behind the yearling's ears, she broached the subject of her leaving. "You know, Nathan, I can't stay here forever."

Nathan, laughing only seconds ago over the frisky horse's playfulness, frowned. The expression in his blue eyes added to his woeful expression. "Why? I thought you liked it here."

"I do. But I need to go home at some point. When I do, just remember you'll always be close to me, in my heart."

"I understand." Nathan nodded. "Ma says I have to look for the silver lining in sad news." He remained silent, clearly thinking. Then his face brightened with a smile. "Pa is letting me work with the horses and he never did before you came."

The lump in Libby's throat grew larger and she smiled back, meeting the boy's earnest gaze. If ever she had a child, she'd want him or her to be just like Nathan.

The horse's neighing interrupted the moment and soon both were too engrossed in training yearlings to worry about her leaving.

Colin's first stop that morning had been the blacksmith shop, where he'd ordered much-needed tack to be delivered within the week. Next, he'd dealt with ordering feed and other necessities. Scuttlebutt about the new track and the newly formed Louisville Jockey Club and Driving Park Association had abounded everywhere he turned. The air had all but snapped with energy and excitement.

With his errands finally out of the way, he headed to the train station. The eastbound train to Shelbyville pulled into the station. He quickly boarded, took a seat, and peered out the window. Colin couldn't wait to see the finished racetrack. Hopefully his horses would be ready to run in the next spring meet.

His thoughts shifted to the boy, and for the hundredth time he wondered what he'd seen out by the oak trees. Had Libby really disappeared then reappeared? Or had his eyes played tricks on him?

Other questions formed. Where had the lad come from? What was he doing out by the two oak trees? Where did he get the clothes? And for that matter, why change? It was all very puzzling.

Liberty Edwards was a godsend, so maybe he came from heaven. Lads that talented with horses didn't show up every day on his farm. Colin decided to have a more in-depth talk with Berta as soon as possible.

The shrill whistle of the train blasted in the air and the big steam engine and four cars slowed to a stop. Colin promptly disembarked, headed to the livery to pick up his horse, and was well on his way home in no time.

At the stables, he left his horse with a handler for grooming and went looking for Berta, who was outside hanging laundry.

"Colin?" She nodded, watching his approach.

He halted near her basket and peered down at the ground, trying to figure out a way to broach the subject of Libby. When he didn't say anything, she bent and pulled a shirt out of the basket, shook it out, and then used a wooden pin to anchor the ends on the line. "Was there something important you needed?" Her questioning glance rested on his face.

"Um…yes…um…" He rubbed his chin with his thumb and forefinger, still thinking. Finally, he decided to just blurt it out. "There's something strange about Liberty Edwards, and I'm betting you know what that is."

"We all have secrets." Berta looked away quickly, but not quick enough for Colin to miss the bit of pink hitting her cheeks, along with a guilty expression clouding her eyes. "Some are worth keeping."

"Oh?" Colin waited until Berta glanced back at him before raising his eyebrows. "If there's something I should know, you'd best tell me."

When Berta remained silent with her attention on the basket filled with clothes, Colin sighed. "I mean the child no harm. I just want to know more about him. Like where he came from and who his people are." He shook his head. "It's not like my farm is on the beaten path."

The blonde woman's cheeks took on a rosy hue as she shook out a pair of long johns and proceeded to hang them on the line.

"How could he just show up out of nowhere?" How had he gotten to the farm, miles away from town? Berta knew more and he wasn't about to leave it alone until she told him everything.

Her lips thinning in a straight line, Berta appeared to be waging a mental battle. Wringing her hands, she looked up at him but Colin could read nothing in her guarded expression.

"What? You know something." He eyed her for several seconds. "I told you I mean the boy no harm, but he's so young. Someone must care about him."

"*Ja*, she is young…" She shook her head. "I meant *he*." Her face grew a darker shade of pink, if that were possible.

Totally stunned and not fooled one bit by her cover-up, he struggled to keep his face blank. "She," he asked, looking at her for substantiation.

Finally, Berta nodded. "She's definitely not a boy," she said, exhaling another long breath.

This whole thing just kept getting more interesting by the minute, he thought, swallowing hard.

"I'm sorry I didn't tell you or Gus, but she seemed desperate to stay. And I figured if she was as good as she claimed, both of you needed her." She reached for another shirt to hang. "Now you know why I didn't want her staying in the bunkhouse."

Unable to disagree with either claim, he remained silent, trying to digest the information. The lad who urged his horses to ride like the wind was a girl. The idea boggled his mind.

After pinning the shirt in place, Berta turned back to him, her features taut with worry. "You'll let her continue working?"

"Of course I will." He wasn't heartless. Besides, he'd be crazy to turn her out when she knew horses. Unfortunately, there went the perfect solution to his problem of hiring a jockey. He couldn't in all good conscience subject a young girl to such a dangerous sport. It had been bad enough when he thought her a boy. Boys grew up and needed a livelihood, so in essence Colin had been helping rather than aiding and abetting an unsafe situation.

Then remembering the other night, he asked, "Do you know where she came from?"

"Only what she told us at dinner." Berta proceeded to tell him. "I'm not sure how much is true. But since she's safe and is a good worker, I decided it wasn't my business."

"Hmmm." Colin thought about this for a moment. "Do you think Nathan might know more about her?"

"'Tis possible." A smile took over Berta's face. "They're thick as thieves. Libby spent the better part of the afternoon working with my boy. Right now, she's helping Gus with one of the pregnant mares. Since Nathan had no stomach for watching a foal being born, you'll probably find him in one of the twin oaks."

Gus most likely had things under control in the stables, especially if Libby was helping with the mare's foaling. Colin made a detour to the trees, which was exactly where he found Nathan sitting on a high branch, kicking his legs in the air.

"Hello, Nathan."

Waving, Nathan smiled. "Hey, Mr. Thorpe."

"Mind if I have a chat with you?" When the boy nodded, Colin started climbing and was soon sitting next to him, legs dangling. "You know Libby pretty well, don't you?"

"Yeah," Nathan said, nodding. "But he's leaving."

"Libby's leaving?" Something akin to disappointment welled up in Colin's gut. He shook it off as impossible. There was nowhere for the girl to go.

Suddenly, the boy clapped a hand over his mouth and his eyes got big. "Never mind," he said, glancing down at the ground.

Colin remained silent, pretending to be deep in thought. Then he said, "What do you know about Libby leaving?"

"I can't tell. It's a secret."

"A secret?" He swallowed his smile. In his experience, it would take no time to unearth the news Nathan held back, but the key was using the right bait. "What if you tell me what it is and I promise to keep it a secret? That way you and I will have a secret."

Nathan considered this for several minutes, then came back with, "Will you let me ride Zeus?"

Colin laughed. Imagine, the little bugger was bargaining with him. Shaking his head at how easily he'd been manipulated, his smile broke free.

"Sure, Nathan, I can do that. So tell me. What's the secret you two share?"

"You promise not to tell Libby I told you?" When he nodded, he added, holding out his hand, "You have to shake on it."

Still smiling, Colin shook it. "OK, now give. What's the secret?"

"Libby's from the future."

"The future?" What the hell? "Where's the future?"

Nathan shrugged. "I dunno, but it's far away. The trees brought him here. That's why I wasn't supposed to tell anyone, especially adults 'cuz they might think he's crazy. You won't think he's crazy, will you?"

Of course it sounded crazy, Colin thought, absorbing his revelation. That just couldn't be. People didn't go through trees into another era. Maybe Nathan didn't understand exactly where Libby was from. It could be some city he'd never heard of. The minute the thought was out, he discarded it. He looked up into the tree's branches and wondered. If the trees took people through time, then why didn't they whisk him someplace different?

He thought back to the other night. Was that why she was wearing different clothes? Because she came from the future? My God, it was unbelievable. At the same time, it all began to make sense. If he hadn't seen her disappear and reappear with his own eyes, there was no possible chance that he would have believed what Nathan told him.

An anxious expression slid over Nathan's face. "Yer not going to fire him, are you? Libby really needs the job and has to stay by the trees in order to go home."

"No, Nathan, Libby will have a job here as long as he needs it. But let's not say anything about where he comes from. It will be our secret."

Nathan's face took on a toothy grin before he said, "Yeah, our secret. So, when can I ride Zeus?"

Colin had to laugh at Nathan's one-track mind. "You'll have to wait until things slow down a bit. Think you can do that?"

"Sure, Mr. Thorpe."

"Good. I'll leave you to your tree. Thanks, Nathan. I think you helped Libby by telling me. Don't forget. It's our secret. Mum's the word, OK?"

"Sure, mum's the word." Nathan's grin got wider. "I like that new word." He repeated it several times.

With thoughts on his newest employee, Colin climbed down and started for the stables. It was bad enough to try to wrap his mind around the lad being a girl. He couldn't fathom the rest.

How had she fooled them all? Except for Berta. But he couldn't blame her for remaining tight-lipped on the subject. Women usually stuck together in times of trouble. He could picture Berta going one-on-one with Gus about Libby sleeping in the bunkhouse. That thought made him smile and cringe at the same time. One thing he was sure of as he neared the foaling mare's stall, Libby was good with horses. She must have had some experience with them to be able to ride and to handle them so well.

"The foal needs to be turned," Gus said as he neared the pregnant mare's stall and took in the scene before him. Libby stood to the side, watching, a fearful expression on her face.

Electra and her foal were in good hands. Colin slipped in to give what aid he could without saying anything. Now was not the time for a confrontation.

Still, he had lots of questions. Being a betting man, he'd bet his favorite thoroughbred, Zeus, that she'd be at the trees after dinner tonight, just like the other night. He planned on being there, too, waiting to get his answers.

Chapter 11

Leaving the newborn colt with his mother after a difficult birth, Colin followed Gus out to the corral to work with the mating stallions. Libby kept busy in a separate pasture, training yearlings. During the earlier ordeal, Colin had watched the child closely, giving him ample opportunity to make out her feminine features. Her gentle cooing to calm the mare had been a dead giveaway. He had no idea how any of them could have mistaken her for a boy when there was nothing masculine about her. While not very old and having a boyish figure, Liberty Edwards was, as Berta so aptly put it, no male.

Shaking his head at their shortsightedness, he marveled at her nerve. Here she was a young girl taken away from her home in the future by—OK, he knew it sounded bizarre—magical oak trees.

Had she really come from the future like Nathan had said? Or had Nathan simply told him a make-believe story?

The problem was, it made sense with what he'd seen—Libby standing in front of him one moment, disappearing the next, only to reappear seconds later.

Colin always kept an open mind to possibilities. While traveling from the future seemed about as farfetched as anything he could fathom, he'd read and studied too much about past cultures not to have a desire to believe in the unbelievable.

Take mythology, for one. Legends that ancient cultures believed, whether Greek, Roman, Hindu or Nordic, all had mystical ideologies behind them. Most cultures stemmed from some kind of belief in magical beginnings as an answer to their mysteries.

Science was just beginning to unravel a few mysteries, but there were still plenty of unanswered questions. During a world tour taken before his marriage, Colin had seen many amazing sights. Stonehenge in England and the pyramids of ancient Egypt left behind plenty of questions that may never be answered. Who was he to question the unexplainable?

"Libby's become quite an asset to the farm in a matter of days," he threw out, just to measure his manager's reaction.

"*Ja.* The lad knows his stuff." Gus went on singing Libby's praises. In fact, the entire time they worked, it was Libby this or Libby that. According to Gus, she could single-handedly run the farm.

At quitting time, Colin was even more confused. How in the hell had this paragon won over his manager so easily? It was all too much. The girl, supposedly from the future, held Berta and Nathan in her pocket and now Gus was raving about her. He needed to find out what was what and he planned on doing so later that night.

Rubbing his hands together in anticipation, he took the porch steps to his house two at a time, hurrying to find his children, intending to spend time with them before dinner. Then after his evening meal, he hoped to catch Libby under the tree. That was the key to solving this puzzle.

An hour later, Colin entered the dining room and nodded at the nannies. "Good evening, ladies." He sat and picked up his napkin to spread on his lap. "I trust you had no problems with the children while I was away?" Thank God Colin had found these two blessings. Neither had married, probably because both were a little odd. Or their spinster status could have more to do with their resemblance to horses. Each woman had a long narrow face dominated by big eyes and a wide mouth. The two pulled back their graying hair into tight little buns, creating stern appearances, which were totally opposite of their manner.

Despite their looks, the Young sisters were two of the warmest individuals Colin had ever met.

"I believe Sam is ready to learn to ride a horse," Minnie said, smiling warmly and recounting the story of his earlier escapades with his younger sister.

Colin sighed and nodded. "Once the busy part of the foaling season is over, I'll have more time."

"Horses are all that child talks about," Maizie agreed. While she prattled on about more of the children's exploits, Colin listened patiently, glad to know his children were so well-loved.

He'd taken on the two shortly after their father had died, leaving them nearly destitute. They needed employment and a place to live. Abby had needed help. The two became indispensable after Abby got pregnant again. In Colin's opinion, Minnie and Maizie had not only taken care of his children, they'd also taken care of his wife during the last year of her life. For that he'd be eternally grateful.

Funny, Colin thought. Until that moment, his dead wife hadn't entered his train of thought since the evening before. He smiled. Maybe he was healing. Lord, he hoped so. The guilt that ate at him because of Abby's unhappiness wasn't helping anyone.

"Ladies." Colin stood when done with dinner and held out both elbows to escort the spinster sisters to the library. "I have to check on my horses. I'll see you in the morning." Colin bowed and hurried toward the oak trees. At the same spot he'd hidden two nights earlier, he made himself comfortable. Though the sun was low on the horizon, it wouldn't be dusk for a while.

Not more than a quarter hour passed before Libby walked down the path, and as before, she moved behind the bushes, emerging minutes later. Sure enough, she'd changed clothes. He watched the girl make her way to one of the trees and look up in total concentration, or a better definition might be in prayer. When nothing happened for a multitude of moments, her shoulders slumped in defeat, or possibly exertion. Colin wasn't sure. She sat at the base of the tree, leaning back to rest her head against its trunk with her eyes closed.

Noiselessly Colin strode over to stand in front of her and studied her without her knowledge. From this angle, he noticed her delicate and feminine features. She would be a beauty in a few years. A smattering of freckles splayed across the bridge of her nose, the only imperfection on a face with flawless skin. Observing her thus, he really had to doubt his judgment at ever believing her to be a boy.

An owl hooted in the distance.

Her eyes flew open.

A startled blue-green gaze met his amused one. As before, Colin felt a jolt go through his system when he looked into the depths of those light eyes. Why this young girl elicited such a response from him, he didn't know. But it was there nonetheless.

Then he spotted what looked to be the deed to his farm tucked into her vest. The spark of heat cooled instantly into icy rage that fingered down his spine.

ɞ

Libby jerked awake and leaned away from the tree. "Mr. Thorpe. What are you doing here?" She couldn't believe he stood in front of her.

Colin chuckled, but there was nothing humorous in the sound. "Funny, I could ask you the same question. In fact, I think I will. What are you doing out here? And that's awfully strange attire you're wearing, Libby." His eyebrows shot up and he continued staring at her with an unreadable expression, until it hardened.

Too dumbfounded to speak, Libby gawked at him. He was dressed much the same as the first time she'd laid eyes on him in the stables. Up close he was devastating to her senses, all male, smelling of leather, horses, and sweat. Her heart started pounding and her mind went blank. What was it about this man that made her lose her train of thought so easily? He turned away and she finally regained a measure of mental clarity.

Then he did the unbelievable and sat down next to her. He brought one knee up and placed his bent arm on the knee, creating an unconcerned pose.

He looked directly at her. His lips quirked in what looked to be a smile, but didn't reach his eyes. "Well? Cat got your tongue?" He hesitated a bit before adding, "I'm waiting, Libby. What are you doing out here? With my deed?"

Uh-oh! Still at a loss for words, Libby knew she was in deep doo-doo, but had no idea how to remedy the problem. What could she tell him? The truth? Yeah, right—that would get her kicked off the farm or put in the loony bin, and then she'd never get home. She let out a breath, thinking. "It's a long story." She started to rise, hoping to escape. "Look, I have to get back now. I just came out for some air."

His arm shot out, straight and firm as a bar, holding her down.

"I've talked to Berta," he said, sighing. "And Nathan, who told me an incredible tale. Now I want to hear your version."

"He told you?" Libby's eyes widened in horror. How could the little bugger give her up? She sat back down and her shoulders slumped.

"Yes, he told me. And as I said, his tale was astonishing."

"Nathan promised he wouldn't say anything," she said, shaking her head. "Wait till I get my hands on him. He's dead meat."

She tried to shoot to her feet, but he halted her movements again. "Whoa there, young lady. Calm down. It's not his fault. You should know better than to tell a ten-year-old a secret."

Having no choice, she settled back down as he continued speaking.

"You can get anything out of one if you know how to ask the right questions, especially one like Nathan. Besides, I promised him I wouldn't say anything and look who's breaking his promise now? But promises are overruled by extenuating circumstances." He paused to take a breath. "When it comes to the welfare of my farm or my workers, I do what I have to do. Nathan's just a youngster, who doesn't know any better. I'm an adult doing what I feel is right, so let's keep this between you and me, OK?"

Libby looked him squarely in the eyes. Wrong thing to do. As much as she wanted to, she couldn't look away. Colin Thorpe had the most beautiful blue eyes. Gazing into them, it was all Libby could do to keep from melting like an ice cube on the spot.

That he seemed as affected by the connection as she was even more disconcerting. Finally, he broke his visual hold and looked out toward the pasture for several minutes before he said, "Well, do we have an agreement? Can we keep this between us?"

"I don't seem to have any choice, do I?" she was able to squeak out without his scrutiny.

"No, you don't. And you might as well be honest with me because…" He turned back to her. "I saw you the other night."

"You did?" She met his gaze again, unable to keep the stunned expression off her face. "What did you see?"

Colin flashed white teeth, moving his attention to the pasture a long moment before adding, "Let's just say I saw enough to make me want to investigate. Now that I've talked to both Berta and Nathan, I want to hear what you have to say."

"Oh, right." Libby snorted. "Like you're going to sit there and tell me you'd believe I came from the future!"

"Is that where you're from?" he countered.

"Would you believe me if I said yes?" she shot back.

"If you told me it was true, then I would at the very least consider it. But what I don't understand is why you'd take the deed to my land with you."

His honest, yet puzzled, tone left Libby speechless. He had every right to be upset that she'd take his deed, but the idea that this man, sitting over a hundred years in her past, had such an open mind—more so than most from her century—was hard to grasp. Her gaze followed his toward the pastures as her mind spun.

Finally, her need to unburden herself and get another viewpoint was too much to resist. She glanced down at her hands and sighed. "I am from the future. Somehow the trees brought me here originally. Best I can tell it was from a wish I made. Unfortunately our scuffle with Smithers resulted in a change in history, which is why I took the deed. I need it to save the farm in my time. I'd planned to return it before I left for good." She reached for the deed from under her vest and handed it to him.

Taking it, he nodded to her jeans and tailored shirt. "So that's why you changed clothes?"

"It's a long story," she said, offering a lopsided smile.

"Then it's a good thing I have a little time." He leaned back against the tree and made himself comfortable. When he turned her way, his glance said he clearly expected her to talk.

For the next hour Libby did just that, telling Colin everything about her job on the farm, her best friend, and her fiancé, Dave. She explained how the trees had called to her and how, after heeding their call, her initial run-in with Smithers now threatened the farm in the future. There wasn't much she left out about the life of Libby Edwards or life on Twin Oaks. He was a good listener, only asking questions here and there for clarification.

When she was done, there was silence between them. The sun had already set, but the light still lingered. Cicadas buzzed, the evening breeze carrying the loud noise throughout the meadows. The tree frogs and crickets eventually joined in, creating a symphony of sorts in the balmy night.

"Let me make sure I understand all of this." Colin's questioning voice infiltrated the other sounds. "You traveled back and forth from the year 2013?" He paused, as if absorbing the news. "And the farm's still intact, even after I'm gone." He glanced at her for verification. When she nodded, he whistled. "Amazing!" Still watching her face, he asked, "Does Louisville still have a racetrack?"

"What do you think," she asked evasively, not wanting to reveal too much information about the future. She had to be careful about changing anything else.

"I hope it lasted. If what you say is true, then I have the closest thing to a crystal ball in front of me." An engaging grin spread across his face. "Can't you at least give me a hint?"

"Time will tell, not me," she said, shaking her head.

He laughed. They discussed the deed and Colin said he'd have a copy made. "But it will take a few days. In the meantime, you can't continue pretending to be a boy, nor can I let you continue to train such unpredictable animals. It's not right."

"No."

He eyed her intently, his mouth forming one tight line. "What do you mean, no?"

"Either I continue as before or I leave." It was an empty threat, since she needed the trees to get home.

"I thought the trees brought you?" When she didn't respond, his lips curled into the semblance of a smile. "I'd like nothing better than to continue as before, but I can't have your safety on my conscience. What if one of the horses throws you? Or worse?" He shook his head, his expression turning to stone. "It's too dangerous for a girl."

Libby blew out a frustrated breath and rolled her eyes. However did women in 1874 put up with such chauvinism? She sent up a prayer of thanks to Susan B. Anthony and others like her, who paved the way for women a century earlier. The fact that it hadn't happened yet made her more than anxious to find her way home. "I've only been thrown once in my life, due to my error. Trust me, I have no intention of letting any horse throw me again. Besides, in my time, we can do just about anything a man can do."

"Really?" He considered this for a moment. "So women in your time vote? Like out west, in the Wyoming Territory?"

"Yes. We vote. We pay taxes. We own land and we fly planes in the

Air Force."

"Air force? What's that?"

"Never mind. Suffice it to say I'm fully qualified to train your thoroughbreds. Just ask Gus. I've gotten more out of Fortuna and Zeus in the two days I've worked with them than you or Gus could get all summer."

Again he was silent. Then he wiped his face and sighed. "I can certainly use your skills, but you're way too young."

Bristling at his comment, she jutted out her chin. "I'm old enough." Jeez, even in this century she was mistaken for a kid. What did she have to do? Wear a sign that said OVER TWENTY-ONE? "I'm a liberated woman and perfectly capable of making my own decisions."

The crinkles near the edges of his eyes deepened when he smiled. "Just how old are you?"

"Like I said, I'm old enough." She tried to keep annoyance out of her voice, but the comment still came out too caustically.

Colin chuckled. "OK, you're old enough. Prickly too. So, women in the twenty-first century go around looking like men?"

Nodding, Libby mentally counted to ten. "We've also earned the right to dress as we please. It took almost a century, but we prevailed. And to ease your mind about my age, besides being engaged, I have two years of college under my belt." This time she was more successful in keeping her tone light while still getting her message across.

Grinning, Colin held up a hand. "Such a feisty woman-child. There's fire in your eyes when you speak. Far be it from me to dictate to you. I'd venture to say I could learn a lot from you." He leaned back against the tree, pulled up a blade of grass, and rested an arm on his knee in his earlier nonchalant stance. "I like you, Miss Libby Edwards from the future." Just before sticking the blade of grass in his mouth, he said, "If you'll continue your charade as a boy, I'll allow you to train."

"Thank you."

"You're welcome. It'll take a few days for me to get the deed copied and notarized. In the meantime, be careful. I don't want any mishaps."

"You won't be sorry." It seemed a good thing that she hadn't been able to return tonight. If she went home with a copy rather than the original, she wouldn't have to risk returning. Now that her secrets were out, she could relax and enjoy her stay for a couple more days. She refused to listen to the voice in the back of her head, warning her not to get too attached to these people. She would have to pretend to be on a vacation.

In no hurry to leave, Colin was silent again.

Libby didn't think he would say anything further, but he proved her wrong by asking, "You're engaged to be married?" She nodded and he said, "Tell me about your fiancé."

"Why do you want to know about Dave?"

"That's his name? Dave?"

"Yeah, Dr. David Phillips." Thinking of Dave, she smiled. "My friend, Bev, calls him Dr. Bull."

"Dr. Bull? As in…"

Libby shrugged and stopped a gurgle of laughter from bursting forth. "Dave can be a little stuffy at times and he doesn't like Bev, so you can form your own opinion about that."

Colin's chuckle zinged through her ears, landing in the soft part of her belly. "It's been a long time since I've sat talking and laughing with someone like this. It seems so natural, sitting here discussing your life in the future as if we did it all the time."

Dusk lurked, but there was still light enough for her to discern his grin when he looked at her. His eyes held such warmth that Libby had to glance away.

He sighed. "This Bev sounds like quite an instigator. Surely your Dave's not so bad?"

"No, he's just a little closed-minded. You know, a brilliant scientist?" Looking at her hand on the ground, she broke off a few strands of grass and shrugged. "Only he shuts his mind off to possibilities. I tried to tell him about my time travel, but he scoffed at the idea. I'm sure he thinks I'm delusional. Now I'm not certain if I want to marry him."

"Why should it matter if he believes you or not? Besides, I thought all women wanted to get married."

"Words spoken like a true man." Libby didn't bother keeping the sarcasm out of her voice.

But rather than offending Colin, he only chuckled after pulling the blade of grass out of his mouth and tossing it aside. He then bowed his head. "At your service. Do you always get your hackles up when someone says something that annoys you?"

"My hackles aren't up." Libby shook her head and crossed her arms. "Why is it that men think all women want to get married?"

"Because it's true," he said. "Marriage is always their ultimate goal. If he's willing to marry you, why should you care whether he believes you or not? He's giving you his name, isn't he?"

"It matters. Times have changed. Marriage isn't the only thing we women want. In my time we don't have to marry to better ourselves. We can marry for love."

"Ah yes, love." His eyebrows inched higher. "And do you love him?"

"You sound so skeptical. Don't you believe in love?"

"I don't know. I've never been in love. I'm not sure it exists." He picked up another long blade of grass and twirled it between his fingers. Then he looked back at Libby with a sad expression.

He appeared so forlorn. His lost little boy expression tugged at her. Libby asked gently, "Not even with your wife?" When he shook his head, she offered a consoling smile. "That's sad."

He lifted one shoulder in a half shrug. "We became friends during the early part of our marriage. I guess you could say we cared for each other. At least, I cared for her, I'm not sure if she cared about anyone but herself. We definitely weren't in love. She hated the farm—hated her life here." He stopped talking and threw the twisted blade of grass on the ground. "I don't know why I told you that." He sighed wistfully. "I guess I feel comfortable here with you." A smile lit his face as he said, "Let's get back to our discussion. You never answered my question."

His smile was too persuasive. Libby returned it. "What question?"

He laughed again, the sound sending a tingling sensation to her insides.

"Going for evasion? That's a good tactic, but not good enough. I asked if you loved your intended."

"My intended?" Libby gave a nervous grunt, ignoring the feeling his laughter was creating on her system. "That sounds so formal."

"Evading again?" He pierced her gaze, raising his eyebrows.

"God, you're tenacious." She focused on her hands and distractedly made figure eights in the ground next to her. "Yeah, I love him, but I don't think it's enough. I need him to believe in me. He just doesn't understand how important it is to me and I don't know how to remedy the problem." She risked a quick glance at him. Her smile turned sheepish. "Listen to me. I'm as bad as you. I don't know why I told you that. You have enough problems without adding mine."

"Me? What problems have I got? We were discussing you. Remember?"

"Well, your wife died. And you have three young children. Even if you didn't love each other, it must be hard not having her here, especially for the kids. I lost my mom. I know how that can be."

He was obviously about to accuse her of evasion again, except that same forlorn look suddenly crept into his expression and his words seemed to stick in his throat. She swallowed hard and couldn't stop the concern or compassion from spilling out in her gaze. The connection she'd felt earlier was back. Her breath caught in the back of her throat as Colin swallowed hard. Breaking the connection, he glanced down at the ground, appearing as uncomfortable with it as she.

"I guess it is hard," he whispered. "I just plow through one day at a time," he said minutes later. "Eventually it does get easier." His voice took on a teasing quality as he added, "You have a way of distracting me from my melancholy thoughts, so I'm glad we had this time together."

"So am I," Libby said, shrugging her shoulders, happy to have the conversation veer toward other topics besides Dave. "I think there is another reason I couldn't return home tonight, you know? Besides the deed."

When she didn't elaborate, Colin looked at her with an expression that said, "Well? What is it?"

"Promise not to laugh?"

His bark of laughter rang out, and Libby slapped at his arm. "I asked you not to laugh."

"I'm sorry," Colin said, a big grin still splitting his face. "I can't help it. Here we are baring souls, and you make me promise not to laugh. It struck me as funny."

"Yeah, well, being stuck in the wrong century is no laughing matter. I only hope I can get home when I need to." She stopped and realized she sounded unappreciative of all she'd experienced up to that point. "Not that you don't have a wonderful place here, and not that I haven't loved every minute of working on the farm and learning all about it. It's just that I don't belong here."

He visibly sobered. "I'm sure you'll be able to travel back when the time comes. Until then, I'll help any way I can. Two heads are always better than one." His voice trailed off. "Finish what you were going to tell me." He glanced at her, then made an imaginary cross on his chest. "I promise not to laugh."

"Oh my God—did you just cross your heart?"

His grin was quick. "Yes, I did. But don't expect me to spit on my palm like I did as a lad."

"Oh, we don't spit anymore—at least, girls don't."

"So the universal cross your heart and spit in the palm still exists into the next two centuries?" At Libby's nod, he sighed. "It boggles the mind what stands the test of time. But enough of your evasion—you do that a lot, you know."

"Do what?"

Colin shook his head. "I rest my case. Finish with your thoughts, then I think we should call it a night. It's getting late. Berta and Gus will be worried about you."

"You're right. I guess I am evading the issue." Stalling, she smoothed out non-existent wrinkles on her jeans. "OK, the way I see it, I originally came here for a reason, like maybe to learn something. At first I had the feeling that maybe I'm here to help Gus with Nathan—teach him about the farm. You know Gus has no time right now?"

At his nod she continued. "Yet when I'm with the family, I get this feeling I was meant to see them. I've never seen a family as close as Gus and Berta's. They are so wonderful and warm. They accept each other and work toward a common goal, a goal both share. Seeing them together makes me realize that I want what they have. Maybe somehow by being around them, I can learn how to achieve that end." She stopped talking. "Or…do you think there's a bigger reason I wished myself here?"

"I have no idea. I'm still trying to wrap my mind around you coming from the future. I'll think on it, though. In the meantime, since you still want to work, tomorrow comes bright and early." He stood and brushed grass off his pants. "I'll see you in the morning. I'm taking over for Gus with the thoroughbreds. We can train them together." He turned and started to walk away. "Good night, Libby."

Before he'd taken ten steps, Libby said in a loud voice, "Thanks, Mr. Thorpe. Good night."

He stopped and pivoted, snaring her gaze. "Do me a favor, will you?"

"Yes?"

"Call me Colin. Everyone else does. We're just not that formal around here," he said, much like his great-great-grandson had done, eliciting a déjà vu moment.

As she continued staring after him, other feelings surged through her system.

He was halfway up the path to the house when he turned around again. "Are you ever going to tell me if there is a racetrack in your Louisville?"

Libby hesitated. "I don't know how much I should tell you about the future."

"Fair enough. Well, till tomorrow." And then he was gone.

Chapter 12

The days raced by in a blur. Near the end of the first week, Colin provided Libby with a notarized copy of the deed. As one week became two, eventually easing into three, Libby tried not to obsess about her inability to return home. Instead she focused on the exhilaration of doing a job she loved, using her workday routine as something to count on. Breakfast in the morning followed by training the thoroughbreds with Colin until the heat set in. From there she helped Gus check on the mares before moving on to the foals, and then training the yearlings with Nathan in the afternoons. Lunch was somewhere in between.

The work was challenging as well as rewarding. Mostly because the men around her took her opinion seriously and valued her contribution to their end goals. That alone was worth every bit of the time spent in the past, and did much to take her mind off the hardships of living without electricity and the Internet. What Libby would give for a hot bath, she thought, trudging down the path toward the trees in another attempt to wish herself home. Her routine now included visiting the trees every night. At this point, she was certainly ready to leave. Yet, no amount of wishing seemed to matter.

Was she stuck here? Her heart skipped beats at the thought. No! She refused to believe that. The trees weren't working. With no idea as to why, the only thing to do was to keep trying. Hopefully, when she did return to her own time, it would be to within minutes of her earlier departure. The thought of having someone in the future worry over her disappearance only added to her troubles.

There was one advantage to her delay. Colin began joining her in the evenings. Libby looked forward to seeing him emerge from the path if she happened to have her eyes open. If not—if it was one of those times she'd closed her eyes, only to open them and find him watching her—a thrill always went through her. It was a rush to imagine that he'd actually sought her out. She was coming to depend on his quiet strength. Too much, if she were honest.

Tonight was no different as she glanced up and watched his approach. A smile lit his expression when he noticed her. Libby crossed her fingers, hoping that he was just as happy to see her as she was to see him.

Warmth flooded her senses when his steady amber gaze ensnared hers, holding her eyes captive for what seemed like infinity. Finally, the spell was broken when he turned to sit down next to her.

As Colin stared off in the distance, Libby surreptitiously studied him. He seemed different tonight. Smoothing out her jeans in an effort to calm her rapid heartbeats, she prayed he didn't realize the effect he had on her. That was all she needed. To be trapped in the past with Sam Thorpe's great—God only knew how many greats—grandfather and him knowing about her crush. Just another destination to add to her guilt trip with Dave in tow, thanks to her constant comparison between the two men.

"So, how was your day?" He tore off a blade of grass and stuck it into his mouth. "How is the foal doing?"

Libby cleared her throat. "Fine." She went on to tell him more about her day, something she loved—that and their common interest in horses. Libby could probably talk his ears off about the subject and he'd listen intently, as if he valued her thoughts. If only Dave could be more like Colin.

"How about yours?" She must have imagined the earlier look because there seemed to be nothing out of the ordinary in his manner as he recounted his day.

"I thought you could wish yourself home," he said after a lengthy pause.

Libby shrugged. "I thought so too."

"You have the deed, so why are you still here?"

"I don't know." She sighed. "But at least I'm enjoying myself."

"I'm enjoying your company." His gaze moved over the landscape as he exhaled. "I mean my words. I feel comfortable talking with you." His attention returned to her face. "I find myself hurrying with my chores in order to come out and meet you under the trees." He hesitated and met her gaze. "Why do you think that is?"

An honest yearning brimmed in his eyes. Libby sucked in a breath.

"I don't know." She swallowed hard and looked at her hands to break eye contact. "I think tomorrow will be the day Fortuna's going to beat Zeus."

Colin's low chuckle seemed to mock her evasive ploy, drawing her focus.

His smile slowly faded, his expression becoming tormented.

Her stomach did somersaults. For a split second, she could have sworn she spied desire in those brown depths. But it was gone in a heartbeat as he took the blade of grass out of his mouth and tossed it aside while his attention roamed over the horizon.

Seconds later his grin was back. "You think so?" he replied, now appearing so under control that her imagination had to be working in overdrive.

Squinting at him, Libby fought to figure him out as he added lightly, "Are you going to tell me about the racetrack and any races that are still run?"

It was the same question she always refrained from answering every night. Libby laughed, glad to note he was back to his normal teasing manner once again. "Not tonight. But you can tell me more about your plans."

"I've told you about them already. I can't see why you won't give me a clue."

She crossed her arms. "Time will tell, not me," she countered, locking her mouth with an invisible key, then adding, "Since I'm not talking, tell me more."

Colin chuckled, the rumble of it zinging straight through her insides. "Fair enough."

The two spent several hours talking about everything and nothing before Libby said, "I think it's time for me to go in. I had a wonderful evening, Colin."

"The evening certainly passes quickly when I'm with you," Colin said in a regretful voice. He stood, then bent to help her rise. "Here. I'll escort you back to the Gundersons' door."

Together they walked the path to the house. At the door, Libby thought for a moment that he would kiss her. But all he did was pull her into his embrace for a warm hug and kiss her forehead.

"Good night," he said, before turning and starting for his own house.

Libby went inside extremely confused. Walking upstairs, her mind was on the hours spent with Colin and whether or not she'd wanted his kiss.

☙

The next morning Libby struggled to keep her thoughts off the man who'd kept her awake most of the night. Walking toward the track to meet Colin for their morning workout, she forced herself to focus on Nathan instead.

Working with the bright boy gave her immense satisfaction. He usually joined her in the stables after his chores. She loved teaching him. Nathan was a natural with the horses, much like his father must have been at his age. The kid was such a quick learner, hanging on anything Libby said. She realized she was getting attached to him. In fact, she was becoming much too attached to all of them. The Gundersons were becoming family. The noisy meals she spent with them were always full of love and laughter. That never changed. Why couldn't they all live in her own time so she wouldn't have to leave them behind?

As she continued walking, her thoughts shifted to her other experiences since Colin's discovery of her time travel. So much had happened in such a short span. The early morning was her favorite time of the day. Riding champion horses around a track and shaving seconds off their time gave her a sense of accomplishment. The elation she derived was like nothing she'd ever experienced.

She'd learned a great deal about riding and racing thoroughbreds in the past three weeks. As her technique improved, the horses began responding and their times improved. Both Gus and Colin had been impressed and her duties increased. She started working with all of the runners.

Colin, looking too handsome for words, came into view and Libby couldn't help but remember last night. Chills tingled down her spine as she thought about how much she loved being with him. He always made her laugh.

That she was starting to enjoy their encounters more and more troubled her greatly. She wasn't sure what she would have done if he had actually kissed her last night, another reason to worry. From the moment she'd first set eyes on him, he'd attracted her. Yet, getting to know him was actually more appealing as was their shared love of horses and the outdoors. Even worse, she saw his vision for the farm as clearly as he did.

"Good morning." Colin nodded as she approached.

"Good morning," she replied, watching him give an order to one of the grooms. Of course, she didn't particularly care for his autocratic manner. Arrogant and confident, he assumed a leadership role, which carried over to everyone on the farm. Including her.

Occasionally, he would say something that riled her. When this happened, he'd look at her with those incredible eyes—eyebrows raised—as if to say, *You really want to test me*? Libby's answer was always a resounding *yes*. Still, it did no good. He'd always win. But that didn't stop Libby from trying. In fact, she was beginning to think he said things to get a rise out of her.

The thought brought a smile to her face. It was still there when Colin, holding two horses tacked and ready to exercise, refocused on her. Dressed much as he'd been the first time Libby saw him, he looked totally masculine and sexy as all get-out.

He smiled. "Your expression's very much like a cat that has swallowed the canary all of a sudden."

Libby's grin got wider. "Oh, and what expression is that?"

Colin's laughing eyes caught hers. Having gotten used to the way his gaze affected her every time their eyes met, she'd come to expect it and accept it. But this look carried something different as he said, adding a wink, "A very satisfied one."

My God. He's flirting with me. The notion brought her up short. She wanted nothing more than to flirt back. Big mistake. Libby had to force herself to remember her fiancé.

Except that when she did happen to think of Dave, she compared him with Colin and he kept coming up short. Unfortunately, that said a lot about their relationship. Colin Thorpe was everything any woman could ask for, but he belonged in 1874 and she didn't.

Libby had no intention of remaining here. Not when she missed everything about the future. Her friends. Technology. Feminism. Advances in medicine. The list went on and on. No one in their right mind would wish to remain without hot and cold running water if they had a choice.

Eventually, the oaks would take her home. They just had to.

In the meantime, she needed to keep her distance from the one who stood not a foot away with the killer smile that always made her heart flutter. Ignoring the flutter now, she broke eye contact and said a little too curtly, "Well, I'm not a cat." She then grabbed the reins from him and started leading her horse to the starting line.

ଓ

The abrupt change in Libby's manner and the tone of her voice stunned Colin. What got her back up this morning? Shrugging off disappointment, he followed her. Within no time they were back to their easy way and the two continued working as if the moment had never happened.

While training, Colin's thoughts were on Libby. After last night, he'd decided that since his time with her was limited, he was going to enjoy what was left of it. That meant spending a little more of the day in her company. She made him laugh; made him forget his problems.

There were a hundred reasons he should keep a tight rein on his feelings, the biggest one being she'd be leaving shortly. Her life belonged in another era. She had a fiancé waiting. Yet none kept him from praying every night on his way out to the trees that her journey to the future would be delayed one more night. Colin could no longer deny living for their mornings together, and every evening he found he was in too big a hurry to join her by the two oak trees. He was wading in too deep, but he couldn't prevent from treading deeper.

The thought of Libby returning to her home left him feeling bereft, so he refused to dwell on it. He'd come to accept that once she was gone, he'd miss her much more than he had his wife—despite only knowing her a brief period. He wouldn't think about that either, or the timeless connection they shared.

The two finished training for the day and while walking back, Colin asked nonchalantly, "I need to check on some fences out by the south pasture. How about accompanying me and taking a ride simply for the pleasure of riding?"

Her face lit up at his suggestion. Then she frowned. "What about my duties?"

"Gus can handle things on his own," he said. "Nathan can even help him now. One afternoon away shouldn't hurt. What's more, you've been working too hard. You deserve a break." He stopped short when he realized he was pleading.

Libby appeared to be waging a mental battle. Finally, she sighed. "I really shouldn't, but somehow I can't muster the energy to refuse such a generous offer." She laughed, the pleased sound sending a signal directly to his groin, one he ignored as she said, "Besides, riding any horse in your stable's impossible to turn down. I might as well enjoy myself to the fullest while I'm still here. No telling when I'll be going home." Colin felt a tug of regret when she sobered and scanned the landscape, adding, "To be honest, I've already gone past the point of involvement with all of you, so one ride won't change anything."

He swallowed hard as guilt lodged in his gut. Unfortunately, guilt did little to diminish his need to be with her.

At Colin's earlier request, Jake had two horses ready and waiting at the stables. He and Libby quickly mounted and rode out together.

After watching Libby with the thoroughbreds every morning for several weeks, Colin could see that she loved to race. More than that, she loved to win. Anticipating this ride, he'd purposely paired her with a horse that would even things out, figuring their ride would eventually turn into a race between them, even expected it. Colin wasn't disappointed as Libby took off.

Laughing, he raced after her. Libby's skill and lighter weight more than made up for Colin's mount's advantages. Even though she rode a mare lacking his stallion's stamina, Libby had the uncanny ability to get more run out of a horse than anyone he'd ever met. He wanted her to be challenged, while at the same time he wanted their contest to be a fair one.

Libby rode hard to keep her small lead. Soon he edged ahead and fought to maintain his ground, fully aware that if he'd been riding the mare and she the stallion, she would have left him in the dust and been happy to do so.

The challenge of staying ahead of her was too hard for him to ignore. He loved meeting any dare she threw out. Colin kept his small lead, but a lead nonetheless. Spotting his destination up ahead, he slowed. So did Libby, conceding defeat, which was something else to admire. She didn't cheat. If she lost, she accepted it. But that never stopped her from trying to best him the next time. With that attitude, there was no telling how much her skills could improve.

Riding at a slow trot to cool off the horses, he pointed. "See that tree at the top of the rise?" At Libby's nod, he said, "That's a good place to stop. The fence I need to check isn't too far away."

☙

Libby had forgotten what it was like to ride for the mere pleasure of it. She hadn't done so in too long, having spent her weeks in the past riding thoroughbreds around a track instead. The feeling—of the horse's power beneath her legs and of the wind on her face—was like nothing else.

There was no place in time she'd rather be than right where she was, having raced Colin through the Kentucky countryside in 1874. The thought should have frightened her, but didn't. She'd been too caught up in the moment, as the two had ridden neck and neck, neither willing to yield the win. She laughed, totally energized. She could worry about it all later—after she beat Colin. For now, she planned on simply enjoying herself to the fullest.

Looking around, Libby recognized the rise as the same place she'd been with Pride that afternoon she'd felt such peace—the same afternoon she'd made the trip back in time. As they rode closer, Libby noticed a blanket with a picnic basket sitting in the middle of it.

Her look turned questioning as she glanced at Colin. He shrugged. "We may be out here awhile. We need to eat sometime. I thought we could enjoy our lunch while we're here as well."

Bad idea, Libby thought, dismounting. It all seemed too romantic. Somehow Libby felt romance wasn't part of why she was stuck in this century. As much as she would love a little romance with Colin, she had to refrain from acting on it. Getting entangled with him in that way would only complicate things. She really didn't need any more complications in her life right now.

Furtively watching him dismount, she grinned. OK, she must have gotten the wrong idea. His laughing eyes and boyish smile did strange things to her insides, but both appeared innocent. How could she refuse his sweet offer of a picnic? Besides, he was right about being hungry. Both needed to eat. This way they could take their time. Plus, she could use a break. What a perfect way to spend a couple of hours.

Libby dismissed her worries, confident that she could handle her wayward thoughts. Despite a few uncomfortable moments last night, Colin had never given her reason to worry about stuff like that anyway. He probably had no intention of romancing her, especially since she was dressed like a boy, hardly the garb of a seductress. That thought made her laugh. No, seduction was most likely not on his to-do list.

"I love the quality of your laughter," Colin said, his wide grin forming. "I can't help but feel cheerful when I'm around you."

He took her hand, leading her over to the blanket. Libby plopped down and watched him tie the horses. His demeanor was definitely happy, but nothing in it indicated he was being anything other than the friend she'd come to rely on. Her imagination was playing tricks on her.

Colin sat down next to her. He seemed as content with the silence as she did before he finally leaned over on his knees and snagged the basket. Then placing it between them, he opened it up.

"Hmm, let's see what we have." He pulled out several items including bread, cheese, and ham. "We won't starve. And we certainly won't die of thirst." The last item in his hand was a decanter of red wine. He rummaged around in the basket and came up with two glasses. "God bless the French. They really know how to make a good bottle of wine. Want some?"

Libby smiled. "If I drink that, I won't be able to beat you on the ride back."

"What makes you think you'll be able to defeat me if you don't drink it?" Colin took the stopper off the decanter and poured two glasses, handing her one. She took it. He continued speaking, making eye contact. "Besides, if I imbibe too, maybe we should wait for our rematch." He then took a drink, steadfastly holding her gaze, clearly daring her to drink.

Tiny alarm bells pealed in Libby's brain. As outrageous as it seemed, she had to mentally shake the feeling that maybe her instinct hadn't been far off base. There *was* something different in his demeanor today, yet he'd never given her any reason to be wary of him. Ignoring the warning, she sipped, keeping her eyes locked on his. The entire time, sensation in her belly grew and she felt herself falling under his spell.

Finally, he averted his gaze to set his wine glass down. As much as Libby shouldn't be thinking of him romantically, she couldn't quite push the idea away as her gaze lowered to his lips. For too many seconds she wondered what it would be like to kiss him.

Good grief.

As his focus returned to the food, she adjusted her legs underneath her and patted her hot cheeks, praying he wouldn't notice what had to be a beet-red face.

Thankfully, he ignored her, his manner once more that of the man Libby had come to rely on. She leaned back against the tree, pondering his seemingly mixed signals. Shrugging off the idea as silly, Libby took another swallow of wine.

After setting up two plates of food, he handed one to her. Colin then moved the basket to the side. With his plate on his lap, he began eating.

"So, tell me more about my land in the future," Colin said, interrupting the easy silence. "Is the entire twenty thousand acres still intact?"

Libby had just taken a bite and contemplated his question while chewing. She swallowed. "I don't know. Twenty thousand acres is a lot of land for one parcel, especially in the twenty-first century. I think some of the land has been sold off at one time or another to developers. This area is still part of the farm, but I think once you get over that rise, Sam's land ends."

"Sam?"

"Sam Thorpe—your great-great—not sure how many greats—grandson. He's a good man. I told you about the farm and the way he's keeping what's left in a trust for future generations."

"It warms my heart to know this survives." He gestured to the green rolling hills.

"Yes, it's a piece of history that few see." At his raised eyebrows, she elaborated. "It's called progress and population explosion. Everyone wants a piece of the American dream. Home ownership. Most of the big farms around the Louisville area are gone, eaten up by developers who build houses. There are lots and lots of houses now where empty land and farms used to be."

"Then I guess I should be happy that so much of mine is left. Tell me more about Louisville. I imagine the city has changed too. You say there are houses everywhere. That seems so hard to imagine, as it's pretty big right now. I can see Louisville eventually growing out to the track we're building, but farther out boggles the mind."

Libby shrugged. "What do you want to know?" Colin had mentioned his trip to Louisville and the meetings he'd recently attended. Over the past week, Libby realized that Colin was referring to the beginnings of Churchill Downs.

"Do they still have horse racing?"

Grinning, she took another bite of food, stilling a rush of adrenaline.

"Is there a derby still run in May on our racetrack," he asked a moment later.

Libby laughed. "You tell me." Imagine being witness to history in the making. The creation of one of the most watched horse races ever, the Kentucky Derby.

"I hope so. Our first derby is set to be run on May 17, 1875." He scrutinized her face as if searching for the future hidden in code there.

"You know I'm sworn to secrecy."

"If only we can become a part of history. It's a dream worth having."

Libby's grin widened at the excitement in his voice. She set her empty plate aside and took another sip of wine. Her mood was mellow as she turned away from the tree and sat with bent legs out to her side. "It's nice out here. I'm glad you invited me."

Glancing over at her, he smiled wistfully. "So am I."

"We have so much in common." Libby sighed. "I don't know what I would have done if you hadn't pushed me to tell you everything. And you believed me. Of course I should have known that you'd have a fancy for the unbelievable."

Colin leaned back on his elbows, stretching out one leg at a time just inches from her, appearing replete from the food and wine. "Oh? How so?"

"Well, everything about this place says you're open to ideas. I mean, you even name your horses after Greek and Roman gods. Everything has a meaning, doesn't it?"

"As a matter of fact, my horses' names do have meaning." Colin was clearly taken aback by her perception. "So you're familiar with mythology?"

Libby smiled. "A little." More than a little. She couldn't be friends with Bev and not be familiar with mythology. Bev believed it was just a matter of time until the mysteries of the universe were uncovered. She was always doing major research on past cultures and legends, dragging Libby with her as she scoured bookshelves and the Internet to prove a point. After reading all about fairies and witches, Greek and Roman gods seemed pretty tame.

"I know that Zeus was a supreme deity or ruler," she said. "His son was Hercules and Aphrodite was Zeus's daughter. Fortuna is the goddess of chance. I'm a little stumped by Asapurna. I know it's from mythology. I'm not sure what it means, though."

"It's Hindu," Colin answered, grinning. "She was a mother goddess. Her name literally means 'she who fills your desires.' "

"See what I mean. Asapurna and Zeus are perfect names for the animals you chose to begin to build your dream."

He chuckled. "I see your point. I'm surprised you caught it. Most people don't."

"It's all too much." Libby sighed and said, "Why couldn't I have met you in my own time?" Then silently amended, *Why couldn't I have met you before I met Dave?*

His brow furrowed. "Surely there are open-minded men in your century? And men who dream?" Leaning in closer on one elbow, he reached for her hand and held it for a minute, studying it. Then he brought it to his lips and kissed it before whispering, "How is it that you know so much about such things as mythology? How is it that you're so perceptive of me and of my motives? Who are you, Libby

Edwards? Some goddess sent here to torment me from the future?"

The bells in her brain clanged louder even as her heartbeat quickened. Libby couldn't take her eyes from him. He was going to kiss her if she didn't do something quickly to lighten things up. She pulled her hand from his and turned. The movement was enough to break the spell.

"Not a goddess," Libby whispered, swallowing hard. "Just Elizabeth Edwards, flesh and blood, trying to find her way back home."

ঙ

Thoughts of having Libby as he wanted, wrapped in his arms and intertwined in his life forever, swam around in Colin's brain. He inhaled much-needed air in an attempt to regain his wits.

For more than a moment, kissing Libby's sweet lips had been the most pressing thing on his mind. Doing so might spoil their relationship, and he wasn't fool enough to risk that. He enjoyed her company too much. She had a way of cutting to the quick of things. Sometimes he even said things just to see her reaction.

"Elizabeth?" he said, eyeing her intently and pushing his daydreams away. "I thought your name was Liberty."

Libby's grin spread. "I lied."

He quirked a brow. "You lied?" Libby had to be older than he'd first thought. She acted like a grown woman, although he'd never known one to be so forthright. A most refreshing idiosyncrasy. If all the women of her century were so inclined, it offered plenty to contemplate.

"I had to improvise when Gus asked. I thought it a decent save. I'm supposed to be a boy, you know. Telling him my name was Elizabeth would have given away the game."

"Elizabeth," he repeated, holding on to his smile over her brazen attitude. "I like it. It suits you." He studied her face. "Of course, Libby suits you too. I bet you have two sides. Libby is the woman-child who flies through time. Elizabeth marries Dr. Bull." Colin had to remember her time in his century was limited. Intuition told him that she would never be truly happy here. As much as he'd love to pursue a lasting relationship, he refused to be the cause of anyone's unhappiness ever again.

"Maybe," Libby said laughing, the sound zinging its way from his ears to his groin. She leaned on her forearms and looked up at the sky. Colin did the same. Billowy white clouds drifted overhead.

"It's so peaceful here," she said.

Colin nodded. "This is my favorite spot." Sighing, he lifted higher on his elbows and, lost in thought, stared out at the green landscape that went on forever.

"Tell me about your wife," Libby asked after minutes of silence. "What was she like?"

"Why do you want to know about Abby?" He broke off a blade of grass and twirled it in his fingers, studying the texture.

"I don't know." Her voice, soft as a whisper, tugged on his conscience. "It just seems that thinking of her makes you sad. I'd venture to say that if you didn't love her, her death wouldn't affect you so much."

He focused on the distant meadows and thought about what she was asking and how to answer her honestly. "Guilt," he murmured, breaking another long pause.

"Guilt?" The question hung in the air.

"You say thinking of her makes me sad? Well, the thought that I was the cause of her unhappiness during our marriage eats away at me." His voice sounded as unsteady as he felt.

She hesitated a moment, then reached for his hand, covering it with her own. The contact was warm as well as soothing, easing the constricting band around his heart.

"You told me the first night we talked that she hated the farm." When he nodded, Libby shook her head. "Surely you know that you aren't responsible for another's happiness or unhappiness."

"I took her away from everything she loved. And for that she never forgave me. Our life together was strained after we moved here. I tried to please her," he said almost desperately, watching a squirrel running for cover and wishing he could be as unencumbered. Glancing at Libby and noting the compassion in her eyes, he swallowed hard and struggled to keep the pain filling his soul from showing in his expression. "I did everything I could think of. Took her into Louisville for the social life she missed in Virginia. Sought to placate her by building her a modern house and buying her clothes in the latest fashion that she claimed to want. No matter what I did, it wasn't enough to make it up to her."

"Oh, Colin, I'm sorry," she said, squeezing his hand. "But you're not to blame. She had a choice. She could have been content here."

"She should have." He grunted. "But nothing short of going back would do. I couldn't go back. You've seen this place. You understand my dream. Why couldn't she," he asked, not bothering to hide the torment he'd held inside for too long.

"Was the farm always your dream?"

Colin nodded. "I knew that I would be finding land on my own and moving away. My father and I have differing opinions on what my life should be. I had to leave the area to build what I wanted."

"I take it she understood you'd be moving away when she married you," Libby asked gently.

Nodding again, Colin sighed. "She didn't think I would."

"Well, there you go," she said. "You two negotiated a marriage and she agreed to it. She didn't need to, but once she did she should have honored her agreement. Steve Harvey says we're all responsible for our own happiness."

"Steve Harvey?" Colin questioned, with raised eyebrows. "Another man in your life?"

Libby laughed. "No, he's someone famous who goes around giving advice that no one listens to. I've never met the man, but Bev swears by him."

"Well, that's good because I'm not up to being jealous of someone else," Colin said, grinning. "Dr. Bull is enough for me."

The bit of distress he noted in her eyes stopped him cold. "I'm sorry. That was forward of me and uncalled for." He offered an apologetic smile and let out a relieved sigh when he saw her relax.

"No problem." She paused a heartbeat then added, "I don't think you should feel guilty anymore. Your wife was wrong."

Her declaration was like a balm on raw flesh. "Are you my defender, Libby?" He looked at her, unable to hide the intense feelings suddenly engulfing him. "Just like that, you're so sure she was wrong. I could get used to having you around. You're definitely good for my soul."

Libby's smile died, clearly indicating he'd gone too far. He swore under his breath, knowing she must be confused with his acting the teasing charmer one minute and the serious suitor the next.

Shaking her head, she sat up straighter as her back stiffened. "I feel as if I'm headed on a collision course with you. I don't want this whole mess to blow up in my face because I haven't been honest." She licked her lips nervously and met his gaze. "Colin, you know I can't stay here, don't you?"

"Of course I know that." His voice rose along with the anger aimed at himself for giving her the need to remind him. "How could you think I would expect you to, especially after what I just told you about my wife? My God, she hated every minute she spent on this farm. Do you think I want the same for you?"

No one could miss the pain in his words, but their effect on Libby tore his heart in two as tears formed in her eyes, began streaming down her face.

"I'm sorry," she whispered. "I didn't mean to suggest that. I'm only trying to be honest."

He reached out and took her into his arms, brushing the tears off with the pads of his fingers. "I'm the one who's sorry. Please don't cry."

Libby only cried harder. Their gazes connected, yearning in hers obvious behind the tears, yearning that drew him. Colin couldn't fight both his desires and hers. Not when her eyes beckoned. And where they beckoned, Colin followed. Right now they were begging him to kiss her. Compelled to yield, he slowly moved his head until his lips captured hers, merely tasting at first. The more he tasted, the more he wanted. He could stay here forever kissing her. She was warm and pliant and the desire to sink into her warmth was more than a craving.

One of the horses neighed and a bird squawked, yanking Colin back to reality. His sanity rushed back like a tidal wave, swamping him with a flood of emotion. Reluctantly, he released her lips. Only he wouldn't let her out of his arms. He leaned back into the blanket, taking her with him, nestling her head on his broad shoulders.

There he lay for several minutes letting Libby cry, thinking he'd give up his dream and go to the future with her if there was a way. The minute the thought was out, he realized how ludicrous it was. Colin had his children to think of. Even if he could take them with him, he had responsibilities and people who depended on him for their livelihood.

His was no longer a dream he could leave.

଺

Her tears spent, Libby lay with her head on Colin's shoulder. For how long, she didn't know. All she knew was that she felt comfortable in his arms—not wanting to move—not wanting to think anymore. It hurt to think. She'd gone well past the point of no return with Colin and done the stupidest thing of all. Fallen in love with him. One kiss told her everything. If he hadn't stopped, if he'd continued and had asked for more, she'd have made love with him out here in the grass. She knew it with every fiber in her being. There was no use pretending otherwise, as she would only be lying to herself.

"What are we going to do?" Her hollow voice interrupted the uneasy silence and floated on the warm breeze.

"I don't know," he whispered. He took her chin by the thumb and forefinger, tipping it so that she could see his gaze. "You feel it too. Don't you?"

Libby looked into his soul-searching eyes and nodded. He kissed her again, a quick brush of the lips, before releasing her, then sat up and began packing. "I think we've both been through enough for one day." Silently, he worked. Finally, he sighed and sat on his haunches. "Libby, I realize your time here is limited. Let's spend what little there is left together."

"That's not such a good idea." She scrunched up her nose, trying to ignore the surge of pleasure swelling within her heart.

"Why?" His earnest gaze sought hers.

Oh, God. He was making this hard. "I can't stay and it wouldn't be fair to you."

"I want to be with you. I think you want the same." Still watching her, he waited until she nodded before adding, "Why not take what time there is?" His voice was insistent, almost pleading. "I'll take whatever you give—whatever you allow. Whether you're taken from me today or next week, the pain is going to be unendurable. Give me some memories to keep me warm when you're gone."

"What are you asking?" Libby knew damned well she shouldn't be considering his proposal.

"I know you're engaged to marry and I have no intention of causing you dishonor. I merely want to be in your company. I'll take a few hours off each day and we can be together doing whatever you'd like."

He stood and reached for the blanket, saying while he folded it, "If you're still here when I go to Louisville, you could accompany me." He placed the folded blanket in the basket and picked it up. "I have to be there on and off for the next couple of weeks. We can take in the social whirl, which will be in full swing. You'll need some clothes—other than boys' garb. There's a shop in Shelbyville." He glanced at her questioningly.

Her breath hitched at the back of her throat. Indecision swamped her. What could it hurt to spend a little time here? Damn! She knew it was wrong, but the caring and acceptance he offered was too tempting to pass up. Stalling, she moved to untie her horse. He followed her and helped her mount.

"Well? What's your answer," he asked, looking up at her.

Meeting Colin's gaze, showing him that her desire and need mirrored his, Libby nodded. "My answer is yes." Mistake or not,

she wasn't about to lose the opportunity to be with him. She had a lifetime in the future to deal with the consequences.

Chapter 13

Colin helped Libby onto her horse and then attached the basket to his saddle before mounting. Their daily rides followed by a picnic lunch had become the norm after three days. It was something he would miss once Libby found her way back home. But he refused to dwell on that as they slowly headed back the way they'd come.

"You know, you never have gotten around to fixing that fence."

Libby's voice drew his attention and it dawned on him what she was referring to. He chuckled. "There is no fence."

"So that first time you *were* bent on seduction? I'm shocked."

"Is that what you think of me?" Colin snorted. "That I would bring a woman-child who flies through time out here to seduce her?" He tsk-tsked.

"No." Libby shook her head.

"I'm glad you think so highly of me. But we should talk about how naive and trusting you are, my dear. If I'd been bent on seduction, you'd be seduced." A blanket of guilt settled over his shoulders for the part of him that wanted to do exactly that, but he shoved it off, refusing to dwell on that too. His intentions were honorable.

She grunted. "Yeah, right."

"The thought has crossed my mind, but I refrained because you're not in a position to accept my offer of marriage," he admitted. He would marry her in a heartbeat if things were different. "Besides, I'm not willing to spend precious moments begging for your forgiveness. The fence excuse achieved my main intent, which was to spend time with you."

"Good save."

"What did I save," Colin asked. "I was being honest."

"Since we're being honest, you deserve to know that I'm more woman than child."

"Thank God." Colin placed one hand over his heart. "It's good to know I haven't fallen in love with a child." Admitting this might not be the best way to keep things on a friendly basis, but he refused to let her go home without knowing how he felt. He glanced at her sideways. "Just how old are you, anyway?"

"Twenty-three." Their gazes connected and for a split second he caught the look of love in her eyes before she blinked. "How old are you?"

"Thirty-two—which makes us nine years apart." It was all he could do to keep his voice light. "Much better than you being half my age."

"You thought I was sixteen?" Her frown erased any remaining trace of affection in those eyes. "That's insulting. It's bad enough to get carded in bars, but sixteen? For that you need to grovel."

"I don't grovel." He grinned, glad to have a topic to bring him back on firmer ground. "What does carded mean? You go into bars? Saloons? Is that allowed?"

Thankfully, Libby's laughter and comments about the future and what women were allowed to do fully divested him of his earlier thoughts. Amazing how women in her time had such freedoms. All the more reason she would never be content in his time. Not with so many constraints to deal with in 1874.

Colin left Libby with Nathan, then found Gus working to bring a couple of horses together. The two were not complying. Every time the stallion came up to the mare on the other side of the dividing fence, the mare would kick out. As he cantered away, she would then try to take a bite out of his hide.

Gus shook his head. "I think it's going to be a day or two for her."

"Well, Gus, sometimes the females of the species are that way." He clapped Gus on the back and added in an amicable voice, "As males, we need to be patient, proceed cautiously, and wait for them to give us a sign."

His manager studied him for a long minute, then grunted. "Are we talking about horses, my friend, or young workers?" At Colin's raised eyebrows, Gus shrugged. "Berta told me some days ago that Libby's female. She was worried I was working her too hard. I figured you already knew her gender by the way you two were acting."

"What do you mean," he asked, surprised.

"The air all but crackles when the two of you are near. Plus, I've eyes, Colin. I've seen the way you look at her. There's yearning in that look."

"I figured you'd find out sooner or later." Colin sighed. "It's hard to keep anything from you."

"Are you sure it's wise to get involved with someone so young? Besides, there is so much we don't know about her."

"Looking out for my welfare or hers?" Colin lifted one sardonic eyebrow.

Gus laughed. "I'm not exactly sure." He sobered. "Why don't you tell me? Whose welfare should I be most concerned with?"

"I'm a little uncertain about that myself." Colin's grin turned sheepish. "But I do know I feel comfortable with her. There's something about her that makes me feel alive for the first time in my life." Silently, he scanned the lush green landscape before glancing back at Gus. "My troubles seem lighter after seeing her smile. It's as if we're meant to be together. Of course, just my luck it's all for naught. She doesn't belong here."

Gus snorted as disbelief welled in his eyes. "What do you mean she doesn't belong here? I've never seen anyone take to this place the way Libby has. It's as obvious as the nose on your face."

"No, you don't understand." Colin shook his head. "This isn't her time, her place."

"It isn't her time and place? Ha, she's here, isn't she?"

"Yes, but not forever."

"No one is here forever. We only have as long as God gives us to make the best of it," Gus said, stroking the mare to calm her.

"You're right, of course. But nevertheless, she can't stay. She doesn't belong here."

"You're not making sense, Colin." Gus's eyes narrowed. "Why doesn't Libby belong here when she's a natural with the horses?"

"Sit." He gestured to the fence railing. "Prepare to open your mind." Gus hauled himself onto the rail and waited silently as Colin situated himself next to him. He hesitated, unsure how to broach the subject. Finally he just blurted it out. "Libby comes from the future. She's from a time over a hundred years from now."

Jaw hanging open, Gus stared at him. He eventually closed his mouth and said, "The future? You mean like Jules Verne's future?"

Colin nodded. Rumor had it that his favorite author had written a futuristic novel that was too pessimistic to publish.

"That's impossible."

"It's farfetched, I know. I'm as shocked by it all as you are. But it's true. She flies through time."

"No," Gus said on a loud snort. "People don't fly through time from the future. That's more than farfetched. It's totally outlandish." Shaking his head, he snorted again. "Maybe she hit her head? Maybe she's a little daft, you know, not all there?"

"Trust me. Everything would be easier if she were a little daft. But I believe her. I saw her come and go." Colin's gaze drifted to the clear blue sky as he thought of how to best explain. "She knows things, Gus," he said, his tone convincing. "I've spent time with her. And as much as it pains me to do it, I have to help her find her way home."

"My God, how can such a thing be possible?" Gus whispered, focusing on the ground as if the answer to the mystery lay in the dirt beneath his feet.

"Who understands everything about the universe? There're plenty of unexplained happenings," Colin replied, in an effort to reassure himself of something he still found incredible.

"Yes, but those are things we can substantiate. How do you prove time travel exists?" The whispered question hung in the air.

"And how do you prove it doesn't, my friend?" Colin countered. Such a dilemma.

Gus drew in a long breath and whistled it out through his teeth. "That's a lot to take on faith."

"Yeah, well, it gets easier as time goes on. I want you to be prepared for when she returns to her own time. When that happens, she'll no longer exist here in 1874."

"You truly believe she's come from the future?" At Colin's nod he said, "And you're sure she has to return?" When Colin again nodded, Gus swore. "I knew it was too good to be true. With Libby's help, things were getting too easy around here. I should have known better than to believe it would last." Gus met his gaze again, holding it for too long.

Rather than risk exposing what lay in his heart, Colin couldn't maintain eye contact.

"My God, you're in love with her, aren't you?"

The question sounded too much like an accusation, telling him he'd been unsuccessful in hiding the truth.

He sighed as Gus added, "Damn, Colin, she's barely out of the schoolroom."

"Don't worry, my good man. She's old enough." A strangled laugh burst forth as he waved off Gus's concern.

"She can't be much older than sixteen."

"Libby's twenty-three, which is old enough."

Eyebrows raised, Gus studied him. "I don't have to worry about your conduct toward her, do I?"

More halfhearted laughter erupted, but Gus didn't appear to find a similar humor in the situation. "I'm serious." He stiffened, and any and all amusement faded from his face. "She's under my protection. If your intentions toward her aren't honorable, I'll have to ask you to refrain from being with her. "

Colin sobered. "You know me better than that. I'd marry her tomorrow if I thought we had a future together. Besides, Libby can take care of herself. She has a way of putting me in my place and is plenty old enough to know her mind. I doubt she'd let anyone take advantage of her, unless it was her choice. Doesn't mean I can't enjoy her company." Gus didn't say anything, merely waited for Colin to go on. "I'm spending time with her. I plan to take advantage of whatever time we have left. Just so you know, she'll continue to be with me in the afternoon for a couple of hours each day. She's also agreed to accompany me to Louisville." When Gus started to object, Colin put up his hand. "I'll find a companion for her. She'll have proper protection. I don't want anyone to think less of her because she's with me. But like it or not, Gus, she's going."

Gus remained silent for a few minutes, obviously mulling Colin's revelations around in his head. Finally he asked, "If what you say is true and Libby can't stay here, what happens when she travels back to her time? I can't help think that you're setting yourself up for disappointment."

Colin took a deep breath as a lonely ache wormed its way to his heart. His gaze roamed over the rolling hills. Several horses frolicked in the distance, holding his attention for an extended moment before his focus returned to Gus.

"No need to worry about me," he said in a pained tone. "I can take care of myself. I'm a big boy who knows the rules."

"That's the problem, Colin. You've always followed the rules and where has it gotten you? No one deserves happiness more than you. I know you didn't have it with Abigail."

"Abby has nothing to do with this." Colin's tone was clipped, expressing his refusal to discuss his dead wife.

"I disagree. She has everything to do with it," Gus practically snarled. "I watched Abigail's bitterness tear you apart. Find another woman." His gaze turned pleading. "If what you say is true, then don't set yourself up with someone you can't have."

"Too late, Gus. I aim to ride this one to the finish."

Gus jumped down and prepared to undo the gate to release the mare. "It's obvious you're set on your course, but what about Libby?"

"What about her?" Colin put his hand behind his neck and rubbed, thinking about the question, not liking the answer. "I know she'd never be happy here forever, but while she's here, I'll do everything in my power to please her."

"What about her happiness when she returns to her future life? If she becomes involved with you, she could be hurt in the end."

"That's her decision to make, not yours or mine," Colin said.

Sighing, Gus said, "I may be overstepping my bounds, but I'm worried. You're more like a brother to me than an employer. Plus, I've come to care for Libby. I'd hate to see two good people suffer because they were foolish."

"Isn't that what love is all about?" Colin said, giving in to another self-deprecating laugh. "We're all foolish when we fall in love. It comes with the territory. I certainly never expected love to happen, but now that it has I need to follow my heart."

"I've said my piece." Gus grunted. "Tread carefully, my friend." His attention returned to the mare. "If you'll excuse me, I need to accommodate our big boy over there." He nodded at the stallion prancing across the paddock. "I'll take this mare in and bring out another that's more ready."

"I'll help," Colin said, thankful to have the subject dropped. Gus's warning came days too late. Like runaway horses in a thunderstorm, Colin's feelings had taken off. He only hoped that Lord Tennyson knew what he was talking about with his poem about better having loved and lost than never having loved at all. He didn't want to contemplate the alternative.

ꕥ

Libby watched Nathan cautiously make his way toward the frisky colt. Her thoughts were not on work, but on her time with Colin. A surge of pleasure shot throughout her system over his comment about falling in love. She couldn't pretend it hadn't affected her. The fact that her feelings matched his lifted a huge weight off her shoulders. Of course, she refused to listen to the loud clanging bells of her conscience. She had the rest of her life to deal with it, once she went home. Colin was in the here and now and she intended to take advantage of the situation while she could. She might never get another chance at experiencing the love he had to offer.

As Nathan worked to secure a bit with lead and halter on the young horse with a minimum of effort, Libby caught movement out of the corner of her eye and turned to see Gus walking in their direction.

"I did it." Nathan's shout was full of pride.

Libby laughed. "You sure did, kiddo." She nodded to the other side of the pasture. "Now see if you can coax him to follow your lead."

"You've done wonders with the boy," Gus said, his gaze on his son. "He's taking to his task as if he were made for it."

"He is his father's son," Libby said, holding a hand over her eyes to block out the sunlight.

Silently, they watched Nathan work until Gus's voice interrupted the quiet. "Colin tells me you're not from around here."

Libby looked up at him and, chewing on the bottom of her lip, thought about how to answer. Finally she shrugged. "Yeah, I guess you could say that. Do you think I'm crazy?"

"Hell, Libby, that's an understatement." Gus took off his hat and scratched his head. "This whole thing is crazy. But Colin believes it.

That's enough for me." He stuck his hat back on his head and tugged it into place.

"I guess that's something." Scanning his expression closely, she asked, "Did he tell you everything?"

"You mean that you're a girl?" At her nod, he added, "Berta told me. But that's not what concerns me now."

His tone alerted her. She lifted her chin an inch and met his gaze. "What concerns you now that you know the truth?"

"I fear the two of you will do something you'll both regret. I know Colin cares for you. If you aren't supposed to be here, I can't help believing that this whole thing is wrong."

"How so?" The yearling she'd been working with yanked his head to the side, trying to pull out of her reach. "Easy, boy," Libby cooed, grabbing the reins and holding tight until the horse calmed. Colin only wanted to spend time with her. How could that be wrong? She glanced back at Gus and stated with more confidence than she possessed, "I know what I'm doing." Wrong or not, she wasn't blind to the consequences.

"Do you?" He stroked the horse while the animal was getting used to the bit in his mouth. "Somehow, I don't think either of you know."

"Everything in life has consequences. Surely the two of us spending time together isn't hurting anyone," Libby shot back, feeling slightly defensive.

"I'm worried is all."

"Worried?" Hopefully, he didn't think she was some kind of Jezebel coming to steal his master's heart. The thought made her smile. "For me or for Colin?"

"For both of you."

"Oh, come on." Snorting and giving a good impression of dismissing his concern, she waved her hand. "Nothing's going to happen. We'll both work to keep things easy between us."

"I doubt it will be that *easy*. The air sizzles when the two of you are together. All it will take is one spark and you both will go up in flames."

Libby felt trapped, unable to look away as he continued, his voice holding more than a warning. "Colin is only a man and at some point he'll want to consummate the relationship. The more he cares for you, the more tempting you become."

Yeah, like she was really a temptation, she thought, shaking her head. "He's always been a perfect gentleman. He won't go where I don't want him to." The fact that she'd been thinking along those lines sent a rush of heat waves to her cheeks. Holding her head down so he wouldn't see her embarrassed flush, she led the horse to the rail and tied him off, then picked up another bit with lead. Dismissively, Libby turned her attention to another nearby colt.

Gus followed, much to her dismay. "You're so sure of your ability to hold him at bay? I know him. He won't stop trying until he gets what he wants. I'm giving you fair warning, Libby. Keep your guard up. If you consummate things, you'll both come to regret it. I don't want to see either one of you hurt when you return to your time and place. Most of all, I don't think Colin will be able to deal with the loss."

"What are you getting at?" Libby halted, suddenly not so sure of her motives any longer. "It's not my intention to hurt him."

"Then don't. The only way you won't hurt him is to stay away from him until you find your way back home."

Her eyes narrowed as she searched his earnest face. "But it's what he wants," she whispered. Or was it something she wanted?

"His wife's actions almost destroyed him. He cared for her. She was nothing but a selfish woman. Thank God he didn't bow to her demands. Still, she made his life a misery and Colin blamed himself for her bitterness." Gus gripped her by the shoulders and his voice became more fervent. "He feels things very deeply—takes responsibilities for others. He doesn't need any more heartache. Think about that and about what your actions will accomplish. Why go looking for trouble?"

Libby closed her eyes, her thoughts becoming a jumbled mess. As much as it hurt to admit it, Gus made sense. She opened her eyes and spoke from her heart. "I won't go looking for trouble, Gus. But I can't ignore him either." Tears sprang to her eyes and she brushed them away, unable to still the pain piercing her heart. "Damn, this is such a mess," she whispered. "I don't think either of us has a choice. All I can do is take it one day at a time."

"I've said my piece. That's all I can do." With head held high, he turned and headed in Nathan's direction.

Watching the two laughing at something Nathan said, Libby couldn't stop second-guessing herself. Maybe Gus was right. Maybe she should keep her distance from Colin.

No maybes about it. As long as she continued to exist in 1874, they should stay away from each other.

Pure pain pierced her soul as she realized she had to try harder to get home. At the same time, she had to make sure that Colin understood her decision. Closing her eyes, she willed away fresh tears at the thought of not seeing or being with him anymore.

How had he become so important to her in such a short time?

Another fact dawned on her, this one not so surprising. Once she made it back to her own time, she and Dave were through. The man no longer owned her heart. Not like Colin did. She wondered if he ever had because what she felt for Colin dwarfed her feelings for Dave.

She should have never considered marrying someone who didn't accept her for who she was. Even when hampered by time and era, Colin had never tried to change her, had actually seemed to enjoy her as a person.

It was with a heavy heart that Libby finished her day. Dinner was a subdued affair. Both Berta and Gus were quiet while eating, seeming to sense Libby's disquiet. Even Nathan and Sarah weren't as buoyant as usual. When the meal was over, Libby set off for the trees and her talk with Colin.

He was waiting for her when she rounded the bend. He'd placed a blanket on the ground.

She sat down beside him with her back against the tree.

"What is it," he asked, clearly noting her turmoil.

Pasting a fake smile on her face, she shrugged and looked away. "How do you know something's wrong?"

He gently rubbed the side of her face with the back of his hand. "Ah, Libby," he whispered. "Because I know you." His hand trailed to her chin and he lifted it up, forcing her to meet his gaze. "Now what's wrong?"

Unable to figure out a way to begin, Libby remained silent. How do you rip out your heart, she thought? Maybe it was better to just plunge in the knife and twist. She took a deep breath. "I think we should stop seeing each other until I go home."

"No! That is not an option." Colin's angry voice reverberated through the early evening. He sat upright and turned to her, his eyes blazing with passion. "How could you even suggest such a thing?"

"What can come of it?" Libby offered a sad smile. "What are we doing?"

He grabbed her shoulders and gave her a little shake. "We're taking advantage of the time left. I'll not be denied."

"You know what will happen if we continue? The end will be harder to endure. Please, Colin, I don't want to hurt you. You have to see how useless it is," she begged.

"You think I would give up one second with you to keep from hurting?" His manner was unyielding. His voice held a steely resolve when he added, "I already hurt from wanting you, so what's a little more?"

Her heart sank. "But I don't want to be the cause of anyone's pain, especially yours."

"You promised, Libby. You said you'd give me the time. Why have you changed your mind?"

"Gus." She sighed. "He made too much sense. He's right."

"Damn his meddling hide." The curse was followed by some not-so-nice words said under his breath. "This is between you and me. Can you honestly say you don't want to be with me?"

"I'm so confused," she whispered, shaking her head slowly. "I don't know what to do."

"We're taking what time there is. I'll not let you renege on your promise. Do you understand?"

The torment in his voice ripped through her, tearing into her resolve. "This is becoming more than we thought. We shouldn't continue."

"No! I accept the fact that circumstances will take you from me, but I can't endure the thought of you purposely keeping yourself from me. If you do, you might as well yank my heart from my chest right now and stomp on it." He pulled her closer. "Whatever is between us is growing. Neither of us has a choice anymore," he said urgently in a low voice before lowering his mouth over hers.

It was nothing like the kiss on the grass during their first picnic. That kiss spoke of love, tenderness, and longing. This kiss spoke of the raging desire she felt pouring from his body. There was nothing tender about Colin's lips rendering a full-blown assault. He continued his onslaught, using his mouth and tongue to ignite in her what had been simmering inside for days. When Libby responded, he released her mouth, raining kisses over her face to her ear.

"Yield to me, Libby," he whispered. "I need you so much." He continued using his tongue to excite, using his mouth to beg. "Please, Libby. Give me memories. Let us give each other memories." He moved against her, leaving her no doubt about where this was headed. "See what you do to me. Feel my desire. Yield to me."

His pull was too enticing, his lips too inviting. More than anything, she needed something to remember of her time with him, too. All she wanted at this point was to yield everything, join with him, and never let him go because the thought of not doing so left her soul empty.

What could it hurt? Libby loved Colin and he loved her. This was just an expression of that love. Plus, she was tired of denying their attraction existed. If a stolen moment in a pasture under two oak trees was all she could have? Well, she'd make the most of it.

☙

Elation surged through Colin when Libby's resistance dissolved into a moan. And when she all but melted and gave him more access to her neck, love and yearning overwhelmed him. The primal urge to mate with her became more than an act of love. It was an act of fate. She was part of him—his other half—no matter that she'd come from over a hundred years to be with him. She would be his for as long as time allowed and he planned to spend every second loving her.

He worked to shed her clothing as well as his own before kissing her again.

"See what you do to me," he asked after releasing her lips. "I can hardly control myself when I'm near you for want of being inside of you. As elemental as breathing, my love."

Her only answer was to bring his mouth back to hers. In tandem they touched each other, discovering what lovers learn when bodies become temples to expand on love. She was as fully aroused as he was when he hovered over her, seeking her gaze. Holding it, he let her see the proof of his love shimmering there.

Having the same look reflected back to him was nearly his undoing. "Forgive me, Libby. It's no longer a matter of honor. It's a matter of life and death." He sank into her warmth and began the eternal dance of love, moving in and out with a song in his heart.

This mating was more than mere sex. Their joining transcended time. He'd remember this night forever.

When Colin could think again, he opened his eyes and moved to place his main weight onto his elbows so as not to crush Libby. He looked into the depths of her eyes and was relieved to find that her eyes, while filled with emotion, held no regret. Her regret wasn't something he wanted. In the end, she'd wanted him every bit as much as he'd wanted her. He felt it down to his soul. They belonged together, despite the fact that their lives were separated by time. That he also felt down to his soul.

"Now that we have that minor detail out of the way," he paused for effect, "there's no question that we'll continue seeing each other. For as long as we have."

"That was sex, Colin, not a minor detail."

"Yes, but that's why you were backing off, isn't it? So we wouldn't go there?" he challenged. "Now it's a moot point."

"Yeah." Libby sighed and closed her eyes. "I can't help feeling that we should have had some restraint. It's going to be hard enough as it is to leave you."

Colin moved to lie next to her on the blanket, pulling her into his embrace and holding her in his arms so that her head rested in the crook of his arm and shoulder.

He kissed the top of her head. "This was meant to be. You can't deny you don't feel it, too. There is nothing in me that will believe otherwise after what just happened. Dave or no Dave, time or no time, we were meant to be together at some point. I'm just glad it happened sooner rather than later." He stopped talking for a few minutes, stroking her arm. His voice was quiet when he continued. "Now we have no obstacles. I'll have no more objections. Look at me, Libby."

Her closed eyes opened wide and she did as he'd asked.

"You are mine for as long as you are here. Do you understand?"

She grinned.

"What's so funny," he asked, a bit offended.

"You! So autocratic—so sure your word is law."

"Your point?" He smiled, knowing her words spoke volumes.

"You're definitely a dominant male, obviously not used to being thwarted."

"You're very observant." Colin's smile turned mischievous. "Will you spend the nights in Louisville with me?" He sighed and brought her hand to his lips to kiss. "I'll have to find you a companion, preferably one that looks the other way."

"Do I really need one?"

He nodded and moved to begin dressing.

"That's so weird," Libby said, stretching. "I can't believe all the social restrictions for women."

"Out here on the farm, things are not as restrictive. But in town, there is definitely a social order. Especially for women of my class." Colin handed Libby the shirt he'd taken off her earlier. "Here, you should get dressed. Someone could come by."

"What do you do when you attend these social events?" Libby shrugged into the shirt and reached for her pants. "I'm curious."

"Oh, I don't know. There are dinner parties—balls with dinner and dancing—and picnics. Someone's always having one or the other." He stopped talking for a minute and stood to put on his trousers. Then he smiled and said, "Soon we'll have thoroughbred racing."

Libby pulled on her pants too, then sat back down to tug on her boots. "It sounds so romantic."

Colin had always looked at the parties and evenings out as a means to an end. Appeasing his wife. He never enjoyed them, certainly never anticipated them. But he was actually looking forward to taking Libby out in public, dancing with her and showing her another part of his world.

Fully clothed, he turned to Libby, who leaned against the tree. He bowed and held out his hand. "Miss Elizabeth Edwards, may I have this waltz?"

"I feel like I'm living a dream." Libby smiled wistfully. "You're actually asking me to waltz. How romantic." Yet, she shook her head and said in a sad voice, "Colin, I can't waltz. Most of us don't dance like that in my time."

"It's easy, Libby," he urged, his eyes filling with laughter.

She finally put her hand in his. He gave a little tug, pulling her onto her feet and into his arms. "All you have to do is follow my lead." Then humming in her ear, he led her around the pasture. After a few moments he glanced down at her. "That's it, you're catching on. It's basically three steps. One, two, three…one, two, three. Feel the music, Libby, feel the love."

And so they danced, gliding in the balmy July evening, the noisy insects accompanying the music in his mind. Colin could stay here forever dancing with Libby.

Chapter 14

The next morning Libby hurried to catch up to Gus as he headed for the stables, praying he hadn't noticed her guilty expression during breakfast. Heavens, just remembering the time spent with Colin was enough to have her blushing for a decade.

Thankfully, she grabbed a brush to groom one of the soon-to-be trained stallions while Gus got busy elsewhere. Done with her task, she stored the brushes and looked up to see Colin enter the stables. A thrill went through her when his gaze zeroed in on hers and he treaded her way.

"Good morning." His smile turned sexy…almost suggestive. "I trust you slept well?"

"You know I did." Heat streaked up her face. "I dreamt of you." Blushing ruined the effect of the flirtatious huskiness in her voice.

Colin halted inches from her, then took her hand and put it up to his lips. "I'd have slept better if you were with me," he said before kissing her hand, acting as a Southern gentleman. Yet the rogue she'd made love to last night came alive in his gaze when he refocused on her. "I missed you."

If Libby's cheeks were red, the hue had to have just deepened, considering the flames shooting out of his intense blue eyes. Her insides melted at that look. "Shush!" she whispered, glancing around. "Someone could hear."

Still holding her hand, he guided her to the back of the stall and double-checked for prying eyes. "No one is about." He leaned in and nuzzled her neck. "I'd tell the whole world if I could. I love you, Libby Edwards. You'd best get used to hearing me say it."

A feeling of dread crept up her spine and she couldn't shake it off. As much as Libby loved hearing his declaration, she couldn't help remembering Gus's warning. She stiffened and took a step back. Clearing her throat, she pushed a short strand of hair behind her ear.

"Don't forget. I can't stay."

He placed his hands on her shoulders to stop her from retreating farther. "I understand, but know one thing. As long as you're here, I'll do anything and everything to show you how much you mean to me. Don't deny me or put up barriers that I'll have to break down. Doing so will only waste precious time."

His confidence was clear in the strong tilt to his jaw and his erect shoulders. It should bug her that he was so sure of himself and her, but it didn't. His assessment was dead-on. "You're incorrigible." To change the subject, she asked, "What are you doing here? I'll be out at the track in a few minutes."

"Evading again," he asked, eyeing her.

"Yes." She fought the grin that broke free. "Now, answer my question."

Colin chuckled. "That's my Libby." He bent his head.

Next thing she knew his mouth caught hers. At first the kiss was gentle, his lips soft. Libby opened herself to the warmth spreading through her. Of their own volition, her arms wrapped around him. He deepened the kiss and it was all Libby could do to hold on to the desire to drop down in the stables and have her way with him.

She tore her mouth away and stared up at him, unable to keep the look of horror off her face. Every time he touched her, she went up in flames. How could this be happening? Dave had never made her forget where she was.

"God, Libby, what have you done to me?" he whispered. "That was meant to be a demonstration for you, not for me." He lowered his forehead to hers. "I can't think clearly for want of you. You've flown through time to torment me and make me want things I shouldn't want."

Tears threatened, but Libby blinked them back. "I don't mean to." Her tone was equally distressed. "I feel the same way."

"Don't cry." Colin pulled her closer, cradling her head with his hand. "I shouldn't have said anything."

If only she could stay in his soothing arms forever as he held and stroked her, making her feel like she was the most important thing in the universe.

Finally, he released his hold and said in a teasing voice, "I did have a purpose for searching you out this morning."

In an effort to mirror his forced lighter mood, Libby picked up the discarded brush and turned back to the horse that had already been groomed. While stroking, she glanced playfully at Colin. "So, don't keep me in suspense. Why are you here? Besides stealing kisses?"

"I wanted privacy." The grin overtaking his face had her insides quivering. "In order to tell you we're going into town this afternoon for new clothes. We'll be leaving after lunch. Now that I've delivered my message, I'd better go before I end up doing something that will delay our day." He turned and said over his shoulder while walking, "I'll see you out at the track."

Watching him saunter out, Libby could only marvel at his restraint. Gus's warning was useless against the attraction that brought them together. She only hoped they both could overcome the heartache when it was time for her to go home.

☙

Later that afternoon, Libby and Colin rode into Shelbyville to visit a dressmaker. Along the way she learned he'd already ordered several garments within days of discovering Libby's secret. Madame Dubois was a talented woman, creating several dresses for Libby based on Colin's description, using materials that had sat dormant since months before Abby's death. He'd bought the material to please his wife, only Abby had turned her nose up at them after expressing the opinion that small-time dressmakers had no clue about the latest fashions. This way he could at least give the woman the orders she'd planned on a year ago.

Besides dresses, he'd ordered all the attire a woman in the late nineteenth century should wear, including chemises, corsets, and other undergarments. Libby's jaw dropped and she had to fight to keep her eyes from bugging out of her head over all of the paraphernalia scattered around the shop. Saying that clothes were different in the 1870s than from her own time was an understatement. Things had definitely changed for the better, she thought, feeling like a trussed-up turkey.

"My designs are simple, *oui*?" Madame Dubois had a definite French accent. "But your slimness is becoming, so simple works, *non*?"

"I don't look the same, that's for sure," Libby replied.

"Oh, *non*, *mademoiselle*, you look wonderful. Here, let's try the ball gowns. Mr. Thorpe, he has a good eye, *oui*?"

Glancing at the two gowns, Libby could only agree. "Yes, these are beautiful. You're very talented." In her own time, Libby hated dressing up. She was more comfortable in a pair of jeans and an old shirt than she'd ever been in a dress. Even at the department store, she preferred slacks.

Stepping into one, she fell in love with the garment—the material and color. Colin obviously had exquisite taste. The fabrics he'd chosen for all of the gowns were vibrant and bold—midnight blue, emerald green, and deep mauves—colors that suited Libby, bringing out her features, especially her eyes. Her skin practically glowed against them.

Libby twirled back and forth, feeling gorgeous, like a princess going to a ball. The material followed in a sweeping motion that clung to her legs until momentum fanned it out again. There was something about playing dress-up that made a woman feel special, she thought, eyeing her reflection in the mirror. The corset did wonders for her figure. It cinched in her waist to add curves to her boyish outline and at the same time pushed up her small breasts. Imagine! She had cleavage for the first time in her life.

Still, another bigger question lurked. How long would it take before all the extra clothing would get to her? Refusing to dwell on the answer, she shook the thought. Without wearing the clothing, she couldn't enter Colin's world. Louisville in 1874 was something she wanted to see and she couldn't do it as a boy.

As she pulled on the ugly homespun shirt and tucked it into the faded dungarees, to Madame Dubois's dismay, another thought crossed her mind. How had Colin explained her presence?

"I'll have someone come out to collect all of this tomorrow," he said as they prepared to leave.

"*Mais oui*, Mr. Thorpe. Oh, and by the way, my sister Giselle will be happy to play lady's companion for the *mademoiselle*. She would love a trip to Louisville." Winking, she said, "Giselle will be discreet."

Colin smiled. "Thank you, Marguerite. Tell her someone will fetch her early on the morning of our departure."

"She'll be ready."

Libby caught their exchange on the way out the door and couldn't help asking, "She doesn't think I'm a lady of the evening, does she?"

"Are you?" The disarming grin spreading across his face did not amuse her.

"I'm serious." Libby swatted at his shoulder. "She probably thinks I'm some hussy. Or…oh my God, she probably believes I'm your mistress."

Colin laughed. "If you're that worried about your reputation, maybe you should marry me."

"It's not funny," she shot back, squaring her shoulders.

"Libby, she's French. They think differently about things like that."

"But that's what she thinks, isn't it?" She glanced at his face for substantiation. At his silence, she wanted to stomp her foot or shake him. "I'm no man's mistress. I won't be bought and paid for." She wagged a finger in front of his nose. "You got that, Mr. Thorpe? I am not for sale. You take the money for those dresses out of my pay. You hear me?"

"OK, only if you promise to stay until you pay your debt," he countered, still grinning. "But you should know that I spent a small fortune on all those doodads. Considering your wages, it'll take a year or so to pay it all back."

"Men!" she huffed before turning and storming off in the direction of her horse. "You're all the same."

"Wait." He reached out his hand to catch her by the elbow just as she grasped her horse's reins.

Eyes blazing, she spun around, holding on tightly to her temper.

"Whoa there, feisty lady." He put up his hands in mock surrender. "If I didn't know better, I'd say we were having our first disagreement." He broke off a moment as if searching for the right words. "Libby…no, not Libby." He hesitated, then looked directly into her eyes, and said, "Elizabeth Edwards, you know damn well I'd never consider you a mistress. You are more a wife to me than my own wife was, even though no vows have been spoken. So, I'll hear no more about the subject."

She stood staring at him until he moved to help her mount. The minute he was seated in his own saddle, he turned his horse in the direction of the farm. Libby had no choice but to calmly follow. Her outward appearance may have appeared tranquil, but everything on the inside was tossed upside down.

The two rode in silence for almost a mile. Every now and then she glanced over at him, noticing his subdued manner, yet not knowing how to deal with it. Finally she asked, "You really mean that? What you said back there?"

"What do you think?" He sighed.

Libby shrugged. "I don't know what to think."

Colin stopped his horse. Libby did the same.

Their gazes reconnected and held for what seemed like forever.

"You have my heart, Libby." They were so close, he was able to reach out and touch her face. Caressing it with the back of his hand, he said, "No matter that I've only known you a short while." His voice was whisper soft, earnest, and the intensity of it sent her mood soaring. "You think I give that lightly? I'd give you my name if I could. I'd love nothing more than to share the rest of my life with you, share all my worldly goods with you, grow old with you. Unfortunately, having what I crave would not make you happy, so I've not voiced my wants. Still, make no mistake, my intentions are purely honorable."

He flicked his reins and started riding again.

Dumbfounded, Libby stared after him. The man had a way of saying the right thing at the right time to turn her insides to mush.

She urged her horse forward and easily caught up. "I'm honored you feel that way." Looking at the lush green scenery, she said, "I'm sorry."

"Let's not spoil our time together," Colin eventually said, ending the uncomfortable silence that sprang up between them. "I regret my words. I should have kept my thoughts to myself."

Libby swallowed the lump in her throat. "Please don't say that. Your words were beautiful. You have my heart, too. When I go home, I don't know how I'll bear it without you." Though she didn't feel like smiling, she forced her lips to form one. "I don't want to spoil our time together either."

"Let's enjoy Louisville." Unfortunately, too much sadness welled in his eyes as he added, "We'll deal with the rest later."

Libby remained silent. Eventually her thoughts turned to another matter that was pressing on her mind. "How are you going to explain me," she asked, voicing her concern.

"Explain you?"

"Yeah. In Louisville." She snorted when it was obvious he had no clue what she was talking about.

"Why would I have to explain you?" Colin glanced at her, his eyebrows raised.

"To those people who have known you for years when they see you with me. They are going to want answers about where I came from. I certainly don't want anyone else to know I come from the future. Which brings us back to my question. Where did I come from? Who am I? Even if they don't ask, they'll be wondering."

"You're right, of course." Colin spent a moment deep in thought. Finally he smiled. "I'm sure we'll come up with something, especially since you're so good at the game."

She laughed, relieved to be back to their easy way.

☙

The next two days flew by in a blur for Libby. During that time, she and Colin had been together as much as possible.

In the evenings, when others assumed they were out under the trees, he'd sneak her to his bedroom through the servants' entrance. Tonight was no different. Like two little kids, they tiptoed up the stairs. Ensconced in a world where no one intruded, he made love to her again and again. It was getting harder and harder to leave his arms when the time came to return to the Gundersons'.

Dawn broke after a sleepless night. Libby hurriedly dressed and headed downstairs. For the next three evenings and nights, Colin would be hers and hers alone. That thought sent a thrill through her. Despite not belonging with him and knowing she should guard her heart at least a little bit, she could no more hold herself from him than she could stop breathing. She loved him and he loved her.

As usual, breakfast was a noisy affair. Libby ate quickly and ignored the guilt lodged in her stomach. She and Gus finished at the same time and both stood. Libby cleared her throat and tried to keep the embarrassment from showing. "I need to go to the big house to dress." Of course they knew of her upcoming trip and about the companion Colin hired. Yet, if they knew of her actions this past week, they'd consider her a Jezebel. Or worse.

Clucking like a mother hen, Berta took Libby aside and gave her a big hug. "You have a good time, *ja*? When you get back, maybe you should consider staying with Colin in the big house."

Blinking back tears, she shook her head. "That wouldn't be right." How had the woman become like an older sister or surrogate mother to her in a few short weeks?

"Gus and I discussed it. We both know that if you two could, you'd marry." Berta pulled her into another bear hug. "I can't remember Colin ever looking so happy. Joy has been in short supply around here. Life can be harsh, which means grabbing on to something good while you can. Colin can make up some excuse to have you there. Only Gus and I will know the truth."

"Thank you," Libby whispered, swallowing hard. "You and Gus have been so wonderful to me. I'll never forget you when I go home. I love all of you."

Still wrapped in Berta's arms, she squeezed and wished with all her heart things could be different.

"*Ja*, we love you too, child." Leaning back, she smiled. "It's so hard for me to get used to your age. Looking at you now, you seem so young. Take care, Libby." Berta released her and nudged her toward the kitchen door. "Now, off with you."

Nathan hugged her, and wiped his tears with his shirtsleeve. "I'll miss you, even if y'are a prissy girl. You're a good frien'."

She hugged him back. "I'll miss you too. Remember what I told you about the horses."

During the walk to the big house, Libby's heart ached. She truly did love everything about this place. Well, not everything. There was plenty she wouldn't miss when the trees took her home. Funny, some of that stuff hardly bothered her anymore. Not as much as the thought of never seeing any of these people did. Libby shoved the negative sentiments aside, determined not let anything destroy the next few days.

She was about to knock when the door suddenly opened and Colin leaned toward her.

"Just think, I have the next three nights with you all to myself," he whispered before kissing her cheek. He straightened, then indicated a woman Libby now noticed. "Giselle, may I introduce my fiancée, Libby Edwards." He turned back to her. "Libby, this is Giselle Franklin. She'll be your companion." He caught her eye and his tone brooked no argument. "She is to be with you at all times in the city. Do you understand?"

Libby nodded. "I understand." Louisville wasn't that bad, but Colin had given her the rundown on what was expected, which in her mind might take some getting used to.

Introductions now over, Libby grabbed her companion's hand. "Come on, Giselle, and help me make sure I'm presentable. Oh, and call me Libby. As someone once told me, we aren't that formal here on the farm."

Colin stood watching them start up the stairs to the guest room. She glanced back to catch his smile. They shared a look for a few seconds as the truth zinged through her. He remembered that night he told her to call him Colin.

"*Oui.*" Giselle's soft accent pulled her attention. "It will be Libby in private. Other times, Mademoiselle Edwards." Her smile was broad. "If I am to be a servant I must act the part. The wealthy in town are touchy about their servants speaking too informally to their employers." They entered the huge room decorated in yellow. "What do you wear today? I will help you dress."

Libby went over to the gown she'd picked out. While Giselle assisted her with all of the undergarments, she asked, "I take it you weren't born here? You and your sister have French accents. I'd love to see France. Is that where you're from?"

"Yes, but I'm only half French. My father is an American."

"So you're French and American?"

"Yes. Papa lived and worked in Paris for the American government, where he met Mamma. We have lived in Shelbyville not quite four years." Giselle talked nonstop while slipping the corset into place and helping her tie the laces. "Papa retired and brought us back to his home. My sister was married, but her husband died of the influenza. So she came with us. Mamma was a seamstress. She and my sister can make the most exquisite creations." Giselle finished trussing her up, reached for the two-piece day dress, as it was called, and helped Libby shrug into it.

"This outfit, along with all the others, fit that description," Libby said, glancing at the transformation in the cheval glass. Despite feeling like a turkey on Thanksgiving, she liked her feminine appearance. "So, your mother was a dressmaker in Paris?" No wonder the gowns were beautiful.

"*Oui.* But Mamma does not work much anymore. She helps Marguerite when she gets busy. Shelbyville is not Louisville, but ladies like to look nice no matter where they live. If they can find what they are looking for without going to the city, they buy it. Marguerite makes other things too. She's quite talented."

As Giselle fastened the back of her blouse, Libby glanced at her companion's reflection in the mirror. She looked like a teenager. She must have left Paris at a very young age. Did Giselle miss her home?

"How old are you," Libby asked, suddenly curious.

"I turned twenty on my last birthday."

"You left your home at sixteen? That must have been hard."

Giselle thought a moment. "It was hard, but not intolerable. My family was with me and soon the new place becomes home," she said, shrugging. "Now I would be sad to leave here. And if I did, I would know that wherever that place was, it would eventually become home."

Libby decided her response was something to reflect upon later.

"There, you are ready." Giselle finished buttoning her dress and patted her shoulder. "Such a change. You go from boy to beautiful woman so easily."

Noting her disapproving expression, Libby laughed. "Boys' clothes are much more comfortable." Not only that, they allowed a person to breathe. Then thinking about Colin's reaction, her smile broadened. How hard could it be to endure a little discomfort for a couple of days?

"Yes, but not so pretty, *non*?"

"No." Still grinning, Libby grabbed her hand. "Come on. I'm eager to see Louisville."

"It is a very nice city with much to offer. Of course, it's not like New York or Chicago and nothing like Paris, but it is closer."

Libby led her out of the bedroom and down the stairs. Funny, how Giselle's description of Louisville in the nineteenth century was very much like her own description of the modern city in the future.

"My God, Libby, look at you!" The thought dissipated when Colin's stunned voice registered. "How I ever mistook you for a boy, I'll never know. You take my breath away."

Libby's gaze sought his. Obvious appreciation shone in those blue depths. Happiness shot through her.

At the bottom step where Colin waited, she curtsied. "Why, thank you, kind sir. You'll spoil me with all of your compliments." She inclined her head at his more formal garb. He was dressed in a vested morning suit with snowy white shirt and cravat. "You're not so bad, yourself. I don't believe I've ever seen you looking so nice." He was a fine male specimen who made her insides quiver. Why, if she met him in her own time, she'd find him just as attractive.

"When visiting the bigger city, one must dress for it. Of course, it's worth it to see you looking so fetching, my dear," Colin said, chuckling.

He tucked her arm in his and led her out to the waiting open carriage. The minute George, the driver Colin hired, saw them coming down the steps, he stood to assist them. Their bags were packed and placed in the storage area. Within moments, George guided the horses down the dirt road.

Birds chirped and insects buzzed as Libby sat back, unwilling to miss any detail about this trip. Seeing Louisville in an era so long ago was like a dream come true. She had to pinch herself to make sure she wasn't asleep. Of course the idea of being with Colin in social situations was more than exciting.

Even his superior attitude tickled her feminine side. Another smile tugged at the edges of her mouth as she surreptitiously watched him through half-lidded eyes. So what if he thought himself supreme ruler of his house? As long as she was in 1874, she'd be by his side.

Chapter 15

As the carriage rolled along, Libby tried to take a deep breath, but wearing a corset wasn't conducive to breathing. How did women in this day and age tolerate the confining clothes? Her gaze landed on her companion. Giselle didn't look the least bit uncomfortable or bothered by the heat.

Air-conditioning was definitely an underappreciated luxury of modern times, she decided, wiping perspiration from her forehead. She glanced out of the dusty carriage from under the brim of her bonnet, wishing she could also chuck the hat. It weighed a ton. She'd never worn one before. Not even to the Derby, where women usually tried to outdo one another for the most creative headgear. The few times she'd attended she sat in the infield with a hundred thousand other partiers. Hats out there weren't a necessity.

"I'm looking forward to tomorrow night," Colin said, drawing her attention. "The Mayfields are holding a ball. I can't wait to show you off."

Libby nodded, wondering what she'd do while he was busy during the day. Besides delivering three horses to buyers and interviewing associates interested in using his stallions as studs, Colin planned on attending meetings about the racetrack. The never-ending search for studs to mate with his thoroughbred mares would also take up a good amount of time. He'd already explained why she couldn't join him. Females had their place and it clearly wasn't in the paddocks.

Three saddle horses were tied to the back of their carriage, along with two others that were sold, together kicking up quite a bit of dust. Libby was excited to see Louisville in the past and Colin was excited about showing her where the new racetrack was to be built.

Several hours later, Libby wondered how much longer their trip would take. She tried not to fidget, but her rear end was numb. With all the shade trees along the route and the absence of concrete and asphalt, she'd have thought it would be cooler. Not so! It was still hot. And humid. What she wouldn't give for a Coke or Pepsi. Her once crisp two-piece cotton dress was wilted with sweat. The tight, formfitting bodice that barely allowed her to breathe earlier now seemed oppressive as did the long sleeves. Puffy at the top, they tapered to the wrist, allowing for little airflow along the arms. The high collar rubbed against her neck, making her yearn for shorts and a T-shirt.

Looking around, she recognized the road they were riding as one of the main thoroughfares out of the city, yet nothing looked familiar. Shelbyville Road or Highway 60 in her time was one of the busiest. This part of the dirt road in 1874 was treelined and narrower. At least it was fairly smooth.

A slight breeze hit her face. She held her head higher, trying unsuccessfully to get cooler air down her neck.

"Where are we?" Libby said minutes later, turning to Colin. Everything around them was rural—nothing but a few limestone walls or wooden fences here and there.

"The town we just past a few miles back was Middletown. We're south of Lyndon, just north of Jeffersontown." Her jaw dropped in stunned disbelief. This area was the site of the future mall where she used to work, she realized as he added, "We still have five miles or so before we reach the city's outskirts. Another hour at the most."

They traveled another quarter of an hour before the road widened. Houses appeared every now and again, hinting that civilization loomed. As they rode farther, Libby began to recognize landmarks as the Crescent Hill area. Homes were a little closer together, but still nothing like what she was used to.

A few minutes later, the stench practically gagged her. Libby covered her mouth and nose with her hand.

"Sorry," Colin said. "There's no avoiding the smell." He shrugged. "Butchertown," he added as if that answered everything. "The porkers do a thriving business, but I wish the slaughterhouse wasn't right off the main turnpike into town."

The road became more crowded. Taking in all the activity, Libby forgot her discomfort. Horse-drawn wagons and single riders coexisted with plenty of pedestrians. Vendors pushed their cars and pawned their wares on street corners. Men yelled, "Meat pies," or "Get your copper pans here." The smell of cooked meat infiltrated her nostrils as did the scent of horses, urine, and earth.

"That's the Louisville Glassworks Company," Colin said, pointing to a building.

She nodded, then noticed people around what looked to be a hand pump set right in the middle of the next street. "What are those people doing?"

Colin looked to where she indicated. "They're filling water jugs. Those are public wells. Louisville's progressive and one of the few western cities to pump water directly to houses. Still, there are some who're squeamish at drinking river water."

Libby hadn't even thought about the water or the microbes most likely living in it. Thankfully, she'd gone weeks without a problem. "I don't know which is worse."

His shoulders lifted in a shrug. "Water is water. The city waterworks is massive and includes a filtration process. It's a matter of taste."

Eventually they turned onto Main Street. The scenery changed, became more congested, and the road widened. Only now it was cobbled, making the ride bumpier. The buildings were side by side, most between two and four stories high. Libby tried to find structures that lasted into the twenty-first century, but nothing looked familiar.

"Our hotel isn't far," Colin said. "We're staying at the Galt House."

"Really?" The hotel was a landmark in her time.

"Yes. I prefer its central location. The original burned some years ago. Of course the Louisville Hotel also offers luxurious accommodations. I have no problem with switching if you would rather."

"I'm sure your choice will be fine." She smiled, then glanced at Giselle, who'd remained silent for most of the trip. Libby cleared her throat, leaned into Colin, and lowered her voice. "So, are we clear on where I come from?"

"Yes," Colin said, chuckling. "You're a friend of the family and lived in Chicago until a couple of months ago when your parents, Thomas and Elizabeth Edwards, died. You came to the farm as a favor to my mother, who was your mother's best friend when they were younger. No one will question it." His smiled broadened. "How can anyone claim you don't exist when the great fire wiped out all family records three years ago? Everything is being recreated by word of mouth. You really are quite inventive, my dear."

"I only hope I don't encounter anyone from Chicago. I have no idea what the city looks like or what's there in 1874."

"Do not worry about that," Giselle said, speaking out for the first time in hours. "I was there six months ago. I can tell you about the city if anyone asks. It is much different than before the fire."

"You've visited Chicago? Before and after the fire?"

Giselle nodded. "My uncle. He lives there. We take the train and visit often."

Really?" Libby fought to keep amazement off her face. Too many of her friends in her own time didn't like traveling. Despite the ease of traveling by air, some never went more than a couple hundred miles from home. Yet here sat Giselle in 1874, who'd traveled from France to New York, to end up in Louisville by way of Chicago. The woman most likely could teach her something about being adventurous.

"You'll have to educate me on Chicago before I go into public. That way, I won't blow my cover."

Her companion shook her head, clearly not understanding. "Your cover? *Qu'est-ce que c'est?* What is that?"

"Sorry, it's slang." Libby laughed. "Blowing my cover means letting people in on my secret, which is that I'm not from Chicago. I don't want people to know that. We invented a cover story to tell people when they meet me. I'm only working on Colin's farm until I can figure out a way to go home. He was kind enough to offer to bring me along on this trip, and hired you to help. It's all very complicated."

Grinning, Giselle patted her hand. "French women are much more tolerant of affairs of the heart. Here, it is such a question of morality. But to me, it seems very judgmental. I think what is in your heart is much more important."

"I'm not sure about the affair part, but my heart belongs to Colin," Libby murmured. The woman was ahead of her time.

"It appears both your hearts are engaged." When Libby's brow furrowed, Giselle added, "I do not mean to be rude. It is just that never have I seen anyone so engaged with each other, *non*? It is no simple affair you two share. I may be young, but I understand *amour*."

Libby glanced at Colin, who'd obviously caught the exchange. Their eyes met. The heat and desire emanating from that gaze zinged her insides. No one could mistake that look.

The lady is right, Libby thought. "Definitely more than a simple affair. Wouldn't you say so, Mr. Thorpe?"

"There's nothing simple about you, Libby," Colin said, offering a lopsided grin.

They were saved from exploring the subject further when the carriage slowed. Colin released Libby's gaze and she turned to peruse the hotel now in front of her. It was grand, yet nothing like the hotel in her century.

She also noticed that the street sign on the corner read Second Street and Main.

This wasn't the same hotel that stood into the next century—hers was at Fourth and Main. The fact that the Galt House was well-known in both times comforted Libby, although she had no clue as to why.

George stepped down, moving to help Libby and Giselle out. Colin was right behind.

"If you would unload the bags here," he said. "I'll have a bellman take them up to our rooms. Your room will be next to mine, George. After unloading, take the carriage and horses to the livery." After giving final instructions, Colin then turned to Libby and Giselle. "I've reserved a suite of rooms for you two. That way you'll have Giselle close by, Libby." He held out both his elbows. "Shall we?"

Now inside the hotel, Colin quickly registered and received instructions along with keys. Arm in arm they set off for the staircase. The bellman preceded them and had the bags in their rooms quickly, despite having to climb two flights of stairs.

"I'll let you ladies unpack," Colin said. He turned and caught Libby's gaze. "Then we can have lunch together before I need to go to my first meeting."

"Do not worry about me, Mr. Thorpe," Giselle interjected. "I find I am quite tired from all this traveling." Then winking at Libby, she took the key to her room, unlocked the door, and went inside.

"Hurry, the bellman's gone and no one is coming." Colin grabbed Libby's hand and pulled her behind him to his hotel room door. He quickly unlocked and opened it, practically shoving Libby inside. Once inside, he wrapped her in a bear hug. "I've been waiting for hours to taste you."

Seconds later, he was kissing her as if she was water and he hadn't had any for days. Then his lips softened. Libby moaned and stepped closer to his heat as he took his time with slow kisses that kindled a fire in her belly. Never before had just kissing made her yearn for more. How was she ever going to leave him?

He released her lips and whispered, "Can you feel my desire, Libby? I swear, as God is my witness, I've hungered for no one as much as I hunger for you."

As his lips found hers once again, she was amazed that his thoughts mirrored hers. Seconds later, all thinking dissipated into sensation after sensation. Colin fingered the back of her blouse and struggled to undo the buttons. He lifted his head and chuckled. "'Tis easier to get you out of your boys' attire. This dress is like a fortress. Here, turn around. I'll need to play lady's maid."

"Damn, that thing is hot," she said, taking off her bonnet. "Do women wear this stuff all the time?"

Colin shrugged. "I never thought about it before, but yes."

Libby turned around while Colin quickly undid the buttons. Once out of the two-piece dress, a sense of relief washed over her, but total liberation wouldn't come until she rid herself of the heinous corset.

The lacy contraption caught and held Colin's eye. A blast of heat rushed to her center. Libby felt sexy and desired as he kissed the swell of one breast and started untying the ribbons.

It dawned on her why women wore this kind of getup when Colin continued undressing her, kissing uncovered spots. "There is something to be said for imagination," he said.

Now naked, she wholeheartedly agreed as Colin picked her up and carried her to the bed. He shed his clothes in record time, then leaned above her before lowering his mouth to hers.

The kiss went on forever. Libby melted, softening even more when he released her lips and groaned. "See what you do to me, Libby?" He took her hand and placed it over his thick arousal. "You only have to look at me and I want you. What have you done to me, Elizabeth Edwards? You've come from the future and stolen my soul."

Libby's brain had already turned to mush. Funny, before that happened, before his hands started roaming over her body, her last coherent thought was how could he accuse her of stealing souls? In Libby's mind, he was stealing hers, bit by bit.

Colin filled her, and except for the pleasure, her mind went blank. When he started moving inside her, using slow, even strokes, she could only feel—until she exploded with the orgasm he seemed to elicit so easily. Seconds later, Colin followed with his own release.

Reality eventually returned and Libby felt him roll over, taking her with him. Without breaking contact, he situated her so that she was on top, kissing her again for what seemed like forever.

Stroking up and down her arms, he released her lips and sighed. "I could stay here forever, wrapped in your love." He broke off for a heartbeat. "Ah, Elizabeth, I love you with all my heart."

Tears blurred Libby's vision. Never before had she felt so loved. So cherished. So complete. Why did it have to happen with someone who was in the wrong century? Why? Like a hamster on a wheel, the question ran through her brain. She laid her head on his shoulder and cried.

"Shush, Libby," he whispered and kissed the top of her head. "'It wasn't my intent to draw tears. I've accepted what is. How can I not? The question I ask myself is would I be better off without experiencing your love? The truth is, one moment with you is better than a lifetime without ever knowing you."

It finally hit her. There was no way she would ever meet anyone else who gave what he did. Men like him just didn't exist in the twenty-first century. Colin Thorpe would always be the love of her life. And he was right. She'd take any time left with him over never having met him.

"I'm sorry, Colin. I love you too. It hurts to know it can't be forever."

"Hush, Libby. My love for you will be forever. We will meet one day in the hereafter. I'll wait."

Blinking back tears, Libby could only stare at him. Their love did seem like something that would last through time. She prayed with all her heart that heaven existed. If it did, she knew she'd be spending eternity with Colin.

"I'm sorry," Colin finally whispered, kissing her forehead after several minutes passed. "I must get dressed, but I don't like leaving you like this. Will you be OK?"

Libby nodded. He pulled away to stand, then began dressing. Libby remained on the bed and watched. She never got tired of looking at his naked body. He was gorgeous, with big broad shoulders, lean hips, and strong legs.

While he dressed, he talked. "I'm not sure what's going on tonight. There is always some party or another. I've been out of the whirl for a time, but it shouldn't be too hard to get an invitation. I'll work on procuring one. My meeting should only take a couple of hours. I'll meet you in the lobby at four o'clock and I'll show you and Giselle a little of the city. Hopefully by then I'll know where we'll be going tonight."

Now dressed, he stepped over to the bed, kissed her, then held out that damned corset. "Here, you need to get dressed too. Come, I'll help do up your stays and buttons. You can't manage by yourself. It wouldn't be good for you to be found naked in my room."

He reached for the crinoline and chemise. Putting them on one item at a time, Libby hated the thought of having to wear the stuff for the rest of the day. Then she smiled. Things really hadn't changed that much. After all, women of her time wore spiked heels and panty hose, and spandex was all the rage for keeping tummies flatter.

Walking over to the mirror situated in the corner of the room after dressing, she stared at her reflection. Twirling, she felt like a girl in them, a new sensation. Dressing in feminine clothes, much to Dave's dismay, was at the bottom of her to-do list. Libby had always been more comfortable in jeans. Too bad she couldn't go around town now in them. Oh well! Despite the discomfort, she figured three days wouldn't be too bad to play dress-up, especially for Colin. In no time they'd be back on the farm where she could wear her boys' clothes and be comfortable again.

Colin stood and kept his gaze on the mirror, catching her eye, seeming interested in the emotions playing over her face. He held out his hand. "You are lovely, Libby. Come. Let's get you back to your own room."

"You make me feel lovely." Inhaling to still the flapping butterflies, she moved to meet him and put her hand in his. "So, what type of party do you think we'll be going to tonight? I can't wait. I hope it's something that will allow me to dress in one of the formal gowns. They are so exquisite. How did you know what colors to choose?"

"Now you sound more like the woman I've come to know than the child I thought you were." Colin laughed and led her out the door. "Supposedly, they are all the rage. I'm glad you like them. You require something that tells others you're no child."

"They do make me feel like I'm all woman, Colin." Your woman, she wanted to add, but didn't. "Thank you. I still plan to pay for them, though. So don't think you're off the hook for that," Libby stated firmly.

By this time, they were at her room. He took her hand and kissed it. "How long do I have to pay penance for purchasing your clothes?" he teased, grinning as he took the key out of her hand and opened her door. Ushering her inside, he added, "Until later, Libby. Rest while you can. You're going to need the energy later."

Her soft laughter broke free. She watched in amused silence as he turned and headed down the hall while whistling.

☙

"Libby, he's such an attractive man," Giselle said as she shut the door. "How I would love someone like that to pay attention to me."

Smiling dreamily, Libby nodded. "He is gorgeous, isn't he? I do feel lucky." Then she remembered her circumstances and amended, "Well, I'm lucky while it lasts."

"Such a silly statement," Giselle admonished, clearly not understanding her comment. "Anyone looking at the two of you together would know it was meant to last. It's obvious he loves you and you him. I'm sure he will marry you."

Instead of telling her why that would never happen, she offered, "I know that before I met Colin, I had no clue about how I could feel about another human being."

"You are so lucky to find someone like that, Libby. My parents have that and Marguerite had it with her husband. Even though they found true love, it is rare." Her smile turned wistful. "I hope to find such a love, but living in Shelbyville doesn't provide me with many to choose from."

Libby was silent for a moment. "Having a soul mate like Colin is indescribable." Then she smiled. "You know, I just had a thought. Why don't you come with us tonight?"

"*Non*, I don't think so." Giselle shook her head. "It isn't done. I'm supposed to be your companion."

"I bet you're used to hobnobbing with wealthy people," Libby said, having none of it. "Didn't you say your dad was with the government in Paris?"

"Yes, but what has that to do with me accompanying you tonight?"

"You've been through all kinds of social situations and are probably more comfortable in them than I am. I hate those types of functions. I'm only doing it because I can't pass up the opportunity to see what it's like. If you tagged along, you could help."

Libby could see that Giselle was seriously considering her suggestion.

"It does make sense," Giselle said after a few moments in thought. "I love parties and dancing. I rarely get the opportunity to attend anything since coming to Kentucky." Her gaze turned reflective again. "In Paris, I was just starting to be allowed to attend them." Giselle smiled warmly and twirled around gaily as if she were dancing, obviously happy, before she plopped back on the bed, sighing. "How I wish you were staying, Libby. You're so easy to talk to. I don't really have a lot of friends outside of my sister. I have to confide. This trip to Louisville is the most excitement I've had in months."

"Do you have the proper clothes," Libby asked.

"Of course. Marguerite makes the most beautiful gowns and I rarely get to wear them. Why do you think I came along on this trip?" She glanced up. "You don't think Mr. Thorpe would mind?"

"No, I think it will work well for our story." Libby laughed. "Help our cover, so to speak, and make it more believable to have my companion accompany me. Don't you think?"

"*Oui*, I like it, especially if I can attend a party. I think we should go out and celebrate."

"I agree." Libby grabbed her hand and started for the door. "I've been dying to see the sights. Colin is meeting me at four o'clock downstairs. We have a couple of hours to kill." She was dying to become better acquainted. "I'm so happy you're here. It's nice to have a friend."

During lunch with Giselle, Libby forgot some of her homesickness. In the past weeks, there were moments where she really missed Bev. Her new companion seemed to fill that void. Giselle was closer in age—more like an equal. Berta was a wonderful friend, but Libby couldn't shake the feeling that the older woman looked upon her as someone to watch over and care for, rather than a confidante.

After lunch, Libby and Giselle went sight-seeing. As the two walked through the crowded streets of Louisville, Libby was taken aback with all she saw. The city looked so different, the buildings unrecognizable. The river, the main focal point without the concrete and steel impediments of the future, was totally new to her. The water's edge was visible as was the steamboat dock. There were no Humana or Aegon buildings. No tall skyscrapers reaching toward the heavens to impede the view.

Bigger than she imagined, Louisville in the past had a strong pulse and was alive. Libby then realized that no matter the time in history, cities were the lifeblood of the country. Activity hummed and the world went about its business, something that probably happened wherever people congregated.

They walked and gawked for a couple of hours, after which Libby's feet hurt. Her walking boots were not made for walking as the song declared. Libby smiled at the thought that not much had changed in that area either. Fashionable shoes of any age hurt the feet after a few hours of wearing.

"I've seen enough. Let's go back to the hotel and have a cool drink." She glanced at Giselle. "How do you put up with all this junk you have to wear? It's so hot."

A look of confusion crossed her face.

"I'm not used to wearing a corset," Libby said, hoping the explanation was enough.

Giselle shrugged. "I don't know. I've never known anything else, so I'm used to it."

On the walk back to the hotel, Libby thought about her adventure. One thing she liked—it didn't seem as hot and humid. Louisville could be worse than hell in July. The river breeze actually made it quite pleasant, despite the sun beating overhead. Besides, they were able to stay in the shade of the buildings, which made the heat easier to bear.

Smiling, Libby imagined wearing a pair of shorts and a sleeveless shirt in this crowd. Some of the ladies she watched go by would have heart attacks if they knew what people in the future wore on an everyday basis. She almost laughed out loud at that thought.

Libby still wondered how these women put up with all the constraints. Besides being dressed to the hilt, almost every woman Libby saw had a hat or bonnet covering her head. Even the men she saw wore hats, which seemed so odd in the middle of July.

"My feet are hurting," Giselle said. "I am glad we're finally back. Next time we should wear more comfortable shoes, *n'est-ce pas*?"

"You have comfortable shoes?" In this century? Libby was struck dumb.

"Of course. There're not so pretty, but sometimes beauty is forfeited for comfort, *non*?"

"I agree." Libby nodded. "Next time, we'll wear more comfortable shoes while walking."

Laughing, the two headed inside the hotel toward the restaurant. They were seated immediately. Libby pulled the ornate timepiece out of her pocket that Colin had given her. It was a pin, but Libby felt funny wearing it, which was why it was in her pocket.

They still had about a half an hour before she would meet Colin.

When their lemonade came, Libby lifted hers in a toast. "Here's to friendship."

She clinked glasses with Giselle as the memory of her and Bev sitting under the two oak trees and clinking soft drinks came to mind.

In response, Libby began to wonder when she'd be going home. The thought didn't cheer her at all.

Chapter 16

A bubble of excitement warmed Libby's insides. This adventure with Colin would continue at an old-fashioned ball tonight. Well, it wasn't old-fashioned for now, but to her it would be like stepping into a painting from times long past.

Someone abruptly stepped too close to her, and she had to pull hard on the reins of Colin's saddle horse. Riding single file along Third Street behind Colin and with Giselle following, she weaved in between two horse-drawn wagons parked on opposite sides of the dusty road that had suddenly become crowded with a different kind of traffic than what she was used to.

The din was totally different from twenty-first century Louisville. There were no interstates or congested streets with cars buzzing, horns honking, or sirens blaring to interrupt the quiet. In fact, the sounds seemed amplified without the background traffic muffling the noise of other activity. People shouting, horses neighing, dogs barking, and wagons rumbling carried on the air for blocks.

Libby tried not to gawk at the incredible sights. Dressed in a rainbow of colors, people walked along the sand-colored road. It was like seeing a Monet painting come to life. Everything moved at a much slower pace here. She wondered if she'd ever get used to seeing the formality of the late nineteenth century. Even more amazing, they all seemed so comfortable. She stretched her legs farther into the stirrups and took a deep breath. Her riding habit wasn't too bad, except for the corset. She'd never get used to wearing one.

Eventually Third Street widened and the traffic thinned. By the time they reached the outskirts of town, they were the only ones on the road.

Libby glanced around at the peaceful scenery. It was quiet enough to hear birds chirping and insects buzzing.

"I can't get over how different it all is," she said to Colin as he came to a stop beside her.

He nodded. "I can't imagine what the area will be like in a hundred years. You're lucky. You've glimpsed both past and future."

Colin dismounted, helped both her and Giselle off their mounts, then led the horses to a tree and tethered them to a branch.

Libby turned a full circle, taking it all in. She pointed. "I think the twin spires are located in that area. I have no point of reference, so I can't be certain. Just think. This is where the tradition begins."

"Twin spires? Hmmm." His eyes followed her hand. "They'll start on it soon. The grandstand will be over there. The track should be ready for the spring meet."

Giselle sighed. "I cannot wait. I love going to the horse races. We went many times in France. There is nothing so exciting as watching the horses run, especially when your horse wins."

"So, you're a gambler?" Colin teased.

Giselle's lips curled into a sly smile. "*Oui*, we all become gamblers when we go to watch thoroughbreds run, *n'est-ce pas*? And after seeing such beauties, picking one to win cannot be avoided."

Colin grinned. "I never imagined you as a gambler. Maybe you're not such a good influence over my Libby after all."

Snorting, Libby swatted at his shoulder. "I hate to break it to you, but I've already been to the track. Too many times to count. Giselle's right. The minute you view the horses from the grandstand, you can't help but become a gambler." Libby sighed, remembering the fun she and Bev used to have. "There is nothing like a day at the races. Even when you lose, you don't mind because it is so entertaining."

"My, my." Colin shook his head, tsk-tsking. "The temperance ladies would have a field day with you two. I suppose you both drink to excess, too."

"I've been known to sport a hangover now and again." Libby grinned, enjoying his teasing. "How about you, Giselle? Ever drink too much French wine? Enough to cause a headache the next day? We mustn't disappoint our host."

Giselle laughed and winked at Libby. "Of course, but only on special occasions."

"I'll have to watch out for you, Miss Edwards," Colin admitted, holding out his hand. "It's time we head back."

Libby smiled, wishing that her time with him would never end.

The horses seemed to sense their journey was ending and trotted at a faster pace. Every now and then Libby would egg Colin on, and a race would ensue. The two would shoot ahead of Giselle, galloping down the road at breakneck speed.

"How did you do that," Libby asked after losing the second of three races. "I should have easily beaten you."

"Skill?" Colin's sideways grin was disarming.

"Ha! I'm more skilled than you. I should have won, and you know it."

"I can't allow that." He shook his head. "Be happy for the one win. Where you're concerned, I fight extra hard to maintain an advantage."

Libby grunted. "That's so macho. You know, Colin, men and women are equal in the twenty-first century. We don't play these little games of one-upping."

"Oh?" He eyed her for a moment too long. "I don't belong to that century, so those rules don't apply. Besides, I like playing games with you, Libby. What's more, as long as we're together, I'll always relish winning."

Libby could only laugh at his audacity. He was the ultimate male. She didn't mind losing to someone as sexy and as potent as he was. It made surrendering that much sweeter.

Back at the hotel, Colin escorted the two women to their room. Before turning to leave, he said, "Be ready no later than 8:15. We don't want to be too fashionably late. Dinner is served at nine."

☙

Libby considered her reflection in the mirror. "Giselle, your sister is very talented. Look how beautifully this dress hangs. The material is gorgeous." She felt transformed, as if she were Cinderella going to the ball. The midnight blue creation fit snugly at the bodice, bustled slightly in the back, and flowed into a small train. The gown, cut low in the front, showed off her sleek shoulders. Best of all, Libby loved having cleavage, which made wearing the corset easier to endure. "You need to pinch me so that I know it's real."

"*Oui*, she is talented, but you make her creation shine."

Glancing at her new friend, Libby smiled. "You are also one to make a dress shine. Look at you. I'd venture to say, you'll turn a few heads tonight."

"I just want to have a good time. I love to dance. Thank you, Libby, for insisting I do this. It is much better than going to dinner alone."

"Why is it that you can go to dinner alone and I can't?" She scrunched up her nose. "I don't understand all the social restrictions."

"There are a lot of rules, but it is not so bad in this country. Not like Great Britain, where they are tedious about how to act. Still, there is one similarity. The rules differ for the working class versus the wealthier class. If one is a servant, she is invisible."

"Seems kind of stupid, if you ask me."

"You will be with Colin. Wherever he goes, they know him. Since you're with him…" Smiling, she shrugged.

"God, I hate rules."

"Most are in place for our safety," Giselle said in a no-nonsense tone. "Not all men are gentlemen, and many take advantage of women if they can."

Libby sighed. "I never thought about the women who went before me and paved the way to equality."

"You are talking about suffragettes, *n'est-ce pas*? *Oui*, I've heard of them. Some men do not like them. You should be careful about what you say in front of Colin's friends."

"Don't worry, I'll be on my best behavior. I've had a little practice with Dave's friends."

"Dave? Who is Dave? Does Colin know about him?"

"It's a long story." Libby looked in the mirror again and patted her head. "I love what you've done to my hair. I realize short isn't in, but it really looks chic. And what is that stuff you put on my eyelashes? My eyes stand out and appear darker, but I don't look made up."

Giselle smiled smugly and winked. "I'll never tell. We French have some secrets."

Moments later, Libby answered Colin's knock at the door.

"My God, Libby," he said, standing in front of her. He motioned for her to turn around. "Look at you! I'll be fending off the men all night."

Blushing, she looked down at her gown. "Thank you." She cleared her throat and glanced at him, worrying her bottom lip. "Social situations aren't my specialty. Dave always said I lacked polish. I hope I don't embarrass you tonight."

"Dave is a fool. You lack no polish, Elizabeth. You're brilliant the way you are, the rarest of gems."

Libby loved hearing his compliments. She slipped her arm into his curved elbow. "You look very dapper, Mr. Thorpe. I'm being escorted by the most handsome man of all."

Chuckling, Colin turned to Giselle, who now stood next to him. After telling her how beautiful she looked, he offered her his other elbow. "Shall we? I will be the envy of all who know me, escorting two lovely ladies to the ball."

He led them down the stairs and out of the hotel to George and the awaiting carriage. Colin helped both Libby and Giselle ascend into the vehicle before seating himself. George climbed on board and they were off.

A mansion soon came into view as the open carriage turned onto a treelined drive.

"Tomorrow, Jameson is having one of his balloon ascensions and fireworks afterward," Colin said as the conveyance slowed, easing behind a line of other horse-drawn carriages.

"That sounds like fun," Libby said enthusiastically. "Who is Jameson?"

"Jameson Claremont. He's hosting the ball tonight."

George stopped the vehicle and jumped down.

Arm in arm with Colin in the middle, the three started up the steps leading to a large veranda.

Hundreds of candles flickered everywhere, shedding soft light into the now darkening night. Men in formal black-tie attire, complete with top hats, escorted gloved women dressed in gowns and matching hats, these colors more Renoir than Monet.

Colin practically had to drag Libby into the huge entryway. "Don't gawk, love. There are people behind us. You'll have plenty of time to take in the sights later."

Amazing, she thought, picking up her pace. It was like stepping into a page from a fairy tale, so much so that Libby felt the magic of the event. Who wouldn't want to attend a ball and dance by candlelight?

This must be what it's like to attend a Derby party that the elite of the city held every year, or walking the red carpet on Oscar night. When she realized there was a receiving line ahead, she froze. "Colin, they're announcing people. Can't we slip in the back?" She didn't want to be singled out in such a public way.

"There's no reason to worry," he said, offering a reassuring smile. "Trust me, Libby. You're the loveliest woman here. No one will say or do anything to make you feel uncomfortable. Otherwise they'll have to contend with me."

Nodding, she forced herself to relax and follow Giselle's lead.

She heard their names being called out as they walked farther into the room until they stood in front of a couple Libby assumed to be the Claremonts.

"Colin, so nice to see you again," the man said, shaking Colin's hand. "I'm glad you're out and about after your loss."

"Thank you, Jameson." He turned to Libby. "May I present a friend of my mother's and her companion. Miss Elizabeth Edwards and Giselle Franklin. Mr. and Mrs. Claremont."

Libby smiled. "So nice to meet you."

Giselle followed suit.

"See, that wasn't so bad, was it?" Colin whispered in her ear.

"No." But this is only the beginning, she thought, still in awe over the scene in front of her.

They were directed farther into the ballroom where Colin signaled a servant holding a tray of champagne-filled glasses.

While sipping champagne, Libby met so many people it was hard to keep track of them all.

Eventually Colin took her drink and set it down with his. "I've been waiting all afternoon to dance with you," he said, leading her in a waltz that she was now comfortable in following. Libby sighed, loving the romance of being swept around the room while the orchestra played. She was living the fairy tale.

"What do you think?" Colin released his hold as the music died. His hand lingered at the small of her back.

"What can I think? It's pretty impressive," Libby replied honestly, looking into his questioning eyes. "I'll never forget this night as long as I live. Thank you for bringing me."

He smiled. "The pleasure is all mine."

"Dinner is served," a servant announced, and several formally-clad waiters steered the large group into the dining room. Never in her life had Libby seen anything so spectacular. Everywhere she looked, there were tables set with enough silver and crystal to fund a small war.

Libby and Colin were seated at the main table, which held at least fifty people. Giselle, all smiles, sat across from them and next to one of the gentlemen she had danced with earlier.

Talk while they ate centered on the new Louisville Jockey Club. There was much speculation. Libby smiled, knowing exactly what the future held.

She also didn't miss the speculative glances from several of the women at the table, at the same time wondering who they were. Did they have designs on Colin? They seemed very interested in what he was doing. A streak of jealousy went through her. The women were gorgeous and sophisticated—much like Dave's colleagues' wives. A horrible thought struck. Once she went home, Colin would be at these women's mercy. Pain ripped through Libby at the image of Colin spending time with anyone other than her. Pushing the disturbing notion away, Libby refused to allow anything to spoil her time tonight.

After dinner Giselle danced, and Colin became immersed in a conversation with Malcolm Webster, his solicitor. His wife, Susan, smiled at Libby as the two men chatted away. "This could last awhile," she said. "Would you care to walk outside and get some air? These events can sometimes get stuffy."

Looking over to find Giselle once again being swept off her feet, Libby nodded. Her friend would be OK for a few minutes.

"How long do you think they'll be talking," she asked as they headed toward the door. Libby liked Susan, in fact had felt immediately comfortable with her upon their introductions earlier that evening.

Susan flashed a wicked smile. "We'll give them about ten minutes to finish. If they haven't found us by then, we'll go looking for them." Though tall and statuesque with striking features—shining black hair, a fair complexion, and ice-blue eyes—she was also a warm, friendly woman with a good sense of humor. Even though she appeared older, she didn't make Libby feel gauche and unsophisticated like the Stepford wives did.

As they reached the outside garden, Susan said, "You're old family friends?" When Libby nodded, she offered a genuine smile. "Colin's one of my favorite people, so it's nice to see him smiling for a change."

Libby glanced back at Colin and her smile widened. "He does seem happy, doesn't he? Did you know his wife?"

"Yes. I knew Abby," Susan said a little stiffly.

Her unexpected change in demeanor threw Libby and she couldn't stop from asking, "What was she like? Was she pretty?"

"Abigail Thorpe was a beautiful woman."

It figures she'd be beautiful, Libby thought as her smile turned into a frown. "I'm still curious about her. I never got the chance to meet her."

"Colin deserved better. I don't like to speak ill of the dead, but she wasn't a pleasant person to be around," Susan admitted, her expression becoming more solemn. "Unfortunately, due to our husbands' relationship, we had to spend a lot of time together." Susan stopped abruptly, clearly embarrassed, as if she'd said too much. "I hope you don't repeat that. I should not have spoken out of turn. She was Colin's wife, and as such she deserves my respect."

"I wouldn't dream of saying anything," Libby replied, squeezing her arm affectionately. "Colin's lucky to have such good friends in you and your husband."

"Well, he's just as lucky to have a friend in you, wouldn't you say?" Susan said warmly. She place her hand over the one Libby had on her arm and added, "I think the men have had plenty of time to talk. Let's go find them, shall we?"

Slowly walking toward the back steps, Libby caught part of a conversation that carried from the corner of the house in the opposite direction.

"She's a friend of the family, so he says. Did you see her hair? It's as short as a boy's. What can that man be thinking to be bringing someone so gauche here?" The woman's voice hesitated. "Besides, he's still in mourning. His wife's been dead less than a year."

Libby stopped short when she realized they were talking about her.

"Oh, Caroline. Mourning never stopped you," said the second voice. "You're jealous because he never looked at you like that."

"She'll never hold him, that's for sure, at least not after he sees me again," the first, more shrewish voice shot back.

Susan also heard the exchange and whispered, "Vile gossip. We shouldn't continue listening." Neither moved as the second voice said, "He never looked at you before, what makes you think he'll do it now?"

"Of course, he never looked at me before. He was married at the time."

"That didn't stop you from trying. Problem is, you haven't figured out that he's not interested in you. He does seem interested in that Elizabeth Edwards, though. Still, nothing will come of it. He's married to his horse farm."

Susan shook her head and flashed a look that said, "Don't believe it."

Knowing she shouldn't eavesdrop, Libby couldn't seem to summon the will to walk away.

"You just don't know men, Emily. He tired of you. He'll tire of his farm. And mark my words. He'll tire of that chit out there."

"You're wrong, Caroline. He didn't tire of me. He chose the farm over me. For you, it's not even a matter of choice."

The voices trailed off.

Libby cleared her throat and glanced at Susan, who shrugged and said with an apologetic smile, "It seems the widows Caroline Hillier and Emily Jones are having a chat about your Colin."

Remaining silent, she nodded.

"I hope you don't take anything they say to heart," Susan said. "Caroline is a viper, who's not happy unless she's sinking her fangs into someone, usually someone else's husband. And I'd heard Colin and Emily were seeing each other until about a month ago. I'm not sure if he broke off things, or if they ended of their own volition. What I do know about Colin—he would not be with you if Emily was his main interest."

Struggling to smile, Libby tried not to worry about something she had no control over. Unfortunately, one question ate at her. What would happen when she left? Colin would definitely find solace somewhere. Somehow, the thought of him spending time with either woman didn't sit right with her. Neither woman seemed to have Colin's best interest at heart. If she couldn't be here, the next best thing would be someone who made him happy, no matter that the idea pierced her heart.

Susan must have seen the sadness creep into her smile, because she grasped Libby's hand and squeezed. "Let's forget their conversation and go and find our men," she said with forced cheerfulness. "I have a hankering for some dancing."

Still gripping Libby's hand, Susan tugged to get her moving in the direction of the house.

The men were in the same spot, apparently waiting for their return.

"Time's up, dear," Susan said, laughing. She released Libby's hand and grabbed her husband's. "Let Libby and Colin enjoy the evening. You can always talk later, but one can only dance at balls."

Colin watched Susan and her husband take to the dance floor before turning to Libby with an outstretched hand. "Come, my sweet. Susan's right. The music beckons. I don't know what came over me. Imagine me forfeiting an opportunity to have you in my arms. It simply isn't done."

As he spun her around the room, his gaze zeroed in on hers, Libby felt as if they were the only two in the room. It was romantic and magical. She could dance with him like this forever, she thought, staring dreamily into his eyes.

If she wasn't dancing, he was introducing her to people. Giselle came and went, staying only until some other young buck came to offer his hand for another dance. Libby couldn't remember a time when she'd had so much fun. The night never lost its magic until Libby noticed a beautiful woman with a calculating stare bearing down on them.

"Why, Colin, darling," she said, ignoring Libby as if she didn't exist. "I didn't know you were out of mourning?" Her smile matched the calculation in her eyes. “So sorry to hear about your wife. I’m sure her death came as a shock to you.”

Colin nodded, his smile identical to hers. “Thank you for your concern.” He turned to Libby and pulled her closer, his stance protective. “May I present Elizabeth Edwards, a good friend of the family. Elizabeth, this is Caroline Hillier.”

Minding her manners, Libby offered a polite smile, but was frozen on the spot with an icy glare. This woman was the consummate Stepford wife, and Libby had no intention of allowing the woman’s tactics to scare her. “How do you do?” Her phony smile amped up ten degrees. “So nice to meet you.” She’d said the same words all night, but this time no one could miss the insincerity in them as she held out her hand.

Caroline extended limp fingers. “Likewise,” she said, her voice dripping with contempt.

Libby risked glancing at Colin and was surprised to see him straining to contain his anger. He truly didn’t like her, thank God, but Libby had to admit, Caroline Hillier was beautiful.

The vein on Colin’s forehead became more prominent and Libby realized he wasn’t merely angry. He was livid. He bowed. “If you will excuse us?” While leading Libby to the dance floor, he added, “I believe this is our dance.”

Once on the floor, Colin relaxed slightly. Shaking his head, with an apologetic smile on his face, he said, “I’m sorry about that. She’s a menace. Don’t mind anything she says. Caroline has always had this mistaken impression that I’m interested in her. I want you to know here and now, so there will be no misunderstandings. I am not interested in her now, was never in the past, and will never be in the future. Is that clear?”

Libby smiled. “Crystal.”

“Good.” He chuckled.

While they danced, Libby reflected on the conversation she’d overheard, but unwilling to spoil what was left of the evening, she refused to dwell on what it meant.

Giselle walked up as the event was clearly winding down. “I’m so sorry, Libby. I was not the best companion. But it looks like you are having a good time, *non*?"

"Yes, very much so."

"It looks like we all had fun," Colin said. "But we should call it a night." Offering his elbows, he added with a smile, "Shall we?"

Arm in arm, Colin escorted them out of the mansion. While they waited for their carriage, another beautiful woman walked up to them.

"Colin, I was hoping I might see you tonight."

He smiled. "Hello, Emily." He turned to Libby and Giselle, and made introductions.

Recognizing the name, Libby stiffened and offered another polite smile. Emily Jones seemed friendly enough, not the cold, calculating woman that defined Caroline Hillier. Still, her interest in Colin was more than apparent. Libby couldn't release the rigid line of her shoulders. "It truly is nice to meet a friend of Colin's," she said with more cheerfulness than she felt. "I've met so many wonderful people tonight."

They made small talk until their carriage rolled up and Colin said, "Can I drop you home, Emily?"

"No. I have an escort, but I appreciate the offer," she said as a man walked up to the small group. "Oh, there you are, Thatcher." Emily placed her hand on his arm. "Let me introduce you to Colin Thorpe."

Libby caught the look that passed between Colin and Emily, wondering what it all meant as they shook hands and made the appropriate comments before climbing inside the awaiting carriage.

On the trip back to the hotel, Libby's curiosity grew. Susan had said that Colin had been seeing the woman. Was he interested in her? "Emily seems nice," she commented a few minutes later. "Tell me about her."

"I've never given you any reason to doubt my love, have I?" He searched her face, his gaze too intense.

Libby cleared her throat, feeling a little foolish for the jealousy that seemed to have planted itself in her stomach and was now growing thorns.

"Emily's in my past and will stay there. Even though you won't be part of my future, you have nothing to fear from the widow." He patted her hand and gave it a gentle squeeze. "I am not a monk, Libby. We had a pleasant relationship for several months. I care about her as a friend, yes. But that is as far as it goes. We ended our liaison well before you and I became intimate. No one has captured my heart like you have, and I doubt anyone else ever will." He lifted her hand to his lips and kissed it. "You have nothing to worry about from Emily. Trust me, my love."

Chapter 17

Colin waited patiently while Libby played maid to Giselle after arriving back at the hotel from the ball. Then Libby gathered up the necessary items and he ushered her into his suite. Now that he had her to himself, he intended to take his time and fully savor their night together. Slowly he undressed her. As her garments fell to the floor one by one, he kissed and caressed each exposed area.

Once Libby was naked, Colin quickly dispensed of his own clothing. He began gently rubbing her foot, following the action with kisses. The sensation caused her to giggle. He did it again and drew the same response.

"I love the sound of your laughter," he said, adding another kiss.

She stroked his sides with a soft caress, an area that the minx knew was sensitive. Colin flinched and glanced at her. Both erupted into gales of laughter and fell back on the pillows laughing.

Their laughter died down and all teasing ceased.

Colin caught Libby's head in his hands. He lost himself in her light green eyes and said in a fervent voice, "I love you, Elizabeth." He kissed her once. Twice. Three times, before adding, "Your love has given me so much happiness in the short time I've known you. I never knew I could feel so alive."

Their lips reconnected for a soul-searching kiss that went on forever. Colin wondered if he would crave her kisses if he had ten years to spend with her or a lifetime, rather than the short while they were given?

Her hands slid up and down his body. Her tender touch made him yearn to hold her and never let go.

"Oh, Libby, you're my light," he whispered. "My world will darken when you leave."

Pain swept into her eyes before she closed them. When she opened them again, they were rimmed with moisture.

"It unmans me to see your tears. I'm sorry, Libby. I don't mean to make you cry." He kissed her face, tasting the salty drops. The action, meant to comfort, soon changed to need—the need to be closer together, to be joined as one. Colin smiled as his erection grew. "See what you do to me. If I had a lifetime with you, I'd never have my fill," he murmured before pressing into her and feeling like he'd come home.

Afterward, Libby fell asleep while he held her close, unwilling to relinquish his hold. He stared into the dark room with a heavy heart.

As dawn crept into the horizon, Colin hugged her closer. The movement was enough to wake her. She opened her eyes and the affection lurking there drew him like manna draws a starving man. He shouldn't want her after last night, but that didn't seem to matter. Coherent thought vanished the second he entered her warmth and didn't return until long after they'd both skyrocketed into pleasure.

She stretched, giving him a sultry look that only added to his desire to keep her close. "I'm feeling very replete and boneless," she purred. "I relished being in your arms the entire night. I could stay this way forever."

Colin sighed and kissed her forehead before making himself comfortable beside her. The love he felt for her was near to bursting in his heart. Libby might not be considered a classic beauty, but she was the most beautiful woman he'd ever known. Her beauty came from within, from her soul. Her presence shed light on all of those around her, especially on him. All night he'd lain awake with an ache in his heart thinking about how dark his life would be without her. No longer content to let her leave without giving her his name, he needed her vows. He brought up the only subject he could think of that would get her to agree to such a thing.

"Libby, I've been thinking." He picked up her hand and kissed it. "What if you're with child?"

"I doubt that I am," she said, dismissing his concerns with a warm smile.

"But what if you are?" he whispered urgently.

"I don't know how to answer that." She sat up, clearly flustered. "What are you getting at?"

"There are ways to prevent conception, but we've done none of them. So, it is possible that you could be carrying my babe right now, correct," he asked, meeting her gaze.

"It's a very slight possibility and if that happened, I'd cherish your child more than life itself. You have to know that."

"Maybe so, but if you've conceived, what about the child? What are you going to say when he or she asks about me?" He couldn't stem the intensity of his feelings from showing in his expression.

Libby inhaled sharply, eyeing him thoughtfully. "Colin, exactly what are you saying?"

"Marry me, Libby. Stay with me for as long as we have left as my wife. I want no bastards hanging over my head in the future. When you go back, there is no way I'll know whether my seed took or not. If you marry me, I'll at least be assured that I have honored my responsibilities. I want my child to know that I cared enough to give you both my name, even though I'm back in the past."

☙

Libby stared at Colin, open-jawed. The man just kept surprising her. Never in her life had she expected him to offer marriage. She closed her eyes, wishing she wasn't using birth control and thinking about what he wanted. God help her, but more than anything, she wanted it too.

"Can we do that here, so quickly?"

"Yes, we only need a judge. I've a friend who can do it without delay. It won't be a church ceremony. That would require several weeks' wait for the banns to be announced. I don't think we have that long." Libby was still speechless, and after a long delay, Colin said, "We can keep it secret, except for Gus and Berta—and a few others. But we can be together without shame. I dislike sneaking around."

She eyed him warily. "What happens when I go home? I mean, if we marry?"

"You go home, and I stay here, but you'll have my name. That's what will happen."

"Will you consider yourself married?"

"Of course I'll consider myself married," Colin said indignantly.

"I don't know about this." Libby shook her head, knowing she was adding fuel to a fire that could easily grow out of control. "I love you enough to want you to be happy and that means finding someone to love after I'm gone." It broke her heart to say it and it hurt too much to think of it happening, but she had to set him free. "Will you do that?"

"Without a crystal ball, I don't know how I'll feel," he said. "Just know that if it's possible for me to find someone else, I will, but don't make it a requirement." He ran a hand through his hair. "I should ask the same of you, but to be quite honest, the thought of you in some other man's arms while I can't have you leaves me hollow. Still, I do want you to be happy. In your time I'll be dead, so you'll in fact be a widow," he admitted tersely. "And free to remarry."

Libby put a hand to his lips. "Don't say that. I don't want to think that kind of thoughts."

"Then marry me. Make me the happiest man in the world."

Blinking back tears, she swallowed hard. "But it won't be forever."

"None of us knows how long we have. Please, Libby. It will rest my fears. I can't live with myself—with the thought of you going into the world without knowing that I cared enough to give you my name."

Tears streamed down her face and a foreboding feeling crept into her heart. "Oh, Colin," she whispered, nodding. "This keeps getting deeper. We should never have made love that night under the trees. All we're doing is prolonging our agony. Yet, I can't fight you. As long as I'm here, more than anything, I want to be your wife. How could I not? You're the love of my life."

"Thank you, Libby," Colin whispered, kissing her tears as he'd done the night before. The gentle action only brought on more tears.

"Shush," he said, then smiled. "I seem to have a knack for making you cry." His smile turned wistful. "Maybe we shouldn't have consummated things, but we can't go back, only forward. At least I'll rest easy, knowing that you'll have my name. Thank you for that."

Libby nodded, wondering how things had spiraled so far out of control. Still, she had no power to stop from falling deeper into love with him. After a while, she quit fighting the draw and could only accept the feelings as something that was meant to be.

Colin held her close for long minutes before kissing her forehead and untangling himself from her embrace. After rising, he started to dress and then stepped over to the side of the bed. "I have lots to do today. Get some more sleep while I'm gone. I'll keep anyone from coming in to clean until later. I'll also make arrangements for our wedding." He bent over and kissed her. "I love you, Libby. I'll be back before lunch."

After watching him leave, she lay back against the pillow thinking about what the day would yield. The foreboding she felt earlier was gone, replaced by the thought of being Colin's wife, which now left her completely relaxed. Somehow it felt right. The idea brought a big smile to her face. Libby closed her eyes. In moments, she drifted off to sleep.

When Colin let himself back into the room hours later, he spied Libby still sleeping peacefully. He moved over to the bed and watched her for a few minutes. Discarding his boots, trousers, and shirt, he lay down next to her, pulling her into his embrace. In minutes he, too, was sound asleep.

Two hours later he slowly woke. He glanced at his timepiece on the nightstand and noticed that it was getting late. He bent to kiss Libby's neck, nuzzling her awake.

She smiled and stretched. Colin felt her grin as he continued nuzzling her. She eventually met his lips with an urgent mouth.

Colin allowed the kiss to continue. Just before he lost all logic, as he had a way of doing when kissing her, he lifted his head. His grin turned into satisfaction personified. "I love waking up with you, but we have no time to dally. I've made arrangements for Judge Henry to do the honors. The Websters will be meeting us at two o'clock."

He arose from the bed and grabbed his trousers. When he noticed that Libby was still lying there with her hands under her chin, watching him, he planted a hand on her bottom, hidden beneath the sheet. Giving it a squeeze, he said, "Come, my love, time's a-wasting."

He moved to pick up his shirt.

Libby sighed. "I'd be perfectly happy to spend the day in bed." She sat up.

Chuckling, Colin stopped dressing and watched her stretch. She reached for the sheet and tucked it under both arms. He laughed as an embarrassed flush rose from her tempting breasts and traveled all the way to her forehead.

She quickly pulled the sheet over her head.

His chuckle receded to a wide grin. "No need to cover yourself.

I've seen it all before." He bent over, pulled the sheet down, and kissed the top of her breast. "And I've tasted it all before. You're lovely. I could watch you forever."

Libby blushed a deeper shade of pink. "I know I'm not well endowed. My boyish shape is hardly one that elicits men's passion."

Colin brought her hand to his lips and kissed it. "Want to bet? You'll always bring out my passion. I'm ready and willing even now to taste you. Besides, your breasts are beautifully shaped and plenty big for my purposes." Then he stood and pulled his shirt over his head and said, "Now quit stalling and get dressed."

"Yes sir, Mr. Thorpe." She jumped up and saluted him.

When done dressing, they went to collect Giselle.

"So, what is on the agenda for today? More sight-seeing," she asked, answering Colin's rap at the door.

Libby grinned. "How about attending a wedding?"

"Really?" Giselle shrieked, practically jumping up and down.

Colin winced and said with a snort, "What is it about women and weddings that always prompts such excitement?"

Libby's grin stayed in place. "I don't have the slightest clue why. We also love babies and have to dance around when anyone turns up pregnant. It's a chick flick kind of thing."

Holding out both elbows, Colin drew his brow together. "What is a chick flick?"

Libby only laughed and waved a hand. "Never mind. Suffice it to say, we women love marriage and babies."

"A fact I'm well aware of. It's a chick flick that I'm having trouble grasping."

They strolled through the hallway, down the stairs, and into the lobby, laughing and bantering back and forth as they entered the restaurant for an early lunch.

After a hearty meal, Colin looked at his timepiece. "We have barely enough time to make it to Judge Henry's chambers." He arose. "Shall we?"

Susan and Malcolm Webster were already there waiting for them.

Judge Henry gathered everyone together and began the ceremony. "Dearly beloved. We are gathered here…"

The intensity of Colin's gaze pierced Libby's heart and stole her breath as the judge asked, "Do you, Colin Thorpe, take this woman, Elizabeth Edwards, for your wife from this day forward, to have and to hold, to love and to cherish, for better or worse, richer or poorer, in sickness and in health, till death do you part?"

Colin nodded, his demeanor sober. "I do."

She kept her gaze fastened on his as the judge turned her way and asked her the same question.

With all the enthusiasm she could muster, Libby said, "I do." She had to pinch herself to make sure she wasn't dreaming when she heard the words, "I pronounce you man and wife. You may now kiss your bride," and Colin captured her lips with his. As Colin slipped a gold ring on her finger, the judge said. "It pleases me to present Mr. and Mrs. Colin Thorpe."

Amazing how a ceremony that took less than fifteen minutes from start to finish produced a sort of transformation. Libby felt different. She knew then that her love for Colin would last her a lifetime. Looking at the smiling faces around her, it all seemed so surreal, like it was happening to someone else.

When all the paperwork was signed, Colin shook the judge's hand, then turned to Libby. "Well, Mrs. Thorpe? How does it feel to be married to someone who loves you with all his heart?"

Libby's heart skipped a beat as she whispered, "I will always cherish the idea of being your wife." She offered a wobbly smile. "Even if it's only for a short while. I love you, Colin Thorpe. For as long as I live, you will own my heart."

"What more could a man ask?" Colin's smile, dulled with sadness, never reached his eyes.

Everyone started talking at once, drawing their attention.

The Websters each gave Libby a hug. Then Giselle stood, waiting her turn. "I wish you happiness, Libby, for as long as time allows." She winked. "Didn't I tell you he wanted to marry you? I can sense these things."

"Thank you, Giselle." Libby hugged her tightly. "I am happy right now. What more could anyone ask for? Good friends and the love of my life all in the same room at the same time." She took a step back and warned, "Don't forget. We're keeping our wedding a secret for the time being."

Giselle smiled warmly. "I know, Libby. I won't breathe a word of it to anyone."

Colin interrupted. "If we want to see the balloon ascension, we need to hurry. I've had the hotel fix us a supper and provide a blanket for the afternoon. Come, you two. We don't want to miss the show."

They spent the rest of the afternoon and evening with the Websters and Giselle at the park-like grounds where hot air balloons had taken off.

Sitting on a blanket, watching the people all around, Libby thought back to events in her own time and noted similarities. Simon Harrington, a young man who'd been at the ball the night before, spotted Giselle and introduced himself. He claimed a spot next to her on the blanket. The Websters had their own blanket, which was laid out next to Libby and Colin's.

Libby couldn't remember a more carefree afternoon. The weather was wonderful, neither too hot nor too cold. The light breeze felt good on her face. Billowy, fluffy white clouds sailed through the sky, every now and again covering up the sun, cooling things off a bit.

On a bandstand in the distance, a band played the latest tunes while couples danced. Libby recognized some of the pieces, but didn't know them by name. Life seemed to move at a much slower pace here in 1874. People of all kinds packed the park—children playing games, men talking with other men, women strolling with parasols, showing off their finest clothes.

When the balloons lifted off, it was another colorful sight to see, again reminding Libby of the Derby Festival. Every year, during the two-week celebration preceding the Kentucky Derby, there was a balloon race with a balloon glow the night before. Maybe that's how the tradition started, she thought, feeling a little homesick and remembering Bev and their tentative plans. But she quickly recovered when she looked over at Colin and caught his smile. She'd be home soon enough. When that happened, there would be a hole in her heart a mile wide. Shoving that out too, she gazed up at the sky and the rainbow of colored balloons that headed for a distant target.

At dusk they enjoyed a sumptuous meal, compliments of the Galt House restaurant. The Websters had brought wine. Libby's glass was never empty from the moment she sat down earlier in the afternoon. Pleased to watch another Derby Festival tradition, she was slightly tipsy when the fireworks started, not long after darkness set in.

All too soon the evening was over. As they headed back to the hotel, Libby marveled over the magic of the last two days and seeing life as it existed in the past. As much as she missed her modern conveniences, she couldn't get over how people truly celebrated simple pleasures. Maybe even more so, because there weren't so many distractions.

There was a *joie de vivre*—a love of life—present in everything they did. Children didn't miss video games; after all, they hadn't been invented yet. Instead, they took pleasure in hitting a ball with a stick and playing hide and seek. Adults didn't care if there were no television or movies to watch. They enjoyed the afternoon's festivities and the conversations at hand.

After observing it all, Libby finally understood it was the people and their interactions that made the world great. That never changed in over a hundred years. It suddenly hit her what a great gift she'd been granted—to remember this time and these people for the rest of her life.

Outside their hotel room, one Colin told her he was happy to be sharing openly with his wife, he opened the door.

"Come here, my tipsy vixen," he said, picking her up and carrying her over the threshold and into the room. He placed her on the bed. "I enjoyed the day with you, Mrs. Thorpe, watching you have a good time. This has been one of the happiest in recent memory. When I'm with you, I feel as if everything's right in the world."

"I think the bed's spinning." Libby giggled. "I can't believe you got me drunk on my wedding night."

He sat down next to her and helped her sit, then began undoing her buttons. "I hope you're not too intoxicated to partake of our wedding night, my dear." He chuckled and continued in a more teasing vein. "I sensed you were a woman to lead me far astray, but I never imagined you'd be too inebriated to consummate our vows."

Libby merely laughed. "Well, Mr. Thorpe, if I'm inebriated, it's only because I want so badly what only you have to give."

Boldly she gripped his shirt and tugged, bringing his lips to hers.

Chapter 18

The room seemed empty when Libby awoke. She vaguely remembered Colin easing out of bed earlier and telling her he wouldn't be long. He promised they'd have the rest of the day together once he concluded his business. She got up, moved to the bathroom, and finished her morning rituals. Her riding habit was the easiest thing in her small wardrobe to put on without help. She slipped it on, shaking her head at the ridiculousness of how much energy it took to dress.

After impatiently pacing the length of the room, Libby finally sat in a chair near the window to wait for Colin.

She checked her timepiece and noted only a half an hour had passed, yet it felt like two. The sun rose higher above the horizon. It was too glorious a day to be inside. Decision made, she hurried out into the hallway.

At Giselle's room, she rapped on the door several times with no response. Figuring she must still be sleeping, Libby glanced longingly toward the staircase. The outside beckoned. Colin's warning about going out alone pricked her conscience, yet it would take too long to wait for Giselle. What could it hurt to take a quick walk on such a perfect morning?

Fresh air greeted her and sunshine warmed her face as she strolled up the block, enjoying the quiet. Most of the shops were closed and the streets were empty of both people and animals. When she reached a cross street, a view of the river caught her attention.

A big riverboat, its paddles slowly pushing the boat north, was a sight to see. It reminded her of the *Belle of Louisville* in her own time, and viewing one in the right setting was captivating. Libby continued walking toward the water, not paying attention to her surroundings until she neared the banks and realized she was utterly alone. She looked around. Everything looked peaceful. Still, something about the stillness bothered her, and the hairs on the back of her neck stood on end.

Birds chirped and bees buzzed, but the sounds did little to ease the sense of dread that shot through her. Feeling a little out of her element, she turned to retrace her steps as Colin's warning replayed in her head.

Someone yelled. She glanced behind her and noted a group of young teen boys headed her way. The thought that they were just kids and shouldn't concern her quickly changed to alarm once she noticed their menacing expressions.

"Looky here. See what the river's drug in, Jessie." Libby took a closer look at the kid who'd spoken and realized he was older and most likely their ringleader. "Looks like we got us a bird ripe fer th' pluckin'."

"Yeah, Kid, look at her in her fancy getup. I bet she's got sumthin' worth stealin'. "

"My thinkin' exactly."

The boys were still a ways from her when she turned around to walk backward up the hill. "Aren't you a little young to be leading kids to accost innocent people taking in the sights," she asked the obvious leader of the pack, piercing a pair of hard eyes with her bold stare.

With every hurried step, Libby worked at maintaining a safe distance, veering in the direction of Main Street. Fear had her heart pumping, but she'd die before she would show that emotion.

"We're old enough and they do what I tell them," Kid answered, not taking his eyes off her.

"What happened to playing stickball or kick the can?" She only hoped she could keep him talking until she reached Main Street.

"Looks can be deceivin'." His laugh held no humor. "Stickball's a little dull for th' likes of these brats. Like me, they prefer more sportin' games."

"So confronting someone alone is sporting to you? Where's the challenge in that? Seems to me you guys are just a big bunch of bullies."

"Doesn't matter what ya call us, we'll still be takin' yer purse. Hand it over."

Still moving backward in giant steps, Libby shook her head. "Sorry to disappoint you, but I'm not carrying a purse."

"Coin's not the only thing someone like you is good for."

Panicked, Libby turned and increased her speed to a full-on sprint.

Even though most of the kids were fairly small, three or four were much bigger than she. Kid looked to be around her age and outweighed her by at least fifty pounds. They *would* hurt her if they caught her.

Her adrenalin pumped, spurring her on. She didn't know how much of a lead she had, if any, but she wasn't about to waste precious seconds looking back to see if they followed.

Someone grabbed her shirt from behind. She fought to pull out of his grasp and he ripped her bonnet off. He snatched a handful of her now uncovered hair, and her head snapped back, throwing her off balance. Pain ripped through Libby. The stench of alcohol that hit her was enough to terrorize her further. She kicked, scratched, and kneed him in the groin with force.

Swearing, he released her to grab his crotch. "Why, you bitch. Get 'er, boys," he yelled.

Libby ran.

Hoofbeats sounded behind her and she increased her speed. As the rider closed the distance, she prayed one of them wasn't on horseback.

A shot rang out.

Seconds later, a horse and rider came up from behind. "Good God, Libby!"

Recognizing Colin's voice, she stopped and looked back. Struggling to control her labored breathing, she noted the others had dispersed as fast as roaches seeking cover when the light turns on.

"What the hell do you think you're doing out here unescorted?"

She slumped with relief, thankful he'd come to her rescue. Until she caught his livid expression that said she'd gone above and beyond recklessness.

Anger, directed at herself, filled her. The sudden desire to go back home—to her own time—made her realize how out of place she felt here in the past. At this point, she didn't need to be reminded of her stupidity. He'd told her not to go out without Giselle and now she knew why he hadn't wanted her to go. She met his heated gaze with a lifted chin. "I was out for a walk, minding my own business."

Heck, she was less than three blocks from her hotel. Suddenly living in 1874 wasn't fun any longer. Worse, she missed Bev. Tears slid down the sides of her face as he dismounted and stormed over to her.

"Are you all right?" He stooped to pick up her bonnet that had fallen in the scuffle and handed it to her.

Nodding, she attempted to tie her bonnet with unsteady hands. "I'm fine, only shaken."

"You should be shaken. When I realized it was you those boys were after, my heart almost stopped," he said, still vibrating with anger. "I distinctly remember telling you to never go out unescorted," he said with a steely edge to his voice. "Did you think I was jesting? And to be alone down by the river, of all places? Do you wish to die?"

"It's broad daylight on a Sunday morning." Her attempt at rationalization only enraged him further.

"So you think the gangs from the House of Refuge stop their brutality to pray just because it's Sunday? My God, Libby, the little thugs are dangerous."

"They're just kids."

"That might be true, but desperation makes them dangerous. They've nothing to lose. Do you realize what would have happened if I hadn't been riding along?" He held out his hand, his expression unyieldingly cold. "Come."

At the hotel entrance, he stopped and nodded. "I need to go to the livery. Go on up. I'll be there shortly." He turned to walk down the road, still leading his horse.

Libby could tell by the sound of his voice and his mannerisms that he was still angry, which did nothing to stop her mood from heading south.

Once in her room, she went over to the window and stood looking out, not seeing anything, wondering how life could be so unsafe for a woman. One couldn't even walk down the street without being fair game for anyone bigger and stronger. Those who'd hounded her had been mere boys. Were they worse once they grew up? Did men think they could take what they wanted if they could get away with it? Was this what it was like for women in the past?

The thought horrified her.

The door opened and closed, announcing Colin's return. She ignored him and kept her unseeing stare on the street below.

He strode farther into the room, and she sensed his attention was directed at her.

"I'm still trying to understand how you could be so thoughtless as to go out unescorted," he finally said. "And down to the river, no less? The area is full of riffraff."

Libby spun around. "I didn't know it was unsafe."

His jaw hardened. "You should have heeded my warning."

"I went for a walk. A simple walk," she said with a sinking heart. She couldn't believe he was lecturing her, even though what he'd asked did make sense now that she'd been attacked. Still, she didn't like it. Not one little bit.

"Why did you disregard my wishes?"

Hands on hips, she gaped at him, feeling as if she had to defend herself. "You think I intentionally disregarded your wishes? That I set out today to see what I could do to tick you off?" Problem was, she knew he had a right to be upset, but it didn't slow her building anger.

"You completely ignored my orders and you know it," Colin countered.

In no mood to be treated like a child, Libby lifted her chin. "For your information, Mr. Thorpe, I'm a grown woman." She'd had enough of Dave's instructions on how to dress and act, which made her a tad sensitive to being ordered about. It didn't matter that Colin was only concerned with her safety and well-being. "I don't need a man telling me what I can and cannot do," she ground out.

His face reddened as the temperature in his voice dropped even lower. "And I'm telling you, as your husband, if you ever do that again, I'll take you over my knee and tan your backside but good. Do you hear me?"

"How dare you!" Incensed, she poked him in the chest with a finger. "You think that because I wear your ring you have the right to tell me what to do?"

"You're damned right I have that right. You're my wife. I am responsible for you. It's my duty to protect you."

"You don't own me. I am responsible for me—no one will ever own me. I told you when I met you that I answer to no man."

Colin ran a hand through his hair. "How can I make you see how foolish your actions were?" He rubbed the bridge of his nose with his thumb and forefinger and took a few deep breaths before his voice gentled. "Libby, this is a different era than you're used to. My world is not the same as yours. Some situations are dangerous and it's up to men to protect their women."

She crossed her arms, not particularly happy to have something she'd discovered firsthand substantiated.

Glancing at her, he shook his head. "I can see that your attitude's still combative. At this point, there seems to be nothing that'll get through to you and I'm tired of arguing about it." He caught her gaze, his dead serious. "I'm sorry if you don't like it, but that's the way it is. Now accept it. I'll brook no further comment on the subject. Do you understand?"

Libby's control snapped. "Oh, I understand, all right," she threw out in her most derisive tone. "I understand that men are Neanderthals in 1874." Ignoring fresh tears, she raised her voice. "I hate being trussed up like a turkey. I hate the restrictive clothes. I hate wearing a bonnet." She grabbed the thing off her head and threw it on the floor. "I hate the fact that there is no electricity, no cars—nothing that I'm used to. Everything here is different. The people are different. Nothing's familiar. I can't even take a walk by myself on a Sunday morning. It's a woman's torture chamber."

She marched stoically to the bed and gave Colin one more defiant look, before sitting down with tears streaking down her face.

An expression of stunned horror flitted over his features. No one spoke for long seconds. Finally, he said in a quiet voice, "I'm sorry you hate it so much, Libby. But that doesn't change my role, which is to make sure you are safe. Don't you see? I died a thousand deaths when I recognized you in that thug's clutches. My heart stopped at the thought that if I had been but a moment later, your throat could have been slit. You attacked him. He wasn't going to let you go after such an insult."

Drained, Libby slumped forward and thought about what Colin was saying. Now that anger wasn't guiding her, she saw his point so clearly. That did nothing to make her feel better, in fact made her feel worse…defeated even. Still, she had to make things right between them.

"I'm sorry, Colin," Libby said with a sigh. "I didn't think. I know you're only doing what you think is best. Thank you for being there for me when I needed you most."

Colin walked over to the bed, sat down beside her, and pulled her into his embrace. He did nothing but hold her while time stood still. Then taking her head with his hands, he kissed her tenderly.

"Promise me, Libby, you'll take care?" he whispered, pulling away. "I know it's restrictive here, but I don't want to see them pull your lifeless body from the river because you've been foolish."

At Libby's questioning look, he sighed and nodded. "It happens."

"I promise." She gave him a tentative smile. "I won't do anything so stupid again."

Colin smiled back and held her close. "Thank you for that."

They sat in silence until she asked, "Who were those kids? They seemed too young to be so hardened."

"They're orphans, the city's discards. There are so many lost children, especially after the war. It's been almost ten years, but still things are tough for some. They are uneducated, untrained, and poor. 'Tis easier for our city's citizens to accept their thievery rather than try to truly help them because it seems no one gives a damn about their future." He was quiet for several minutes before asking, "So, they've done away with social injustice and poverty in the twenty-first century?"

"Not entirely," Libby said, shaking her head.

"Are there no lost children in your time?"

His question brought to mind the thought that maybe things really hadn't changed in over a hundred years. Only the twenty-first century's problems were different; still dangerous, but different.

"Yes, there are a lot of lost children in my time. I guess no matter how things have changed and advanced, there's still a bit of familiarity about them."

"I'd venture to say that the area where these children live is dangerous," he said, smiling sadly. "Do you go unescorted into areas where such children exist?"

Catching his meaning, Libby sighed. Yes, there were dangerous areas in her city. As much as it galled her, she had to admit the fact. "Point taken."

His smile turned gentle as he took her face in his hands and kissed her again. When he lifted his head, his intense blue gaze trapped hers. "I'm glad I finally got you to understand. I love you. 'Tis not my desire to hamper your freedom, but remaining safe requires it."

She nodded and he changed the subject. "Have you eaten?"

Libby shook her head.

"Are you hungry?"

Keeping her eyes on his, Libby nodded.

"Come. Let's go find Giselle and have lunch. I'm starved."

He stood and pulled her up with him. Together they walked to Giselle's door.

"We're getting a bite to eat," he said when she opened her door. "Would you care to join us?"

Readily agreeing, Giselle grabbed her bonnet, rushed out into the hallway, and took Colin's offered elbow. They walked to the hotel dining room much the same as the day before, only this time the mood wasn't quite as jubilant.

Colin was unusually quiet during lunch. He was pleasant enough, just not as carefree and happy as he'd been earlier. Libby figured he was still upset about the incident. Heavens, *she* was still upset about it too. Nonetheless, his subdued manner started to alarm her. She'd come to know him pretty well in the past month. He seemed to be withdrawing from her and she sensed his mind was far away, not on lunch or what she and Giselle had been talking about.

"Where are we going tonight," she asked, trying to draw him out.

He shrugged. "Tonight, Malcolm and Susan have invited us to dinner." He smiled and added, "Sorry, ladies. No dancing tonight."

Giselle's smile was wistful. "I had such a nice time last night. I'm not used to these late evenings. I slept in today, but I'm still tired."

Libby agreed. "I would prefer a quiet evening."

"Well, ladies? What should we do this afternoon? I can have George bring the carriage around. We can drive around and view the sights."

Both Libby and Giselle nodded. For the next few hours, they toured the city by horse-drawn carriage. Every now and then, Colin pointed out a house or home of one of those he knew. Other than that, he didn't partake of the conversation.

As the afternoon turned into early evening, Libby became more apprehensive. Though polite and as charming as ever, Colin seemed distracted.

"Are you sure you aren't still mad at me for this morning?" she whispered to him when Giselle stepped out of the carriage ahead of them.

He offered the same sad smile he'd given her too many times that afternoon and patted her hand. "No, my love. I'm no longer angry. I have a lot on my mind, is all." He leaned in to give her a gentle kiss on the cheek before jumping out of the carriage and helping her out.

Libby blinked back tears of frustration as Giselle drew her aside and asked, "Is everything all right between you and Colin?"

Smiling, Libby nodded. "Of course. I think we're both tired after last night." Giselle might remind her of Bev, but Libby thought it best not to mention her troubles despite the need to unburden herself. Another wave of homesickness enveloped her. As Libby allowed Colin to escort her upstairs to their room, she really missed Bev.

Colin remained aloof as he helped her dress for dinner.

During the ride to the Webster home on Third Street, he was more open and talkative, which eased Libby's mind somewhat. Still, she sensed he was having the same kind of doubts she was having. She didn't belong here and she missed her own time, but the thought of leaving him behind was unendurable. Not after all that had happened earlier that day. She also worried that she might never go back. That thought tore her in two. Part of her wanted to stay with Colin forever, and the other part wanted nothing better than to go home, where men were normal and life existed on a more enlightened plane.

After a pleasant evening with the Websters, a couple she truly enjoyed, Libby sat next to Colin on the ride back to the hotel and realized he'd lapsed back to his uncommunicative self.

"Will you please tell me what's wrong?" The need to make things right between them was stronger than ever.

He glanced at her and something flickered in his gaze. Sadness or weariness. Libby wasn't quite sure, but there was definitely something he wasn't telling her.

"Why do you assume there's something wrong," he asked.

"Because of what happened this morning."

He smiled. As all his others that day, the smile held no joy, only resignation. "That's over," he said, patting her hand. "I'm just weary. I will certainly enjoy falling into bed tonight. It's been a long day." He then stretched out his legs and his attention went to the passing scenery.

Libby sighed, not liking this side of him at all. If only he'd tell her what was eating him, then she could fix it. What really scared her was the idea that she couldn't.

Chapter 19

Their hotel room door closed with a final click and noise from the bustling Galt House lobby died, encasing them in silence. Colin drew Libby closer, wrapping his arms around her. She smiled. He seemed to be himself again. Engulfed in his warmth, she breathed in his scent—one of horses, leather, and sweat. Totally male and totally Colin Thorpe.

Her spine relaxed one vertebra at a time as his strong hands worked out the knotted tension. A nice ending to a day that had begun so horribly, she thought dreamily, shoving any remaining images of her attack to the far reaches of her mind, along with all of the doubts that had hounded her during dinner.

His lips caressed her face, a gentle and soothing balm for her hurts. Eventually, his mouth found hers. The kiss went on and on. Libby could stay in this suspended state of pleasure for a lifetime. Only she didn't have a lifetime, she remembered. But she wouldn't dwell on that either.

He lifted his head and turned her. Playing the lady's maid, he undid each button, taking his time, adding feather-light caresses along her bare arms or fingering the lace before dipping beneath with a soft touch where the mound of her breast met material. His warm, moist mouth slowly followed. Her head fell back, giving him more access. Exquisite ripples of heat rushed to her core, extending outward, sending warmth from head to toe.

Her dress dropped to the floor.

With hands on her shoulders, he gently repositioned her to face him. Then he worked on untying the nineteenth-century corset that worked with vice-like effectiveness on her midsection. Inhaling deeply, once freed of the hated garment, she focused on what his hands were now doing, languishing in more sensations.

As many times as they'd made love, Colin's actions felt different tonight. He still kissed and touched, but the quality in his hands seemed altered. There was a reverence in his touch, a hesitance in the slow and tentative contact. She fought to discern this new mood. It seemed as if he were trying to mark her with his hands while also trying to remember her with those same hands. But as soon as the thoughts were out, they dissipated. She couldn't concentrate when he used his skillful mouth and fingers so well, kissing and caressing. As her last item of clothing floated to the floor, Colin picked her up, carried her to the four poster bed, and gently laid her down.

He quickly divested himself of clothing before joining her. Still, Colin seemed in no hurry, keeping his pace slow and deliberate. Kissing…caressing…touching…stroking…making love with painstaking precision. Libby moved in response to his touch, offered herself up to his glorious lips. His skillful hands. By the time he stretched out, leaning over her, she was desperate to have him inside her. Once there, she craved to find the release she knew was forthcoming. Still, Colin kept his strokes unhurried, as if savoring every lengthy, extended, exquisitely slow thrust, tormenting her further. Libby fought to take the lead and increase the rhythm. But Colin would not yield control, continuing his deliberate in and out.

She moaned. The sensation of pleasure built, went on forever with each thorough stroke of her insides. When the wave came and absolute ecstasy engulfed her, she and Colin launched into simultaneous orgasms that didn't subside for long moments. Libby felt drained. She'd given him her body and soul, just as he had.

Fully sated and unable to move in the afterglow of their lovemaking, Libby's thoughts drifted to her earlier emotional meltdown that Colin witnessed after saving her from being brutally attacked. Or worse. Neither mentioned their fight or what preceded it. Remembering his preoccupation during the day and at dinner, everything now converged, permeating her brain in tormenting images. How could she have disregarded his warnings? She shouldn't have gone out alone and she shouldn't have been so upset over his autocratic attitude. His anger and concerns had been totally justified, given the era. In hindsight, she understood that now. But everything had hit at once and she'd reacted without thinking.

In a flash of insight, it dawned on Libby what he'd been doing—saying good-bye with his body. The thought rent a searing stab to her heart.

Tears streamed down her face. Never had she felt such pain.

☙

Colin felt her sobs and a sorrow of his own swept through him. Dying inside because he had no answers, he lifted up on his forearms and lowered his head to kiss her wet eyes. His mouth followed the trail of tears.

In a sob-wracked voice Libby said, "You're saying good-bye. Aren't you?"

He could only nod as he rolled over, not breaking contact with the woman he would love for all eternity. He held her within his strong grip, feeling helpless. Her out-of-control weeping pierced him to the core. His tormented whisper filled the air. "Yes, Libby." He stroked her soft arms in an effort to ease her pain, struggling to ignore his own. "I have to let you go."

"But what if I can't go back?"

"Have you really been trying," he asked solemnly. "Or simply been delaying the inevitable?"

Her tear-soaked eyes sought his, their grief overwhelming, even as they conveyed that she understood his meaning. After that first night, when he'd confronted her, she hadn't seemed in any big hurry to wish herself back. What's more, he hadn't wanted her to.

"Why?" she whispered seconds later. "Why not take all the time we've got?"

Anguish slipped out of his gaze, poured out in his voice. "Don't you see? I've been so selfish. You don't belong here. The longer you stay, the harder it will be for me to let you go." He broke off to swallow a lump in the back of his throat. "I was merely fooling myself. Pretending you would come to love my time and all I have to offer, that somehow you would be happy here. After the incident today, I realized I was living a delusion. When we were arguing, I saw such unhappiness." He sighed and wiped his face. In an effort to help her understand further, he said, "I saw the truth. This situation is too similar, too reminiscent of the experience with my first wife. I'd rather you go back to your own time than witness your becoming a bitter and unhappy woman."

"But, Colin, I'm not like Abigail."

"I know you could never be like Abigail. Still, you don't belong here. You belong in a different era and I won't risk having your unhappiness on my conscience. I no longer fear losing you. I'm now more afraid of changing you. I love you too much to allow that to happen." He pulled an unruly curl from her damp face and gentled his voice. "I want to remember you the way you are tonight."

He caught her gaze again, showing his resolve. "My mind is made up. When we get back to the farm, I want you to try *harder* to go home." At the shake of her head, Colin placed his hands on each side of her face, halting her and forcing her to see how much it meant to him. "Please, Libby. Abide by my wishes. Don't make this any more difficult. With every breath I take, I want you to stay. At the same time, I know that's not possible, and I accept it. You already possess all I have to give. You have my heart. You have my name, and anything I own, I'd yield to you. But it's not enough to keep you here." He held her stare. "You know I speak the truth."

Eventually she nodded her agreement as fresh tears tracked down her face.

He snuffed out the gas light and hugged her to him. Her gut-wrenching sobs filled the dark room. While Libby cried, all Colin could do was stroke her back in an attempt to comfort her with his touch.

"I've always known when the time came to return to my own century, leaving you would be heartbreaking. Reality is so much tougher than I imagined," she whispered, once she stopped crying. "I feel as if my heart is ripping in two."

With her tears spent, she finally drifted to sleep, lulled by his words of endearment and soothing touch. Lying awake, Colin held Libby close, as if doing so would keep her with him.

Though he wished with every fiber of his being for a different ending, he'd never regret loving her. She was his life, and insisting she return to her home took an enormous amount of willpower. She wasn't like Abby, but Libby would never be totally content in his world either, so he had little choice in setting his beautiful butterfly free. He wouldn't be the one to steal the dust off her wings, keeping her from flying again—eventually killing her.

☙

The morning dawned all too soon for Libby.

Silence reigned as she allowed Colin to help her into the carriage before he hefted himself up to sink into the seat beside her. Even Giselle was quiet, having picked up on their somber mood.

George quickly stowed their luggage, then climbed onto the driver's box and flicked the reins to get the horses moving.

As the carriage turned onto what was Highway 60 in her time, Libby stared out the window, focusing on all she'd be losing. She didn't want to think, didn't want to feel anymore. Doing both hurt too much. If only she had something to deaden the pain, she thought, praying for numbness to set in. Keeping her gaze on the scenery around her, she tried to memorize everything she saw. Her thoughts shifted to Gus's warning.

She smiled wanly. Gus wasn't wrong about the pain. But he'd been wrong about regretting her actions. How could she ever regret loving Colin or making love with him? Time spent in his arms was worth every bit of the pain she now endured. Nothing could change the fact that she loved him with all her heart, and she felt his love in return. She would remember him and the feeling for the rest of her life.

They had created memories that would remain etched in her mind's eye forever. Seems Colin's insistence of making some had been right on. Her smile widened. Then she chuckled. Why deny the truth? Colin Thorpe had been a hard man to ignore, which had been part of her problem from the moment she'd stepped into 1874.

Her small laugh caught Colin's attention. He looked up and his features broke into a wobbly grin. "It's good to see you smile again," he said. He glanced at Giselle, whose attention was focused on a book she was reading and whispered, "For a while there, I was afraid I'd taken the light of your smile from you."

"It's not your fault we fell in love," she whispered back.

"No, I don't think either of us could help falling in love." Colin cleared his throat, leaned in so that only Libby could hear. "But I regret pushing you to consummate our love. I should have taken Gus's words to heart. I'm sorry I hurt you, Libby. That was never my intent."

"You haven't hurt me," Libby murmured. "You know as well as I that we'd have ended up the same way eventually, no matter what we did to prevent it." Given the level of attraction between them, she was more surprised with how long they waited, despite the conservative nineteenth-century setting. "I'm only glad we didn't waste more precious time," she said a little louder. "While I wish the circumstances could be different, I could never be unhappy over loving you." She reached for his hand, brought it up to her lips, and kissed it. "Thank you for giving me the world in such a short time."

Giselle, obviously catching the last of the conversation and clearly not understanding what had happened, eyed them curiously. Finally she asked, "You talk as though you are leaving. I thought you couldn't go back yet?"

Libby's voice was as wistful as her smile when she added, "It seems I need to try harder." She'd confided in Giselle the day before after her companion questioned something Colin had said. Considering the era, Giselle had taken the news well, despite Libby's opinion that she really hadn't believed it. She would definitely believe it once Libby was gone.

"Wait." Giselle put up a hand. "I thought you were staying as long as you could. Why have you changed your mind?"

When Libby explained about her attack, Giselle's eyes grew the size of quarters. "Where was I? Why were you out alone?"

"You were still sleeping. I didn't want to disturb you."

"Oh, Libby, you should have woken me. I thought you knew how dangerous it could be."

Libby gave a soft snort. "Obviously not. I know it now."

"That explains why you are a little subdued, but I still don't understand why you are going back so soon. I was hoping we'd have a little time together before you left."

"I thought so too." Libby's smile became sadder as she glance at Colin. "Let's just say the incident made us both realize that I haven't tried very hard to go home in a while. I've foolishly been prolonging my departure."

"I'll miss you," Giselle whispered. She appeared to be fighting back tears.

"Don't cry." Libby shook her head and grasped her hand. "You've been a good companion these past three days." She squeezed reassuringly. "I will always treasure our friendship. You never judged me or judged my actions with Colin."

For the rest of the ride, her sadness was—if not completely forgotten—pushed to the side a bit. Libby didn't want her final hours with Colin to be filled with sorrow. She wanted him to remember her with the same happiness and love they'd shared during most of her stay. Sorrow would come later.

Once they arrived, Berta had Sarah fetch Gus and Nathan. Both came running from the stables. She then led the group inside to her big kitchen table, insisting on fixing lunch while Colin offered an abbreviated version of what had happened, that Libby was going home and why.

No one seemed happy with the news, but they accepted it without a word, as if they sensed talking about it would be unpleasant. Questions could wait until after Libby was gone.

While eating, Libby looked around the table and studied each face. Gus, Berta, Nathan. Then her gaze shifted to Colin, who nodded. These people had come to mean so much to her in such a short time. Colin wasn't the only one she would miss. Libby loved each and every person in the room. They'd become family. She swallowed the lump of sadness at the realization that she would miss them all much more than she thought possible. Unwilling to add to the somber mood with her thoughts, she kept them to herself.

Thankfully, Colin sensed her thoughts and kept his mood light for the rest of their meal. When done, she and Colin took one more ride out to their spot. He laid out the blanket. For long moments they did nothing but hold each other. This time Libby knew their lovemaking would be their last so she drew it out, much as he'd done the night before. She memorized the feel of his face in her hands, the shape of his muscular shoulders and chest, and she worked her way lower. When he entered her, Libby blinked back the moisture filling her eyes. This would be a joyous union. Tears would come later. As release took her, she wrapped her arms around him and whispered in his ear, "You'll always be my hero, Colin. I'll love you forever."

With their passion spent, Colin brushed back a lock of her hair and said, "We'll meet again in the hereafter, Elizabeth Thorpe."

As he helped her mount, she took one last look at the same place they'd first picnicked in the grass. She'd remember this spot forever.

Finally, her inevitable journey's end drew closer. Libby changed into her own clothes and walked up to Colin's front porch, where everyone she'd come to love had gathered. Gus, Berta, ten-year-old Nathan, and Giselle stood there, each wearing sad expressions. Even Colin's three children had made an appearance. His oldest looked like a miniature Colin, and Libby swallowed regret that she'd never had the chance to get to know him. The two girls were adorable, especially the baby. All three would hold a special place in her prayers because they were motherless. Her biggest wish for Sam, as she took his hand, was that Colin would find a woman worthy of these kids.

Once the children were ushered upstairs with their nannies, Libby had no more excuses to prolong her task.

"Good-bye," she whispered to Berta. "Thanks for taking me in."

She turned to Gus and hugged him. He shed a single tear and shook his head, clearing his throat. "I'll miss you. You're the best damn horseman I've ever known."

Unable to answer, she just nodded and moved to hug Giselle.

Colin's gentle good-bye kiss, one which spoke of a thousand wants and wishes never to be fulfilled, was almost her undoing. After releasing her lips, his eyes were misty.

"Good-bye, Elizabeth Thorpe. I'll love you forever," he whispered, gently pushing her toward the trees.

Colin thought his presence might hamper her chance for success, so with an aching heart, she quickened her pace, too afraid if she didn't hurry, her wish to go home would be halfhearted.

At the trees she closed her eyes, wishing and praying really hard to go home, unwilling to disappoint him.

In less than a minute, the ground gave way and the earth shook. Everything seemed to break apart. She felt herself falling and knew she was hurling forward in time. Her mind went blank as the world around her flew by in a hazy blur.

☙

Colin stared at the empty doorway Libby had walked through for an endless moment before following. He made his way to the twin oaks and stopped at the same spot he'd hidden that night—when she'd disappeared and then reappeared in a matter of seconds. Stepping farther in the shade to wait, he wanted to know the exact moment she'd be carried away in time.

His wait wasn't a long one.

Not more than five minutes elapsed when, standing in the shadows, he watched Libby cease to exist in 1874. He remained rooted, staring into the space where his life had vanished.

Eventually he slowly walked up the hill, feeling as if his heart had been torn asunder.

Upon entering, Colin didn't care that the house was shrouded in darkness. Abovestairs, Sam laughed at something Minnie said as she readied him and his sisters for bed. The sound didn't provide the usual joy it should have. He'd heard that children's needs had a way of helping one overcome grief. He prayed it was so. He thanked God for the purpose to carry on. At this moment, he needed his children more than they needed him.

Heading for his study, he wondered how he would bear the dimness without Libby's sunshine lighting and warming his world. As far as he was concerned, his days would be darkened forevermore.

Chapter 20

Libby opened her eyes. Pride stood in the spot where she'd left him, calmly eating grass. She jumped up to retrieve her cell phone and noted the time and day. It seemed like a lifetime away, rather than mere minutes.

Her wedding ring glinted in the sun, drawing her eye. She held out her hand, lovingly tracing the edges of the ring with her forefinger as a stabbing pain pierced her soul. How would she ever survive without Colin—without all the people she'd come to love in the nineteenth century?

Tears blurred her vision as she mounted Pride and urged the stallion to the one spot she'd be near her love in this century. At the gate of the peaceful cemetery, she quickly dismounted and scrutinized the stones, beneath which lay generations of Thorpe remains. She found the one she sought and collapsed in a new round of tears after reading the epitaph.

Here lies Colin Thorpe
Husband to Elizabeth
Whom he loved
All the days of his life

Clutching the grass covering Colin's grave, she sobbed, feeling the loss all over again.

Emotionally spent, she rose to pick up Pride's reins. In a fluid move, she mounted the stallion, but her shoulders drooped on the slow ride back to the two oaks. Moving in a grief-filled haze, she tied Pride in the same spot. She needed more time to collect herself before taking over her duties here in the future. The kids she was supposed to teach to ride this afternoon would have to wait.

She didn't know how long she sat under the trees, staring out at the landscape and seeing nothing with tear-glazed eyes. A squirrel running up one of the massive trunks drew her focus. She watched him for a moment, then looked around. Everything appeared so different. Somehow, this didn't feel like home anymore. A sad smile formed. This *was* home, but her home was no longer where her heart was. She felt displaced. Like she didn't belong in her own time and era. A semblance of a laugh rolled up. What a stupid thought. Of course she belonged here.

She then remembered Giselle's words when Libby had asked her about leaving Paris and moving to Shelbyville, Kentucky, a town completely opposite of the larger foreign city.

Soon the new place becomes home. "I'd be sad to leave here," she'd said. "But if I did, I'd know that wherever I went, I would eventually feel at home."

When had 1874 become home to her and why hadn't she realized the fact before she left the past? It dawned on her just then that she'd most likely always had the choice to leave. Nothing had changed. She couldn't get to the future during those earlier attempts because she'd never wanted to leave the past badly enough. She'd prolonged her visit intentionally.

Bev's words during their picnic under these same trees came back to her.

Of course you'll be able to come home. Just wish it like before.

Yes, Libby had never lost the ability to get home. Just like Bev had said.

Too bad she couldn't go home now.

Suddenly, her posture straightened. Wiping her eyes, she wondered. Could she? If 1874 was now home to her, would wishing herself back work? Excitement surged through her at the thought. Yet, if she could, was that something she should even attempt when nothing had changed?

Or…had it?

Her love for Colin eclipsed all else, but was returning to him—to all that 1874 had to offer, *or not* in this case—something she could live with? Wouldn't do to return just to change her mind and then have to endure another departure, something she felt neither of them could survive.

This is it, she thought. Decision time. No more wasting energy on things that wouldn't make her happy. She had to truly think about her choice to be with Colin. Or not.

Her friendship with Bev was her main reason for returning to the twenty-first century. Fashion was near the top, along with technology, including air-conditioning, computers, communications, and transportation. She thought of her cell phone left in Pride's satchel. Did texting really matter? Did technology and progress? Did *things* make her happy?

She shook her head. No. Colin's love did.

But what about all the negatives in 1874? Could she get past them?

The lack of amenities was a pain. The attitude of the people bugged her. Still, she discarded their stuffy, moral righteousness as happenstance. People in general hadn't changed. They just hid behind hypocritical actions, which Libby realized was only a minor irritation. After all, the twenty-first century held hypocrites. Those individuals she cared about in 1874 were warm, loving, and accepting, neither narrow-minded nor self-righteous.

The one negative Libby had trouble with was the way women were treated in 1874. Could she tolerate such backward thinking? Would Colin's love be enough to overcome that?

Dave was no longer a consideration, but the thought of leaving her father saddened her. What made her sadder was their relationship, which wasn't a close one. After her mother died, he changed. Libby always felt as if she'd disappointed him somehow because she loved the farm so much. She even wondered if he'd miss her if she weren't around. Not the best father-daughter relationship. Still, it was hers and it would be hard to give it up, even if the Gundersons' approval and love had somehow compensated for her father's emotional distance in the past.

She sighed. It all came back to Colin and the chance to build a life with him on the stud farm. She shared Colin's dream of breeding and training some of the best horses in the country, and she loved the work.

In the end, her decision rested on her love for Colin versus her love for her best friend.

Without Bev, her life wouldn't have been as full. Friendships like theirs would last forever despite not being together.

Bev's toast suddenly came back to her. To friendship! May it last through time!

What would Bev say? A half laugh, half sob burst free with the simple answer. She'd want what Libby wanted. Her best friend loved her enough to let her go, just as Colin had. In fact, Bev, a romantic and a firm believer in fate, wouldn't be happy to learn that Libby had even considered picking friendship over love.

Pride whinnied when Libby jumped up to grab her cell phone out of his saddlebag to text her friend good-bye and explain why she couldn't wait. Bev would understand.

Libby was too afraid that if she didn't go now, she might never get the chance again.

Somehow fate, in the form of a quest to save the farm in the future, had taken her back to 1874 where Libby had found what she'd never dreamed she'd been looking for. Who she was and why she existed.

Bev would be *very* disappointed if Libby didn't follow her destiny and live it to the fullest as fate had dictated. Grinning, she glanced up at the oaks as her decision became final.

Closing her eyes, she relaxed and wished. *Please, please take me home.*

Chapter 21

Twin Oaks Farm—in the future

Bev neared the two oak trees and saw Thorpe's Pride right where Libby's text had said the mare would be. She swallowed her sadness, stared up at the green canopy, and whispered, "Godspeed, my friend. I wish you all the happiness you deserve."

She then untied Pride and said to the horse while leading him back to the paddock, "Even though it's here in black and white on my cell phone, it's still hard to believe."

With Pride taken care of, she went in search of Sam and Doug. It would be hard enough to sell them on the idea of Libby living in the past, but no way Dave or Mr. Edwards would buy it without proof. Hopefully, Libby did what she said she would do and left them messages.

If only her friend could have said good-bye in person. Bev understood her reasons. Hell, she'd urged her on, but a hug would have been nice. Arms-deep in the birth of the newest foal on the farm, Bev hadn't been able to break away and Libby hadn't wanted to risk waiting.

Pulled out of her thoughts as both men headed her way, Bev wondered how to best go about her task. How did one impart such news? Just blurt it out or ease it into conversation?

Deciding on a direct approach, she said once the men were within earshot, "Libby went back to 1874 to find your deed."

Two faces stared at her with incredulous expressions.

"By God, that's not funny," Sam said, frowning.

"I didn't tell you that to be funny," Bev replied in a patient tone. "It's true." She then went on to explain what she thought happened, ending with, "My best guess is she wished herself back to gain a copy of the deed and decided to stay." She smiled wistfully. "I'm the only one who knew. Well, she did tell Dave, but he didn't believe her."

For several long seconds Sam gaped at her. "She met my great-great-grandfather?"

Doug looked as if he didn't know what to think and kept quiet.

She nodded. "I know it's a lot to take in."

Sam shook his head. "Dammit all, Bev, no one can come and go through time."

"She can. She did."

As if absorbing it all, he rubbed the back of his neck. "I remember Libby's unease about the trees. But how is it possible that the twin oaks called to her? There has to be some other explanation." He sighed. "You're asking me to believe the impossible."

"Well, there is one way to find out," she said, handing him her cell phone. "This is the message I received before she left." As he read, she added, "We only have to check beneath the trees to find the copy of the deed she buried there."

"As incredible as it seems, it won't hurt to take a look." He broke off for a moment. "We should notify her father and that young man she was going to marry. They have the right to know what's going on, and I want them present when we search. Will you call them?"

Bev nodded, wondering how to prepare for the distasteful task of calling Dave Phillips.

଼

Responding to the knock, Bev opened Libby's cabin door and Dave walked past her into the room. Mr. Edwards hadn't arrived yet.

"Where's Libby," he asked. "What's happened? Why'd you call?"

"Hello, Dave. It's nice to see you, too."

"Don't be a smartass, Bev. It's unbecoming." His dismissive gaze caught hers. "Did you say something to her to cause more problems between us?"

Bev stared open-jawed. Was he for real? "This wasn't my doing." Well, technically it was because it was her idea to go back for the deed. Still, Colin Thorpe sounded like a dream man for Libby, much more so than the man in front of her.

"She's finally agreed to dinner so we can talk, and an hour before I'm to pick her up, you call and tell me she's gone. I know you put her up to it."

"You are *so* predictable," she shot back. Just like Dave to blame her for a mess of his own making. If he hadn't acted like such an ass and tried to turn Libby into a Barbie doll, her friend might never have fallen in love with a nineteenth-century heartthrob.

"I'd rather be predictable than look like you," he said, eyeing her up and down.

"Oh, really?" Grinning, she sauntered toward him. She picked up his tie, fingering the fine silk as he leaned away, warily watching her. "I bet you have twenty just like this. And let me guess. More dark navy suits and only white shirts hang in your closet?" She dropped the tie and patted his chest, tsk-tsking. "You're about as colorless as they come."

Shaking his head, Dave walked to the window and stood looking out.

Except Bev needed to vent, not just because she missed Libby, but because he'd always treated Bev as if she were beneath him, an attitude that had bothered her from the get-go. What did the guy have against her? "You know what your problem is, Dave?"

"No, but I can see you're dying to enlighten me."

"Of course." A satisfied smirk snuck out as she nodded and sat. "Your problem is you can't see beneath the surface of an individual. It's too bad, because you miss so much."

"Spare me," he muttered under his breath. The disbelieving look sliding over his expression as he slanted a glance in her direction added to his tone. "That's utter bullshit."

"Oh?" Stretching out her legs and leaning back in the chair, she held his gaze. "I'll prove it. What do you see when you look at me? Not that I don't already have a good idea. But tell me. Do you look beneath my surface?"

"OK, I'll play your game." His gaze took a trip over her body. "I see a pain in the butt with a loud mouth, spiked hair, and too many earrings."

"I thought so," she countered with a forced laugh. "For your information, Dr. *Predictable* Bull, I'm graduating from U of L *summa cum laude* in pre-med. I put myself through school, though my parents can buy and sell you. I've already been accepted to three med schools, which I probably won't attend because I've got my heart set on vet school. I'm sure you never knew those details. Why? Because you can't look beyond the cover, especially if you don't like what you see. You assume the worst."

Dave's jaw clenched as a bit of red hit his cheeks. "Oh, yeah?" he said in a growl. "While you're listing my faults, let me tell you this, Ms. Colorful. If all that's true, then you're just as bad. Hiding who and what you are behind the hair and rings. Joke about me all you want. At least I don't hide from life. I know who I am, and I'll not make any excuses to you because you find me predictable." With a dismissive turn of his shoulders, he refocused on the window.

A knock sounded.

"Saved by the bell," Bev muttered as she headed for the door, relieved to have the diversion. She didn't want to think about the thread of validity running through his words.

Tom Edwards entered, concern written in bold print across his face. "Have they found any sign of her yet?"

"No, Mr. Edwards," Bev said, shaking her head. "Now that you're here, why don't you sit down?" She looked over at Dave and nodded to the table. "You too, Dave."

Dave raked an impatient hand through his hair. "I only want to find Libby, talk some sense into her," he murmured, turning back to the window. "Then get the hell out of here."

"Please sit." Bev motioned toward the chair.

Sighing, Dave moved to sit in the chair she indicated and waited. When she hesitated, his eyebrows rose. "Well, you've got our attention, so tell us what you couldn't over the phone. Where's Libby?"

"You won't like what I have to say." Bev curled a fist, holding back the urge to hit him. "And knowing you, you won't be open enough to believe, but here goes." She flashed him a mocking smile. "She went back in time and decided to stay."

"Come on, Bev." Dave laughed. "That's the best you can come up with?"

"What makes you think this, Bev?" Tom Edwards said, interrupting the snide reply on the tip of her tongue.

"Well…" Bev cleared her throat. "She's gone back before," she said, glancing at him. "I know it's hard to believe, but it happened—the first time when she was fourteen."

Tom noticeably paled. "Go on," he said, swallowing hard.

"A few weeks ago, after Libby started working on the farm, she went back to 1874 to—" She shrugged. "The why doesn't really matter. Anyway, she returned and told me about it. Then Sam was having legal problems with clearing his title. Somehow the deed to his property went missing and there's no record of it. Libby went back to retrieve a copy of the original. She thought something that happened on her first visit created the change." When Dave scoffed, she threw him a heated glance and said, "You can leave if you don't want to hear the rest."

Dave opened his mouth to speak, but Tom raised a hand. "I'm interested in what she has to say." Then turning back to Bev, he still looked awfully pasty when he nodded. "Please continue."

Bev sighed. "As crazy as it sounds, she left earlier this afternoon and traveled back to 1874. She returned briefly. We texted back and forth and said our good-byes." She cleared her throat and pushed a strand of hair behind her ears. "She was in a hurry to get back. She promised to leave messages for everyone under the twin oaks." She left out the part about her finding her dream man. Hopefully, Libby took care of that. "The oaks had some kind of magic. She wished to go back in time and they took her."

Dave stared at Bev until he shook his head and snorted. "I know Libby thinks she can travel through time. Hell, she even tried to convince me, but come on, Bev. You can't really buy into her games? Flitting around time like you're zipping to the store and back is impossible."

"I don't care what you think. It's true."

Tom Edwards gripped Dave's shoulder, his expression solemn. "I believe her, Dave."

He gaped. "You can't be serious, Tom. They're daydreams or her imagination working in overtime. There's always some explanation."

"Come with me." Tom started for Libby's bedroom. "I need to show you something."

Both followed him into the room.

At Libby's dresser, Tom rifled through her jewelry box, grabbed an earring, and glanced at Dave, holding it up. "See this?" When Dave nodded, he continued speaking. "This earring belonged to Liz, my wife. It went missing the night we decided to have Libby. That same night Liz told me an incredible story." Fingering the earring, Tom paused. He glanced up with a gaze full of pain. "She was upset, thought she was imagining things because this kid claiming to be her daughter appeared out of nowhere, telling Liz she loved her and that she was sorry for the things she'd said. Apparently, this daughter from the future took the earring with her and then disappeared right before her eyes." He set the earring back in the box and sighed. "We had no idea what happened and quite honestly, I'd forgotten about the incident until after Liz's death."

"That's when she wished under the trees to see her mother," Bev said. "The trees allowed her to go back."

Tom nodded. "When Liz died, Libby was inconsolable. She wasn't eating and lost interest in outside things—was basically in a deep depression. Her doctor suggested this place," he said, indicating the farm outside the bedroom window. "I've always been leery of Twin Oaks because of the night she came home from her two-week stay. That same night I went to check on her and saw Liz's earring in her hand. Now, how or why it happened, I don't know. But I do know she met my wife before her birth and left with the earring. The whole idea bothered me. I felt that somehow, at some point in the future, I'd lose her just like I did Liz, so I tried to keep her from this place."

Bev stared. "Wow. I had no idea."

"The two have always seemed connected. And now she's vanished, which only confirms my earlier fears." Tom glanced at Dave. "I think we should go and see what's under the trees."

Dave murmured something under his breath.

"What?" Bev donned her most innocent expression. Despite feeling so wretched with never seeing her best friend again, she felt immense satisfaction at seeing Dr. Bull brought down a peg or two. "I didn't catch that."

Ignoring her, Dave kept walking. "Trust me, you don't want to know." When he got to the front door, he stopped. "Are you coming?"

he yelled to Tom. "Let's get this over with. The sooner we dig up nothing, the sooner we can look for Libby."

Bev sidled up behind him, taunting, "A predictable disbeliever till the very end. Why am I not surprised?"

Dave grunted. "You know, Bev, someday that big mouth of yours will get you into trouble."

"Says who? You?" Fighting with the guy somehow took her mind off missing Libby.

"Children, please," Tom said. "Let's go. You two can fight when I'm gone."

A chagrined expression flitted over Dave's face. He offered an apologetic smile. "Sorry."

Embarrassed, Bev remained silent as Tom asked, heading out the door, "Where're these trees?"

"Not too far," she said to his departing back.

Along the trail, they joined Sam and Doug, both carrying shovels. The small procession headed to the trees.

At the center of the oaks, Bev halted, then pointed. "The text Libby sent told me to look in this area, in front of where Pride was tied."

The men started digging.

They dug about a foot, when Sam shouted, "I think I hit something."

All eyes focused on the ground beneath his shovel. They each took turns and dug faster.

Seconds later, they pulled out a rusty old strong box, an antique lock securing it.

The group quickly advanced to Sam's study where he worked on the lock with a penknife while Bev and the others watched with interest. After a few minutes and a little finessing, the small lock gave. Sam opened the box and pulled out a journal, four letters—each separately addressed, and a notarized copy of Sam's deed to Twin Oaks.

They all stared at the aged letters addressed in Libby's bold scrawl as Dave whistled. "Well, I'll be damned."

ଔ

When Libby's equilibrium returned, she grinned at the scene before her. Eighteen seventy-four. Exactly as she'd wished. Never had she been so happy to see the familiar oaks without the other trees. She could only marvel over how much this stud farm had come to mean to her in such a short time. Pushing to her feet, she wondered how much time had passed. Hopefully she could spare Colin from enduring her same pain.

Anticipation flowed through her. For the first time since she'd made her decision, Libby was struck with exactly what *coming home* meant. It meant they could be together. Always. She could be a part of Colin's life without the fear of ever having to leave again, and they could build their future together. Plan together. Dream together.

She laughed, hugging herself, before turning and running toward the house. At the top of the porch steps, she slowed, surprised to find everything ominously quiet. Were his children in bed already? Maybe she'd been gone longer than she thought.

"Colin," Libby called out softly, tiptoeing through the dark hallway, stopping at the library door. She hesitated, then knocked. "Colin?" She opened the door and slipped inside.

Slivers of light spilled from the shade-drawn windows, creating shadows in the darkened room. Catching movement, Libby could barely make out Colin sitting behind his desk, holding a filled glass. A decanter of what looked like either whiskey or bourbon was within his reach.

"What's this? A ghost who's come to haunt me?" Colin's anguished whisper filled the air, sending chills down Libby's spine. "I can't get you out of my mind and now I'm having visions." He lifted the glass and took a long swallow. Then he closed his eyes and leaned back in his chair, not moving a muscle.

Libby watched in stunned silence, unsure of what to do. "Colin?" She tentatively stepped farther into the room. "Are you all right?"

Colin opened his eyes. In the barely lit room she could see his bleak expression. "Ah, the apparition speaks. 'Tis funny, but you sound just like her. Have you come to torment me more? Is it not enough to haunt my dreams? Now you haunt my waking moments? Maybe if I drink enough, I'll be able to get you out of my mind. Out of my heart. Out of my soul." He took another long swig, slamming the glass on the desk. "Go away, vision. Leave me be." He then leaned back and shut his eyes once more. "I don't want to feel any more."

Why was he acting so strange? Apprehension filled her. It couldn't have been more than thirty minutes since she'd last seen him.

She rushed up to his chair and knelt beside him, taking his hand.

"Colin. It's me, Libby. I'm not a dream. Open your eyes."

His eyes opened and in a heartbeat, joy replaced sorrow. "Libby?" He shook his head, as if clearing his mind. "My God," he whispered. "It is you." A jubilant smile lit his face and tears lurked at the edges of his eyes. "Somehow you've come back to me." He gripped her wrist, tugging her up and onto his lap. Lowering his head to an inch over hers, he murmured, "How can it be? I saw you disappear."

Libby closed her eyes as his mouth made the final connection, and poured every emotion she felt into the kiss. This is where I belong, she thought as his strong hands drew her closer. When they broke apart, she softened her smile. "I came home." She kissed her way up the side of his face, brushing his black hair off his brow and kissing to the lids of his amber eyes. "I wished myself home. Now that I've found where I belong, I'll never leave again."

"Please, Libby." Colin wrapped his arms around her, hugging her to him. He laughed, planting kisses everywhere…her face…her chin…her neck…all the way to her ear, whispering in between the kisses, "Tell me you mean your words. I can't survive another parting."

"Oh, Colin, I'm sorry I left."

"I let you go once. I don't have the will to do it again." His audible anguish tore her heart in two. "I'll do whatever it takes to keep you here, by my side, till death do us part. Do you understand?"

Nodding, she met his gaze, hers becoming blurry, wondering how she had any more tears left. "I should have known I could never be happy without you."

"And I should never have let you go." Grinning, he stood and rearranged her in his arms. As he carried her toward the door, he said, "You are my life, my love. I need you so much."

Libby smiled into his shoulder. "My sentiments exactly."

He took the stairs two at a time.

Once in their bedroom, Libby looked around and sighed. Home. She now had no doubts. Her decision to come home had been the right one. At the four-poster bed, he stopped. His arms went slack. She slid the length of him, well aware of his full arousal signifying the need he spoke of, increasing her own awareness. Her own need.

They came together like two lovers who'd been apart for too long. Neither could stop touching, kissing, stroking, nibbling, as if not believing their good fortune. Within minutes, Colin had Libby naked. Seconds later he rose above her to find his way home.

Libby's last coherent thoughts before the storm of his passion swept her up were of Colin, of the rightness of loving him, of being in this place and time. Where he was concerned, she gave all she had. He was her love and she was his.

ଔ

When Colin could think again, he lifted off Libby, situating her right where she belonged, with her head on his shoulder, wrapped in his embrace. He kissed her brow, let his head plop on the pillow, then closed his eyes. Now that his mind had cleared, it didn't take long for his thoughts to gather, as all of the reasons he'd sent her home resurfaced.

"What about my century? And all you hate here," he asked, the question intruding further into his cocoon of contentment. "Nothing has changed. I meant my words. I won't see you unhappy."

Libby put a finger to his mouth, but Colin pushed her hand aside. "Can you truly be happy? Giving up all in your own time?"

He felt her smile.

"I'm not Abigail." She lifted up on her forearms, leaning close enough for him to see the seriousness in her eyes. "I'm taking responsibility for my choices. I can easily live without twenty-first century advances. What good are they, if I can't share them with you?"

"What about the restrictions for women here?" Colin countered, still unconvinced. "I have no qualms about you working on the farm in boys' clothes if that will make you happy. But you can't wear boys' attire all the time. I'll expect you to dress in the evenings, and because of the racetrack, I'll be traveling back and forth to Louisville. I want you with me so the world will know you're mine, not hiding here. While in town, you'll need to dress the part and follow convention. Can you? Can you be happy abiding by those strict rules you hate?"

She lowered her head and kissed him. Thoroughly. Then lifting her mouth, she grinned. "Of course I won't like it but I accept the rules, and I promise to abide by your wishes when we're in town. After all, no place or time is ever completely perfect. Besides…" She winked. "I think I like dressing up and looking beautiful for you."

Colin chuckled. "Libby, you are beautiful to me no matter what. Whether in boys' clothes or a stunning ball gown, I'll always see perfection." Seconds later, their lips met.

Chapter 22

"I guess we should open them and find out what happened," Sam Thorpe said after passing out three letters and staring at the one addressed to him.

Bev peered in silence at the envelope in her hand. Her eyes misted.

The tearing of envelopes rent the air before the sound changed to rustling as she, like the others, began reading.

Dear Bev,

This is the hardest letter I've ever written. As I put pen to paper, it dawns on me that I will no longer be able to confide in you, share drinks at Giorgio's with you, or hug you. Your friendship gave me the courage to find my destiny and meet my fate. Without you in my life, I wouldn't have had the guts to do so.

You deserve more than a text saying good-bye, for sure. My main regret is not waiting that afternoon to give you one more hug and kiss good-bye. I was too worried I wouldn't be able to get back to Colin and forgot to take time for what was important. I hope you will forgive my impulsive selfishness.

I miss you so much and probably will for the rest of my life. You are always in my thoughts and prayers. Never a day goes by when I don't think—what would Bev do—or what would Bev say to that? I'm smiling right now because I'm imagining your own smile as you wish me well, only too glad I had the spirit to follow my dreams.

Those dreams led me to Colin Thorpe. Once I found him, I couldn't give him up. He's become my life. I know you'll understand and be happy for me. My biggest wish for you is that you find your destiny. I pray fate gives you a love like I have with Colin. Bear in mind, your love for me is what I will always remember and cherish most. You always believed in me and I'll always believe in you.

Your loving friend,

Libby Edwards Thorpe

PS: We've changed the name of Colin's farm to Twin Oaks because the trees are what brought us together. We've left explicit instructions about them, so they will still exist in your time. I've begun a journal, to be buried in the box when I die, along with an indisputable copy of Twin Oaks's deed, ending my original quest.

Dead silence permeated the room while the occupants absorbed the meaning of their letters.

A couple of tears had dropped to the page as Bev had read, and just as Libby had predicted, she felt her smile widen.

Sam's voice intruded on the silence. "My God, it doesn't seem possible even with proof." He finished his and handed it to Doug, shaking his head.

Stunned, Dave appeared to have lost his voice.

Tom wiped a hand over his eyes and offered his letter to Bev. They exchanged and both continued reading.

Dear Dad,

I have taken my time writing this because when I decided to return to 1874, I thought I could easily leave you without regrets. We were never close and I always felt as if I had let you down somehow. Over time, I've realized I do have a few regrets overshadowed by the fact that we never understood each other.

Now that I'm a mother with more wisdom, I can view your motives in a different light. I know you loved me and only wanted my happiness. I am happy. I am where I want to be and my life is complete with Colin Thorpe. All of this must be hard to imagine. Traveling through time is a little unbelievable. My only wish was to find a place where I belonged. Once I discovered that place, I had to stay.

I began a journal with the details of my life. As I age, I'll record my thoughts and those thoughts will always include you. Please try to forgive my actions, understand them, and be happy for me.

Your loving daughter,

Elizabeth Edwards Thorpe

Bev then scanned Sam's letter that he'd handed her.

Dear Sam,

I know you will be surprised to read this, as I'm sure anyone who finds I've decided to remain in the past would be. I want to thank you for hiring me, but I find I must give notice. I hate to leave you in a lurch, especially with Thorpe's Pride, but I no longer had the choice to return to the twenty-first century. Working with Pride's predecessors will have to suffice. My life—my love—my everything—is here in 1874 with Colin Thorpe. To leave a time where I found I belonged, to return to a place where I felt like I never fit in, was something I could not do.

I don't know how or why all of this happened. All I can say is I'm glad it did. It was a matter of fate and destiny. My fate and destiny took me back to the beginning of your stud farm and that is where I am truly happy. I only hope you and Doug can be happy for me.

Sincerely,

Elizabeth Edwards Thorpe

Dave finally found his voice. "It's like we've stepped into *The Twilight Zone.*" He set his letter aside, turned to Libby's dad, who by this point had noticeable moisture filling his eyes, and clapped him on the shoulder, squeezing. "I don't know what to say, Tom, except that I'm sorry."

"I'm OK, Dave," Tom said, clearing his throat. "The saddest part is the regret. I should have tried harder to understand my daughter while I had the chance." He smiled wistfully. "But I have what I've always wanted. Libby's happiness. It seems she's found it."

While the others in the room consoled one another, Bev couldn't resist reading Dave's letter as it sat open on the desk.

Dear Dave,

By this time you've obviously discovered how wrong you are about my time traveling. Sorry about the "Dear John" letter. No one deserves that. But the only other option would be to delay my trip back to 1874 or return at some point to meet with you. I couldn't risk either. I'll never leave the past again.

I placed your engagement ring in the oak tree on the right, just before I zapped back. Look for an indentation where the branches divide. There is a little nook big enough to hide it.

I did love you, you know. I even believe that you may have loved me to some extent. But face it, Dave. You never accepted me for who I was. I was never good enough and you never really believed in me. We weren't meant to be. I know that now after finding a man who not only accepts me as I am, he loves me, and he believes in me. I don't have to change. To him I am perfect, faults and all.

I wish you well, Dave, and hope that someday you'll find someone you don't have to change.

My sincerest regrets,

Libby Thorpe

Bev finished and looked up to see Dave watching her.

"I guess I owe you an apology," he said, offering a semblance of a smile. "Nothing like eating a little crow to put a humble taste in my mouth. I'm sorry I didn't listen to either of you when you tried to tell me. God, what a fool I am." He shook his head and started for the door. "I need to retrieve my ring. Should make a good keepsake to remind me of my arrogance and my stupidity."

"Wait, Dave, I'll go with you," Bev said, running to catch up with him.

Dave stopped and threw her a suspicious look. "Why? So you can gloat?"

"No, I'm past all that." At his raised eyebrows she smiled, then shrugged. "OK. Maybe I'd like to gloat. But I won't. I needed to get out of there." Her nod indicated the room they'd left. "It's too sad."

"Suit yourself." Dave walked on, quickening his pace.

At the trees, he reached up and felt around the tree trunk where the branches separated. Seconds later, he pulled out his ring.

Scrutinizing his face, Bev noted his forlorn, almost subdued expression as he stared at the solitaire before pocketing it. "You really love her, don't you?"

"Of course I do. How could you not love Libby? She is—" He cleared his throat, which sounded as if it was tightening with grief, and swallowed hard. "She *was* genuine. I never understood until it was too late what I had in her." He hesitated. "Do you know the saddest part of all?"

"No," Bev said softly. "What?"

"I was too self-absorbed and concerned with my needs to understand hers. Plus, I didn't appreciate her for who she was. I only hope she's found the happiness she deserves." He blinked several times and wiped at the edges of his eyes with the back of his hand. "Now that I understand what she wanted, I want the same thing. Yet, somehow I doubt I'll ever be lucky enough to find it."

Epilogue

One Month Later:
Libby accepted Colin's help in dismounting from atop Hercules after barely losing to Fortuna. "I can't believe how much faster she's gotten."

They'd been working most of the morning and this was their last run before moving on to the stables.

Giselle, having led Fortuna in a walk, stopped to pat the horse's long neck. "She outdid herself."

The mare whinnied and shook her head in the air, as if in agreement.

As Giselle headed in Gus's direction, Colin handed Hercules off to a handler, then wrapped an arm around Libby's shoulders.

"Are you happy?" He asked the same question at least once a day.

She sighed, looked around, and answered truthfully. "Very." Her days were full of challenge. Not only with her role as trainer, but with mothering three wonderful children. Sam, Melanie, and baby Rebecca desperately needed her love. How easily they returned it, which made up for ninety percent of her loss.

The other ten percent came from her friendship with Giselle, who'd demonstrated an ability to ride and train Colin's horses and was now living and working on the farm. They had become fast friends and now worked side by side. Her company eased the heartache of missing Bev.

Libby thought of her friend in the future constantly and continued the daily practice of sharing her life by writing in her journal. She missed her dad too. It would have been nice to say good-bye properly. She'd been in too big a rush to be reunited with Colin, and would always feel a small twinge of regret when she thought of her dad. She hoped that in sharing her life, her father might come to understand her better and be happy for her in what she'd found.

A new family and others who loved her.

She leaned her head against Colin's wide chest and smiled warmly. "Yes. I have exactly what I need to be happy." She offered one last glance in the direction of the twin oaks, the farm's new namesake and wondered how they knew. They truly were magical.

~~ The End~~

Author's note:

While I did take quite a few liberties in the telling of this story there are several facts I wanted to make note of in doing my research for this book.

First of all, my main characters did not exist in the 1870s, but some of the men mentioned did. Men such as Merriwether Lewis Clark, Jr., who was a visionary and a main promoter of the new track. He spent years researching and promoting his idea. Three hundred and twenty men invested one hundred dollars each and signed the Articles of Incorporation for the Louisville Jockey Club and Riding Park Association on June 22, 1784. That was enough to start the ball rolling for the new grandstand and track. There are several men who dreamed and their dream is the legacy of the Kentucky Derby. The first Kentucky Derby was run on May 17, 1875. From the very beginning it has been hyped as a big party and has only gotten bigger over time.

Of course, no Derby would be complete without the horses. Diomed won the first Epsom Derby in England on May 4, 1780, the same race the Kentucky Derby was fashioned after. He was later sold to an American and he set the stage for the beginning of the American Thoroughbred. Lexington (1850 –1875) carried his blood. Aristide won that first Kentucky Derby back in 1875 and his dam was sired by Lexington. Lexington is probably one of the most famous thoroughbreds in the history of American thoroughbred racing. In 1866 Woodburn Farms bought him from Richard Ten Broeck for fifteen thousand dollars, an unheard of amount in 1866, but not as much as the millions of dollars Kentucky thoroughbreds sell for today. Fifty-two of the first sixty-one derby winners carried Lexington's blood. The champion sired six-hundred colts or fillies. Of these, two hundred and sixty were winners. During his reign, he was dubbed as "the most successful stallion in History."

About The Author

Sandy Loyd is a Western girl through and through. Born and raised in Salt Lake City, she's worked and lived in some fabulous places in the US, including South Florida. She now resides in Kentucky and writes full time. As much as she loves her current hometown, she misses the mountains and has to go back to her roots to get her mountain and skiing fix at least once a year.

As a sales rep for a major manufacturer, she's traveled extensively throughout the US, so she has a million stored memories to draw from for her stories. She spent her single years in San Francisco and considers that city one of America's treasures, comparable to no other city in the world. Her California Series, starting out with Winter Interlude, are all set in the Bay Area.

Sandy is now an empty nester. Time Will Tell is the first in a series of connecting historical romances as well as a couple of contemporary romances. To date, she has published eight books besides Time Will Tell—four contemporary romances and four romantic mystery/suspense /thrillers. She strives to come up with fun characters—people you would love to call friends. And we all know friends have their baggage and when we discover what makes them tick, we come to love them even more. She doesn't skimp on the romance. And because she loves puzzles, she doesn't skimp on intrigue, either. Yet whether romantic suspense or contemporary romance, she always tries to weave a warm love story into her work, while providing enough twists and turns to entertain any reader.

Games, Giselle's story, is due out July 2013, followed by **Temptation**, the third in the series, due out in August 2013.

Email her at sandyloyd@sandyloyd.com or visit her website at www.sandyloyd.com. Like her on Facebook to keep apprised of her releases www.facebook.com/sloydwrites. Follow her on Twitter @sloydwrites.

Games – Book Two in the Timeless Series

Below is an excerpt of Games, a historical set in Kentucky in the months preceding the first running of the Kentucky Derby.

Simon led Giselle into the library and over to the table with four chairs in one section of the large room.

While walking to the bar, he asked, "What game would you like to play?"

Giselle giggled and Simon grinned. "Maybe I should rephrase my question. Before I do, though, would you like a glass of sherry?"

"*Non*," she said, bestowing a wide smile and a firm shake of her head. "I want what you are drinking."

Lifting an eyebrow, Simon met her gaze. "Isn't that a bit strong?"

"*Non*, you forget I lived in Paris. I have come to love French brandy. Bourbon is not much different." At his scoff, she countered, "What? You do not believe me?"

"No. It's not that." He laughed and poured two stiff drinks. "I believe you. I just wonder how well you hold your liquor."

"Why not bring the drink over here, Simon, and I will show you. Bring the bottle, too. We may need reinforcements."

Her comment earned another laugh. "My, my! I'm learning all kinds of things. Imagine a little French lush. I never would have guessed."

He placed the drinks along with the bottle on a tray and strode toward her. With a minimum of movement, he put the tray on the table and handed one drink to her while picking his up.

He sat down next to her just as she spoke.

"You know, I should not be in here with you."

He glanced at her, and took a drink. Then he set his glass on the table and began shuffling the cards. "All right, I'll bite. Why not?"

Eyeing his actions, she brought her glass to her lips and took a lengthy sip before answering.

"Because you are a bold one, Simon Harrington. And I do not know what to make of you."

His rich laughter rose up and filled the air. "And you amuse me, Giselle. Why is that? I can't remember laughing so much or enjoying a woman's company since the last time I was with you."

She smiled coyly. "So that is why you ignored me during dinner. Because I amuse you?" she asked, keeping her smile in place while her eyebrows shot up.

"No." He began dealing the cards. "I ignored you at dinner to have your company after dinner. It appears my ploy worked. Didn't it?"

Giselle picked up her cards, rearranging them before setting them down and taking another drink. Suddenly she burst into laughter. She shook her head, grinning. "That is simply too devious."

While arranging his cards, Simon lounged back in his chair, allowing a nonchalant expression to move over his face. "One does what one must," he said offhandedly.

"No wonder I find you so entertaining." At his shrug, she asked, "So, what are we playing?"

"I thought we'd play poker, since you seem so familiar with male vices. Five card draw."

"I have to warn you. I am pretty good at poker," she countered. Her grin returned, reaching her eyes.

"Naturally," he murmured, giving in to the urge to curl his lips into a wide grin.

"What are we betting with?" She leaned toward him, clearly getting into the spirit of the game.

"I don't know. We can use matchsticks if you'd like. Or money?"

"Playing for matchsticks sounds rather boring." Giselle's smile turned smug when she added, "And I have no need of money. Why not raise the stakes and play for something we both really want from the other?"

Her provocative dare drew his attention. Something about her expression didn't bode well. He straightened, clearing his throat. He hesitated. "I'm not sure that's a good idea."

"What is the matter, Simon?" she whispered, her voice challenging. Hell, everything about her challenged him. The gleam in her eyes, the secret smile she flashed, even the way she held her head when she goaded, "Are you losing your boldness?"

He shook his head, working to ignore her taunting ways. Trouble was, he couldn't ignore her for long. Not the enchanting woman he glimpsed in front of him, dressed so provocatively, throwing out challenges.

His amusement grew. Knowing he only wanted one thing from her right now and also knowing if she knew what it was, she'd run for her life, he grinned. "Are you going to push until I get it back?"

"Of course," she said slyly, more laughter bubbling up.

The minx was enjoying herself immensely. Watching her, he tamped down a desire to wipe clean the teasing gleam emanating from her eyes, replacing it with one of passion. Not his best idea. Though stuck, he wasn't sure he wanted to get unstuck. Shrugging, he said, "Very well. I'll play it your way. What's your bet?"

"My company after dinner tomorrow night. If I win, you do not have it. If I lose, you have it. Now, what is yours?"

Simon was silent as ten seconds ticked by, then another ten. With his eyes on hers, he mulled over his options for dealing with the chit and wondering at the craziness of actually considering his bet.

"A kiss," he said, backing down at the last minute.

Her trill of light laughter danced in the air around him, mocking him.

"Oh, Simon, I am disappointed in you. That is hardly worth playing for."

He held his tongue while discarding three cards, then looked over at her with a raised brow. "How many?"

"One. Would you like to raise the bet?" she asked mischievously, her eyes alive with humor, still mocking him.

Biting back his smile, he tried not to be amused. "Not when you only take one card, I don't."

"I could be bluffing."

"Maybe. But I don't think so," he said confidently. "Let's see your cards."

"Smart man." She turned over two aces and two tens. "What do you have?"

He flipped his cards, showing only a pair of fives. When she started to rise, he put his hand on her arm, effectively stopping her.

"One more and we can raise the stakes," he goaded, with a closed expression sliding over his face.

"I already have what I want," she said, shaking her head. "Why should I take a chance on losing again?"

"Same reason I took your first bet. Because you're a gambler at heart and can't resist the challenge I'm throwing out."

She sat back down, considering his claim while meeting his eyes. "*Oui.* If you lose, you lose not only my company, you will have to spend time with Minnie and Maizie."

"All right. I can agree to that."

When he didn't say anything further, she prodded, "What is your bet, Simon?"

He shrugged. "I'm going for broke. You may not like it."

"I will not know until you tell me, will I?" she threw out haughtily. After another long pause, Giselle urged impatiently, "Well?"

"I want a night with you. Not just the evening, but the full night."

She laughed. When she could speak again, she said, "Let me see if I have this correctly. You want me to bet my company for full night against your spending a little time with Minnie and Maizie? I hardly think the two are comparable."

"You asked and I bet," Simon explained, shrugging nonchalantly. "You certainly don't have to take me up on it. I merely thought to make it more interesting…up the ante, so to speak."

"Oh, it definitely does that," she agreed. "I have never done anything so outrageous in my life and I am not sure if I want to, not for one measly evening with Minnie and Maizie. It hardly seems a fair trade."

"Then think of something so it is fair. That is, if you're not too afraid to take me up on a real game with real stakes," he dared, taunting her further, causing her eyes to narrow while her gaze seemed to be searching for some answer in his face.

"Let me think." Finally, she glanced at him, her expression curious. "If I spend the time with you, what will be expected of me?"

"Nothing but your company. But I reserve the right to change your mind about certain aspects of your visit."

"You mean you will try to have your way with me?"

He chuckled. "Something like that."

"And if I do not want to, you will accept my decision?" she asked tentatively, her expression becoming guarded.

"Of course. I only want willing women in my bed. There's no thrill in forcing myself on someone, even though some find the idea sporting." His gaze pierced hers while he added, "Make no mistake, Giselle. I *do* want you willing in my bed and *that* will be my goal for the night."

The blush spreading up her face told him she was probably still an innocent. It also made him rethink the craziness of this game. But once he put the offer out on the table, he wasn't about to back down. He wanted her too much, and his reasoning where Giselle Franklin was concerned had taken a holiday long before this.

Giselle licked her lips in a nervous fashion. "I see. And you would do this, despite what you saw and heard this afternoon."

"That's between you and Bradford," he whispered solemnly, his expression hardening. "This is between you and me. The two have no connection."

"You are willing to spend the night with me, ply me with sweet words to gain my acceptance, and you are not concerned I may have feelings for someone else?"

"Do you?" he asked a little too quickly.

"Do I what?"

"Have feelings for Bradford," he clarified, leaning back in his chair, holding her gaze. "I couldn't quite make that out from your words. It's obvious he does for you, but are they reciprocated? Are you going to marry him?"

"What if I said yes?" Giselle asked quietly, swallowing hard with a searching expression.

"Then I would fight doubly hard to have you."

Her eyes narrowed in confusion. "That does not make sense."

"It does to me," Simon stated firmly. "I asked a few simple questions. Are you in love with Bradford and are you going to marry him? How hard can they be to answer?" He asked his impatient questions in a curt voice as irritation spread along his spine.

"You do not ask much, yet you ask too much," came her tormented reply. "I cannot tell you how I feel about Bradford, nor can I say I will ever marry him at this point. But my question for you is why does all this matter if I am but a game to you?"

He gave a self-deprecating laugh and answered honestly. "Who says I have to be rational in my dealings with you? Look at it this way. I'm wagering a night with an inexperienced virgin in the hopes I may sway her into making love with me. I must be mad. How many men have you flirted with over time, Giselle? How many men have tried and failed to woo you? One hundred? Two hundred? Are you worried that I could succeed where others have failed?"

His words caused her to look closely at his face again, but he still allowed his expression to yield nothing.

"Why are you doing this? I do not understand."

"Neither do I," Simon said, sighing. "Are you going to take the bet or not?"

She remained silent, the entire time Simon held his breath, not totally sure of her answer. He gave a sigh of relief when she said, "I cannot take it for the original bet. You would have to agree to leave me free every evening you are here."

"Done," he said quickly, then picked up the cards and hesitated. Snaring her gaze, he asked, "You're sure you want the bet? I don't want you to cry foul if you lose."

She stiffened and threw her shoulders back. Her expression resolute, she took a long swallow of her drink, almost choking on it.

"I will honor my bet, if you will," she said, once her coughing fit ended. "Now, deal the cards."

"Anything you say, my dear." Simon smiled at her confident expression and the bravado voiced in her words. "Good luck."

He shuffled the cards thoroughly before dealing them. When he was done, he put the deck facedown and picked up his hand, keeping his face blank while arranging his cards.

He took three cards out of his hand and laid them on the table. Glancing at her, he raised a brow. "How many?"

She closed her eyes and sighed. "Three."

Simon dealt her three cards as well as himself. He lounged back in a nonchalant pose, his serious gaze meeting her wary brown one.

"What do you have?" he asked, his voice coming out in a whisper.

"Nothing." She laid her cards facedown, looking at him with a turbulent expression in her eyes.

His breath came out slowly as he laid his cards on the table. "Looks like a pair of fours beats nothing."

She stood and said softly, "Can I honor my part tomorrow night? I need some time to come to terms with my folly."

He nodded and watched her walk proudly from the room, wondering the entire time if he'd gone completely mad. What had possessed him to suggest such a thing? He leaned his head back against the chair and closed his eyes, seeing only her laughing brown-eyed stare dancing around in his brain, mocking him. And he knew nothing short of having her would erase the image from his mind.

Available at Amazon.com.

Made in the USA
Lexington, KY
22 September 2017